GW00600874

INTRIGUE

Seek thrills. Solve crimes. Justice served.

A Colby Christmas Rescue
Debra Webb

Wyoming Undercover Escape
Juno Rushdan

MILLS & BOON

A COLBY CHRISTMAS RESCUE
© 2024 by Debra Webb
Philippine Copyright 2024
Australian Copyright 2024
New Zealand Copyright 2024

First Published 2024
First Australian Paperback Edition 2024
ISBN 978 1 038 93549 6

WYOMING UNDERCOVER ESCAPE
© 2024 by Juno Rushdan
Philippine Copyright 2024
Australian Copyright 2024
New Zealand Copyright 2024

First Published 2024
First Australian Paperback Edition 2024
ISBN 978 1 038 93549 6

MIX
Paper | Supporting
responsible forestry
FSC® C001695
www.fsc.org

Published by
Harlequin Mills & Boon
An imprint of Harlequin Enterprises (Australia) Pty Limited (ABN 47 001 180 918), a subsidiary of HarperCollins Publishers Australia Pty Limited
(ABN 36 009 913 517)
Level 19, 201 Elizabeth Street
SYDNEY NSW 2000 AUSTRALIA

Cover art used by arrangement with Harlequin Books S.A.. All rights reserved.

Printed and bound in Australia by McPherson's Printing Group

A Colby Christmas Rescue
Debra Webb

MILLS & BOON

Debra Webb is the award-winning, *USA TODAY* bestselling author of more than one hundred novels, including those in reader-favorite series Faces of Evil, the Colby Agency and Shades of Death. With more than four million books sold in numerous languages and countries, Debra has a love of storytelling that goes back to her childhood on a farm in Alabama. Visit Debra at debrawebb.com.

Books by Debra Webb

Harlequin Intrigue

Colby Agency: The Next Generation

Disappearance in Dread Hollow
Murder at Sunset Rock
A Place to Hide
Whispering Winds Widows
Peril in Piney Woods
A Colby Christmas Rescue

A Winchester, Tennessee Thriller

In Self Defense
The Dark Woods
The Stranger Next Door
The Safest Lies
Witness Protection Widow
Before He Vanished
The Bone Room

Visit the Author Profile page at
millsandboon.com.au.

Dear Reader,

Nearly a quarter of a century ago, I submitted a story to Harlequin Intrigue. It was called *Safe by His Side* and it was the first story in a new series idea I called the Colby Agency. Some of my writer friends said I shouldn't submit a series idea since I was an unpublished newbie but I did it anyway. I've always had a habit of doing things my own way. And good thing, too. To date, sixty-two books in the Colby Agency have been published, and I have received so many fan letters. Victoria Colby became one of the most beloved characters of my writing journey.

It's been a while since I visited Victoria, and her grandchildren are all grown up now. But time hasn't stopped this power couple. She and Lucas are still providing the most discreet private investigations. I realized it was time to put Victoria and her family back on the page. Look for many new Colby Agency: The Next Generation stories to come. Don't worry, Victoria, Lucas and the other characters you've come to love are still there. If you're new to the Colby Agency, you'll love these stories, as well. Each one is a stand-alone journey, so no need to play catch-up. Don't miss a single one!

Best,

Debra

CAST OF CHARACTERS

Victoria Colby-Camp—The head of the Colby Agency. Victoria never backs down from danger... but her weakness is her grandchildren. She will do anything to keep them safe.

Jamie Colby—Victoria's only granddaughter. Even at twenty-five, Jamie has made a name for herself in the world of spies and danger. But this will be her biggest test of all.

Kendrick "Kenny" Poe—An agent from the International Operations Agency—the first global initiative of its kind. Kenny drops everything to help Jamie.

Abidan "Abi" Amar—He is a private contractor with more secrets than the NSA. Can Jamie and Poe trust this man to help save her brother?

Luke Colby—The youngest member of the Colby family. When Luke is kidnapped, the whole family must do whatever necessary to rescue one of their own.

Lucas Camp—He and Victoria began as friends before she was married to James Colby, Lucas's best friend. But after James's death, Lucas spent the rest of his life keeping Victoria safe. When she agreed to be his wife, it was the best day of his life.

Dr. Quinton Case—He has perfected a neurosurgery technique that can save lives...but can he protect the lives of his own family?

Friday, December 21

Four Days Before Christmas

Chapter One

Victoria Colby stood at the window in her office that looked out over the street. This was one of her favorite places in the world and certainly she had traveled broadly. But here, in the Colby Agency offices, this window was her happy place. Watching the snow fall so close to Christmas was just icing on the cake. The winter storm had started two days ago, and the snow hadn't let up since. But, as Lucas reminded her, the storm wouldn't get in the way of their plans this year, so why not celebrate the deepening blanket of white?

It was the season after all.

Her heart felt heavy at the idea of not spending the holidays with her family. It was tradition. But that was impossible this year. Of course, she was literally surrounded by her agency family. Victoria and Lucas couldn't deny having an amazing extended family here at the agency.

And as wonderful as that was, it wasn't really the same.

The whole truth was that celebrating would be a lot more enjoyable if, for one, she didn't feel like her family were scattered so far and wide this holiday. And, secondly, she was worried sick about Tasha, her son Jim's wife. Jim and

Tasha were in Sweden and not for a vacation either. Tasha had been diagnosed with a rare type of cancer. Fortunately, Victoria had been able to get her into a cutting-edge research study that was showing very promising results with its participants. Victoria desperately needed this treatment to work. The idea of her son losing his wife—her precious grandchildren losing their mother—was simply unthinkable.

More unnerving at present: the children hadn't been told about the diagnosis. Tasha and Jim wanted to wait and see how things would go before telling their daughter and son. No point ruining their holidays as well, Jim had insisted. Victoria sighed, her heart heavier still. It wasn't like her grandbabies were actually children. Jamie was twenty-five now. Victoria still couldn't believe her granddaughter was so grown-up. She smiled and traced a melting flake of snow down the glass. Jamie had done everything early. Graduated high school and university years before her peers. Every three-letter government agency on the planet had sought her out well before she had that degree in her hand.

But Jamie had done what Jamie always did—exactly what *she* wanted to do. She had accepted an invitation to be one of only twelve Americans with the brand new International Operations Agency—or the IOA. Practically no one had a handle on exactly what this new multi-country agency was really, but the promise of great things was certainly being bragged about in all the highest places. This agency would extend far and wide, interweaving many allies together in a way never done before.

Victoria was extremely proud of Jamie for choosing a route with global implications, though she had to admit she would have preferred to have Jamie coming on board with the family business. The Colby Agency represented Victoria's life's work. She worried that after Jim there would be no one in the family to carry on the important work they did here.

Her grandson Luke, on the other hand, was just preparing to enter the last semester of his final year at university in Nashville, Tennessee. He was far less in a hurry to get on with his life. Another smile tugged at Victoria's lips. As a child, he had been so like his father. Extremely curious but not quite ready to jump in with both feet. He'd changed his major twice in his freshman year, before finally deciding to go into medicine and transferring to premed at Vanderbilt.

Victoria couldn't wait to see him spread his wings and come into his own.

With all that was going on in their lives, the kids wouldn't be coming home for Christmas either. Everyone—the world it seemed—was too busy. This made her far sadder than perhaps it should have, but this would be the first year that no one in the family had stayed in or come to Chicago to celebrate.

Lucas appeared behind her, and Victoria turned to him. "I fear it's going to be a lonely Christmas."

He touched her cheek with the backs of his fingers. "It's never lonely as long as we are together," he reminded her. "We're alive and well. We'll have plenty to celebrate."

Of course, he was right. She leaned into his strength, and they watched the snowflakes swirl and fall. Whether the family was here or not, it was going to be a beautiful few days. All of Chicago lay under a blanket of perfect, white snow giving the busy and at times troubled city such a peaceful appearance. How could anyone who loved this city not feel the magic of the season? At their ages it was important to enjoy each day all the more.

Victoria should be grateful, and she was. Who could blame her for missing her family?

"Slade mentioned," Lucas said, "that he and Maggie

planned to drop by after dinner at her mother's house. It will be nice to see them and to spend some time with Cody."

Another grandchild who was growing up so very fast.

"That would be lovely." Maggie's mother had no one else and Victoria certainly wouldn't selfishly resent the woman for having at least some family for the holiday even if it meant that Victoria and Lucas were alone. She and Lucas were so very lucky to still have each other.

The reminder that they would indeed have some family dropping by for the holidays brightened her spirits. Although they had not known about Slade until he was a grown man, he was as much a member of this family as anyone else. He had been raised by an evil woman who had done all in her power to turn him against Lucas, his biological father. But time and circumstances had changed that painful connection into a good, solid and loving relationship. One for which Victoria was immensely thankful. Lucas had sacrificed a great deal for his country. He deserved all the happiness that came his way.

"We should send everyone home after lunch," Victoria suggested. It was Friday after all, and the agency would be closed next week. All open cases had been closed by mid-December.

It was something they strove for each year beginning on the first of November. Having the last of the year's cases basically buttoned up by the holidays wasn't always possible, but they worked diligently toward that goal. There were some cases that simply couldn't be wrapped up so neatly in a certain time frame, but all efforts were made. This was good for her investigative team and for the clients they served.

Victoria had to admit that as careers went, she and Lucas had certainly enjoyed unusual ones. She, Lucas and James

Colby, her first husband, had begun their young lives together along with their careers working in the government. James and Lucas had been CIA—eventually leading a special black ops group like no other. In time, when Victoria and James had started a family, they had left the more dangerous work serving their government and started a private investigations agency.

But the past had not been ready to let them go and had drawn them deep into a whole other level of danger.

Victoria pushed the painful memories away. They had survived the nightmares and the tragedies and, thankfully, she and Lucas had found their way to each other in time. Although they had tried retirement and moving to a warmer climate, staying away from Chicago and the agency they had built was impossible.

"That is a very good idea, my dear." He kissed her cheek and then nuzzled it with his own. "Do you have something in mind for this evening?"

Victoria smiled. "I suppose we could be like the typical family and spend the weekend watching Christmas movies and baking cookies."

Lucas chuckled. "I don't think anyone would accuse us of being typical."

Victoria thought of the many, many cases they had investigated. The many times they had barely survived with their lives. "Oh yes, sometimes I forget that we're not like other couples."

During their nearly half-century-long careers, they had been kidnapped, shot at, had bombs left for them, had their entire office building burned down and, of course, one or both had been left for dead numerous times. Thankfully, they had always survived. At times by the sheer skin of their teeth.

Funny how even now, looking back at all those horrific situations, each one had been just another day at the office. And now, their granddaughter was following that same path with the IOA. Luke—not so much. Her grandson had chosen Vanderbilt University in Nashville for his premed work, where a great deal of amazing research was happening. And since Luke was a die-hard country music lover, Nashville was the perfect setting for him.

"I was thinking," Lucas said, "that we might consider a quick trip to Paris. I know how you love that city. A few days there would be a welcome change of pace. We'll be closer and available to rush to Sweden if Jim and Tasha need us. We can have the kids there in a matter of hours if need be."

Victoria held back her first response and mulled over the proposal. "You know, that's actually not a bad idea." Christmas in Paris. Yes. That would be very nice. "I'll run it by Ian and Simon to make sure they haven't made out-of-town plans already."

To her knowledge, none of the primaries at the agency were planning to travel out of town. She turned to her husband. "This was really a great idea, Lucas."

He smiled. "I already have reservations at the Shangri-La. I spoke to Jim yesterday and he was in agreement that he would prefer that we enjoy ourselves for the holidays and not wait around to hear news from Tasha's procedure."

So her husband and her son had been conspiring together. "Do you have flights already as well?" His smile widened to a grin. Why had she even asked? "This really is quite perfect, Lucas. Thank you."

Her cell vibrated against her desk. Victoria started for it and Lucas headed for the door. "I'll inform everyone that I told you about your Christmas present."

She should have known. "So everyone but me knew about this?"

"Not everyone." He grinned, then slipped out of her office.

Victoria shook her head. "Probably everyone but the janitor," she murmured with a laugh.

Luke flashed on the screen of her phone and Victoria's smile spread wider. "Luke," she said in greeting, "how wonderful to hear from you."

Her grandson was always busy, but even still he found a minute here and there to call his grandmother. He had probably heard about Lucas's surprise as well.

"Grandmother."

Victoria's smile faded. The clear and present fear she heard in her grandson's voice had her heart stumbling. "Luke, are you alright?" Had something happened to Tasha and Jim had already called the children? Dear God, she prayed that was not the case.

Had Luke been in an accident? He was speaking to her, which had to mean he was all right...wasn't he?

Or what if something had happened to Jamie?

A fresh wave of fear pounded in her veins.

"Listen to me very carefully, Grandmother," Luke said. "They're only allowing me a few moments to speak with you."

Victoria suddenly calmed. Inside, she went completely still and quiet while her instincts—the ones she had honed over nearly half a century—elevated to the highest state of alert. "I'm listening."

"They want ten million dollars. You have forty-eight hours. But you are not to do anything at all until you receive additional instructions." A pause. "I love you, Grandmother."

The call ended.

"Luke!" Victoria's heart burst into a frantic staccato. "Luke!" She stared at the black screen.

Victoria rushed from her office and paused in the private waiting room just outside the door. She immediately thought of Mildred, her dear assistant of so many years. How she wished she were here now.

Her new assistant gazed up at Victoria with a kind smile. "Is everything all right?"

"Rhea, I need Lucas, Nicole, Ian and Simon in my office *now.*"

Rhea was fairly new, but she recognized there was trouble. Rather than bother with her phone, she ran from the room to personally gather everyone.

Needing to leave her own cell phone free, Victoria reached for the phone on Rhea's desk and called Chelsea Grant. Chelsea was their very best at tracing cell phone calls. "I need you in my office. Now please."

Five minutes later, those closest to Victoria were assembled in her office and she had provided the details of the call from Luke. She struggled to maintain her composure. Memories from when Jim had gone missing at age seven ripped at her insides. *This is not the same. Not the same.*

"The call came from the Nashville area," Chelsea confirmed. "But I'm having a difficult time narrowing down an exact location. The call bounced all over the Volunteer State like a football in a final play free-for-all. If another call originates from that phone, it's possible a drop in signal strength could create a hesitation in the smoke screen they're using. All I need is a call using that phone which lasts a few minutes and a couple of strength hesitations. The signal will automatically go to where it's strongest— where it originates."

"Thank you, Chelsea." Victoria turned to the others. "Thoughts?"

Ian Michaels and Simon Ruhl had been with Victoria

the longest of all her outstanding investigators. Nicole Reed Michaels, Ian's wife, was another of her most trusted. Between the three of them they had a world of experience and knowledge. More important, they were highly skilled in the art of evading danger and recovering assets.

"I'm hearing nothing from Interpol or our friend in the Mossad," Ian said. "My impression so far is that we're dealing with a domestic situation."

"I agree," Nicole confirmed. "My contacts in the CIA, the State Department and the NSA have heard no recent chatter related to our agency or anyone close to it."

Victoria wanted to be relieved at least a little, but she was not. She turned to Lucas. "What are you hearing from Thomas Casey?"

Like Lucas, Thomas Casey had once been a ghost of the highest order. A man who knew all things and who could go in and out of all places—wherever in the world—like smoke undetected. Their contacts and assets were scattered far and wide. But with that level of reach came fierce enemies...fierce competition.

"Ian and Nicole are correct," Lucas said, "this is not an international situation. This is someone closer to home."

"My contacts in the FBI—" Simon went next "—have confirmed rumblings in the southeast but nothing necessarily high level. Yet, they are not willing to take a bigger connection off the table."

Nicole rolled her eyes. "That's just like the Bureau. Always trying to make a situation bigger than it might be."

Simon shrugged. "They have agreed to put out feelers at the university and in the neighborhood where Luke lives."

"In my opinion," Ian said, "we should be heading in that direction even now."

"Luke said I was not to do anything until I received further instructions." The worry and uncertainty had Victoria's heart pounding again. No matter how many times she had faced life and death, knowing that a member of her family was in danger tore her apart inside.

"We should at least call Jamie," Lucas offered. He paced from the conference table to where Victoria sat on the edge of her desk, his trademark limp more visible than usual. He too was worried. These sorts of situations were far harder to tolerate at their ages.

And yet, they would die before backing down. She hoped whoever was behind this understood who they were dealing with.

"I don't want to call her," Victoria said, "until we have something more to share. At this point we know basically nothing."

Lucas leaned against Victoria's desk, putting himself next to her. "You're right, of course, but I feel as if we're doing nothing at all to alleviate the situation."

"The only part that gives me any relief is that Luke sounded somewhat calm despite the fear I heard in his voice," Victoria offered. "His tone was not as frantic as it could have been." Whether the rationale should or not, it gave her some sense of peace.

Nicole looked up from her tablet. "I've moved the requested ten million to a separate account—the one we generally use for ransom demands."

"Very good." Victoria should have already thought of that herself. Perhaps turning seventy-one last year had slowed her cognitively more than she'd realized. No. That wasn't true. There was absolutely nothing wrong with her brain. This was a problem with her heart.

And she was terrified.

"Luke has numerous friends," Simon mentioned, scrolling through the notes on his phone. "I've cued up a list with contact details in the event we need to start tracking them down. His professors. His class schedule. We have everything we need to begin a thorough search for him." His gaze settled on Victoria. "Whenever you say the word."

Her instincts urged her to act, but...the grandmother in her feared not following the directions given.

"We know from our contact at Nashville Metro that his car is at his condo. It hasn't left his parking space," Lucas said.

All their vehicles were tagged with state-of-the-art tracking devices. But having Nashville Metro confirm as much was good news indeed. "Which suggests," Victoria pointed out, "that wherever he is, someone picked him up or that person is at his condo with him." The latter was not likely since they all had panic buttons in their private homes as well. She felt confident Luke would have found a way to trigger that alarm.

The Colbys had suffered more than their share of losses. They did not take chances.

And yet, this ransom situation had happened just the same. Victoria felt powerless.

His cell phone had been turned off and the battery removed as soon as the call had ended, limiting its use as a tracking device. Victoria suspected his phone had only been used to ensure Victoria understood they did indeed have Luke in custody.

Ian said, "Nashville Metro have reported nothing in the way of hostage situations. There have been no new kidnappings in the past seventy-two hours. This appears to be an isolated event."

Nicole looked to Victoria once more. "I've run the enemy list through the steps and found no new activities."

Over the course of the past half century, the Colby name had amassed a good many powerful enemies. The activities of those enemies were closely monitored at all times. It was a necessary evil in the world of high-level investigations. The trouble was that new enemies cropped up and old enemies found fresh ways to hide. It was a never-ending cycle of discovery and catch up.

"Then we wait," Victoria said. There simply was no other choice. Waiting was far more difficult than taking action, but it was, at times, necessary.

Victoria's cell chimed with an incoming call.

Her heart rushed into her throat.

Jim.

"Don't tell him anything," Lucas urged.

As difficult as that would prove, Jim was thousands of miles away and could do nothing about what was happening here. He certainly didn't need the additional stress.

"How is Tasha?" Victoria decided coming straight out with the question was the best way to prevent herself from blurting the truth. Worry twisted inside her, slicing like barbed wire.

"She came through the preparation for the procedure quite well. The doctors are very hopeful."

Her son's voice sounded strained and so very tired. "This is wonderful news," Victoria said, fighting the sting in her eyes. Jim did not deserve this—whatever the hell it was. He had been through enough. Far more than most people were aware. His body bore the scars from the physical torture he had suffered from the moment he went missing as a child. The mental scars had taken years to put behind him. They would never be forgotten, but he had built a wonderful life and Victoria wanted nothing to tear that sweet life apart.

He had paid far more than his share already.

"She'll rest today and then the procedure will go as

scheduled tomorrow. If it's successful, we should know by Monday."

This was far sooner than Victoria had expected. If this did not go their way...no, she couldn't think that way.

"Is there anything we can do, Jim?" Victoria offered. "We all have you and Tasha in our prayers, of course."

"That is much appreciated, but we are hanging in there. The staff here is working diligently to make our time as stress free as possible."

"I'm so glad." Thank God. *Thank you, God.*

"I should go and be with Tasha. Please let Luke and Jamie know we're doing fine."

"I will," Victoria promised. "Don't worry about anything here. We have everything under control."

"Thanks, Mom. Love you."

Victoria's chest tightened. "Love you." The call ended and for a bit she stared at the dark screen and struggled to hold back her emotions.

Lucas placed his hand over her free one. "You did what you needed to do."

She nodded. Lowered the phone and looked from one of her dedicated friends to the next. "Whatever else we do, we must—"

Her cell chimed again. She gasped as the name on the screen flashed.

Luke.

"Let it ring once more," Chelsea said.

The phone chimed again, and Victoria answered. "Luke?"

"Grandmother, you will receive a letter of instruction from a special courier in fifteen minutes," he explained. "You are to follow the instructions in this letter very carefully. They have explained the first part of the instructions and I am supposed to pass that part along to you now."

His voice gave the impression of calm, but there was no missing the hum of fear just beneath the surface. The sound of it tore at her soul.

"Whatever we need to do," Victoria said. "Just name it."

"Besides the ten million dollars, there is something he needs and there is only one person who can get it for him."

Him. The person behind this was a man. The information wasn't surprising and wouldn't narrow things down much, but it was something—a small piece of the bigger puzzle. "All right. I'm listening."

There was silence on the line.

"Luke?"

The sound of struggling echoed in Victoria's ear. She held her breath, fear tightening her throat like a snake coiled around it. "Luke, is everything all right?"

"Yes." His answer was strained. "I don't want to tell you but I…" A breath blasted across the line. "I have no choice."

"It's all right, Luke. Tell me what you need, and I will make it happen."

"They want Jamie. She is the only one they will allow to do this. If anyone else tries…they say they will…*kill* me."

Panic rushed into Victoria's chest. "Luke, I—"

"Wait for the courier, Grandmother."

The call ended.

Terror slammed into Victoria, making her jerk with its impact.

"I'm calling Jamie now," Lucas said. "As soon as I know where she is I will send the plane for her."

Dear God. Victoria held tightly to the phone no matter that the connection to Luke was lost, her eyes closing in horror. Now they wanted her other grandchild.

Chapter Two

Los Angeles
8:45 a.m.

Jamie Colby watched the guy dressed as Santa stroll down Hollywood Boulevard. It wasn't like there was much of anything open. Just a diner or a coffee shop here and there. A tourist trap or three selling tickets for bus tours to the homes of the stars and other popular sites.

Jamie climbed out of her rented car and stepped to the sidewalk. "Santa has a new follower at three o'clock," she murmured for the microphone disguised as a necklace draped around her throat.

The guy in jeans and a torn T carrying a sign begging for donations had pushed away from the storefront he'd been holding up for about an hour and strolled after Santa. Both looked a little worse for the wear, like they'd slept in their clothes for a few days or a week. Not exactly a top-of-the-line Santa. More a low-rent version. *Who wants their kids sitting on the lap of a guy that sleazy looking?*

But Jamie wasn't complaining. Working an op in LA around Christmas was way better than rambling around her apartment in DC. It was cold and wet in DC. Today in LA—Hollywood actually—it was a pleasant sixty-eight degrees with the sun shining. In a couple more hours the streets would be filled with tourists and life would be buzzing like bees in a honeycomb.

She liked the sunshine and the life beat of this place.

The only downside in her opinion was that after an entire month of hanging around the LA area, Jamie still hadn't stumbled upon any big celebrities. A few unknowns and lots and lots of wannabes. The city was always awash with people who wanted to possess just a little bit of the magic that came from Hollywood. The problem was most would never know what it was like to be a celebrity. Most would work in the service industry or something not exactly legal until they disappeared into obscurity or went back home to Kansas or wherever with their tails tucked between their legs. It was not a journey for the faint of heart.

Jamie had to admit that she'd had the dream once—at fourteen. She'd been in love with the idea of a career on the big screen. What young girl hadn't flirted with the idea? But her grandmother had known exactly how to change her mind. She brought Jamie for a weeklong stay in LA. They'd seen the sights and they'd also seen the parts that no one wanted to talk about—Victoria Colby had made sure of the latter. The reality of life in a big city that was really like a nation of its own with all the issues and ups and downs that went along with a huge population was not such a fairy tale. Bottom line—not everyone could be a star.

Jamie smiled when she thought of her grandmother. Victoria had a way of clarifying all things. She missed her so much. It was snowing in Chicago right now. Jamie wished she was going home for Christmas, but she was on assignment here and her parents had taken a long overdue vacation to Europe. Luke was staying in Nashville to be a part of a special program between semesters. The guy was always looking for ways to gain extra credit. Jamie didn't get it. Anything beyond a 4.0 GPA was totally unnecessary in her view. But good grades had always come easy for her. Luke had to work for his.

"Heads up, Colby."

The words whispered in her earpiece brought her back to full attention. Santa was still making his way along the sidewalk, crossing over Vine. The errant beggar had gained on him to the point of nearly overtaking him.

"It's going down soon," came the voice in her ear.

Jamie picked up her pace and made an agreeable sound for those listening, including her partner.

Every move she made—every move her team made— was under close scrutiny. No one wanted this new agency to fail. But the powers that be weren't interested in throwing money after a new venture that on first look seemed too similar to the ones they already had. In truth there were already far too many government agencies—particularly secretive ones—in the opinion of some. For IOA to survive it had to provide something none of the others did and it had to be better...in every way.

Jamie wanted to be a part of making that happen. Like her grandmother, making a name for herself and a good career just wasn't enough. She wanted to make her special *mark*. A mark no one else had made.

Her friend Kendrick Poe would say she was overthinking it, but he'd already made one hell of a mark for himself so he should totally understand even if he pretended his accomplishments were no big deal.

Besides, just being a Colby set the bar damned high.

For a girl, Luke would say.

Jamie bit back a grin. Her little brother was certain he would go far higher than his big sister.

Not if Jamie could help it.

She was all for her brother going as far as possible as long as she went further. They'd been fiercely competitive—especially with each other—forever.

Up ahead, the beggar guy moved in a little closer on Santa.

Time to move.

Jamie added another click to her pace and walked past the beggar. He glanced at her, but considering her too-tight jeans and cropped sweater he didn't appear to consider her a threat.

Too bad for him.

She had just powered in front of Santa when she turned over her supercool right ankle boot and threw her full body weight into the guy in the red and mostly off-white velvet.

They both went down, landing uncomfortably on the concrete sidewalk.

Beggar guy stared in astonishment for one seemingly endless moment before hurrying away. He'd missed his shot. Too bad. Too sad.

"I'm so sorry!" Jamie cried as she attempted to right herself and Santa. "Are you all right, sir?"

He should be all right, but he smelled way wrong. Inside, she shuddered. Santa needed a serious shower and a freshly laundered suit. He smelled a little like sweat and a lot like alcohol. Jamie really hoped the stain on the front of his jolly jacket wasn't dried vomit.

The man scrambled for his red hat and tugged it back on before allowing Jamie to help him to his feet.

"I'm fine," he insisted, looking around exactly like a criminal would.

When would people learn? If you wanted to do a job well—even an illegal one—you had to get your act together and leave the booze at home.

"Oh no." Jamie dusted at his coat, noting how the right sleeve had come loose from the body of the jacket at the seam. "You tore your jacket. I hope you weren't on the way to a scheduled Santa visit."

"No." He shook his head, then backed away just enough to look her up and down. "You okay, little girl?"

She smiled and resisted the initial response that shot to the tip of her tongue. She was no little girl. The term was probably just the way he referred to all females younger than him, which would include most of the population in the LA area.

"I think I twisted my ankle." She winced. "I should have been paying better attention to where I was going."

"Probably on your phone," he grumbled, testing his own weight on first his left foot, then his right.

Apparently, he actually had twisted an ankle. Could make her job easier.

"I'm so sorry. Really." She offered her arm. "I insist on seeing you to your destination."

She noted the way he stared beyond her. "Beggar guy is coming back around," the voice whispered in her earpiece. No wonder Santa was staring.

When the collision had occurred the other guy apparently crossed the street and now he was retracing his steps. He had a mission. Good for him. Too bad he'd failed already.

"Well...er..." Santa nodded. "I could use the help."

He was old enough, maybe even close to her grandmother's age. No one would be surprised at him asking for help after a spill at his age. Beggar guy would just have to back off for a bit.

"How long have you been playing Santa?" Jamie asked

as they walked slowly forward. She purposely set the pace slow to buy time and to wear on beggar guy's patience.

"Off and on since I hit sixty-five. The cost of living in LA is difficult on a fixed income."

"I'm sure." LA living wasn't easy on a great income. "So, you're a lifer?"

"Born and raised," he said with a glance over his shoulder.

She chuckled. "I'm surprised you're not an actor or a former one." He actually looked like the type.

"Who says I'm not." He glanced at her this time. "Never judge a book by its cover, little girl."

How ironic. She'd just been thinking the same thing.

"We have a newcomer to the party."

The warning echoed in her earpiece. Time to wrap up the chitchat.

Jamie reached to her left hip pocket as if she were reaching for her cell and slipped out the lightweight handcuffs. She'd slapped the first cuff on Santa's wrist before he realized what she was doing. Simultaneously, she tugged him toward the No Parking sign and snapped the other cuff to the metal post.

Then she whirled and confronted beggar guy who had stopped to stare in shock at what she'd done.

Didn't see that one coming, did you?

There were a few pedestrians on the street. No one wanted to whip out a gun. Well, at least not Jamie. She hoped to do this the old-fashioned way by kicking beggar guy's butt. And then he reached into his jacket and came out with a weapon.

Damn it.

She kicked the beggar's gun out of his hand before he had it fully leveled on her. Santa was shouting and attempting to tug himself free. *Good luck with that.*

"The newcomer is coming at you," she heard from her earpiece.

"Great," she muttered as beggar guy dove at her. She rolled him into a hold with one arm locked around his throat and her legs locked around his, prying them apart to prevent him from gaining purchase on the ground. Good thing her tight jeans were made of spandex. When he continued to resist, she pounded his head into the concrete a couple of times, and he relaxed.

Newcomer was suddenly on top of her then.

This one was dressed like Batman and wasn't going down quite so easily.

He flipped Jamie onto her back and had both hands around her throat. She clawed at his face. Before she could get in a good dig, his head suddenly jerked to the right and then his body flew off her.

"I thought you might need a hand." A long-fingered hand reached out to her.

She looked from the hand she recognized to the guy in the Wolverine costume.

Poe.

"Really? Wolverine?" Jamie took his hand and allowed him to pull her to her feet. "I had this, you know."

"I'm sure you did," Poe agreed, "but Santa was causing a scene and we don't need that."

The old guy was shouting at the top of his lungs and people were stopping to stare and point. Cell phones were coming out.

Time to go.

"Where's the car?" she asked as she freed Santa.

"Half a block up on the right."

"Let's go, Santa." She secured the newly freed cuff to

her wrist. She wasn't letting this guy out of her sight and certainly not out of her reach.

By the time she ushered him forward that half a block or so, Poe had hopped behind the wheel. Jamie opened the rear passenger door and she and Santa climbed into the back seat.

"What's going on here?" Santa demanded.

When Poe had peeled away from the curb, she glanced back to ensure the two followers were still dragging themselves off the ground.

"Not to worry, Santa," she assured him. "We're not sending you back to the North Pole yet."

"Am I under arrest?" Santa demanded. "I need to see a badge. And aren't you supposed to read me my rights?"

"What's wrong with Wolverine?" Poe demanded from the front seat as he took a right on Sunset Boulevard.

Jamie checked behind them to ensure they weren't being followed. "I had you figured for a Deadpool guy."

"Where are we going?" Santa demanded.

"Don't worry," Jamie assured him. "We're going to take very good care of you, Santa."

Poe took Sunset all the way to where it transitioned into West Cesar Estrada Chavez Avenue and then a left on North Main to Our Lady Queen of Angels Catholic Church. This was the drop point. If they were lucky, they would get in and get out without a confrontation.

No one wanted to cause turmoil in a house of God just days before Christmas.

They parked across the street and surveyed the area.

"If they're in the church already..." Poe said without completing the thought.

Jamie understood. If the others were in the church already, they were in trouble. In truth, they had no way of confirming how many of the *others* were on this.

"Let's assume we got here first," Jamie offered.

"Whatever you say." Her partner wasn't so optimistic.

Poe got out and leaned against the closed driver's side door to keep an eye on their destination.

While he got the lay of the land, Jamie needed to convince Santa to cooperate. "Look, I don't know why you needed an exit strategy today, Santa," she began, "but I would prefer to keep breathing so don't give me any trouble. Got it?"

His face wrinkled with confusion. "What in God's name is an exit strategy?"

Clearly the man had not watched enough James Bond. "Someone wants you dead and we're here to make sure that doesn't happen. We extracted you before you reached the location where you were supposed to die, on the corner of Hollywood Boulevard and McFadden Place."

"I was meeting my nephew for lunch."

"I'm sorry to tell you this, but your nephew or someone close to him set you up." She unlocked the handcuffs and tossed them onto the floorboard. "I need you to stay close to me, Santa."

He nodded, the movement unsteady as if the news had knocked him for a loop. Probably had.

The rear driver's side door opened. "We seem to be clear to proceed," Poe said.

Which meant he actually couldn't be certain. Evidently the communication link had dropped. The voices in Jamie's ear had disappeared.

They were on their own without the assist of handy electronics.

Santa eased out and Poe stepped closer, shielding the older man's body with his own.

Jamie emerged on the opposite side and surveyed the sidewalk and the strip mall beyond it on the passenger side, then she crossed around to the other side of the car with Poe and their Christmas package.

"Going in the front door." Poe glanced at her.

Jamie nodded.

They hurried across the street and to the double entry front doors of the church, Santa in tow between them.

The doors were locked.

What the hell?

"Side door," Jamie urged.

They moved around the front right corner of the church, going for the side entrance. Their destination was the door beneath the portico that allowed for dropping off parishioners under the cover of an awning. All they had to do was reach it before they encountered trouble.

Jamie kept a close watch on their surroundings. No one behind them.

No one in front.

No running or shouting.

So far, so good.

Her pulse kept a rapid staccato while they hustled along the side of the building until they reached the secondary entrance. They entered without hesitation.

Inside was dark.

The side door opened into a quiet corridor. Taking a left led to the main sanctuary. Right went toward restrooms and a family room for breastfeeding mothers. Jamie had studied the layout.

"Why are we here?" Santa asked in a too-loud whisper.

"You'll be picked up here," Jamie assured him. At least as long as things went according to plan. She kept that part to herself. No need to get the guy riled up again.

Santa stalled, tugging to free his arm from her grip. "I don't understand."

This was not the time. "As soon as we ensure your pickup detail is here, I'll explain as best I can."

The sound of the door they had entered only moments ago opening had Jamie and Poe parting ways. He went toward the main sanctuary, while she ushered Santa into a coat closet near the restrooms.

The coat closet was actually a room with plenty of hanging space for coats, shelves for hats and hooks for umbrellas. It had once been the only restroom and had housed several stalls, so it was fairly large for the purpose it now served.

"I think there must have been a mistake," Santa whispered.

Jamie pressed a hand to his mouth in hopes of getting the message across without having to say the words out loud.

Under her sweater, in the band that kept her cell pressed against her abdomen, her cell vibrated with an incoming call. Control, the people in charge of this operation, would not contact her via her private cell phone. If the comms link was down, someone would contact her or Poe in person.

The call was more likely a distraction.

She hated the idea that someone might have gotten her private cell number, but it happened. If that proved to be the case, she'd need a new number after this. Always a pain in the butt.

Footsteps in the corridor outside the coat closet had her bracing. She scanned the room and then ushered Santa into the farthest corner from the door. She grabbed the two big coats that someone had left behind and camouflaged him as best she could.

She was about to leave it at that when she noticed the open lid on the built-in wood bench that ran the length of the wall. She tapped Santa on the shoulder and pointed to the big bench. It was at least two feet from front to back. Slightly taller than that and several feet long.

He shrugged and then climbed in. Jamie poked all signs of red velvet into the bench and closed the lid. She placed an umbrella atop it and quickly moved toward the door. She flattened against the wall next to it.

Perfect timing. The door opened. She stepped back, keeping the door between her and whoever was coming in.

As soon as the door started to close, and she spotted the back of the head now swiveling on a pair of broad shoulders, she knew it was not a friend. Definitely a foe.

She reached up, boring the muzzle of her weapon into the back of his skull. "Stop right there."

Surprisingly, he did as she asked.

"Put your weapon on the floor and kick it aside," she ordered.

Rather than bend over to do as she asked, he did what she would have done, he began to lower in the knees.

Oh well, if that was the way he wanted to play it.

Just when he would have twisted to put one between her eyes, she squeezed her own trigger, sending a bullet into his right wrist and sending the weapon he'd been holding flying toward the floor.

He swore. Grabbed for her.

She pressed the muzzle between his eyes. "Don't make me shoot you again. I won't be so nice about it this time."

He glared at her, but his hands went up, blood running down from the right wrist.

The door flew inward again, but this time it was Poe.

"Well, hello," he said to the guy with the bullet wound. "I see you met my partner."

Five minutes later, their pickup crew had arrived, and Santa was on his way to safety.

Jamie had no idea why the man had needed assistance or even who he was. She had no need to know, any more than Poe did. Their mission was to provide him with an exit strategy from his planned engagement and to get him to this church.

They might never know what value he represented, but they had accomplished their mission and that was all that mattered.

Once they were in the rented car, headed away from Our Lady Queen of Angels, Poe said, "You hungry? I'm starving."

Completing a mission was a big rush and it always left her hungry. "How about we get out of LA before we stop."

He hitched his head in acknowledgment. "How about we drive down to the Santa Monica Pier and find something to eat and listen to the ocean roar."

"Somewhere in Malibu will be quieter," she argued. "Too many tourists on the pier."

"Works for me."

Like her, her partner wore jeans and a pullover. His was a UCLA sweatshirt. He was a year older than Jamie and had darker features—brown hair, brown eyes—that sharply contrasted her blond hair. They had been friends for almost two years now. He was a good friend. They teetered on the edge of something more, but work always got in the way. Probably for the best. Who had time for romance?

Her cell started vibrating again, and Jamie reached beneath her sweatshirt and pulled it free of its hiding place.

G flashed on her screen.

She smiled. Her grandmother. "Hey, Grandmother," she said. "Is it still snowing in Chicago?"

"Jamie, we have a problem."

Fear trickled into her blood. "What kind of problem?"

"It's Luke. Someone has taken him, and he needs our help." Victoria's voice trembled on the last word.

There were things she should say. Like how terrible it was to hear this news and why would anyone target Luke? But her throat had closed, and she couldn't seem to make her jaw work.

"Jamie." The male voice she knew as well as her own underscored just how serious the situation was. If her grandmother was so upset…

No jumping to conclusions. Her heart stuttered again, and she managed a breath. She had to listen carefully. "Yes, Grandpa." She swallowed at the lingering tightness in her throat. "What's going on?" Calling Lucas Camp "Grandpa" was like calling a grizzly bear a kitten.

"Colby One will pick you up at the Van Nuys Airport at one. We'll meet you in Nashville."

Poe was splitting his attention between her and the road. He couldn't hear the conversation, but he obviously saw the terror on her face. "What's going on?" he urged.

Jamie made a decision then and there. They had completed their mission. Time off was a given. It was only a matter of how much. "Inform the pilot I'm bringing a friend. I'll see you in Nashville, Grandpa."

She ended the call, and Poe's gaze locked with hers. She explained the situation, the need to scream crawling up her throat. She had to stay calm. Focused. "We have to find him. I…can't…" Big breath. "I can't let him down."

"Don't worry," Poe said softly. "We won't fail… We never have before."

He was right…but this time was different. This was not just another mission… This was her little brother.

Chapter Three

Nashville
4:00 p.m.

The private airfield near Nashville was off the beaten path, but then Jamie suspected that was why it had been chosen. Whether it was the fear that their calls were being monitored or could potentially be so, there had been radio silence during the four-plus-hour flight from LA to Nashville. She'd contacted their superior at IOA and notified him that she and Poe would be out of reach for a few days. Since they were due time off after an operation it was no problem.

Poe had helped Jamie keep herself together. Not an easy task when she was worried. Luke was not like her. He hadn't embraced this undercover, secret agent life. He was a total pacifist—a man focused on learning how to help others with medicine. Although Victoria had insisted they both learn how to use a handgun, Jamie would bet Luke had not touched one since.

"That's your grandmother?" Poe asked as he watched Victoria emerge from the limo that had arrived.

Jamie smiled. She tried to think how Victoria Colby-Camp appeared to others. A mature woman with silver threads in her dark hair. Tall, trim, well dressed. She looked a good twenty years younger than her age. From all appearances she might be your average attractive, wealthy middle-aged woman.

Except there was nothing average about Victoria.

"That's her." They had used a different airfield. Having two jets arrive from Chicago at the same place would have roused suspicions. Jamie rushed to her grandmother and hugged her as hard as she dared. Even so, she was impressed at the slim, toned body she felt beneath the layers of clothing. Victoria not only kept her mind sharp, but she also kept her body lean as well.

"Jamie." Victoria drew back and looked her up and down. "We don't have a lot of time, so we need to talk fast."

Renewed worry twisted in Jamie's belly. "What can you tell me?"

"Let's talk inside."

Jamie turned to her grandpa, who was watching them across the top of the vehicle. She smiled. "Hey, Grandpa." She hitched her head toward the man waiting behind her. "This is Poe. We work together."

Lucas Camp pointed a gaze at Poe that likely sent a shiver down his spine.

"Sir." Poe gave him a nod.

"Poe," Jamie said, drawing his attention in her direction, "this is my grandmother, Victoria."

Her mission partner nodded. "A pleasure to meet you, ma'am. I've heard a lot about you." He glanced toward Lucas. "Both of you."

Victoria nodded before ducking back into the passenger compartment of the limo. Jamie climbed in behind her. Lucas settled on the seat next to Victoria, and Poe dropped next to Jamie opposite her grandparents.

"What in the world happened?" Worry about her little

brother had torn Jamie apart during the flight here. She wasn't sure how much more of the not knowing she could handle.

"I received a call this morning," Victoria explained. "It was Luke. He said I would receive instructions via a courier and that I should do nothing until I received those instructions. The only thing he could tell me before hanging up was that it had to be you who carried out the instructions."

Jamie and Poe exchanged a look.

"Then, we can safely assume," Poe suggested, "that this someone is aware of your particular skill set."

Jamie nodded. "Agreed."

Lucas said, "We have some idea of what your work entails. What aspects of that work do you believe has put you in someone's crosshairs?"

Jamie thought about the question for a moment. "As you know," she explained, "our agency operates a very diverse team to resolve issues all over the world. Sometimes, like today, our assignments seem sedate."

"Like picking up a Santa-for-hire," Poe clarified, "before he was neutralized and delivering him to a safe location."

Jamie went on. "We have no idea who this Santa was or why someone wanted to terminate him. Frankly, it seemed like the sort of assignment any cop in the LAPD could have handled. But there was a reason we were sent in to do it. We just may never know what that reason was."

"I can shed a little light on that one," Lucas said.

Poe frowned and shared another look with Jamie.

"You have no idea," she said, laughing. "Grandpa isn't who you think he is." This was truer than she would ever be able to convince her friend or anyone else.

Poe gave a nod. "I see."

"Your Santa arrived in LA from a visit to Santiago last

Friday. His wife's mother passed away unexpectedly."
Lucas shrugged. "We'll stick with calling him Santa. You
may not realize based on his condition today—he has felt
a little under the weather the past couple of days—but he
was booked solid with many appearances at some very
large malls and department stores."

Jamie got it now. "He would have come into contact with
a lot of people over the next few days."

Lucas nodded. "By tomorrow, the incubation period will
be complete and Santa will be highly contagious with the
virus he contracted at the funeral."

"I take it he had no idea," Jamie suggested. No wonder
he'd been self-medicating with alcohol. He probably felt
like hell and was attempting to cheer himself up.

"None. Eleven other targets were discovered and picked
up in the past twenty-four hours. Your Santa was the last."

"Wow." Poe shook his head. "No wonder we had to take
all those shots when we received our orders."

"There's no reason to believe you were exposed," Lucas
explained. "The date and time your Santa was exposed was
known so he wouldn't have been contagious yet, just feeling a little under the weather from all the changes happening in his body."

Victoria shook her head. "I liked it better when we could
see the attacks coming." She took a deep breath. "At any
rate, based on the instructions delivered by the courier Luke
told us about, there is a certain surgeon in Nashville who
has perfected a previously basically impossible-to-do brain
surgery. The first successful procedure was completed just
three months ago. There have been two more each week
since and though this is an amazing step, this surgeon is
the only one so far who has managed the feat. The hope
is that he will be able to train others, but it's not going to

be easy, and worse, it's going to take time. For those who have inoperable brain tumors, time is not on their side."

"There is a great deal of fiery rhetoric in the medical field just now," Lucas said, picking up from there, "as to whether this surgeon, Dr. Quinton Case, should be wasting his time trying to teach others to do the surgery or just doing the surgery. He can only do two or three per week because it is incredibly tedious and both physically and mentally exhausting."

Victoria said, "How do you decide which patients will receive the surgery and which won't during any given week? How many lives will be lost while time is taken away from surgery to attempt teaching others?"

"Wow, that's a hard one." Jamie searched her grandmother's face. "But, as horrible as what you're telling me is, what does this have to do with Luke?"

"We can only assume that our kidnapper has someone close to him who needs this surgery since all he wants is the surgeon."

Jamie held up her hands. "Wait. This dude wants me to kidnap this surgeon and deliver him to his location of choice?"

"You have approximately seventy-two hours—or until five o'clock on Monday. At that time, if the surgeon has not been delivered to the drop-off location, Luke will die."

Jamie's heart sank. She turned to Poe. "Though I appreciate your desire to give me a hand with this, I think this is where your participation ends. I can't ask you to do this."

"No way." He shook his head. "I'm not walking away."

"I won't argue with you, Kenny." She wouldn't waste time or energy doing that.

"Then don't because I'm not leaving until you do." He leaned deeper into the seat.

"You should consider what she's trying to tell you," Lucas argued. "There is nothing we can do. In fact, this… right here…is as far as our participation can go. The instructions were explicit. Once we have passed the information along, any involvement on our part or the part of our agency will prompt an immediate termination of the deal. No exceptions."

Jamie turned to her grandfather. Then it was decided—she was on her own. "Under the circumstances, I would suggest you get on with this briefing and go."

Victoria shook her head. "There are steps we can take to prevent you having to do this."

Jamie understood. They could make a preemptive strike. Grab the surgeon and then do the negotiating. "But we both understand how risky that option is. The same with going to the FBI. Anything we do puts us in a situation where we can't guarantee the outcome for Luke."

Victoria shook her head again. "Even following their rules, there are no guarantees of the outcome, Jamie. As you're well aware, things can go wrong either way. People can go back on their word."

"Then there's nothing to talk about." Jamie looked to Lucas. "Let's get this done and the two of you should be on your way. It doesn't take a lot of imagination to figure out they likely know about your arrival, and they'll be watching for your departure."

Lucas passed Jamie a brown envelope. "This tells you everything you need to know about your target. The drop-off location will be given to you nearer the grab time."

Jamie accepted the package. "Thank you."

Lucas shook his head and looked away.

"The limo will drop you at the first transition point

where you'll receive the next set of instructions," Victoria said.

"As you said, they know we're here and we have been instructed," Lucas said, his voice tight, "to get back to Chicago."

"I'll take care of this." Jamie looked from her grandfather to her grandmother. "Luke will be fine. I promise." She hesitated a moment. "I'm assuming you haven't told my parents."

"We've been instructed not to tell anyone," Victoria confirmed.

Jamie reached out and took her grandmother's hand. "I will get this done."

They hugged and then Jamie hugged her grandfather. There were so many things she would have liked to say, and she was confident her grandparents felt the same, but there was no time.

Luke needed them to remain calm and to move quickly. All else would have to wait.

Excalibur Court,
6:30 p.m.

JAMIE HAD WAITED at the airfield until the Colby Agency jets had taken flight. Watching her grandparents leave knowing she had to stay and get this done had been extremely difficult. This was her little brother's life, and her grandparents were the strongest, most capable people she knew. She suddenly felt utterly lost and desolate.

The driver had then brought them to a house in a very high-end neighborhood. The house was apparently unoccupied and sat in a cul-de-sac on a hillside overlooking the home of Dr. Quinton Case. Well, calling the place a home was a bit of an understatement. The Case's estate was a massive property ensconced amid more than a hundred acres of treed serenity.

The house on Excalibur Court had been staged with everything they might need—at least on first look. The supersensitive telescope setup allowed them to see—to a degree—inside the home of Dr. Case. Everything from climbing equipment to serious weapons and one hell of a muscle car getaway vehicle had been provided.

There was food and drink, but Jamie wasn't consuming anything in this house. She'd had the driver stop at a local market where she'd picked up food and water. She and Poe had searched the house for wires and cameras. They'd found numerous devices, though they couldn't be sure they'd found them all.

Whoever had set up this op was good.

Strangely enough, a note for Jamie *and* Poe had been left on the kitchen island. The person who had composed the note claimed to have known she would bring Poe with her and the items he would need had been made available as well. This included clothes and weapons. To Jamie's way of thinking, this was proof whoever was behind this knew both her and Poe.

Poe had spread the map and step-by-step instructions on the dining table. Whoever was funding this op had thought of everything—literally.

"On Sunday night, Case is having a holiday party at his home," Poe said. "And that's when you're supposed to nab him."

"The presumption," Jamie said, "I assume is that this is a time when he will be most vulnerable. Preoccupied. Distracted."

The man was surrounded by security at all times, particularly at his office and at the hospital. Understandable, she supposed. But it was sad that because of his success in creating a lifesaving procedure his life was now in danger.

"No question," Poe agreed. "I'm thinking…" He leaned against the edge of the table. "I find it interesting that they assumed you would want me to come because there was nothing in the instructions about me and no one has showed up to put a bullet in my head or ask me to take a walk. Instead, they left clothes and weapons for me."

"Seems like they know me—us—pretty well," she agreed.

"Makes sense I guess since it doesn't seem like a one-person operation if you ask me," he pointed out.

"Since we haven't been given more detail other than the strike is on Sunday night, I'd say it's too soon to tell. But I tend to agree with you. I'm wondering if we'll be given additional backup when the time comes."

Jamie walked into the living room and up to the telescope. The wall of floor-to-ceiling glass doors opened fully to the balcony outside by sliding away like a movable wall. Not so great this time of year, but amazing for extending the entertaining space to the outdoors in the summer. She peered through the lens and directly into the entrance hall of the grand manor that was Dr. Case's home. "The real question in my mind is getting him out of those woods."

Poe joined her at the wall of windows that looked out over the dark landscape. "Getting him out of the house shouldn't be so difficult. There are numerous egresses. It will only be a matter of evading staff and security. The cameras will be another issue altogether, but they may be providing information on the security system. One would hope."

"It's the woods," she repeated as she surveyed the darkness between this house and the target. "He's not going to come willingly, and we have to be extremely careful with him. Any injury could put him out of commission. That would defeat the whole purpose of nabbing him."

"And therein," Poe said, "lies the answer to why we are here."

Jamie straightened away from the telescope, following his train of thought. "They need him for his ability to do this procedure."

"Which means," Poe picked up where she left off, "our employer either intends to start a school for surgeons who want to be like Case, or, as your grandmother suggested, he has a loved one with an inoperable brain tumor who doesn't have the time left to wait his or her turn for the procedure."

It wasn't necessary to say the rest out loud just in case they were being monitored. Even now, Victoria and her people would likely be running down known patients in need of the potentially lifesaving surgery only Dr. Case could provide. Even if they narrowed the list down to the precise patient and therefore the perpetrator of this plan, would there be time to find Luke wherever they had hidden him?

The risk was entirely too great to take.

The sound of clapping had them both spinning to face the threat. "Bravo."

Poe reached for his weapon.

Jamie was too busy picking her jaw up off the floor. Even if she hadn't seen his face, she would have recognized that hint of a British accent anywhere. "Abi?"

Abidan "Abi" Amar stood near the French doors that led to the living room. He clapped one last time before dropping his hands to his sides. "Jamie." One eyebrow reared up. "Kendrick Poe, I presume," he said to Poe. "A man whose claim to fame is that he purports to be a distant relative of Edgar Allan Poe. How very interesting."

"Actually—" Poe put his weapon away "—my claim to fame is the well-known exit of no less than a dozen Americans from al-Qaeda in Yemen. Everything else I've done in my short career is just icing on that very large cake."

Abi gave a nod. "I may have heard something about that."

"What're you doing here, Abi?" Jamie crossed her arms over her chest and eyed him suspiciously.

To say his appearance was a surprise would be a vast understatement. Abi was not a terrorist, though many might say his reputation suggested otherwise. Be that as it may, her knowledge of him provided some room for error in that assessment.

Abi was a contractor who worked doing whatever he was paid to do—within some vague lines that only he could see. In other words, he wasn't a real bad guy. Just one who did things that were not always legal for money.

He colored outside the lines and he loved every minute of it.

"It is my job to oversee your work," he announced. He surveyed Poe up and down. "Although, I must say my job may have been easier without this complication."

Poe's face darkened. "Excuse me?"

Jamie held up a hand for Poe as she walked toward Abi. "So, you're my backup in this?"

"That is correct."

"Wait a minute, Jamie," Poe argued.

Again, she gave Poe her hand. "First, Abi—" she looked directly at him "—I would not trust you to have my back under any circumstances. Ever. Second, if this...whoever-he-is...that took my brother has you, what does he need with me? I can't fathom why he would *complicate* this situation with additional players. More room for leaks and other issues."

The last was the real question. Abi's skills were equal to Jamie's, maybe greater since he was older and had more experience. He had been offered a position at IOA without even putting his name in the hat or competing in any way, but he'd turned it down. He much preferred being his own boss. He didn't play well with others.

If the person who took Luke—who wanted or needed Dr. Case—had Abi on the payroll, they really didn't need anyone else for a straightforward op like this. In fact, the scenario made no sense at all.

"You see," Abi said, "trust is a very important part of this very delicate situation. I think my reputation for being available to the highest bidder preceded me and the trust level wasn't where it needed to be."

"Good point," Jamie agreed. Abi was just as likely to abduct the doctor and sell his services to someone else as to go with the guy who hired him.

Abi went on, "This is also the reason, I suspect, that they took your brother. A little insurance to keep you focused."

Abi was very handsome by any standards. Tall, muscular, black hair and eyes. Jamie stood no more than three feet from Abi and already the physical draw wanted to overpower her. No way. She had been down that road once. Besides, she could only have one focus right now: rescuing her brother.

The very last thing she intended to do was get involved in any way with this man. He was dangerous on far too many levels.

"What do you know that we don't?" she demanded.

"Really? I'm not sure we have the time to cover everything."

Poe shook his head. "This guy is a real comedian."

Obviously, Poe had picked up on the sparks flying between him and Jamie. She'd have to work harder to smother that connection.

"I know that we only have one shot to achieve our goal because our target is leaving for a holiday on Monday." He shook his head. "Can you imagine? He is the only surgeon who has the ability to do this surgery and he dares to take a vacation." He laughed. "Doesn't say a whole lot for his level of compassion."

"You ever heard of burnout?" Poe tossed back at him.

Both men had a point. "All right," Jamie said, redirecting the conversation. "So we have to get him during the party on Sunday night or risk him getting away before he can do what your employer needs him to do."

"*Our* employer," Abi countered.

"What's the plan to get into the house?" Poe asked.

"You don't need that information yet," Abi said. "You will learn each step as needed. That's the most secure way to move forward."

She and Poe exchanged a frustrated look.

"For now, there are other security issues that need to be addressed. I'll need your cell phones and we'll conduct a little pat down."

"You can't be serious." Jamie shook her head. "No way."

Abi turned his hands up. "It's your choice but you know the consequences."

"Fine." She passed him her cell. There was no option for resisting. "Just do it."

With visible reluctance, Poe held out his cell phone as well.

Abi took the phones to the coffee table, gave them a

quick check and then added what was no doubt a tracking device or bug of some sort.

"You are to make no unauthorized calls until this is done." He handed each one their phone back. "You are not to leave this house until the job is finished."

"I take it you're here to stay." Not really a question in Jamie's opinion. He was here for the duration, she suspected.

"I will be here until you complete this mission."

"Look me in the eye," Jamie demanded, "and tell me that you do not have orders to terminate anyone when this is over." Not that she was afraid of him getting the upper hand on her. She wasn't. She was every bit as good as he was one-on-one. But she was worried about what might happen to her brother even if she did get the doctor. And his family. Would Case's family be harmed? As for Poe, like her, he could take care of himself.

"I have no termination orders," Abi said. "Unless, you fail to follow through with your instructions and, I will be honest with you, I declined that part of the deal. If you opt out or fail, your brother's execution will be carried out by someone else, but mark my word, it will be carried out."

She supposed she couldn't ask for more than full disclosure.

"There is just one issue," Abi said.

Here it came. Damn it.

"Your friend here," Abi said with a glance at Poe. "He was not part of the plan."

Poe visibly braced.

"Which means," Abi said, "that I have the less than pleasant duty of informing my employer of the modification."

"Please," Jamie said bluntly, "you have had ample time to do this already. Obviously, you had a clue it was happening because you provided clothes for him."

"Actually, those are mine."

Jamie held up both hands. Oh. She hadn't thought of that. "Whatever. I want Poe here. He's with me—to watch my back. Deal with it."

She held her breath. Hoped to hell he would allow her this one concession.

For a long moment, Abi only stared at her. Finally, he looked away. "You're lucky I'm feeling generous." He shrugged. "Besides, we might need him for a distraction of some sort if we get into trouble."

"I don't plan to get into trouble," Jamie argued. "That's your MO, not mine."

Abi laughed. "Well, let's hope you can keep that record. This is not going to be as easy as it sounds."

The fact that he had inside information compelled her to believe him. "Tell me about the hard parts."

"Dr. Case has a body double."

Dread dragged at her gut. "Are you serious?"

"I am indeed. The most difficult part will be making sure we take the right guy and that we keep his wife and daughter out of the line of fire."

What kind of doctor hired a body double?

"You have some way of proving who the real Dr. Case is?" God, she hoped so. Because all she had was a photo of the man.

"I do and it's foolproof. But that doesn't mean he will make this easy."

Jamie shrugged. "It doesn't have to be easy. It just has to be doable."

She would do whatever necessary to save her brother's life—even give up her own.

"It is doable," Abi said.

"No more issues with or questions about Poe," she pressed.

Abi shook his head. "I will handle the situation."

Poe scoffed. "Somehow I figured that was the answer all along, otherwise you might have to get your hands dirty."

Abi chuckled. "You might be smarter than I anticipated."

The standoff lasted about five seconds. Poe said, "You mentioned a pat down." He gestured to Abi. "Why don't we get that part over with? Jamie and I like to know who we're working with—what he carries, what he's hiding. Things like that. You want to go first?"

Jamie rolled her eyes. *Let the games begin.*

Saturday, December 22

Three Days Before Christmas

Chapter Four

Excalibur Court,
8:30 a.m.

Jamie wiped the steam from the mirror. The shower had cleared her head a bit. She'd barely slept last night. She couldn't stop thinking about Luke and how he must be feeling.

Her little brother was a good guy. His need to help others was so clear in his every decision. The fact that he wanted to be a doctor said so much about him. She had to make sure he came through this safely. No one should be kidnapped and held against his will, but Luke was one of the last people on the planet who deserved such treatment. Jamie wished she could claim credit for even ten percent of his good works. The man was always donating his time and/or ability to one cause or another.

There had been times when Jamie worried that this made him vulnerable. It wasn't that she didn't agree with the work he did, but he had to be more careful to protect himself. He was a Colby. This made him a target far more so than he wanted to admit. She'd warned him time and time again that he had to be careful. He shouldn't just blindly trust anyone.

She scrubbed the towel over her skin. That wasn't fair.

Just because he had been targeted and taken hostage did not mean he hadn't been careful.

When she'd dried her body and whipped her hair into a damp ponytail, she put on the jeans and sweatshirt that had been provided. Her host had thought of everything. Clothes. Shoes. Toiletries. The scariest part was that these were toiletries she would have chosen.

She suspected Abi had taken care of those details or at least helped with that part. Or maybe he'd been the one to think of it period. He was quite a diva when it came to personal comfort. No matter. She had carefully checked every single item for tracking devices and anything else that could be used to monitor her movements or subdue her in any way. As she'd done so, her mind had conjured images of her and Abi together...their bodies entwined.

She rolled her eyes and put the thought out of her head. She knew firsthand how he liked things. She and Abi had a thing for a little while late last year. It hadn't been a big deal. She'd run into him after a long and exhausting assignment. She'd had a feeling he'd picked her out of the pack and zeroed in on her. Maybe she was being paranoid, but it had felt that way. There were plenty of others in the agency he could have targeted.

Of course, his decision to go after her had nothing to do with this current mission.

She gave her reflection one last look. There were several items on her to-do list today and she wasn't standing for Abi getting in her way. He might be in charge of babysitting, but this was her op.

When she opened the bedroom door, the smell of coffee had her ready to moan. The house was a large one with five bedrooms—each with its own bath—and a large center great room with its impressive balcony and telescope. Oh, and the infinity pool was inspiring even in the window. The steam rising from it this morning told her it was heated.

"Good morning, sleeping beauty," Abi announced as bread popped out of the toaster.

"Who slept?" she grumbled. She felt confident her grandparents hadn't slept last night either. Like her, they were probably terrified for Luke. She hadn't been able to stop thinking about him.

She stilled, then glanced around the room. "Where's Poe?"

"He's having a look around outside. Checking out the ride that's been provided to you."

Of course he was. *Men.* "I have some things to do."

Abi passed her a plate loaded with toast, each slice smeared with a plop of guacamole. "Great. I'll go with you. Poe can hold down the fort."

"Sorry, but where I go, Poe goes." The toast actually looked quite good. He'd chopped up tomatoes and sprinkled them across the top. She took a bite. This time she did moan.

"You need coffee."

As if it hadn't been fourteen months, two weeks and three days since they'd seen each other, he prepared her a cup of coffee with exactly the right amount of almond milk creamer.

"What is it you want, Abi?" He was up to something. This was another thing that had kept her awake last night. It wasn't like him to be so attentive unless he wanted something more than he'd stated. Then again, she supposed it was his job to keep her focused and content until the job was done. Whatever the case, trust was not something she would be tossing out for him.

"It's my job to ensure you have everything you need and are fully prepared for the op."

She decided the coffee was too good to spoil with a long conversation, so she ate her toast and drank it while it was hot. When she finished her coffee, she asked the burning question. "Why aren't you doing the job? Why kidnap my brother and force me to do something I'm sure you can do yourself?" They had talked about this last night and the trust issue, but she still wasn't convinced he'd been completely forthcoming on the subject.

Abi sipped his coffee and appeared to consider her question. "My employer wants the best and I assured him you are the very best. Think about it—this is not the sort of situation you wish to leave to chance."

"Your employer has a family member who has an inoperable brain tumor." It wasn't a question. They had tiptoed around this issue yesterday too.

"What's on your agenda?" Abi asked, ignoring her question. "You mentioned things you needed to do."

She considered the man and wondered what in his life had formed his decision to go down this murky path. His father had been a high-ranking member of the Mossad and after retirement, his role in Israeli politics became noteworthy. But Abi had been raised by his mother in London and he had not chosen to serve either country in any capacity. He served only himself.

"Initial stop—my brother's condo. I want to have a look around."

"You believe there's something more going on than what you've been told in your briefing?"

She took her cup and plate to the sink. If he was expecting her to do the dishes because he had cooked, he could forget it. "I don't believe or disbelieve anything. I simply wish to have a look at my brother's home."

He gave a nod. "As you wish."

"Later we can go over the plan." She might as well understand how his employer expected this to go down.

"We won't be going over the plan until we are ready to move."

This she found troubling. "You're assuming there's no room for error in your plan. How can you be so sure the plan doesn't need to be tweaked?"

"The plan is perfect."

"There's no such thing as a perfect plan," she argued.

He smiled. "I'll agree to disagree."

The door opened and Poe joined them in the kitchen. "Morning." He looked from her to Abi and back. "Everything okay?"

"We're going to Luke's condo to have a look around."

He nodded, his expression giving nothing of his feelings away. "Can we talk for a minute?"

"Sure."

"Let's take a walk," Poe suggested. "Outside."

"Sure." She flashed a smile for Abi. "We'll be just outside." She wanted a look around out there anyway.

On the way out the door, Jamie grabbed her coat—the one provided with the other items for this op. Poe had nothing but the windbreaker he'd been wearing in LA. Not exactly suitable for December in Tennessee.

Once they were outside and walking around the infinity pool overlooking the wooded valley below, Poe turned to her. "What's the deal between you and this guy?"

With all that was going on, this was what he needed to talk about?

"Nothing." She surveyed the valley and the house that sat in the middle of those woods. The house was their target. Getting in and out of there with the surgeon in tow would never be easy. Whatever Abi thought, the sort of man who had a body double on staff no doubt had serious protection wherever he went. He would not go with Jamie willingly.

On top of the idea that there was a good chance they would end up dead just for trying to get to him, there was the idea of what would happen if they were successful. The authorities wouldn't rest until they solved the case. Beyond that, there was the concern that the surgeon could end up injured or dead.

Luke could end up injured or dead.

So many things could go wrong.

"Come on, Jamie. I can see there's a connection. How do you know this guy?"

"I bumped into him late last year after an assignment for the agency. He attempted to infiltrate my cover. The op was over, so I don't know why he bothered. Maybe just to see if he could. To flirt."

Poe held up his hands. "Maybe I don't want to know." He visibly shook himself. Maybe from the cold. "So I've thought about the layout down there." He looked toward the surgeon's home. "The security protocols he used the last time he hosted a party and his personal security team are detailed in the package Abi provided. The chances of getting in and out of there will be slim. Very slim." He shook his head. "I have a really bad feeling about this."

She smiled sadly. "It's not like I have a choice. I have to try."

"I did some research on Case as well. He's not exactly known as Mr. Personality. I don't think your friend's employer understands that he could very well refuse to do the surgery."

Jamie had considered this could be an issue. "I suppose we'll just have to convince him somehow."

"But we can't make him," Poe argued. "We can put a

gun to his head, but we cannot make him do the surgery. Torturing him or shooting him won't be an option."

"You're saying you don't think the plan is a good one."

He moved his head from side to side. "The doctor will need proper motivation."

Jamie thought of the photos of the doctor and his family she had reviewed. "He has a kid. A little girl."

Poe nodded. "Ten years old. Take the kid for leverage and there won't be any trouble getting him to go along with whatever he's asked to do. I'm guessing that's why Abi isn't sharing more details. He knows you aren't going to like it."

Fury roared through Jamie. "On top of that, it's another reason why he isn't doing this on his own. He'll focus on the kid while you and I whisk away the surgeon."

"That's what I'm thinking. There's a hell of a lot of room for error, especially with a kid in the mix. I don't like this, Jamie."

She swore. She hated when people used kids for leverage. "I don't either."

A quick review of their options was pretty straightforward: do as they were told or do as they were told. "We'll go with the plan as far as we can," she said, feeling suddenly tired. "From there, we'll do what we have to do to ensure everyone survives."

"This friend of yours," Poe said. "Any suspicions he'll double cross us when the job is done?"

"There's always that chance. We just need to be ready for anything that comes our way."

Jamie's attention shifted to the house. Abi was watching them from the other side of the wall of glass. He knew a lot more than he was sharing.

The question was, would it get them killed?

Douglas Avenue,
10:20 a.m.

LUKE'S CONDO WAS a wreck. And as much as Luke despised housecleaning, this was more than just his indifference to chores. The place had been ransacked. She shouldn't be surprised, and she wasn't. Not really. More unsettled. This was Luke's place. His things.

Jamie moved through the condo slowly, taking her time to look at any and all items. The space wasn't that large so with both Poe and Abi prowling around it was on the cramped side.

She tidied the place as she went. Touching Luke's things relieved her somehow. Relaxed her to a degree. He was her little brother. She loved him. She'd always taken care of him.

"There were three of them," Poe said. "Two who pilfered through his things, one who interrogated him."

Jamie hoped the interrogation hadn't included any torture. "I haven't spotted any blood."

Poe shook his head. "Me either."

This was good. She watched as Poe moved around the space, pausing to linger and then tracing his fingers over an item. Poe read crime scenes like no one she had ever met. Just being in the room and touching the victim's things could pull him in deep enough to practically see through the eyes of the victim.

It was an uncanny gift.

Jamie moved on to her brother's bedroom and picked through his things. She tidied what she could and made a pile of what should be in the laundry hamper.

"Finding anything relevant?"

She turned to find Abi propped in the open doorway. "Nothing yet."

"It doesn't appear anything—including your brother—was damaged in the search."

"The question is, why did they need to search? If my brother was simply leverage, what were they looking for?"

"Perhaps—" Abi pushed away from the door and walked deeper into the room "—he refused to cooperate with their questions about you."

"So they were looking through his underwear drawers for information on my whereabouts?"

A smirk twitched Abi's lips. "One never knows about siblings."

"Ha ha." She smiled at the framed photo on the dresser. The fam—their mom and dad and the two of them. If anything had happened to Luke...

No, she couldn't go there.

"I'm sure you knew how to find me," she said as she exited the room.

Abi followed. "I suppose I should have mentioned as much."

"You weren't here when they picked up Luke?"

"I'm afraid not."

That explained the search.

"Did you suggest they use my brother as leverage?" The thought made her furious. She clamped her jaw shut to prevent saying more than she should. Staying on good terms was imperative—at least for now. She could punch him in the face later. When this was done.

He made a big deal of appearing to consider her question. "I may have suggested the concept."

She so wanted to kick his butt.

"Well, at least now I know who ruined my Christmas."

She put the pile of soiled clothes in the hamper and walked to the kitchen. She took her time and had a look around. She didn't really expect to find anything useful here, but she would be remiss if she didn't go through the steps. At the front door, she paused to open the coat closet. She picked through the offerings until she found something suitable for Poe.

"You need this more than the windbreaker." She passed the leather coat to him.

"Thanks."

She turned to Abi. "Where are they keeping him?"

"I'm afraid I have no idea."

Probably a lie. "Why can't I see him? Verify that he's okay."

"You'll see him when the op is complete. You have my word that he is okay."

"Is that supposed to make me feel better?" This man would say whatever he was paid to say. They both knew this to be true.

"I would certainly hope so." He looked from her to Poe and back. "Are we ready to go back to the house?"

Jamie walked to her brother's desk and sat down. She tapped the trackpad to wake the computer. It was up and running and required a password. She didn't attempt to access the system. No need. Her brother was too smart to leave information too readily accessible. She opened the two shallow drawers and picked through them. Nothing of particular interest. Sharpies, pens. She hadn't really expected there to be anything helpful as to his whereabouts, but she wanted to buy time. She was in no hurry to get back to the Excalibur house. But there was one other thing she wanted to find out.

"I'm finished." She stood, pushed in her chair and headed for the door.

They locked up and descended the stairs that led down

to the ground level. Jamie surveyed the street and postage-stamp-size yard that served two condos. The place was like her brother—efficient, well thought out, minimal. He didn't like wasting time. And he didn't like a lot of stuff.

Jamie settled into the passenger seat while Abi slid behind the steering wheel. Poe climbed in the back. She was sure he wasn't very happy about being relegated to the back seat, but someone had to take one for the team.

"We should stop for lunch." She shrugged. "Since we're out, I mean." Mostly, she just didn't want to rush back to the house. And she'd like to see if anyone was following them. She hadn't spotted anyone on the way here. Going back might be a different story.

Nashville was not Abi's home turf. Jamie knew far more about this city than he did—only because her brother lived here. Despite being in charge, out here in the wild, Abi was just one of them.

"Why my brother and why me?" The story he'd given her up to now just didn't fit in her opinion.

"Your reputation precedes you," he said, absorbed in navigating traffic.

"I'm still not buying it."

There was something he was leaving out. Something relevant. And even if there wasn't, it kept him trying to assuage her concerns. She liked making him work for his comfort.

"Perhaps it's best not to dwell on the whys and just do what we must do."

"How did he find you?"

He glanced at her. Now there was a question he hadn't been expecting. "I have a certain reputation."

This was true. "What're you doing? Advertising on the dark web now?"

"I shouldn't answer that question."

Keeping an eye on the exterior mirror on her side, she said, "I'm still not convinced of why they need us both." She and Poe had discussed the idea of Dr. Case's child being a target as well, which would certainly require more than one pair of hands.

But it didn't have to be Jamie or her brother.

"We'll have food delivered to the house," he said as he pointed the car in that direction.

And there it was. This other thing that nagged at her. He wanted to keep her at the house until it was time for the op. Was he concerned something would happen? That she would be injured somehow, making her useless for the purposes of the operation?

As if fate had decided to answer her question, a black sedan appeared in the passenger-side mirror. It was a ways back, but she watched as he made turn after turn and the sedan did the same. Oh yeah. They had a tail.

"Does having me here have something to do with my grandmother?" She hadn't considered the idea until now. The Colby name was internationally known. Mostly she was making conversation while she watched their tail.

"This only has to do with you and your participation in achieving the proper outcome. Trying to read something more into it is a waste of time."

He was sticking to his story, which suggested he could possibly be telling the truth.

But she wasn't ready to let him off the hook just yet.

"Your father was kidnapped as a child."

The question startled her. Jamie glanced back at Poe. He knew about what her father had gone through. They were friends. Good friends. She'd shared more with him than she did with most. She shifted her attention to the driver.

But she hadn't shared any of that with this man. Finding this information wouldn't be so difficult, but the question was why did he consider it relevant enough to look into?

"He was. He was taken at seven years old and wasn't found until more than two decades later. My grandparents thought he was dead, so they had stopped looking."

"You know what happened to him during that time?"

"Why are we talking about this?" Poe demanded.

"It's okay," she said to her friend. Then, to Abi, she said, "I do. Why do you ask?" To say this line of questioning was making her tense was an understatement. She did not like the idea of feeling a comparison between her father's and her brother's kidnapping situations. No one who knew those circumstances would.

"No reason. I was just curious."

That was a lie. Until just this minute, she hadn't really considered who his employer was. Now she was more than a little concerned. Was he somehow connected to her family? Or their past?

She suddenly wished she could speak to her dad.

"You ask a lot of questions," Poe said, likely noting her uneasiness.

Abi laughed. "Curiosity killed the cat."

He made a sharp turn and then gunned the accelerator. Oh, she got it now. He wanted to distract them from the fact that they had a tail.

"You got some idea of who our tail is?" She looked to Abi for his answer.

His jaw hardened. He never took failure well. "Not to worry. We will lose him."

"Are you sure?"

He sent her a hard look and then took another treacherous turn.

This was a secret mission with a secret target and a secret benefactor. Who else could know their plan? At first, Jamie had wondered if it was part of some security detail. It didn't appear to be someone Abi wanted on their tail.

As they drove, seemingly tail-free now, he watched the mirrors closely. Took several more unnecessary turns in Jamie's opinion. She thought of the doctor—their target. He was just a man, but one with very special talents. At this time there was no one else like him in what he could do. He was uniquely necessary to fulfill a need that could be fulfilled no other way.

What was that ability worth? A lot, apparently. Enough to go to great lengths to make this happen.

There was still something—a piece she was missing. Perhaps it was irrelevant in the grand scheme of things, but she couldn't shake the nagging sensation that there was something more she needed to know...to understand.

Poe could feel it too. She saw it in his eyes whenever they grilled Abi this way.

Jamie made a decision. She had to ask this burning question. "Before we move into position for the op, I'll need to know the part you're not telling me."

Abi laughed. "You should let this foolish idea go. You have my word, Jamie. There is nothing else to know."

Funny, that did not make her feel one iota better.

"And that answer," she said, glancing at him, "is why I will never trust you, Abi."

"You can trust me, Jamie. This is a simple matter of monumental importance. That's all. The weight of the concept is misleading on a basic implementation level. Don't overthink it."

The man so loved throwing those opposing adjectives together.

"I hope you're being straight with me, Abi. I don't want either of us to regret this thing you've decided we must do."

He flashed her one of those grins that made breathing difficult. "No regrets."

Then why did she feel as if she regretted it already?

Chapter Five

Excalibur Court,
2:00 p.m.

Abi excused himself and went outside to take a call.

He hadn't stopped for food. But Jamie got why he hadn't.

"I don't like this." Poe stared beyond the wall of glass doors and watched Abi pace back and forth next to the infinity pool.

Jamie braced her hands on her hips and met her friend's gaze. "I'm with you, believe me. If something is going wrong this early in the game, we're in trouble."

"You're thinking of that tail he struggled to lose."

She nodded. "That was my primary reason for wanting to go out today. He's making this all seem so pat—as if everything is in place with no concerns. This—" she looked to the man outside "—is a concern."

Poe turned his back to the outdoor space and fixed his worried gaze on Jamie. "You know when you have this feeling deep in your gut that something is really, really wrong but you can't quite put your finger on the problem?"

Jamie flattened her palm against her belly. "Right here. The same place that lets you know when you need to cut and run."

"Yeah." He glanced over his shoulder at the man outside. "I'm not saying your friend is setting us up, but he knows this is off somehow and he's just going along as if it's all good."

Yeah, she'd picked up on that. "The good news is I didn't get the impression at Luke's place that there was a truly violent struggle or any of the usual issues we should worry about."

Actually, that could be good or bad, but she had decided to see it as a good thing. Victoria had heard Luke's voice. For now, the situation appeared to be running along without any glitches—with the exception of the potential tail they'd had to lose. If the plan played out the way they had been briefed, then hopefully Luke would be released tomorrow night.

She wasn't thinking beyond that. It wasn't like a person or persons could be kidnapped and everyone involved just walked away as if nothing had happened. There would be repercussions. And, frankly, it wasn't like she could pretend she had immunity in the kidnapping of a prestigious doctor—if this went down as planned.

Since Abi appeared in no hurry to get back inside, Jamie decided to use the time wisely. Who knew how much time she and Poe would have alone?

"What do we know about this Dr. Case?" Poe asked. "I mean, really? Beyond the bio on his website and in the file Abi provided?"

"I was just thinking the same thing," Jamie admitted. "The basics are that he graduated from Vanderbilt, then went on to specialize at Johns Hopkins. He spent the next dozen years building his claim to fame in neurosurgery."

Poe glanced outside to ensure Abi remained preoccupied. "Early this year he completed the first successful surgery removing a previously deemed inoperable brain tumor. Since that time, he's completed many more such operations. But he's only one man."

"And patients from all over the country are frantically trying to get on his schedule."

"While he," Poe said, "is talking about cutting back on the number of surgeries he's doing in order to train more surgeons to do the same."

"But the patients are desperate—they're facing death sentences without this surgery." Jamie started to pace. She could only imagine how the patients felt. If the doctor was doing all he could, then this wasn't easy for him either.

"The bottom line is," Poe went on, "what does your friend's employer want with Dr. Case?"

"Ostensibly, this lifesaving surgery for himself or a family member."

"Either way, the man—woman, whoever—has the means to go after what he wants no matter that it's not legal."

"He has the means but he doesn't have the time to wait," Jamie agreed. "So he's buying a place at the front of the line." Certainly not fair but there were those who would do whatever necessary to get what they wanted.

"If he's smart he has created a plan that ensures he will walk away from this without revealing his identity." Poe shrugged. "It's the only possibility that makes sense. Why would he want to live only to go to prison?"

"Which suggests it's a family member, so he doesn't care." Jamie frowned. "The one hitch in that plan is the doctor. How does Abi's employer protect his identity from the surgeon himself?"

"I don't see how he can." Poe considered the idea for a moment. "Unless it's all carefully choreographed in a way that Case does his thing and then he's taken away. The employer's personal physician will take it from there. Which would mean he'd require a private surgery suite."

"Why the Colby Agency?" Jamie shrugged. "I mean, the agency is the best, but there are other players out there who could help with this op. I haven't seen or heard anything as of yet that makes me believe I have a particular skill set that this guy couldn't find in another operative."

"But," Poe said with a look that underscored his words, "it's you this guy—" he hitched a thumb toward Abi "—wanted to play with."

She couldn't deny the possibility. "Maybe, but Abi is smart. He wouldn't allow his personal feelings to get in the way of a successful mission. He's too good for that."

"Then we have to assume there's a personal connection between your family and this mission. Or perhaps that's what he wants us to believe."

That was the part that worried Jamie. Which was true?

"I need to have a closer look around here." She surveyed the large great room. "Can you keep Abi preoccupied when he comes back in while I have a look around?"

"Sure. We'll just pretend to be mates," he teased in a faux British accent.

Jamie shook her head at her friend, glanced toward Abi and then hurried out of the room. She made her way up the stairs and went straight to the bedroom Abi had chosen for himself. He'd made the room assignments. Considering the clothing and toiletry selections he'd prepared for her, he'd had access to this property for at least a day or two before they arrived.

She opened the door and walked into his room. The bed was unmade. The rumpled sheets kept her gaze lingering longer than they should have. She forced her attention to the nightstands next to the bed. She quickly went through the drawers of each. The only personal item she found was a cell phone charger. She moved on to the dresser where she rummaged through his underwear and socks, taking care to feel for any items that might be hidden inside.

She found nothing in the drawers or under them, so the closet was next. Two blazers and three shirts hung on wooden hangers. Jamie checked the pockets and then the extra pair of shoes standing neatly on the carpet.

There was nothing in the room that he wouldn't want anyone to find.

Jamie walked out of his room and closed the door the way she had found it. Abi was too savvy to leave anything lying around that might give away some aspect of his plan. She went through her and Poe's rooms, double-checking for bugs. She found nothing.

Downstairs, Abi had come inside.

"Since we weren't able to stop, I'll order lunch," he announced.

Jamie wasn't sure she could eat, but she kept that to herself. Food was essential to gain energy. "Anything but pizza." She had eaten pizza two nights in a row on the previous mission.

Poe laughed. "Yeah, the only food available near that last motel was pizza."

"No pizza," Abi assured them. "I was thinking Mediterranean."

"Works for me," Poe announced.

"I need to check in with Victoria," Jamie announced. She needed to know what was going on.

Abi looked up from whatever app he'd chosen to use for ordering food. "As long as I can hear the conversation, I don't have a problem with that."

Jamie nodded. "Understood."

Poe caught her gaze. "I think I'll take a nap until the food comes."

Sounded like Poe had some looking around he wanted to do as well. He disappeared upstairs, and Jamie put through the call. Her grandmother answered on the first ring. "It's me," Jamie said, wishing she could be there in person to talk to her. She'd likely been waiting for a call all day.

"Are you okay, Jamie?"

She smiled. She loved the sound of her grandmother's voice. So commanding and yet so caring. "I'm good, yes. We went to Luke's condo today. I didn't find any readily visible cause for alarm."

"Have you spoken to him?"

"No. Maybe I'll get to later." Jamie chewed her lower lip. There was a lot she wanted to say but holding back was the smarter choice. "Any news from Mom and Dad?"

Her mother hadn't been herself lately. Jamie was glad she and Dad were on vacation and not in the middle of this mess.

"I did," Victoria said. "They're doing well. Just missing all of us. I assured them we will all be fine for Christmas. They should enjoy themselves and relax."

"That's exactly what they should do," Jamie agreed. "I hope you gave them my love."

"I certainly did. Jamie..."

She heard the worry in her grandmother's voice. "Really, Grandmother, I'm fine."

"Please be careful. I wish there was more we could do."

"Knowing that you're standing by is enough."

They talked a few minutes more before Jamie was able to say goodbye. She so loved her grandparents. Victoria was the epitome of all that Jamie believed was right in this world. She hoped to be able to accomplish just a fraction of what her grandmother had done with her life. Her grandfather too.

"What's the ETA on the food?" She tucked her cell phone away.

"Should be here any minute." Abi searched her face, her eyes. "I find it difficult to believe your grandparents aren't up to something. But I haven't picked up on any chatter from the Colby Agency."

"They would never do anything that might endanger Luke or me."

"You're lucky to have people who care about you that way."

She felt like that was an opening, but decided not to take it. "I'll find Poe. Let him know the food will be here soon."

Giving Abi her back, she hurried from the room and up the stairs. She found Poe in his room, staring out the window toward the home of Dr. Quentin Case.

"Abi says the food will be here soon."

Poe glanced at her, then waited for her to join him at the window. "I can't figure out what he thinks he's accomplishing by keeping everything a secret until the last minute. You know there's a reason that we're not going to like."

"I know." She leaned one shoulder against the window frame. "The only reason to do that is if he thinks I'll have an issue with the proposed execution of the op."

"The house is right there." He nodded in the direction of the mansion in the valley below. "Why not just spell it out now? It's not like we can't put together a number of scenarios in our heads. We've done this sort of thing too many times."

"Maybe he's worried we'll give him the slip and share the details with the police or with someone else who can stop him." This wasn't the sort of global issue the IOA dealt with, but they would certainly not hesitate to send an extraction team to recover two of their agents. Except contacting anyone at all was a risk she wasn't willing to take. Luke's life hung in the balance.

"Unless," Poe countered, "the employer is Abi himself."

Now this was an avenue she had not considered. "You may be right." Wow. She knew Abi's family. There was his father. His mother. No siblings. No spouse as far as she knew.

"Whatever he's planning," Poe said, drawing her attention back to him, "I don't want you taking the risk too far. You have to protect yourself, Jamie."

She frowned. "Why would I not protect myself? It's the first rule of any op. You can't complete it if you're down for the count."

Poe laughed. "You always do that. Deflect. I just don't want you to throw caution to wind for this guy. He's not worth it, Jamie. He's using you and Luke."

Yeah. She recognized Poe was right on that one. "I'm aware."

He reached up and tucked a strand of hair behind her ear. "You're important to me, Jamie. Our work is sometimes dangerous—maybe not so much when we're plucking Santas from trouble."

She laughed. "Even Santa needs rescuing sometimes."

"True. Just be careful. I don't trust this guy at all."

She hugged him. Closed her eyes and inhaled deeply of his unique scent. "Don't worry. I plan on taking you home for Christmas when this is finished."

She'd made that decision the moment this whole thing started. She wanted her family to know this man. The realization surprised her a little...but in a good way.

10:00 p.m.

JAMIE STOOD ON the patio and stared toward the Case home. The place was lit up like an airfield. If the family had company tonight, it wasn't obvious. No cars parked in the front cobblestoned parking area. Even from here she could see the massive fountain with its flickering lights that sat in the middle of that parking area.

According to Google, the house where Dr. Case lived had only been built two years ago to the tune of several million dollars. He'd built the house even before perfecting the surgical procedure that had put him on the map. He had two children. A son who had started Harvard this past fall. And a daughter who was only ten years old. His wife wrote children's books and spent a lot of time volunteering. Good for her. She was also a nurse, but she donated her time to a clinic in downtown Nashville.

By all accounts, the family was highly respected and more than a little revered in the area.

All the more reason for Jamie to see this through one way or another. Someone had to protect that family during this… Whatever it was. She just hoped she wasn't going to be caught in a situation where she had to choose between her brother and a member of the doctor's family.

So far there had been no mention of weapons, but she wasn't naive enough to believe they were going into this thing unarmed. Particularly considering Case had serious security. There would be weapons, and anytime weapons were involved, trouble was just one tiny mistake away.

That would be the problem. Getting in and out without triggering a gunfight with the doctor's security team.

As if she'd voiced the issue out loud, Abi joined her

on the patio. He surveyed the valley below before turn-ing to her.

"It's cold out here," he pointed out.

Her body suddenly realized he was right. She shivered. "I hadn't noticed."

He laughed. "I see that."

She wrapped her arms around herself. "Not that cold. Remember I grew up in Chicago."

He removed the jacket he was wearing and draped it over her shoulders. "I remember."

The warmth from his body immediately seeped into hers. "Thanks." She tugged the coat closer around her.

"Your friend has been pacing the floor for hours."

Poe had paced the floor down here until only a few minutes ago and then he'd called it a night only to pace the floor in his room.

"He's restless."

"He needs to chill." Abi crossed his arms over his chest, the cold night air obviously getting to him since he'd given his jacket to her.

"Maybe he could if you'd give us some insight into how this is going down."

"I'm afraid I can't do that. You will know exactly what to do when it's time to move."

She heaved a frustrated breath. "That's no way to run a railroad," she argued. "Preparation is always key in any operation. Preparation of all players."

He shot her a grin. "Trust me. I have thoroughly pre-pared for this. For all of us."

"Tell me one thing." She turned to him and fixed her gaze on his.

"One thing," he agreed.

"Does someone in your family need this doctor's help?"

If this was personal, the situation was all the more dangerous. Personal was never, ever good.

"No one in my family is involved. This is not personal,
Jamie. You have my word."

"Good." She considered what she should ask next. "How
did you learn of this mission?"

"So what you really want is two things," he said, eyebrows raised.

"The one thing was just me getting started."

He smiled. "I see that." He exhaled an audible breath.
"I was approached by a representative of my employer."

He looked directly at her as he spoke. Gaze open. No
blink, no flinch. So far he appeared to be telling her the
truth.

"Are you completely comfortable with the plan?" She
had worked with Abi before. He was good. Damned good.

"The plan is flawless. You do not need to worry about
the plan. I have considered every possibility. There are no
weaknesses...no holes."

"Your reputation is impeccable when it comes to planning and executing a mission," Jamie confessed. "I saw
firsthand when we worked together how capable you are."

"Capable." He chuckled. "A good word, I suppose."

"No other aspect of anyone's ability is relevant if it's
not capable."

He seemed to weigh her words a moment. "We spent a
good deal of time together during that mission."

They had spent a considerable amount of time together,
and they had shared a *moment*.

The memory had her cheeks heating. She was thankful it was dark to prevent him seeing that she'd blushed at
the memory.

"We worked well together," he pointed out.

"We did, but—" Jamie looked directly at him "—it can't be like last time."

Her brother's life was in the balance. She could not allow herself to be distracted.

"The mission hasn't started yet," he argued. "Who knows what we'll find time for before we're finished?"

"Did you drag my brother into this just so you could force me to be involved?"

"How do you know Luke isn't my employer?"

The question startled her. This was something she had not considered. She thought a moment about the possibility. To her knowledge, Luke had no significant other just now. He would have told her. But she couldn't say with complete certainty that there wasn't someone he wanted to help. He was always doing things for other people—especially those in need. This seemed a little over-the-top for his ability. He had a sizable trust fund, but it wasn't like he could withdraw that kind of money without permission.

Unless that was what the ten-million-dollar ransom was about.

The thought had her gritting her teeth for a moment. No, she decided. No way.

"Luke would have come to me if he'd needed help with something like this." Jamie was certain. He wouldn't have gone about it this way. No way.

Abi searched her face, her eyes. "I did not and would not have taken your brother hostage in order to get your attention. It's important that you understand that was not my decision."

"Can you guarantee me he's safe?"

"I can assure you that he is perfectly safe."

"Then you trust your employer enough to take that risk?"

He frowned. "What risk?"

"The risk that if something happens to my brother, I will make you pay."

His frown slid into a grin. "I am very well aware of what would happen to me if I was responsible for trouble with your brother."

"Just so you know, I won't go in without being fully briefed and feeling confident that all is as it should be. So don't go suggesting it's time to go with the idea of filling me in on the way. I will refuse."

"I'm aware." He tugged the lapels of the jacket a little closer to ensure she stayed warm. "We will go through everything very carefully before we move in."

So they were invading the house.

"I'm assuming we have invitations to the party," she said, mostly just to see what he would say.

"Better to be invited than to have to figure out another way in."

"Your employer is powerful."

"Of course."

That he was rich went without saying. "But he isn't powerful enough to get the one thing he wants more than anything else."

Abi's gaze collided with hers. "There are some things even money cannot buy."

Which told her that Abi's employer had already approached this doctor and been turned away.

"For all those other things," Jamie suggested, "there are people like you."

Abi smiled. "If not me, someone else would do it. At least if I do it, I do it well."

No question. The upside was that what she knew of Abi was as close to good as a mostly bad guy could be.

"I know what you're thinking."

She sort of hoped he did not. "And what's that?"

"You're thinking 'What is a bad guy like me doing trying to help someone do a good thing—like kidnap a doctor to save a life?'"

"The thought occurred to me, yes." It wasn't the usual job Abi was known for.

"You're wondering," he went on, "if I might be growing soft in my old age."

She laughed. She couldn't help herself. Abi was only thirty. "Didn't cross my mind."

"When I was approached about this mission," he explained, "I could not say no. By this time tomorrow you will understand my reasons."

"I'm sure you're aware that no one involved is going to walk away from this legally speaking." It wasn't a threat, merely a statement of fact.

"I have a plan for that as well."

He sounded so certain of himself. "I just hope your plan is as good as you seem to believe it is."

He traced a fingertip down her cheek before dropping his hand. "I have never failed. Never. You are aware of this."

She resisted the need to shiver at his touch. "Just because you've never failed doesn't mean you won't."

That was the part that worried her the most. There was always a first time for failure. And the first time was always the worst.

Chapter Six

Kenny stared out the window at the house below their position. He was more than a little worried about this operation. Not for himself, but for Jamie. And Luke. He didn't trust this guy Abidan Amar. At all.

He was aware of Amar before today. He'd heard Jamie talk about him, but only a couple of times. Now that he'd seen the two of them together, he understood why. They'd shared something when they did that operation together. No question about it. As ridiculous as it sounded, he was working hard not to look and sound as jealous as he felt, but it wasn't easy. If he was completely honest with himself, he would own the fact that he had very deep feelings for Jamie. But first and foremost, they were friends. Best friends. He didn't want to risk damaging that relationship. Not just because they worked together fairly often, but also because she meant a great deal to him. If necessary, he would gladly be just friends forever.

He thought of that one kiss they had shared. A smile tugged at his lips. It had actually been a part of the mission they were working together at the time. But he'd felt the connection as real as breathing. Good God, how he'd felt the connection. He'd been really careful since then. If a move happened between them, it would be because she initiated the action.

Jamie was the real deal, with an amazing family that he respected so much. She'd invited him to family celebrations on a number of occasions and it was during their shared downtime that he really felt the pull. Whatever happened, he was giving her plenty of space and plenty of time to make a move.

The sound of footfalls on the stairs told him she was coming up to the second floor. He moved soundlessly to the door and leaned against it. She hesitated outside his door and his heart bumped hard in his chest. Three seconds, then five elapsed before she went on into her room and closed the door. She'd wanted to say something or...

Give it a rest, Kenny.

Whatever she'd pondered during that brief pause, her sense of professionalism had prevented her from saying or doing whatever had crossed her mind.

For the best. For sure. This wasn't the time to get personal. Too much was unknown, and Luke's life hung in that precarious space of uncertainty.

Whatever this thing was that Abi was up to, Kenny would do everything in his power to protect Jamie and Luke. He almost laughed at the idea of Jamie needing him for protection. Backup, maybe. But she could certainly take care of herself and any jerk who would suggest otherwise did not know her at all.

Still, he worried that she trusted Amar far too much. Kenny didn't trust him one little bit. From that haughty accent of his to the way this whole thing was shaking down, Kenny didn't like it...at all.

He needed to sleep. He climbed into the bed and forced

his eyes closed. He thought of Jamie just across the hall.
The way she smiled… The sound of her laugh. She was so
beautiful and so smart.

If they got through this…maybe it was time he told her
how he felt.

Maybe.

If he didn't lose his courage.

Sunday, December 23

Two Days Before Christmas

Chapter Seven

Excalibur Court,
7:00 a.m.

To her surprise Jamie had managed to sleep. Maybe sheer exhaustion had helped. Whatever the reasons, she was grateful to wake up somewhat refreshed. It was always easier to stay focused with a few hours of sleep under one's belt.

When she was a child, her grandmother had always warned that a lack of sleep stole one's waking life. Stole one's ability to function...to remember. Jamie had always taken sleep very seriously because of those warnings.

For the past hour she had been lying in her bed, mulling over the things Abi had said last night. He had a plan for not only getting the mission completed successfully but also for ensuring no one was arrested. She actually could not see how he planned to make that happen, but she could hope.

What they were about to do was illegal. Not just a little crime either. This was kidnapping. A felony. This wasn't the sort of dance on the edge you walked away so easily from. Though she might be able to argue that in her case she had no choice in the matter since her brother's life was at stake. She was, to a large degree, being forced to participate. Still, the powers that be would wonder why she hadn't called the proper authorities. Fear for her brother's safety was a fairly good defense. Their phones were monitored—no unauthorized calls. To go against that edict was to risk Luke's life. As for Abi, he was assuredly breaking numerous laws with no mitigating factors to provide relief. He no doubt expected to get away scot-free.

The Colby Agency had the best attorneys in the country but that worry wasn't a priority right now. Jamie wasn't really worried for her future. As long as she avoided shooting anyone, she could potentially see her way clear—legally speaking—of this business. Whatever happened, her endgame was to rescue her brother. Optimally, she would do this without harming anyone else or getting herself shot.

Keeping Poe out of trouble was her top priority next to rescuing Luke. She would not allow Poe to be hurt by this mess. When she'd come to bed last night, she had lingered outside his door. The need to talk to him, to just be with him had been almost overwhelming. But she had made the right decision.

They were good friends. Very good friends. Since that kiss, it had become harder and harder to pretend she didn't feel other things for him. But she didn't want to harm their friendship in any way.

Poe was the reason she'd been so vulnerable to Abi last year. Even before the kiss that she and Poe had shared, she'd been attracted to him. Funny how those things happened when you were least expecting them.

Get your head on straight, Jamie. After a quick shower, she tugged on the wardrobe selection for today. The fact that Abi had known what size jeans she wore wasn't such a big surprise. That he'd done so well selecting items she would feel comfortable in was an added plus. The sweatshirt sported a Chicago Cubs logo. She shook her head.

Nice of him to try to make her feel at home. She pulled on a pair of socks and the sneakers she'd worn from LA. She wondered if the Santa she and Poe had rescued fully understood yet that they had saved his life. Sometimes targets were so flustered about being plucked from whatever their circumstances that they never got that they were damned lucky to still be breathing.

She brushed her hair and pulled it into a ponytail. She and Poe needed to discuss a potential exit strategy—for him anyway. This wasn't really his fight and he needed to know she would understand if he ducked out.

But he wouldn't. She knew him too well. She and Poe had been friends for a while now. Good friends. She understood that if he had his way, they would take their relationship to the next level. He had never said as much and was fairly subtle about it, but the signs were unmistakable. Not happening. Jamie didn't want to risk what they had. It sounded cliché, but it was true. Falling in love wasn't on her agenda just now anyway.

She was young. They both were. They had plenty of time to fall in love. Her grandmother would be the first to say Jamie should stay focused on her career for now. All the rest could come later.

She removed her cell from its charger and tucked it into her hip pocket. Since this mission was to go down tonight, maybe Abi would be ready to share the details this morning. No matter that she wouldn't say as much, on some level she understood his hesitance. The sooner he shared the ins and outs of the mission, the sooner she and Poe could consider options for reacting differently than was intended. The sooner a leak could happen. He was just practicing extra careful precautions.

She walked to the door, leaned against it and listened.

All quiet. She eased the door open and looked both ways. Hall was clear. The distinct scent of coffee wafted from downstairs and had her leaning in that direction. But before going down, she wanted to see if Poe was still in his room.

Across the hall, she listened at his door. She didn't hear anything so she rapped softly on the door. "Poe," she whispered, "you up?"

Usually, he was up before her. It was possible he was already downstairs, but since she hadn't heard voices, she suspected not. She couldn't see him and Abi standing around in the kitchen staring at each other without exchanging at least a few words.

Then again, maybe she could see them glaring at each other, circling the room like two wrestlers about to tangle.

She knocked again and when no answer came, she opted to give the knob a turn and see if the door was locked. It was not. It opened with little effort. The room was empty. Bed unmade. No surprise there. Poe wasn't exactly the neatest dude on the planet. He would insist he had other assets, and he would be right. She had never met anyone who could read a scene the way he could. He almost had a sixth sense when it came to seeing the details. The FBI had wanted him so badly, but like her, Poe had wanted to do something different…something maybe more relevant.

Certainly, this operation had not been on either of their agendas.

Since the bathroom door stood partially open, she checked in there and found no sign of Poe. A towel hung over the shower door, suggesting he had showered before leaving the room or before bed last night. She wandered back into the hall. Maybe he had gone downstairs, and he and Abi actually were down there staring at each other, waiting to see who broke first.

Listening intently for any sign of life, she descended the stairs and made her way through the living room and into the kitchen.

No Poe. No Abi.

Then she spotted Abi on the patio, savoring his coffee. Steam rose from the mug he held, matching the steam wafting from the pool. He stared toward the house belonging to the doctor. She wondered if he was suffering second thoughts about what he had agreed to do.

Where the heck was Poe?

She made a full round of the first floor. Checked the powder room and the small library. She even had a look out the front windows. No Poe.

Worry started its slow creep around the edges of her mind. Poe wouldn't just leave without telling her where he was going. Besides, she was fairly confident that Abi wouldn't allow either of them to leave until this was done.

When she still found no sign of Poe, she opened the door onto the patio and joined Abi. "Good morning."

He gave her a nod. "Morning." He frowned. "No coffee?"

"I was looking for Poe. Have you spoken to him this morning?"

Abi's gaze narrowed. "I haven't seen him this morning. Did you check his room?"

"I did. He doesn't appear to be down here either." Now she was getting worried. Her nerves jangled. Poe wouldn't just try to leave without telling her. Her worry turned to suspicion, and she had a bad feeling that Abi knew more than he was telling.

"All right. Let's have a look," he suggested. "We can cover more ground if we split up. I'll go outside. You go through the house again."

She shook her head. "No. You go through the house.

I want to look outside." She'd already been through the house.

He started to argue but then decided against it. "Fine. Just keep a low profile. There are neighbors up here."

Jamie walked to the front door, pulled on her coat and headed outside. Excalibur Court was a single, dead end street. There were about a dozen large houses that circled the short street. The ones on their side overlooked the valley below where Dr. Case's house sat nestled amid the thick woods. On the other side of the street, the houses backed up to another cul-de-sac. The area was thickly wooded so there was some amount of privacy despite the number of houses.

Jamie walked to the end of the drive and surveyed the cul-de-sac. There were no vehicles in the driveways. There were probably rules about leaving a vehicle outside the garage. There was one dark sedan at the end of the cul-de-sac parked in the common area. She watched it for a moment. Didn't see anyone inside. The street was quiet. A breeze whipped through the air, reminding Jamie that it was almost Christmas and cold. Lots colder than in LA.

She liked the Los Angeles area, particularly the weather, but she spent most of her time in DC. Went with the territory of her work. She never knew where her next assignment would be. So far in the past year she had been assigned in all directions. Poe had worked with her on three missions.

Worry niggled at her again.

Where the hell was he?

She called his cell. Three rings and it went to voice mail. "Hey, where are you?"

A deeper worry started to gnaw at her. He wouldn't just leave like this. Not possible.

She walked around the yard. Ventured several yards into

the woods at the back of the house. No sign of Poe. She called out his name a couple of times with no response. This was wrong. Then she went back in the house.

Abi was on his phone.

Maybe Poe had called him with an explanation? But why wouldn't he call Jamie?

She kept her cool until Abi ended his call. Then she demanded, "Was that him?"

"No. It was not. In fact, that was a colleague who is monitoring the comings and goings on the roads in and out of this development and he says no one has come in or gone out this morning."

She wasn't surprised that he had backup watching the street. He would be a fool not to have support nearby. It would be nice if he shared details like that, but arguing about it right now wasn't an option.

"Something's wrong." Jamie moved to the wall of glass doors that led out onto the patio and looked out over the valley below. "He wouldn't just leave."

Abi joined her. "Are you sure about that?"

She turned on him. "What I'm sure about," she said pointedly, "is that if he isn't here, then something has happened to him and since you're in charge of this operation, it's your job to know what that is."

He moved his head side to side in a somber manner. "I have not seen him this morning."

"Then I suggest you back up the footage on your security cameras and see what happened." If he dared to tell her there were no cameras, she might just have to punch him.

He nodded. "I can do that."

In the living room, he picked up the remote to the television and turned it on. Then he opened a drawer on one of the side tables and withdrew another remote. This one he pointed at the television screen and made a number of selections.

A new app opened, and several views of the house appeared on the screen. He ran the video back and, sure enough, just before daylight, Poe exited a side door in the kitchen.

"You didn't set the alarm?" This was ridiculous. Why would Abi take that sort of risk?

"I did set the alarm before I went to bed. I can only assume he disarmed it. It was armed when I got up this morning, which is why I didn't consider that he'd gone outside."

Poe was good. Figuring out a way around the code to disarm the security system wasn't outside his purview, but why would he do that without telling her?

"The question," Abi went on, "is why would he leave?"

"It would not be because he wanted to," Jamie argued. If Abi was accusing Poe of something he could just back off. Poe would never double-cross her. She gestured to the screen. "Are there exterior cameras?" It was a silly question. Who had such an elaborate security system inside and then nothing outside?

Another click of the remote and they were looking at the yard around the house. The front was clear. So was the back. The view extended to the woods. While she watched, Abi ran the video back until it showed Poe as he walked out that side door.

Jamie held her breath as she watched him walk around the iron fence that separated the pool area from the rest of the yard. He continued past this area and straight toward the woods.

"This is wrong," Jamie said, outright fear rising inside her now.

"We should go out there and have a look," Abi suggested.

He led the way to the same kitchen side door that Poe

had used. They exited the house and walked the cobblestone path toward the grassy area between the pool and the woods.

There was no way Poe would leave like this without telling her. *No way.* There had to be something about this that she didn't know. A call from someone who had warned of imminent danger. Something.

Once they were in the woods, the lack of light made seeing any disturbance of the underbrush difficult. Jamie stood still and visually searched the area, looking for any indication that a person had cut through that underbrush.

Then she saw what she was looking for. A bent twig on a limb. She headed in that direction. Abi was right behind her. She inspected the bushes and the ground. Someone had definitely been through here recently.

She turned on the flashlight app of her phone and scanned the ground. The light flashed over something shiny.

Her heart bumped harder against her sternum.

She reached down and sifted through the leaves. Her fingers hit a cool and firm object.

Her gut clenched as her fingers curled around a cell phone.

The screen of Poe's cell instantly lit with the missed call notifications from her attempts to reach him.

She started forward, looking for more indications of where the brush had been parted. Her heart pounded so hard she couldn't catch her breath. Why would he come out here? Why wouldn't he tell her whatever was on his mind?

A thought occurred to her, and she whirled on Abi. "You didn't plant any tracking devices?"

He looked away before answering the question. "Only on you. I wasn't expecting you to have company."

Fury roaring through her, she started to search once more. If Poe was lying out here injured, she needed to find him.

Abi didn't argue or question her actions. He just followed suit, picking his way through the brush and searching the same as she did.

An hour later it was obvious they weren't going to find him.

The underbrush became spotty as they neared the drop down the hillside. At that point there was no longer any indication Poe had been out there.

They went back in the house and watched the security footage. Poe went into the woods, but he never came out.

This was wrong, wrong, wrong.

Jamie paced the floor. Where would he have gone? She supposed he could have cut left and come out around one of the other houses.

"I need to check with the neighbors." That was the only possible next move.

"You can't do that," Abi argued. "We cannot call attention to ourselves."

"I don't care. I need to find my partner—my friend."

Abi held up his hands. "What you need is coffee."

Had he lost his mind? "I don't need coffee."

He poured a cup and placed it on the island. "Just sit down and drink. We need to think."

She took a breath and then did as he asked. She slid onto a stool and picked up the cup. She hadn't had any coffee this morning and suddenly she needed the caffeine desperately.

"First," Abi suggested, "let's approach this logically."

She drank from the cup rather than taking a bite out of his head.

"Let's consider the reasons Poe would leave." He gestured to her. "You know him better than me. What do you think?"

"Someone may have called him with information he couldn't ignore."

"Do you have the pass code for his phone so we can see who he has spoken to?"

She made a face. "If I did I would have already checked. All I saw were the latest notifications and that was where I called him. To see beyond that I would need the pass code."

"We can assume someone may have called him not only with news he couldn't ignore, but also with something he didn't feel he could share. Does he have family who may have needed his help?"

Jamie shook her head. "No one he's close to."

"What about your employer?"

"Maybe. But I can't imagine why he wouldn't have told me." That was the part that made no sense at all. Poe would not just leave like this...not while leaving her behind.

"Then we have to assume it's someone from this end."

She was surprised that Abi made the statement. "Is there someone who wanted to stop this mission? Maybe someone who feels it's the wrong move?"

"That's always possible, but I was not informed of this if that is the case. I can make some calls. See if there's something I should know. Check with my people to see if he's left the area."

Why the hell didn't he just say that already?

"I would appreciate that." She took a breath, forced her nerves to calm. "He wouldn't leave like this without telling me unless he felt there was no other option."

"Drink your coffee," Abi said again. "I'll make some calls."

He walked outside onto the patio. Jamie watched and

finished off her coffee. There was a chance Poe could have decided to take a risk to put protective measures in place. Not that she was going to share this with Abi. Poe didn't trust Abi. He was concerned about how this would shake down and, in Jamie's opinion, there was reason to be concerned. Poe may have believed that the best way to head off trouble was for him to bow out, making it look as if it was not voluntary. Then he would take up a position to watch, to be in place in the event Jamie needed an extraction.

It was an option they always discussed for their joint missions. It wasn't one they'd ever had to use. More important, they had not talked about the option in this situation.

Whatever the case, the fact that he didn't share his decision with her may have been to allow her to look completely uninvolved to Abi.

If that wasn't the case, then something bad had happened to Poe and Jamie was really worried. The possibility that Abi could be involved was all the more troubling.

If he was injured—or worse—and someone wanted answers about what they were doing, Poe was in serious trouble because he had no real answers. Until now, Abi had shared basically nothing with them beyond the name of the target.

Which, she supposed, was the point. You couldn't tell anyone what you didn't know.

For Poe, that could end up being a very bad thing. Not having the answers his abductor wanted wouldn't keep him alive.

Chapter Eight

2:00 p.m.

Kenny struggled to stay put as he watched Jamie take a walk around the cul-de-sac. She was still looking for him. She'd come outside and looked around several times. The worry and despair on her face cut straight through him.

He hated, hated, hated doing this to her, but it was necessary. It was the only way to provide any possible protection for her in the hours to come. He didn't blame Jamie for doing what she had to do. Her brother was being held hostage. She had no choice but to go along with what Amar wanted.

On some level, Jamie considered him a friend and Kenny couldn't say that he was an enemy, but what he could say was that the man was for sale to the highest bidder, which made him something worse than an enemy in Kenny's opinion. At least you knew the ultimate intentions of your enemy. There was no way to know for sure about a man like Amar. Where was he going with this? What did he expect to happen when all was said and done?

This was the trouble for Kenny.

Amar would do whatever necessary to accomplish his mission.

Kenny was not going to give him free rein to do as he

pleased. There had to be options for egress if the mission went to hell. Since Amar refused to share the details, Kenny had no choice but to intervene. Jamie was far too personally involved to fully trust her instincts.

He'd awakened early this morning and made the decision. He had to do something. Couldn't just wait. Waiting too long never proved to be the right strategy.

Jamie had no idea, but Victoria Colby-Camp had given him a burner phone to use for contacting her. He had not used it inside the house because he couldn't be sure what sort of monitoring Amar had going. The man was well prepared. Instead, Kenny had taken a walk around the cul-de-sac, much like Jamie was now, and made the calls. Victoria knew where they were, and she knew the identity of the target.

When he'd shared his concerns with Victoria, she had agreed that he had to make a move. With her blessing, he felt certain his decision had been the right one. Even Victoria felt Jamie wasn't thinking clearly. She was too worried about her brother. She was following orders toward that end. She would not be happy that he had voiced the concern to her grandmother, but he hoped it would prove the right move in the end.

Kenny watched Jamie walk back toward the house. The one he had chosen as his hideout was empty. The only unoccupied one in the cul-de-sac. The owners appeared to be on vacation. Perhaps visiting with family for the holidays.

The burner vibrated and he answered. "Hello."

"Kenny, we have some updated information."

Victoria and her team had been working to put together a list of potential patients suffering with inoperable brain tumors who possessed the means to put together an operation such as this one.

"I'm listening."

"We have a list of five patients in the state of Tennessee who have the means to take on an operation of this scale. We've put an investigator in place near the residence of each. Beyond that, we have another half dozen across the southeast who fit the same profile. I'm leaning toward the patient perpetrator as being local. Someone who would know Dr. Case's reputation well. Someone who had been exposed repeatedly to the headline-making leaps Case had taken in the field of neurosurgery."

"Sounds like you have the situation covered as well as anyone could." Good news in Kenny's opinion. "I've seen Jamie walking the cul-de-sac. She's still looking for me. She appears to be fine. Visibly worried, of course."

"I'm certain she's concerned," Victoria agreed.

"I'm uncomfortable misleading her this way," he admitted, "but it feels necessary. I'm trusting she'll understand that if I'm making a move like this, it's for the best."

He was good on that part, no matter that it felt wrong.

"Thank you for letting me know that you've had eyes on her. I've sent Ian Michaels to your location. He'll take a position the next street over. He has a vehicle for you if you need one." She confirmed the house number where Michaels would be waiting.

"Excellent." Kenny felt some sense of relief at the news. "I plan to try and keep eyes on Jamie, but I have no idea how they plan to get to the house where the party will take place. Amar claims to have invitations for tonight's party, but he could be lying."

"Lucas has done some careful research into Abidan Amar. His reputation is not quite as terrifying as I had feared, but he has a history of playing fast and loose with risk. I don't want him doing this with the lives of my grand-children."

Kenny could imagine Amar doing exactly that. What he couldn't see was Jamie or Luke as "grandchildren." But he understood and the idea made him smile. "The security system he has in place won't allow me to get close to the house again, but I left the bug you provided in the main living space. Hopefully, I'll hear the plan when he finally reveals the details to Jamie. Otherwise, I won't take my eyes off the place and when they move, I'll move."

"Keep me posted," Victoria urged. "We are prepared to do whatever necessary to help."

Sadly what they could do was limited. Any mistake could cost the life of the youngest Colby. They had no idea where Luke was or who was holding him. Outside interference could set off a deadly chain reaction.

"I will," Kenny assured her. "Thank you, Victoria."

He ended the call and considered that for months he had heard Jamie talk about her grandparents. He had done some deep research and despite how nice and normal they seemed, Jamie hadn't exaggerated one little bit. The Colby Agency was unlike any other agency of its kind. Victoria and her husband, Lucas, were legends, as were most of the investigators. If Kenny were in trouble, he would definitely want the Colby Agency on his team.

Frankly, he hoped to get to know them better in the future. He hoped to get to know Jamie a lot better as well. There were moments between them that made him believe the idea was possible. Either way, their friendship was invaluable, and he would do whatever necessary to protect that relationship.

Amar's voice sounded and Kenny turned to move closer to the speaker of the receiver.

Amar had apparently gotten a phone call.

His responses gave Kenny basically no information. Hopefully he would relate the update to Jamie when the call ended.

Whatever was going down was scheduled to do so tonight. Kenny needed to be prepared to intervene if necessary. To provide backup for Jamie either way. Listening and watching until there was a move was the only way for him to actually have her back. Had he stayed at the house, Amar would have made all the decisions and Kenny would have had no choice but to follow his orders. Amar would have possessed all the power.

This was the right move—as difficult as it had been to walk away from that house knowing he was leaving Jamie behind. The decision gave him some leeway to move as he saw fit.

The conversation between Amar and his caller appeared to be coming to an end.

Kenny held his breath. He couldn't afford to miss a word.

"Was that your point of contact?" Jamie asked.

"It was."

Kenny hoped the man intended to provide more detail than those two words.

"Do we have some change or addition to the mission?" Jamie prompted.

"Nothing I need to share at this time."

Her sigh was audible. "Really, you're going to stick to that worn-out line? Why even bother to involve me in this if you're going to keep me in the dark?"

"I have my orders, Jamie. When I can tell you more, I will. Every step of this operation is a strictly need-to-know basis only. You're familiar with how this works. I know you are. Let's not get bent out of shape with the rules."

"When you decide to stop playing games, let me know."

The sound of her walking out of the room wasn't what Kenny had hoped for. Maybe she was bluffing in an attempt to prod him into talking.

Then again, he had to admit that hearing her tell him off like that gave him a little kick of satisfaction.

As satisfying on a personal level as the exchange was, the real question was, how long did the guy intend to keep the details from her?

This was not the proper way to run an operation.

Chapter Nine

2:30 p.m.

"Jamie, wait!"

She hesitated at the bottom of the stairs. She was over his secretiveness. If they were in this together, he needed to tell her what the hell was going on. Good grief, they were only hours from when this thing was supposed to go down.

And Poe, damn it, was nowhere to be found.

She took a breath and turned to face Abi. "This thing is scheduled to go down tonight and you're still keeping me in the dark. Why am I even here?" She braced her hands on her hips. "You apparently intend to do this entirely alone. What am I? Arm candy?"

He laughed softly, then looked away. "You surely could be, but we won't go there." He blew out a breath then. Obviously not looking forward to coming out with it.

She braced her hands on her hips, out of patience. "Are we in this together or not?"

"There's been a slight change," he said. "Nothing to worry about. Originally, we were scheduled to arrive at eight tonight but now we're to be there at seven-thirty. I'm not pleased with the sudden change, but I can only assume some other sort of intelligence became available, prompting this schedule change."

The fact that he was genuinely upset seemed to suggest he was telling the truth. Either way, she was over this whole cloak and dagger game. They were on the same side after all.

"I need you to walk me through what's going to happen tonight. This beating around the bush has gone on long enough."

"All right. Let's sit down and I'll walk you through it."

It was about time. She followed him back to the living room area. He went to the bar and grabbed a couple of bottles of water and passed one to her. If not for that sudden phone call, she would be convinced his decision to share had something to do with Poe's absence. She hoped that was not the case.

"We will arrive at the party like any other guests. I've seen the list of invitees, and none are familiar to me. I'm assuming I will not be familiar to any of them. Same goes for you. Which is part of the beauty of the situation."

"Is there some aspect of his private residence that has been deemed more accessible than, say, the hospital or his clinic?" The private residence of a man such as Dr. Case likely included serious security services and a well-trained security team.

"The hospital where his surgery privileges are has state-of-the-art facial recognition for everyone going in and coming out," Abi explained. "It wouldn't prevent us from coming in, but it would not forget our faces. I'm sure neither of us wants that to happen."

"A good reason to rule out that location," she admitted. A hospital with facial recognition technology. Wow.

"His clinic is not equipped with technology quite so advanced, but the location creates a difficult exit strategy. Too congested…too many cameras on the surrounding buildings."

"I suppose the fact that the clinic operates only during regular business hours, daylight hours, creates a problem of its own."

"The cover of darkness is always an ally," he agreed.

"I'm sure there will be security cameras at the doctor's residence." Really, she was confident this was the case.

"You're right, but we have access to the system so no issues there."

Of course they did. Abi was too good to move forward without that key piece of intelligence.

"There will be some sort of precipitous event," she suggested. "A distraction?"

"A power outage. It's not so unique, but it will work and it's not so unusual this time of year."

"You have the layout of the residence?" Familiarizing herself with the floor plan would be useful. As for the power outage, that was always a workable strategy. Power outages happened—as he said, particularly during extreme temperatures. Living this far outside the city proper was asking for additional issues when it came to utilities.

"I do." He pulled out his cell and opened an image. "We enter via the front as one would expect."

The front door appeared to open into a large entry hall. He moved on to another image that showed a photo of the entry hall.

"Security will be here confirming that all who enter are on the list. From there we'll follow the others into the grand hall."

The grand hall was an area that branched off into a living room, dining room, library and—well beyond all that—a kitchen. Any one of those rooms was larger than the entire first floor of this house. The grand hall worked like a massive hub connecting all the other rooms. It made for the perfect area to linger in groups without interrupting the flow of those filtering into and through the other rooms.

"Once we're in," he went on, "we'll mingle, have hors d'oeuvres and a nonalcoholic drink. Just to blend in."

"Where is our egress?"

He slid the photo left, moving to another image. "Our priority exit is through the kitchen. We have two secondary options. Through the French doors in the library and off the back terrace outside the main living area."

"What's the layout for transportation around the property?" She'd looked at the house and property via the telescope, but some aspects were blocked from view by landscaping and other obstacles.

"We'll have two options for leaving. A helicopter from the doctor's helipad. This would give us a sort of emergency style departure. The hope would be that other guests assume there has been an emergency and the doctor had to go. The other option is via a limo that will be standing by in the front roundabout."

So far she had no complaints.

"What method of inducement do you plan to use to ensure his cooperation?" This was the part that concerned Jamie the most. She hoped he didn't intend to use drugs or physical coercion. Despite her reservations with either of those avenues, the problem was, there weren't that many other options. At least none she liked any better.

"We have that covered," he said as he closed his phone and slipped it into his hip pocket.

"Meaning?" she pressed. "Are we going in armed? Will he be drugged?"

"No drugs. No weapons."

She and Poe had discussed the possibility that the man's child would be used to gain his cooperation. "Then we're using the kid." Dread congealed in her gut. She hated the idea. Hated it even more than the drugs or weapons.

"You have my word," he said, his gaze pressing hers, "if it becomes necessary to use the child, she will not be harmed in any way."

Damn it. She knew it! "You can't make that promise. Things go wrong. Accidents. Mistakes. You can never predict how people will react to these situations."

Abi held up his hands as if to quiet her, which made her all the angrier. "This will happen quickly. In an orderly manner. There will not be time for mistakes or accidents."

People always thought a simple plan would go easy—no glitches. But there was no simple plan when it came to abducting another human. Not unless you rendered them unconscious.

The plan sounded perfect. Well thought out. Concise. Except all of that would go out the window when Dr. Case or his wife understood what was happening. If a guest happened to overhear…it would all go to hell in a heartbeat.

"You can't be sure of anything. Not one single thing that involves another human."

"You can't be sure I'm wrong."

She wasn't going to argue the point with him. Moving on, she said, "You've mentioned that we have a very narrow window of opportunity. Why is that the case? It's a party with guests who will be coming and going. Is there some sort of step or arrival—maybe a departure—that will happen that somehow renders our plans unusable? Is something turning into a pumpkin at a certain time?"

He didn't answer right away. And he didn't laugh. Mostly he stared at her, obviously attempting to decide how to answer.

He was just as worried as she was, but he would die before he would admit as much.

"It's the kid, isn't it?" Jamie shook her head. He might as well just spit it out. "It has to happen before she's tucked in for the night."

"Something like that," he confessed.

"I'm not good with this." But what could she do? Her brother's life was on the line. "If anything goes wrong—"

"I will not allow the child to be hurt," he insisted. "Really, you have my word on that."

She didn't doubt he meant what he said, but he could not guarantee the child's safety or the doctor's cooperation. He could only deduce the outcome based on common human behavior. The odds might lean slightly in his favor but there were no guarantees.

"What happens if the doctor is injured?" Had his employer thought of that? What they were about to do posed significant risk to all involved. "Then no one will have the benefit of the lifesaving surgery only he can do at this time."

"We can talk about what-ifs all night," Abi said. "But it's our job to make sure the what-ifs don't happen. We get the doc and his daughter out with no hitches. We do what we have to do and everybody's happy when the night is over."

Jamie held up her hands in surrender. Further discussion was pointless. "Moving on, please. At this point, I need some sort of assurance from you that your employer had nothing to do with Poe's disappearance." The facts were troubling. She had not heard from him, and his cell had ended up on the ground in the woods behind the house. If he'd been taken by someone involved in all this, why hadn't they heard anything? If he'd decided some other action was necessary, why hadn't she heard from him by now?

"I have no idea why or how he left other than what we found on the security system." Abi shrugged. "He told me nothing. I saw and heard nothing."

"You don't receive any sort of notification when some-one enters or exits the house?"

"This is not my house. I'm a guest here just as you are. I had no reason to want to monitor who went in and out. It was only relevant if we were here and frankly, I wasn't expecting you or Poe to cut out on me."

"He wouldn't cut out without a reason," she said to en-sure Abi understood this wasn't Poe just cutting out.

"You want to know what I think?" He braced his hands on the island. "I think he decided he didn't need to be part of this."

Jamie shook her head. "No way. He wouldn't do that. He would never leave me in the lurch."

Abi shrugged. "Maybe I'm wrong. I guess we'll find out tonight. If he shows up and tries to interfere, we'll have our answer. If he doesn't show up, we'll have an answer as well."

Jamie shook her head again. "You'll see." She wasn't standing around here and throwing her friend under the bus. She knew Poe too well. He had either set out on a plan of his own because he knew something was rotten with this one or someone had taken him. End of story.

She thought of his cell phone and worry dug deep be-neath her skin. She desperately hoped her allowing Poe to come here with her wasn't going to be the reason he…

No. She wasn't going there.

"Let me know when you're ready to move." Jamie needed a few minutes to herself. Some time to decompress and get her head on straight. Tonight, was far too important to go into it rattled like this. Psyching herself up for a mission was always a smart step.

Abi touched her arm to slow her departure. "I'm counting on you, Jamie. I can't do this without you."

"Yeah."

Jamie had never felt so torn. This was not like her usual missions. It was wrong. More wrong than anything she'd ever been asked to do. But it was also the only way to save her brother.

She couldn't say no...couldn't walk away.

And because of that she had no choice but to do all within her power to ensure that Dr. Case and his daughter cooperated—but also that they survived this thing unscathed.

For the first time since she was a little girl, she wished her grandmother were here beside her to give her an assist. She could use some of Victoria's wisdom and strength right now.

Lionheart Court,
7:30 p.m.

JAMIE EMERGED FROM the limo that had picked up her and Abi. He waited for her outside the car, looking too handsome in his black suit and black bow tie against the white shirt. His dark skin and black hair gave him the sophisticated look of a foreign diplomat. In his jacket pocket was a red handkerchief.

Her floor length sheath was the exact shade of red as the handkerchief. So were her very sleek high heeled shoes. None of which was made for running or for tackling an enemy.

After seeing the formfitting dress, she'd decided to wear

her hair up in a French twist. Seemed appropriate. Whatever others thought of them being at this party, they certainly made a handsome couple. Jamie felt as if she'd arrived at senior prom with the most popular boy in school, but couldn't remember why she'd decided to come when none of her friends would be here. Only this boy who was so handsome and far too charming.

There were always strangers involved with her missions, but these were not simply strangers. These were civilians who had no idea that this party had been targeted by someone who had so much money at his disposal that he could choose to disrupt this gala and the life of the man hosting it to get what he wanted.

Jamie took a breath and cleared her head. She knew what she had to do. Fretting over the details wouldn't get the job done.

Abi took her hand and draped it over his arm. "In case I haven't already told you, you look amazing."

She smiled at the man who held the door open as they entered the home of their target. "You look quite fetching yourself, Mr. Amar."

He flashed her a smile.

Once they were deep into the entry hall, he leaned close and whispered, "Do you think we look so nice that they'll never suspect we're here for nefarious purposes?"

"As long as they don't look too closely."

He smiled. "Touché."

Apparently, the doctor had many friends. The crowd was larger than Jamie had expected for a family holiday gathering.

They entered the grand hall, and it was like entering a Christmas wonderland. Beautifully decorated trees…garlands and ribbons…so tastefully done. The scent of cedar hung in the air. Holiday music played softly from speakers hidden somehow in the architecture. The ceiling towered two stories above, looking exactly like something from a European castle. The floor was marble and the furnishings were museum quality. Servers strolled about with their trays. But Jamie wasn't the slightest bit hungry or even thirsty.

"Recognize anyone?"

She had seen photos of Case and his family on the internet and on Abi's phone. Jamie spotted Dr. Case near the massive stone fireplace almost immediately. He was surrounded by what she presumed were colleagues. Maybe close friends. This didn't feel like a family holiday gathering. This was almost certainly a business function accented with holiday decor.

"Several other surgeons," he said, leaning close enough for her to feel his lips brush her forehead. "A number of local politicians."

Interesting. Abi had certainly familiarized himself with those in the doctor's orbit. Not surprising really, she decided. This was exactly what she did when prepping for a mission.

She spotted Case's wife. She too wore a red dress. Jamie glanced at Abi. "Am I wearing red because she is?"

He smiled. "It's a very good color on you. Far better than on her. And your blond hair is natural, unlike hers."

Hovering near Mrs. Case was her daughter. Ten-year-old Lillian Case. And of course, she wore a red dress to match her mommy. Oh, dear God. Jamie felt sick at what could go wrong.

"Do you have any assets here or nearby?" She gazed around at the lavish crowd. Some part of her hoped to spot Poe. Damn it. Where was he? "Someone to call upon for backup in case we need it?"

"No assets inside. Just the two of us."

At least he wasn't ruling out the possibility of backup somewhere on the property.

Better than nothing.

Jamie considered the most likely tactic for making this happen in a crowd of this size, in a house of this size.

"I'm guessing the family has a routine for their daughter. A certain time to go to bed. Mommy tucks her in, and Daddy pops by for a good-night kiss. Where's the nanny? Have you made arrangements for disabling her?"

"The nanny tucks her in. Then Mommy and Daddy go to the room for a quick good-night. It's all very affable and everyone disappears quickly. The nanny goes home after. But tonight the nanny is not an issue. She's on vacation for the next ten days."

One less potential liability.

"You know—" Jamie glanced around in search of a server "—I think I might need a real drink after all."

"Allow me," Abi said before making a slight bow and then hurrying to the nearest server.

Jamie watched Mrs. Case for a moment and then her husband, the doctor. She wondered if either could possibly comprehend how their lives were about to change. The ability to breathe suddenly felt unnatural, difficult.

This was wrong.

And yet she was helpless to stop it.

Abi reappeared with two flutes of bubbling liquid. Jamie accepted hers and took the smallest sip. "Thank you."

"Case's wife writes children's books."

Jamie nodded. "You mentioned that, and I spotted it on her Wikipedia page."

"Her latest is *The Fish in My Dreams*. It's about a little

girl who dreams of swimming deep into the ocean with fish on her feet instead of shoes."

Jamie laughed. "Sounds like something her daughter dreamed and told her about."

Abi nodded. "That's what she says in the dedication to her daughter."

Jamie slipped her arm around his. "I'm guessing we should tell her how much we loved the book."

"The daughter will remember you talking to her mother," he agreed.

The whole point.

Jamie led the way across the room. Mrs. Case looked up as they approached.

"Mrs. Case," Jamie said, her smile broadening, "I'm Jasmine Colter. I just wanted to say how very much my little niece enjoyed your new book."

Lillian leaned closer to her mom, her cheeks pink.

"It's Lillian's story really." She beamed down at her daughter. "She has very vivid dreams."

Jamie nodded to Lillian. "Such a great story, Lillian. I hope you'll be telling more stories with your mom."

Lillian smiled finally. "Ducks are coming next."

"Oh my. You're writing a story about ducks?"

Lillian nodded. "For next year."

"How wonderful. We'll be sure to get it."

They chatted for a moment more until another guest arrived to share her praise for the book. Jamie and Abi wandered to the other side of the room.

"We are twenty minutes out," he told her.

Jamie left her barely touched glass on a tray. "I think I'll drop by the powder room."

"I'll be right here." His position allowed him to see the wife, daughter and the doctor.

Jamie nodded and headed through the lingering crowd.

Taking a bathroom break while wearing a dress like this was never fun. But she might as well take advantage of the opportunity. No way to know when she'd have another chance. Ducking behind a bush wearing this wouldn't be so easy.

She made quick work of the necessary business. After a swift wash of her hands and check of her hair and makeup, she smoothed her dress. It was almost showtime. Maybe they would all get through this without a glitch, and she would be on her way home tomorrow with her little brother in tow.

"Hang in there, Luke." She hoped she would be seeing him soon.

She exited the ornate powder room and went in search of her date. Well, *date* wasn't really the right term. *Partner in crime.* No sign of the mother and daughter. She surveyed the room again. She spotted them by the larger Christmas tree. It was then that she noticed their dresses fit particularly well with the holiday decor. Every last thing was meticulously coordinated.

"They'll be going up soon," Abi told her. "When the doctor goes up, that will be our cue."

"Have you heard from your getaway driver? You've confirmed that all is as it should be?" Her nerves were jangling.

"I have. All is exactly as it should be."

"When and how will your employer release Luke?"

His gaze collided with hers. "Once Dr. Case is at the designated location, you will be taken to Luke's condo, and he will be there waiting for you."

"And when will the doctor be returned to his home?"

"By noon tomorrow I'm told."

She wondered if he would be considered missing or kidnapped during that time. If so the police and the FBI would launch into action. Or would he simply be made to call his wife and assure her that he'd had an emergency at the hospital?

"Until then," Abi said, drawing her back to the conversation, "he'll be caring for an emergency situation. It happens all the time. His wife and daughter will think nothing of it."

Jamie searched his face. He'd just lied to her, or he'd made the sort of mistake he shouldn't and he'd glossed right over it.

"Does he usually take his daughter with him to emergencies?"

Abi stared at her for a long moment. "Before the mother realizes she is missing, little Lillian will be back in her room."

"What will she tell her mother? Another dream for a book?"

Suddenly all the holes in his elaborate plan were far too visible and Jamie had a bad, bad feeling swelling in her gut.

He smiled. "Sounds like a bestseller."

As long as no one died or was gravely injured, she reminded herself. Jamie settled her gaze on the doctor. How did a man like him—who possessed a skill like no one else—get through each day knowing he could only save a few? How did he decide who he would save and who he would let go?

Did he have the typical god complex associated with some in the profession?

Even as she asked herself this question, his shoulders seem to visibly slump beneath the weight of his success.

Or maybe she wanted to believe he cared that much. After all, imagine the dedication and work required to reach the sort of skill level he possessed. To achieve what no one else had.

She would soon know how he saw himself. More important, how he saw the patients in need of his help.

She hoped for the sake of all involved that he would be reasonable...not that there was anything reasonable about what was coming.

Chapter Ten

8:40 p.m.

Mrs. Case motioned for her daughter who was admiring the many decadent looking desserts spread across silver trays. Or perhaps it was the chocolate fountain in the middle of that table that had her mesmerized.

Either way, Lillian turned away empty-handed and skipped toward her mother. Almost bedtime. Sweet treats were apparently off the menu.

Jamie wondered if it was Abi's appearance at the dessert table that had alerted the child's mother. He'd insisted on finding something chocolate.

If his sudden need for chocolate hadn't made Jamie suspicious, seeing Dr. Case withdraw his cell phone from his jacket pocket for the first time since their arrival certainly did. The doctor turned from the trio to whom he'd been engaged in conversation. The three continued with whatever discussion they'd been having but the doctor's posture changed dramatically as he listened to the more personal conversation.

Abi appeared next to her with a delicious looking offering. She shook her head. "Something's happening."

She'd no sooner said the words than Dr. Case ended his

call and moved back toward the trio he'd abandoned. She didn't need a listening device to get the gist of what he was saying. His body language spoke loudly and clearly as he patted one man's shoulder and gave nods to the others. He was excusing himself.

Next to her, Abi suddenly reached for his cell phone.

Jamie ignored his subdued murmuring. She was far more interested in what was happening with the doctor. He crossed to his wife and daughter, said a few words, then dropped a kiss on each of their cheeks.

He was leaving.

He hurried from the room. Jamie drifted toward the front of the great hall, then on to the entry hall just in time to watch him disappear through the front double doors with no less than four men dressed in black accompanying him. Members of his security team, no doubt.

When she turned back to find Abi, he was moving in her direction. He put his arm around her shoulder and leaned close to her temple. "There's an emergency at the hospital."

"Are we staying here to await his return or going to the hospital?" She smiled up at him as if they were sharing secret love messages.

"We go with the doctor."

A final glance at the wife and daughter showed the wife smiling with friends and the daughter having wrangled a dessert without her mother noticing. The other guests appeared unconcerned about the doctor's abrupt departure. The servers continued offering drinks and finger foods and the music played on.

Jamie followed Abi from the house. The night was colder than when they'd arrived or perhaps it was only because the anticipation-fueled adrenaline related to what could happen had worn off, reminding her she'd opted not to wear a coat.

Abi said nothing until they were in the car traveling away from the house. "You'll find a change of clothes in the back seat."

She'd expected there would be a change of clothes for them at their next destination, but she hadn't anticipated it being in the car. Turned out to be a good decision.

She tucked up her dress and slid somewhat awkwardly over the console into the back seat. A pair of jeans, a sweater and sneakers were folded neatly on the seat. When had he done this? She supposed he had not. More likely someone had prepared everything to his specifications.

Unzipping the dress wasn't exactly the easiest feat, but she managed. She eased the luxurious fabric down her hips and over her legs.

"You have everything under control back there?" He glanced in the rearview mirror.

"I do." She pulled the sweater over her head and tugged it into place. She kicked off the heels and slipped into the jeans. This was a relief. She'd always felt more at home in jeans than in anything else.

She folded the dress and placed it on the seat, then set the shoes atop it. A quick search of the floorboard using the flashlight app on her cell helped her find a pair of socks. When the socks and sneakers were on, she was set, except for her hair. Making quick work of the task, she removed the pins, shook her hair free and then did a quick braid. It was best if she didn't look anything like the blonde in the red dress from the party.

"Any idea on how this changes our plans?"

"We'll wait until—"

Jamie's gaze swung to the rearview mirror. She didn't have to ask why he'd suddenly stopped talking. The bright lights filling the mirror provided the answer.

They had a tail.

"Brace yourself." Abi's fingers visibly tightened on the steering wheel.

Rather than risk looking back, Jamie braced her feet against the back of the passenger seat and eased down low in her seat.

The crash of metal was followed by a hard lurch forward as the other car rammed them. A new wave of adrenaline rose inside her.

Abi righted their forward momentum. "There's a weapon under my seat if you can get to it."

Jamie eased down into the floorboard and felt around under the driver's seat. The weapon sat snugly in a holster that had been secured to the bottom of the seat. A bit of creativity was required to remove the weapon from behind since it had been installed with the driver in mind.

"Got it."

She eased up into the seat, keeping her head low.

"He's coming again," Abi warned.

Jamie got onto her knees facing the rear window and watched as the vehicle neared. It was impossible to determine if there were more occupants than the driver. She powered the window down and leaned out as far as she dared.

"He's coming," Abi warned.

Jamie closed one eye and focused on the front passenger side wheel barreling toward her. She took the shot.

Tires squealed as the car seemed to spin sideways and rush backward. In fact, it was only because they were going forward that the distance stretched out between them.

"Bravo!" Abi shouted.

The car rocketed forward as he pushed the accelerator for all it had to offer.

Jamie powered the window back up but kept her focus

on the disabled car. It was dark, black maybe, and it wasn't moving.

Once it was out of view, she climbed over the console and settled back into the front passenger seat. She placed the weapon on the console and secured her seat belt.

"Who could have known about your plan?"

He slowed for an upcoming traffic signal. "I don't think this was someone who had advance knowledge of our plan. I'm thinking this was more like security picking up on our interest in the doctor's departure from the party."

"You're suggesting they monitored the guests who left when or soon after the doctor did."

"I am." He made a left turn.

"Maybe."

"Either that or your friend Poe tried taking us out of the game."

Of course he would come up with that scenario. "No. Poe would have followed us and then confronted us at our destination."

"At least one of us has faith in his motives."

"Whoever that guy was, if he works for the doctor, he's going to notify security at the hospital. They'll be watching for us."

"No problem." He glanced at her. "I have a plan."

Two more turns and he pulled into a slot in a parking area between two other vehicles. When he'd shut off the lights and the engine, he shifted in his seat to face her. "There's a sweater back there for me and a pair of sneakers. It might be easier for you to reach them."

The two items were in the floorboard after the erratic driving. She released her seat belt, got on her knees in the seat and reached into the rear floorboard. She passed the sweater and then the sneakers to him. His grin told her he'd enjoyed seeing her in that awkward position. She rolled her eyes.

His jacket, shirt and bow tie flew over the seat. He tugged the sweater over his head and rolled it into place. He powered the seat back to facilitate changing his shoes.

His cell vibrated and he took the call. "Yes."

Jamie surveyed the area. A multistory building sported a Nashville Eye Center logo. The hospital that was their destination, Saint Thomas, stood across the street. On that side of the street there were steps leading up to the parking area, making their current position well camouflaged from anyone who might be watching for their arrival. *Good move.*

He put the phone away and turned to her. "A patient he operated on early this morning developed an issue, which is why he's been called back here. We're going to hang around and then follow him back to the house." He sent her a pointed look. "At a safe distance and in a different car, of course."

"Of course."

They exited the car and headed across the street. The wind whipped across her face, making her flinch. Despite knowing that Poe wasn't the one who had followed them, she couldn't help looking around. Where the hell was he? She glanced at Abi. If he was responsible for whatever had happened to Poe...

She wasn't prepared to go there just yet. There had to be another explanation. Poe would not abandon her under any circumstances. However, as she'd already considered, he very well might take a different tactic to help with whatever he feared was coming.

She had every intention of giving him the benefit of the doubt either way...until there was no longer room for doubt.

They didn't enter the hospital through the lobby. Instead, they used the garage entrance. It was open twenty-four hours a day and since they had not arrived at the garage in a vehicle, the chances that security had spotted them via the cameras was unlikely. The cameras were only at the entrance and exit. Crossing over a short concrete wall in an area well camouflaged by shrubs near the entrance had protected them from view. Then they took the stairs to the level where the sky bridge crossed over to the hospital. Too easy.

"You have some idea of where we're going?" Jamie asked as they moved along the corridor. So far no one had paid attention to their arrival.

"Surgery, I presume." He flashed a smile.

Maybe it was that hint of a British accent, but his answer grated on her nerves. Of course the doctor was here for a possible return to surgery but that didn't mean she and Abi would be hanging out there. The goal was not to be spotted by the doctor's security team.

Careful to avoid eye contact with anyone they passed, they wound through the hospital until they reached the entrance to the surgery center. From there it was necessary to fly under the radar. Visiting hours were over and the usual excuses for their presence were no longer available.

Three people were seated in the surgery center's waiting room. Jamie assumed they had friends or family who'd had to undergo emergency surgery. Then again, for all she knew, surgeries were scheduled all hours of the day and night.

"You wait here," Abi said. "I'll have a look around. See if there's a need for anything beyond just hanging around."

If this was a true emergency with a patient, they had nothing to worry about.

"Whatever you say." She walked into the waiting room and took a seat where she could watch the corridor through the glass wall. If any dudes in all black showed up, she was following.

Abi watched her for a moment before going on his way. She pulled out her cell and then put it back. She couldn't call Poe. His cell was back at the house, disabled. Damn it. She thought of the car that had followed them on the way here. Case's personal security couldn't have known they were at the house on Excalibur...could they?

Why would they? The doctor's personal security team wouldn't likely have gotten a heads-up on a potential kidnapping plan.

Would they?

Only if Abi's employer was very, very bad at keeping secrets.

Then again, it could be as Abi suggested and the follower had been a member of Case's team who'd followed them from the house to ensure they weren't trouble...except she wasn't buying the idea that they would go so far as ramming a guest's car. Following it, she could see. After some time to mull it over, she was confident Abi had gotten that one wrong. Or simply gave her the story to cover the fact that he had no idea where the car had come from.

A man in scrubs and a surgical gown entered the waiting room and one of the two women who had already been present when Jamie arrived rushed toward him.

They spoke, heads together, for a moment, then the man patted her on the shoulder and left.

Standing in the middle of that waiting room, the woman lapsed into tears, her hands covering her face.

Since no one else moved to go to her, Jamie did. She grabbed the box of tissues on the table next to her chair and walked over to where the woman stood crying. "Are you all right?" Not exactly the most original conversation starter, but there it was.

The woman looked at her, eyes red and filled with tears. Jamie offered her the box of tissues.

She tugged a couple free. "Thank you."

"Would you like to sit down?" Jamie asked.

The woman blew her nose, dabbed at her eyes and then shook her head. "I'm fine. Really. I'm only crying because I'm so grateful."

She glanced around the room. The television was set to a news channel with the sound muted. The two anchors' words scrolled across the bottom of the screen.

"Do you mind if we step into the corridor?" She shivered. "It's really cold in here."

She was right. It was cold as hell in here. "Of course." Jamie followed her into the corridor. "You were saying you were grateful."

She sagged against the glass wall as if she could no longer hold her weight. "It was all just a mistake."

Since they were at a hospital—the surgery area of the hospital—a mistake wasn't necessarily something for which to be thankful.

"My husband had surgery this morning." Her face furrowed into a frown. "A brain tumor. We were so incredibly thankful when the surgery was a success. But then tonight the nurse insisted on calling the doctor back. She said my husband was having a possible bleed—a brain bleed."

Jamie made a horrified face. "Oh, that sounds terrifying."

"It was. The strangest thing was that he seemed fine. But after she told us this and gave him something in preparation for a second surgery, he had a seizure." She clasped her hands together against her chest as if in prayer. "I was certain I was losing him." Her lips trembled.

"But he's all right now?"

"It's the craziest thing. Dr. Case's assistant—" she made a face "—not assistant but resident or whatever he is. A doctor," she said, frustrated at herself, "who works with Dr. Case said that everything was fine. It was some sort of error."

So this was why Dr. Case had been called back to the hospital. A mistake. Jamie wondered how often something like that happened. "Do you recall the nurse's name?"

The other woman made a face and shook her head. "The resident or doctor asked me that as well. I believe it was Johnson. Brenda or Beverly Johnson." She flattened her hands to her chest. "My Lord, I have to call our daughter and my husband's sister. They're all waiting to hear. Fearing the worst, I'm sure."

"I'm certainly glad all is well, Mrs...? I'm sorry, I didn't get your name."

"Teresa Mason. My husband is Johnny." She smiled, her lips trembling. "And he's going to be fine. The doctor said so."

"That's wonderful. My name is Jamie, by the way. Can I walk you back to his room?" She mentally crossed her fingers. If this woman's husband was Dr. Case's patient, then Jamie was sticking close to her for as long as she could.

"That would be so kind of you. They said he would be back in the room very shortly. I want to be there when he arrives."

Jamie walked alongside the lady who rambled on and on about the two of them, she and her husband, having recently shared their fortieth anniversary.

"How did you hear about Dr. Case?" Jamie asked. "I understand it's tough to get on his schedule."

"Oh my, yes, it is. We were so very lucky in that he was on call when Johnny lost consciousness. We had no idea anything was wrong. Dr. Case is the only reason he survived that brain tumor. We had no idea it was even there."

Jamie was surprised that surgeons like Case were ever "on call." Then again, she wasn't that familiar with the way physicians' schedules worked and certainly she had no idea how much of their time was owed to or pledged to a particular hospital.

"The other doctor said Dr. Case would pop into the room once Johnny was settled."

Jamie would try her best to hang around until Case arrived. No reason to believe he would recognize her. Once they were in the room she should shoot a text to Abi. He might not be aware of the ruse that brought Case to the hospital.

In Jamie's opinion the whole thing screamed of a setup for when the doctor left the hospital. He would have only a few security guards with him. Far less backup than he had at his home.

She and Mrs. Mason had just entered the room when Mr. Mason was rolled through the door on a gurney that looked more like a bed. Since there wasn't a bed in the room, Jamie assumed it was not just a gurney.

"He'll be groggy for a while," a nurse explained as she and a colleague moved his bed in place. "And he may sleep off and on. But don't worry. We'll be watching him closely."

Mrs. Mason parked herself next to his bed and took her husband's hand in hers. "Thank you so much," she told the nurses. "I appreciate all you do."

Jamie wondered how many people bothered to express their gratitude in this way.

The nurses made their way out and another figure entered.

Dr. Case.

Jamie stayed put in the corner by the visitor's chair. She avoided direct eye contact. She felt confident he wouldn't recognize her, but why take the chance.

"Mrs. Mason, thankfully we did not have to go back in. As my associate told you, we determined that all was well. We'll take another CT scan in a couple of hours just to be sure. Once that's completed, I'll let you know those results as soon as we have them. But I'm confident you have nothing to worry about."

"Thank you so much, Dr. Case."

He gave her a nod, then looked to Jamie. "May I speak with you in the corridor?"

Holy cow. Was he speaking to her? Since he stared directly at her, she assumed so. Mrs. Mason was whispering softly to her husband.

Jamie mustered up a vague smile. "Sure."

Maybe he had recognized her.

Oh hell.

Once they were outside the room and the door closed, he set his attention on Jamie. "Were you here in the room when the nurse told Mrs. Mason I needed to be called?"

Aha. They were attempting to nail down the reason this happened. "No. I'm sorry. I wasn't here." At his frustrated look, she shrugged and offered, "I went for coffee."

"Anyway," Case said. "I'm here now and I'll be hanging around for a while. Just as a precaution."

Obviously, he was worried this Nurse Johnson had done something more than make a fake call. Damn.

"If you or Mrs. Mason notice anything unusual, don't hesitate to call for assistance."

"We will. Thank you."

Case walked away. By the weary set of his shoulders, he

seemed exhausted. His day had begun very early and certainly had not ended the way he had anticipated.

She decided to call Abi rather than bother with a text.

"Where are you? I'm in the waiting room."

She gave him the abridged version of what had occurred. "Doesn't sound like Case is going home anytime soon."

"I'll make some calls about this fake nurse."

"Dr. Case feels overly safe here at the hospital," she said, thinking about how he'd come to the room alone. "He didn't have any of his security personnel with him when he visited the patient's room. Considering what just went down with the nurse, I'm not so sure that's a good thing."

"That is a very astute observation, Colby," Abi said. "I'll have to ensure he's made aware of this oversight."

Jamie had no idea how he intended to make that happen.

"You want me to hang around here? Case said he would be stopping back by?"

"Yes, please do. I have something else to look into."

"I'll let you know when I see him again." She ended the call and put her phone away.

At the Mason's door, Jamie knocked softly and pushed the door inward far enough to step inside. "Mrs. Mason, Dr. Case will be back after the next CT is taken. Do you need anything for now? My friend is still in surgery, so I have some time if you need anything."

"You are so kind. I'm good for now though."

"Great." Jamie frowned. "They seem a bit concerned about this Nurse Johnson."

Mason made a distressed face. "It's so strange. It makes me wonder if she was even a nurse or if she was high or something."

Jamie wondered the same thing. "What did she look like?"

"Brown hair. Short and spiky." She scrunched her face

in thought. "Kind of tall." She shrugged. "I always think anyone taller than me is tall. But a couple or three inches taller than me for sure. Thin. Kind of willowy."

"I'm sure they'll get to the bottom of it," Jamie assured her. "They have cameras everywhere here. Maybe she was from one of those temp agencies." Jamie shrugged. "There are so many staffing shortages these days."

If the point of this nurse's lie about Mr. Mason was to get Dr. Case back to the hospital, why would she just disappear without completing the rest of her mission? Had her backup failed to step up? Or had the plan not been executed as of yet?

Which meant Dr. Case could be in danger right now.

"I think I'll take a walk," Jamie said. "You sure I can't get you anything?"

Mason shook her head. "No, thank you." She exhaled a big breath. "I really appreciate your help tonight. You were so very kind."

"You're very welcome, but it was nothing. Just being a good human."

As soon as she was in the corridor, she called Abi again. "I think we might still have a problem."

"I was thinking the same thing," he said, sounding breathless. "Case is in the doctor's lounge. I'm close by. Two members of his security team are stationed at the door. So far no word on who this nurse is or who is behind whatever went down or is going down."

"Then we're not going anywhere until he does."

"You got it. We need to know where he is every moment until we make *our* move."

Hopefully someone else wasn't going to beat them to the next move.

Chapter Eleven

Chicago
Colby Residence,
11:00 p.m.

Victoria opened a box of ornaments she'd had for at least thirty years, maybe forty. How time flew. There were dozens of boxes of decorations and here she was trying to pull this all together at nearly midnight. But she certainly couldn't sleep.

She stared at the tree. On the way home last evening she'd insisted that Lucas stop at the pop-up Christmas store on the corner and pick out something lovely. They'd thought they wouldn't bother with a tree this year since no one would be home for the holidays anyway and the two of them were set to go to Paris.

But she wasn't sure she could go. Not until she knew for certain that Jamie and Luke were safe. She suspected Lucas had picked up on her hesitation, which was why he didn't question her request for a tree.

She picked up a glossy green ornament. How could she leave with all this uncertainty hanging around them like a dark cloud? Tasha's situation remained unknown. Luke was missing. Jamie had been forced to throw in with a man Victoria did not trust to find her brother.

"You should come to bed, dear."

She looked up as Lucas entered the room. He wore those favorite pajamas of his. She smiled. The blue ones that made his gray eyes look so bright. She loved those pajamas too. She loved him. So very much.

"I thought I'd hang a few ornaments." She draped the green ornament on a branch. The smell of cedar had filled the house and she so loved it. How foolish she had been to even consider not putting up a tree.

It was a tradition. She and Lucas always had a tree.

Lucas joined her and picked out a blue ornament from the box. "I love these ornaments."

They were plain. No glitter or painted flowers or other symbols of Christmas. But there were literally hundreds of them. Red ones, pink ones. Silver, gold, blue and green. Even a few white ones. By the time the branches were loaded with ornaments, they would be beautiful.

"Wait. Wait." Lucas held up a hand. "We have to put the lights on first."

How had she forgotten the lights? "That was always your job," she said, not wanting anything to do with that chore. "I'll make hot chocolate if you string the lights."

He gave her a look that suggested he wasn't quite sure that was a fair trade, then he smiled. "Hot chocolate sounds lovely. Perhaps you'll add a little rum to mine."

"Mine too," she agreed.

Victoria padded into the kitchen. She set a pan on the stove and added the milk, then turned on the flame. While the milk heated, she combined the chocolate and sugar and added it to mugs. Hot chocolate was a winter favorite around here. If it snowed, they had hot chocolate. She glanced out the window over the sink. The snow was still coming down. The weather forecast predicted it would snow all night.

It was beautiful and a little heartbreaking. It would be the perfect time to have everyone together. But that wasn't going to happen.

This would be the first time they'd been spread so far and wide at Christmas. Victoria couldn't help feeling a little nostalgic and a lot sad.

Her cell vibrated in the pocket of her robe. Her heart rate sped up as she pulled it free of the silk. It was Kenny. "Kenny, do you have news?"

"I'm at the Saint Thomas Hospital in Nashville."

Victoria's heart dropped into her stomach. "Is everyone all right?" Please, please let her grandchildren be safe.

"Yes. Jamie is here. I've seen her. She and Amar followed the doctor from his house to the hospital. But I was careful that neither she nor Amar saw me."

"Was going to the hospital part of the plan?"

"No, ma'am. Whatever happened, it was some sort of emergency. The doctor left the party and Jamie and Amar followed not far behind. There was a small incident en route with someone who was following them. I've sent the license plate information to Michaels in hopes we might learn who it was."

More thumping in her chest. "What sort of incident?"

"The unidentified driver attempted to run them off the road. He might be someone who works for the doctor and who thought their following him from the party was suspicious, but I'm leaning more in the direction of another outside source."

Dread congealed in Victoria's belly. "Someone else who wants to, perhaps, kidnap the doctor."

"I fear so," he said. "I'm also concerned as to how this stacks up based on what you've learned about Dr. Case."

The additional intelligence her people had collected certainly shed a bad light on Dr. Case, but there were always two sides to every story. At this point it was best to reserve judgment.

"Very well," Victoria said, the next step clearing in her mind. "Given what we know, I believe it's time for you to return to the team."

"I agree. At this point I feel too removed from what's happening to be useful."

"Call me as soon as you've made contact with Jamie again."

"Will do. Good night, Victoria."

The call ended and she said a quick prayer for Jamie and Luke as well as Kenny and Amar. The smell of scorching milk shook her from the worrisome thoughts.

"You need some help in there?"

She shook off the troubling thoughts and emptied the milk, then started over. "Just giving you plenty of time to string those lights."

"Ha ha!" he called back to her.

She looked out the window and this time she couldn't help smiling. Why was she so worried about Jamie and Luke? They were Colbys. They would get through this and complete the mission too.

It was the Colby way.

Monday, December 24

One Day Before Christmas

Chapter Twelve

4:00 a.m.

"Your people have no idea who set this event in motion?"
Jamie was having a difficult time getting past the notion
that Abi and his backers had no idea how this *mistake* went
down.

He kept his focus on the dark highway as they drove
back toward the Case home. The doctor and his entourage
were half a mile ahead. Abi had carefully kept his distance
since leaving the parking area at the hospital.

"If my people have intel on last night, they're not sharing the information with me." He glanced at her through
the darkness. "Frankly, unless there's a reason for me to
know, I actually do not care to hear about it."

Now that was a cop-out. "Please. Do not try to spin this
for me. Remember who you're talking to, friend. This is
not my first rodeo."

The entourage up ahead took the turn to Lionheart Court.

Abi slowed, giving them ample time to move farther
along the private drive leading to the doctor's home before
they reached the intersection.

He blew out a long, low whistle as they passed that exit.
"At least we know he made it home without being whisked
away by a competitor."

Jamie waited until Abi had blown past the turn the doctor and his team had taken and then took the next right on Lady of the Lake Lane, which would take them to Excalibur. Following the doctor hadn't been an option. They had been at the hospital keeping an eye on the situation for hours. Case hadn't wanted to leave until he was certain all was good with Mr. Mason.

Jamie hoped the patient's continued stability meant he was out of the woods for good. Mason and his family would certainly have a lot to celebrate this Christmas. To find yourself on death's door and then suddenly pulled back by the skill of a surgeon was the very definition of a miracle.

Abi pulled into the garage of the Excalibur house, and she wondered again where Poe was and what in the world he was doing. If he had come here to help her and he'd ended up in trouble, she would never forgive herself.

She should call her grandmother to see if she had heard from him. Though she couldn't see Poe calling Victoria and not calling her, there could be a reason she didn't understand. She got out of the car and reached back inside for the dress and shoes she had worn to the party. Abi tucked his weapon in his waistband and grabbed his discarded clothes as well. There were things she wanted to say, but right now, she wanted a long, hot shower and a couple hours of sleep.

She wasn't sure either would happen, but she could hope.

Abi reached for the door of the house and stalled. He instantly reached to his waistband and the weapon he had tucked there not ten seconds ago as he got out of the vehicle.

He jerked his head toward her and she stepped to the side of the door. Abi held the weapon ready and eased in through the door that Jamie could now see stood ajar.

She gave him five seconds and then she followed.

They moved through the main room and had just entered the kitchen when the overhead light came on.

Jamie blinked.

Poe leaned against the sink, an apple in his hand. "Took you guys long enough to get back."

Abi growled and lowered his weapon. "I could have shot you," he warned.

"Good thing you didn't," Poe shot back.

Jamie skirted around Abi and the island to stand toe-to-toe with Poe. "What the hell, man? Where have you been?"

He smiled. "Good to see you too."

Now she was just steamed. "You disappear—leaving your phone as if you've been attacked and dragged away. What was I supposed to think?"

He had better have a good explanation. Right now her temper was pushing toward the out-of-control mark. This was not in any way shape or form the slightest bit comical.

"Your doctor's body double was on the move."

Abi made a face that said he wasn't buying it. "What exactly does that mean?"

"I took a walk. Early. I took those very nice binoculars you had in the kitchen down by the cliff and had myself a look around. While I was watching I saw someone run out of the house. He seemed in a panic." Poe shrugged. "Like the devil was after him."

"That happened this morning?" Jamie shook her head. "Yesterday morning, I mean?"

"That's right. When I zoomed in, I thought it was Case— Dr. Case. Two men—security, I presume—rushed out and tackled him."

"How do you know it wasn't Dr. Case?" Jamie glanced at Abi. The man she spoke with at the hospital had to have been the real Dr. Case…right? He hadn't actually done any surgery. He only met with the patient and viewed a CT scan.

Uncertainty swelled inside her. What if it wasn't him?

"I can't be certain, of course," Poe admitted. "But amid all the yelling—not that I could hear any of it well enough to understand what was being said—another figure appeared at the front door. I zoomed in and he, I think, was the real Dr. Case. He started pointing and barking orders, which would seem to confirm my initial conclusion. The two security thugs dragged the other *Dr. Case* into the house."

"How does this explain why you disappeared?" Abi asked, his distrust showing.

"Apparently, while I was watching this go down, there was another member of the security team watching me. I took off in a direction away from the house so he would hopefully believe I had come from a different location. I dropped my phone and didn't want to risk going back for it."

"So where have you been?" Jamie demanded.

"Well, I thought I was in the clear, but I ran right into the guy. He took me down to the house and that's where they kept me until about two hours ago."

Jamie had known Poe for a while now. She trusted him completely, but there was something wrong with this story. No, what was wrong was with the way he was telling it. "You're saying you've been held hostage all day and night?"

"In the basement. I could hear the music when the party was going on."

"How did you get away?" A cold hard knot formed in Jamie's gut. So maybe he was telling the truth.

"About nine o'clock last night, a guy walked in and told me I was free to go. I walked back up here, but the two of you were gone."

"I'm finding this a little difficult to believe," Abi said. He looked to Jamie. "Are you buying this?"

"Are you okay?" Jamie searched her friend's face. "I mean, really okay?"

He nodded. "I don't think they intended to shoot me or anything. They just wanted me out of the way for a while."

Jamie turned to Abi. "Can we be certain the man at the hospital was the real Dr. Case?" Damn, this was not good. Luke's life depended on them delivering the surgeon—the real, miracle producing one.

A single moment of hesitation elapsed and in that fleeting second, Jamie knew Abi was about to lie to her.

"I can't be certain."

Now Jamie was furious. "You said you could tell the difference."

"Wait, wait, wait," Abi argued, stepping forward, bellying up to the island, "I would need to be close to him to confirm it's really him. He has a birthmark."

"Oh. My. God. Birthmarks are like tattoos—they can be recreated. Faked!"

"Not this birthmark. It wouldn't be so easily faked. It's a deep scar beneath his ribcage. He could certainly have had it repaired at some point in his life if he'd chosen, but creating the same look wouldn't be an easy task—particularly if you only wanted it to be temporary."

Jamie told herself to remain calm. Arguing with him would accomplish nothing. "As long as you're certain."

"I'm certain."

"What're we doing now?" Poe asked. "I got the impression they thought I was the trouble they'd maybe heard a rumor about. Then they let me go. I figured whatever was supposed to happen had happened, but then you two came back. So apparently, it didn't."

"We were at the party prepared to carry out the mission and there was an emergency at the hospital and Case had to go there," Jamie explained. "He just got back home. We followed him there, then came here."

"Whatever happened over there this morning," Poe said, "and tonight, it feels like something totally unrelated to what we're here to do."

"Did you hear anything while you were there?" Abi asked, his own concern visibly growing.

"I was in the basement, so not much. Except there was a lot of moving around. Big sounds like furniture."

Jamie considered what she had seen at the doctor's home. "Everything appeared to be in place. It didn't feel like there were items missing."

Abi turned his hands up. "Maybe it was just the cleaning and prep for the gala."

Poe shrugged. "I guess so. I'm just saying that's about all I heard while I was down there."

"Were you provided with food and water?" Jamie could see them sending someone down with water at least.

"A guy brought a tray at lunchtime and then later in the evening—before the party started."

"You didn't see anyone else the entire time?" Abi pressed.

"No one."

"I need to think about this." Abi glanced at Jamie, then left the room.

The sound of the glass doors opening and then closing told Jamie he'd gone onto the patio, probably to watch the house below.

Poe looked at Jamie then. "There's something off with this. He's not telling us everything."

Jamie nodded. "At this point I don't think I can even pretend he's being completely up front." She looked directly at Poe then. "I was really, really worried about you. I walked the cul-de-sac." She exhaled a big breath. "I was scared that you were in real trouble."

Poe took her by the arm and ushered her toward the stairs. He looked to see that Abi was still on the patio. "Come with me."

They hurried up the stairs and into the en suite of the room Poe had been using. He closed the door and turned on the shower.

"That story I gave downstairs was for Abi."

Her anger flared again. She had suspected he was not telling the truth. "Poe, what does that mean?"

"It means I am worried about what's happening here. I do not trust this guy. He is lying about too many things."

Jamie waffled between thinking he could be right and lashing out. "What things exactly?"

"I talked to your grandmother."

His words stunned her. "What?"

"I told her my concerns and she did some digging. This guy Case didn't start out being the good savior surgeon that everyone thinks. He purposely only performed certain surgeries. The patients he chose paid him huge bonuses under the table. That's why he has a body double. He fears for his life. But that seems to be shifting so I don't know exactly what's happening. This is just part of the talk about him."

This was not what Jamie wanted to hear. It didn't represent the way Case had presented himself at the hospital.

"His body double is actually his identical twin brother. All of this—" he glanced at the door, then lowered his voice "—all of this is wrong. Whatever Abi is doing it's not what he says he's doing. If some rich guy wanted the surgery, all he would have to do is pay the bonus price."

Jamie thought of the Mason family. How could they

have paid a bonus for surgery? Why wouldn't someone—anyone—file a complaint about this?

"Your grandmother gave me this information," he said. "I couldn't have known otherwise. Her investigator, Ian Michaels, is here in case we need backup." He pulled a weapon from his waistband at the small of his back. "That's how I got this."

Jamie felt sick. "I'm not saying you or my grandmother is wrong, but there has to be an explanation. Abi wouldn't do this." There was bad and then there was *bad*. "And what you're saying about Case just doesn't fit with the man I met last night."

"I'm with you, Jamie. Whatever you decide. I swear I am. I just need you to think long and hard and decide if there's a chance you might be wrong."

"I get it." She did. She really did. "You have my word that I'm taking all that he says with a grain of salt."

"Good."

A knock on the door made them both jump.

"Is this a private party or am I invited?"

Jamie and Poe shared a look. Poe shut off the shower and opened the door. Abi walked in, making the bathroom seem far smaller than it had been moments ago.

"Who wants to tell me what's going on?" He folded his arms over his chest and leaned against the door frame.

"We've learned some information that seems to counter the intelligence you have," Jamie admitted.

Abi looked to Poe before meeting her gaze. "And where did you get this intelligence?"

"My grandmother." She squared her shoulders and crossed her arms over her chest. "I trust my grandmother implicitly."

"What is this intelligence?" He looked between the two of them again.

"Dr. Case is charging bonuses from the patients he chooses to help. His so-called body double is actually his identical twin brother."

Abi nodded. "Well, your grandmother's intelligence is not without merit."

Fury blasted Jamie. "You didn't think I needed to know any of this?"

"Well, there are mitigating circumstances that prevented me from telling you these things."

Jamie held up her hand. "Start from the beginning and tell me those things now. Right now."

"Shall we retire to the living room where it isn't quite so stuffy and humid?"

Jamie sidled past him. She had not been this furious in recent history. These two men were people she trusted. Well, Poe more so than Abi, but she trusted them both on some level. And one or both were yanking her chain in a very dangerous game.

If not for needing to stay in complete control for her brother's sake, she could definitely use a drink right now. This was beyond nuts. When she reached the great room, she couldn't sit down. Instead, she leaned against the bar and waited. Poe took a position next to her. Abi sat on the sofa with an I-see-how-it-is face.

"Dr. Case has an identical twin brother who was used as his body double when the need arose. And, for a while, it did appear that he was choosing patients who paid a bonus for his services. But then, about two months ago he learned that his twin brother was scamming his patients. He was pretending to be the surgeon and, in a way, filtering the patients. Only those who were prepared to pay a huge extra fee under the table were put on the surgeon's schedule. When he found out, Dr. Case chose not to press charges since the man was his brother. Instead, he warned that if his brother ever showed his face around him again, he would see that he paid for what he had done."

Jamie could see where this was going. "So the scam was discovered and remediated before your employer was in need of surgery. Since Dr. Case never chose patients in this way, he would cut off his hands before agreeing to such a thing."

"Exactly. Which leaves us with the plan as I've lain out to you already."

Jamie turned to Poe. "Sound plausible to you?"

Abi rolled his eyes. "Really?"

"I can see that scenario happening," Poe said, ignoring Abi. "Nothing the Colby Agency found opposes the possibility of that scenario."

"Knowing all that, what do we do now?" Jamie asked. "My brother is still caught in all this."

"While we were at the party," Abi explained, "I left a couple of bugs in the house. Popped a couple of tracking devices on cars. We're just waiting to hear there's movement."

"Is the Case's vacation still on?" Jamie asked. How long were they going to be in a waiting stance? She needed to find her brother and get him out of this mess.

"The vacation is still on. At some point this morning, the family is supposed to prepare to leave. The time is being withheld for reasons that are obvious."

"If the family loads up to go on vacation," Poe said, "there will be all manner of security involved. Are we going to end up in a shootout?"

"We are not. We will step in before they get into the family limo to make their escape," Abi explained.

"Have you spoken with your employer since the emergency fiasco? Any update on who this fake nurse was?" That still bugged Jamie.

"We have reason to believe someone else has decided to make an attempt on the doctor."

Having one desperate individual ready to cross so many lines to make something happen was one thing but to have two—at least—competing to achieve the same goal was more than a little disturbing.

"How do we know there won't be additional attempts?" Jamie started to pace. She couldn't help herself. The situation was not contained at all. There were far too many variables.

"We have no control over what others do," Abi argued. "We can only move forward with our own plan until some sort of roadblock pops up in our path and then we go around it." He looked directly at Jamie. "That's why I told my employer we needed the best."

This conversation was feeling repetitive. "I appreciate the vote of confidence, but this is far too risky for comfort."

Poe added, "My gut says that we should move on our own count and not based on the movements of others."

"Waiting could be a mistake," Jamie agreed. She turned to Abi. "It gives the other team more opportunity to try a second strike."

"We are not moving prematurely," Abi argued. "There is nothing to be gained by jumping the gun, so to speak."

"Let's talk about this," Jamie pushed back. "We just spent six hours at the hospital because someone posing as a nurse called in a fake emergency. Now, we're tired—the security supporting Dr. Case are no doubt tired as well. And we're standing around here as if we have all the time in the world and no one else is even thinking about this sort of thing."

"All right." Abi pushed to his feet. "I will call my employer and see if he will agree to our moving forward now."

He walked outside and closed the glass doors behind him.

Poe turned to Jamie. "We need to be prepared. Luke is depending on us to ensure this goes down right and, frankly, I'm losing any and all confidence in what he's doing."

"I'm with you and ready to go," Jamie assured him.

"I should call Victoria and let her know what's happening."

Jamie shook her head. "I should call her."

"Sure. She'll be happy to hear from you."

Jamie took out the cell and put through a call to her grandmother. It was even earlier in Chicago, but she wouldn't mind.

"Jamie, are you all right?"

She sounded so worried, and Jamie's chest ached at the idea. "I'm fine, Grandmother. We're on standby for the moment. We had a false alarm and the mission had to be delayed but we should be moving out soon."

"Poe is there with you now?"

"Yes, he is. He's updated me on everything."

"Good. I'm not sure Abi's employer is on the up-and-up, Jamie."

"I know. I'm worried about that too. Hopefully we'll know something soon. I'm ready to move."

"Just be careful. You have a guardian angel."

Jamie smiled. "I will, Grandmother. Don't worry, I know."

They said their goodbyes, and Jamie ended the call just as Abi returned from his private call.

"We will be moving out shortly," Abi announced. "We have a very short time for any final preparations."

"Thank God." Jamie took a breath. "I just need one last assurance from you, Abi, that this man—your employer—is properly prepared for the intentions he has laid out. This is a very delicate situation. If I note even the slightest hint that some untoward situation is going down, I will not help make that happen."

"No one," Abi insisted, "wants to keep Dr. Case alive more than my employer. You can rest assured that every precaution will be taken to protect him and his family."

Jamie turned to Poe. "Are you still prepared to do this? I will understand if you want to walk away. If any part of this goes wrong…"

There was no need to explain. Everyone in the room understood exactly what she was saying.

"I'm in," Poe said. "We do this together." He turned to Abi. "The three of us."

Abi nodded. "Thank you."

"Let's do it," Jamie announced.

Abi gave her a nod as well. "It is the right thing to do."

As long as no one died…she could live with doing whatever she had to do to save Luke.

She hoped that guardian angel her grandmother had sent was ready as well.

Chapter Thirteen

Lionheart Court,
7:00 a.m.

Jamie scanned the area around the house as the sun peeked above the trees.

It was almost time.

She, Poe and Abi hovered in a group of trees at the edge of the wooded area. Beyond their position was the landscaped yard that surrounded the home of Dr. Case.

Half an hour ago they had received word that they should move into place. The three of them had come down the hillside, which surprised Jamie. She'd expected to go in a vehicle, but Abi assured there would be a vehicle waiting for them when the time came. He had better be right.

"You're going in through the front," Abi said to Jamie. "Poe and I will approach from the rear."

Sounded easy enough. *Not.* "Do I have a cover?" Going in via the front door surprised her. Security was inside and around the house. Not just one or two either. They had already established that there were a lot of security personnel. Whoever answered the door was not going to let her in without one hell of a good explanation.

Abi smiled. "You talked to him at the hospital, did you not?"

The memory of the woman who'd started to cry in the waiting room pinged her, followed immediately by the flash of recall with Jamie and the doctor chatting in the room belonging to the woman's husband. Jamie had walked right into that one.

"I guess I did," she admitted.

Abi glanced at his watch.

When had he started wearing a watch? Apparently, he'd added it for the final step. She didn't recall him wearing one to the party. Change always set her on edge.

"You should go now." Abi turned to Jamie. "A car is coming up the driveway now. You're trading places with the driver."

Jamie spotted the headlights at the farthest end of the drive just before the two round orbs went out. "See you inside," she said to Poe before disappearing into the trees.

Sprinting through the trees wasn't so easy, but she managed. There was just enough daylight to prevent any head-on collisions with the flora or face-plants after tripping over roots. The car stopped as the driver somehow realized she was near. Probably a tracking device in the clothes she was wearing. Abi wasn't one to take chances. A good thing, she supposed.

The driver's-side door opened and the man behind the wheel emerged. He walked right past Jamie and into the woods without a glance or a word. Weird.

She watched until he'd disappeared and then she climbed into the car. Maybe she was accustomed to working with team members she knew and liked. This was strange territory.

After putting the car into Drive once more, she rolled slowly toward the house. When she reached the fountain that sat in the middle of the parking area, she slowed to a stop. By the time she put the car into Park and shut off the engine, a member of the security team was at her door.

She opened the door and started to get out, but he held up a hand. The weapon still sheathed on his hip warned that he was dead serious about her staying in the vehicle. "Let's see some ID."

"My name is... Jamie *Mason*. I'm here to speak with Dr. Case about his patient, my uncle, and what happened at the hospital last night."

He passed along a summary of what she'd said to whoever was on the other end of his hidden communication device. A few seconds later he evidently received a response because he stepped aside and said, "You're cleared to come inside."

Jamie wondered again how Abi had set her up for this. How could he have known that she would approach the woman in the waiting room? Calculated guess? The idea also made her wonder if the whole thing had been a setup. Clearly, the incident with the patient had been... But the wife in the waiting room? Had the fake nurse sent her to the waiting room rather than allow her to stay in the room? Made sense if the supposedly accidental meeting between her and Jamie was the plan.

She followed the guard to the front door. He led her into the entry hall and then disappeared back through the door they'd entered.

Eight, no ten suitcases of varying sizes were lined up in the entry hall ready to be loaded into a vehicle. The family was ready to head off to some ski slope loaded with fresh white snow or some city glittering with ritzy shops. Maybe she should take a vacation. Her parents were in Europe. She couldn't remember the last time she'd actually taken a vacation. Or a holiday for that matter.

She traveled extensively with her work but that wasn't the same.

At all.

Work usually involved being stuck in some location where the target could be monitored 24/7. Once she'd spent days in a jail cell with a target for a cellmate. It was almost Christmas, and she had no idea if she would even be spending it with family, maybe her grandparents, or completely alone.

If you can't save your brother...what difference does the holiday make?

She blinked away the thought and focused on what she had to do. Dr. Case was the key to rescuing Luke. She had to keep that in mind above all else.

Movement at the far end of the larger hall snagged her attention. She focused on the man striding her way. *Dr. Case.* At least she hoped it was the real Dr. Case. What if it was his twin brother?

She steeled herself against the worries and readied to spin a tale that would keep her in the house until Abi and Poe showed up. At least she assumed that was the point.

"Ms. Mason." Case studied her a moment, a frown working its way across his forehead. "I checked on your uncle a little while ago and he was doing fine."

"He is," Jamie agreed. "One of the nurses said you and your family were leaving for an extended vacation and I really felt it was important that I speak with you before you go."

"I wouldn't call this an extended vacation," he offered. "We'll be gone the rest of this week and through the weekend, but I'll be back at the hospital on Monday." He studied her another moment. "What is it you need to speak with me about?"

Damn it, Abi. Come on.

"The nurse," she said. "The one who triggered the false alarm. Johnson, I believe her name was."

He nodded. "The hospital is working with the police in conducting an investigation. To my knowledge she hasn't been found as of yet."

"I think I saw her back at the hospital this morning and I didn't know who to tell." This obviously was a lie, but she was winging it. If she had to buy much more time, she wasn't sure how that was going to go down. The doctor was clearly already suspicious, and she was basically holding her breath.

He reached into his pocket and withdrew his cell phone. "Did you inform security?" He tapped the screen and pressed the phone to his ear.

"I told the nurse on duty at the desk—the one near my uncle's room."

For a few seconds, Case was preoccupied discussing her assertion with whomever he had called. Then he thanked the person and ended the call.

"Security is keeping an eye on everyone who enters the building. There has been no sign of her coming through any of the entrances."

Jamie made a face. Damn. Of course they were monitoring the comings and goings after the incident. "Well then, maybe she never left."

This appeared to give him pause. He withdrew his phone and made a second call. He passed along this suggestion, then hung up.

"Thank you," she said before he could start asking her questions. "I was just really worried about my uncle's safety, and I wasn't sure anyone would actually listen to me. You seemed so kind and so concerned. I felt the need to come straight to you. I'm so sorry for the intrusion."

"Daddy! Daddy!"

Lillian rushed into the room. Her pink sweatshirt sported a popular cartoon character. The pockets of her jeans were trimmed in pink and then there were the furry pink boots. The kid liked pink for sure. She glanced at Jamie, then smiled.

If the kid recognized her...

"This must be your daughter," Jamie said before the child could say a word.

Case smiled. "This is Lillian. She's very excited about the trip."

Jamie smiled. "Well, anyway, thank you, Dr. Case, for hearing me out and making sure my concerns are taken seriously."

This was it. She was out of time and options.

"Have a nice holiday, Ms. Mason."

"I thought your name was Jasmine."

Jamie's pulse reacted to the girl's statement, but she kept her smile in place. "That's right. Jasmine Mason. Most people call me Jamie."

The child frowned as if she wasn't sure that was correct.

"Have a lovely vacation," Jamie offered before turning to the door.

"How do you know Ms. Mason?"

Jamie cringed at the question he'd asked his daughter. The doctor realized something was off.

"We talked about the books," Jamie said, turning back to them and using a last-ditch effort to control the narrative.

Come on, Abi. Damn it.

"I told her about the ducks," Lillian said, her cheeks turning pink again. "I think she liked the idea."

"I absolutely did," Jamie said.

The front door suddenly burst open, and Jamie almost sighed with relief.

But the man who barreled over the threshold wielding a weapon was not Abi or Poe. Not unless they had found ski masks to don after parting ways with her.

"On the floor," he shouted.

Lillian threw herself against her father.

"What's going on?" Case demanded. "Rodgers!"

"Rodgers is not coming," the man in the mask said. "And neither is anyone else on your security team. Now get on the floor. Face down!"

He pointed the weapon at Lillian. "Now!"

Case lowered to his knees, taking his daughter with him. "Let's do as he says, Lilly."

Jamie was sinking to her knees when the guy pointed a look in her direction. "You," he ordered, "take the kid and wait outside."

"What?" Jamie pretended not to understand. Where the hell were Poe and Abi?

"Do it!" The masked man nudged the kid with his foot.

Lillian cried out. Her father tried to pull her into the protection of his body.

"It's okay, Lillian," Jamie said as she moved in the girl's direction. Jamie kept her attention fixed on the guy with the gun. "We'll just step outside for a minute."

More bodies flooded the entry hall. Two, no, three more wearing the same masks. All armed. What the hell was going on?

"Take the kid outside," the first man repeated.

"Come on, Lillian." Jamie offered her hand.

Dr. Case stared up at her, his grip firm around his daughter's arm. "What're you doing?"

Jamie looked directly into his eyes and tried her best to

show him with her own that he could trust her. "Whatever it takes to stay alive." Lillian took Jamie's hand. "I'm not going to let anything happen to you," Jamie promised. She shifted her attention to the man with the gun. "We're going outside like you said."

He jerked his head toward the door. "Now!"

Jamie held on tight to the girl's hand. She hovered close to Jamie, her slim body shaking with fear. Outside, two more cars had arrived. They sat askew as if they'd skidded to stops and were left where they landed.

Since the guy in the mask hadn't given any specific instructions about what they were to do once they were outside, Jamie hurried around the far left corner of the house and disappeared into the landscape, using mature shrubs and miniature trees as cover.

The girl was sobbing now. "Where are we going?"

Jamie drew her down into a squat behind a clump of large shrubs. "Be as quiet as you can," she whispered. "We don't want them finding us out here."

"What about Mommy and Daddy?"

Jamie hadn't seen Mrs. Case. "Was your mommy upstairs?"

Lillian nodded. "She told Daddy she had one more bag to pack."

"Okay. Let's stay calm and see what we can find out." Which really meant stay put until Jamie could figure out what the hell was going on.

So far she'd heard no gunshots—always a good thing. But where the hell were Abi and Poe and whatever backup Abi had put in place or ordered or whatever? Everything had fallen apart and she had no clear idea of what to do from here...except protect the child.

Jamie gauged the distance to the car she'd arrived in. It

was still parked near the fountain. If she could reach that car, she could take the child out of here, tuck her away in the Excalibur house and then come back to see what she could do with the unexpected takeover in the doctor's house.

None of what was happening made sense.

She leaned closer to Lillian and explained, "I need to get you someplace safe."

"We can't leave Mommy and Daddy," she whimpered.

"Listen to me, Lillian," Jamie whispered with all the urgency she could muster. "I can't help your mom and dad while I'm taking care of you. I need to settle you someplace safe so I can help them. That's what they would want. Trust me."

"I can't leave them," the girl insisted.

Shouts echoed from the front of the house. The door was open again. Someone was coming out or going in. Judging by the furiously raised voice, the coming or going—whichever it was—was not voluntary. Jamie listened intently to make out the words. Someone was not happy with how something had been done.

"Find her!"

She heard those words clearly.

"Now!"

They were looking for Lillian. A new wave of tension poured through Jamie. She considered the distance from their hiding places to the woods. It wasn't the direction she'd wanted to go, but she was out of options and quickly running out of time.

Jamie pressed a finger to the little girl's lips. Hoped she understood that it was imperative that she didn't make a sound.

If they could make the tree line, Jamie would find the

way to the house. She would call Victoria, then Ian Michaels. Poe had said he was close by. He could help.

Jamie clasped Lillian's hand in hers and gave it a squeeze. She leaned closer once more and whispered, "We're going to try and make it up the hill through the woods. Just be careful where you step and stay close to me and try not to make a sound."

Lillian nodded her understanding.

Holding tight to her hand, Jamie headed for the tree line. She wanted to go faster, but she wasn't sure how Lillian would do, so she set her pace to match the girl's.

The beam of a flashlight suddenly obstructed their view.

"Hold on there," a voice commanded.

Not Poe. Not Abi.

Damn it.

Jamie froze. Lillian did the same, gluing herself to Jamie's side.

"You were supposed to wait by the cars."

"No one told me where to wait."

"Well, I'm telling you now. Let's go?"

The beam of the flashlight shifted and in the moments it took her vision to adjust, she spotted the weapon in his hand.

"Fine," Jamie said, feigning frustration. She wasn't really sure what her part was supposed to be in this. Did they think she was someone else? Maybe the nanny who was on vacation. Who knew if their intel was up to par. Either way, it was best to play along until she had a better grip on what was going down.

The man with the gun ushered them back to where the two poorly parked cars waited. Another of the team opened the back passenger door.

"Get in," their guide ordered.

Jamie ushered Lillian into the car and slid in next to her.

"What about Mommy and Daddy?" Lillian cried softly.

"I'm sure they'll be fine," Jamie lied. What else could she do? No doubt these thugs were here for Dr. Case. He was far more valuable than anything else they might find in that house.

Jamie just couldn't say what the intent was.

For now, the only choice was to ride this out and see where they landed.

8:15 a.m.

THE DRIVER HAD stopped at the end of the long driveway leading away from the Case home and forced Jamie to put a sack over her head as well as one over Lillian's. Then they'd driven away. Upon arrival at their destination, an older house and certainly nothing in any of the subdivisions near the Case home, they'd been allowed to remove the sacks. A quick glimpse at the digital screen on the car's dash showed they had driven nearly twenty minutes and approximately twelve miles. The new location had to be something off a different road. Jamie had tried to keep up with the turns. There had been about four. A couple of lefts and a right, possibly a second right or at the very least a slight fork to the right.

The driver had then sequestered Jamie and Lillian to a bedroom inside the new location. Evidently the house was unoccupied since there was no bed, just an old futon. The place appeared to have been empty for a while considering the dust and cobwebs. Not to mention it smelled musty.

"I'm scared." Lillian hugged herself. "I need to go home."

Jamie pulled her into her arms and held her close. "I will get you home, Lillian. Don't worry about that."

Jamie had seen only one guy. But he had a weapon. Still, he couldn't be everywhere all the time. All Jamie needed was an opportunity to make a move. She was banking on the idea that Abi would have planted a tracking device on her somewhere. He was too careful—too determined to cover all the bases—not to do so. At least she could hope.

One way or another, Jamie intended to get this child out of danger.

The sound of the guy's voice drew her to the wall between the bedroom and whatever lay beyond it. She cupped a hand, pressed it to her ear and then to the wall.

"We're here. Yes."

He was checking in. If Jamie was lucky, he would give away something about the plan. There had to be a plan.

Another issue she tried not to dwell on was what this situation would do to their timeline. Luke's face flashed in her mind. How long would it be before whoever had taken Luke would lose patience? Or maybe decide to cut his losses? Her gut clenched at the idea.

Not going there. Not yet.

"We'll be ready," their captor said. "Yes. Half an hour. Good."

Something was happening in half an hour.

Were they moving to a different location?

Jamie couldn't wait around to see what that would entail. Not to mention there was a strong possibility help would be coming to assist with the move. She needed to get the kid out of harm's way before any sort of backup arrived. She could not just wait around, assuming Abi would have her location and he or Poe would come to their rescue.

Her odds were far better right now, in this one-on-one situation.

She glanced at the girl. Keeping Lillian safe complicated everything. But if Luke were here, he would tell her to protect the kid at all costs.

Jamie drew in a deep breath and walked to the door and banged on it. "I need the bathroom."

A cliché request, but if it worked, she could live with it.

After the sound of something metal being handled— a lock maybe—the door opened. The man still wore his mask. That was a good thing. It meant he didn't want them to be able to identify him. To some degree, this suggested there was a perception that the hostages would at some point be released. Otherwise, what would revealing his face matter?

"Down the hall." He jerked his head left.

Jamie reached for the girl's hand.

"No. She stays here."

Jamie shook her head. "She's scared. She needs to stay with me. We're only going into the bathroom."

"If you give me any trouble," he warned, "I will kill you both."

"Don't worry. We're not going to give you any trouble."

Lillian clung to Jamie as they made their way to the end of the hall. Jamie took in all the details she could of their location as they made the short journey. Typical ranch house with a narrow hall. The doors along the hall opened into the three bedrooms—all basically empty like the one they'd been locked in. The final door, at the end of the hall, was a bathroom that sported generic beige tile along with harvest gold fixtures.

"Don't close the door all the way," he ordered.

"Got it."

In the bathroom, she left the door ajar. "Why don't you go first?" Jamie suggested.

While Lillian did her business, Jamie studied the small

room. There was a window, but it looked painted shut. Getting out the window wouldn't likely be easy. She checked behind the shower curtain and under the sink, careful not to alert their keeper.

When Lillian was done, Jamie relieved herself, using that time to continue her study of the small room.

Once they had washed their hands and exited the room, she asked, "Any bottled water around here?"

"You couldn't get a drink from the sink?" He gestured to the bathroom.

Jamie shrugged. "No cup or glass."

He swore and stamped back down the hall. Jamie took Lillian's hand and followed him. The hall opened into a small living room that fronted a kitchen-dining combination. The rest of the house was unfurnished other than a couple of plastic chairs. Definitely vacant. Probably a rental.

In the kitchen there was a six-pack of bottled water on the counter. No dust, which told her it had been provided for this operation.

"You can each have one but don't ask for anything else."

Jamie passed a bottle of water to Lillian and then took one for herself. "Thank you."

"When are my mom and mad coming?" Lillian asked.

The man looked at her for a long moment. He grabbed a bottle of water for himself, twisted off the top and took a long swig. Then he said, "Don't worry, kid. As soon as we get what we need, you'll be back with your family and on the way to your fancy vacation."

Wouldn't it be great if it were that simple? The trouble was that Jamie couldn't assume he was telling the truth.

"Let's go," he said with a gesture toward the end of the house where the bedrooms were.

Holding Lillian's hand, Jamie led her back to the bedroom. She'd been right. A padlock had been added to the door. Once they were inside, he locked it.

Jamie slowly walked the perimeter of the room. This bedroom was on the back side of the house. She peeled back the dusty paper that had been taped to the window. She squinted to see beyond the dirty glass. The overgrown grass in the small backyard led right up to the woods. Definitely an advantage.

Next, she checked the lock on the window. It moved. She set it to the unlock position. The window was an old one—wood, not vinyl or aluminum. The screening was long gone. The issue with wood windows was if they had been painted without being moved up and down afterward, then often, they were glued shut. Not so terrible if one had a utility knife with which to cut them loose.

She turned to Lillian and leaned close to whisper in her ear. "Talk to me about the vacation. Try to sound natural."

Lillian nodded and started talking. "We're going to New York."

"Wow, that sounds exciting." Jamie braced herself, her hands on the wood sash. She pushed. The sash didn't budge.

She took a breath and tried again. Pushing upward with all her strength. The sash moved the tiniest bit, giving her hope.

"I hope it snows," Lillian was saying. "We almost never get snow here."

"That would be nice," Jamie said. She readied herself and tried again. This time the sash moved about three inches.

While Lillian went on about all the sites in New York she wanted to see, Jamie braced her hands on the bottom of the sash this time and shoved upward.

The window went up another four or five inches.

Jamie glanced toward the door and nodded to Lillian to keep going. Then she shoved one last time with all her might.

The sash went up as far as it would go. Jamie shook her arms to release the throbbing tension.

Now all they had to do was climb out.

Jamie went first. She surveyed the backyard but saw nothing of concern. She motioned for Lillian to climb out.

"I'm sure your mom will take you shopping." Jamie talked while she helped her make the drop onto the other side.

"I hope so," Lillian said, her eyes wide with worry.

Jamie glanced left. Not that way because they would have to pass the kitchen window and the back door.

She pointed right and to the woods. Then she leaned close. "Keep as quiet as possible, but move as fast as you can."

Lillian nodded.

Jamie took her hand and started moving away from the house that was to have been their prison...or maybe their grave.

Chapter Fourteen

Stonewall Drive, Nashville,
9:50 a.m.

Kenny struggled to control his anger until they had the doctor and his wife settled in the great room of Amar's employer. Another rich guy, apparently, who had decided his life was more important than the doctor's, the Case family's or any-damned-one else's.

But that wasn't really the reason Kenny felt so furious. He was mad as hell because Amar had seen trouble coming and he had hesitated long enough that Jamie and the doctor's kid had been taken by the other team—the other set of bad guys.

Kenny walked out onto the terrace where he could properly pace and mutter the swear words burning inside his throat.

Like the doctor's home, there was a pool and all the usual trappings of überwealth. The home was older than the one on Lionheart Court, but the location was likely the draw. Kenny shook his head. What the hell was he doing here?

They had kidnapped a surgeon and brought him to this place.

He told himself he'd made the right decision. Jamie's brother was being held hostage. It wasn't like he could ignore the situation and he sure as hell didn't trust Abidan Amar to straighten this out. So he'd come along. He'd dove in and done what he could to help. For Luke. For Jamie.

Now Jamie was missing too.

The French doors opened, and Amar joined him on the terrace. Kenny looked away, not trusting himself to look the guy in the eye.

"We have a problem," Amar announced.

Kenny wheeled on him. "You think? Like who the hell took Jamie and the kid? Do you have a handle on that situation?"

"Unfortunately, I can't say who took them. A competitor it seems who isn't looking to save a life, but is positioning himself for a ransom demand."

Kenny took a breath and told himself not to punch the guy. Doing so would not fix the situation and right now they needed to figure out how to help Jamie and that little girl. This was not the time to allow emotions to reign.

Of course Amar couldn't say who had taken Jamie and the kid. He'd totally missed whatever happened this morning. He and his people should have picked up on the trouble in the air.

"Your people were already on the ground when the other guys showed up—and there was only three of them. Three! They came in right under the noses of your people and walked away with Jamie and the girl."

If there was ever a situation that screamed of incompetence, this was it. Kenny struggled to regain his composure. Amar was not incompetent. Kenny knew this. He was just angry. Even the best plan could go awry. He also knew this firsthand. Rather than focus on pointing to how badly Amar had failed, they both needed to focus on how to rescue Jamie and the child.

"You are correct," Amar agreed. "There is no excuse for what happened except to admit that someone on my team failed. However, I've just been told that we have some security footage that may help us nail down who these people were and hopefully find them."

Kenny was over simply talking about this. They needed to act. To do that, he had to focus and to focus he had to find calm. "What is the problem you mentioned?"

"Dr. Case will not move forward with the surgery here until his daughter is found."

Well, Kenny didn't blame him. He'd been kidnapped. His family had been dragged from their home and his daughter had ended up God only knew where. Why would he cooperate? Only a fool would do so.

"What's your plan?" Surely the man had a strategy for straightening out this screwed up mess.

"I'm glad you asked." Amar's sly smile was more of a smirk, and it seriously rubbed against Kenny's last nerve. "We have someone waiting to see us downstairs in the game room."

Kenny followed him back into the house, beyond the great room and down the stairs to the walkout basement. It was like another house, the floor space no doubt as spacious as the layout upstairs.

Amar turned down a hallway to the left, which led into another large room with doors leading to the outside. A man wearing black, as they all had been this morning, was secured to a chair in the center of the room. He glanced at Kenny, then Amar, before looking away. His own smirk suggested he was not worried about whatever they had come to do.

Never a good sign.

"Mr. Reicher."

He turned to Amar as he approached, but said nothing.

Kenny stayed back a few steps and watched. This was Amar's show. He'd give him some time to see if he could pull this debacle together. Jamie liked the guy. Respected him. He must be better at this than he'd shown so far.

"Your girlfriend—Darla, I believe, is her name—and her baby are on the way here. Is there anything you'd like to share with us before they arrive?"

Reicher's face paled a little. "I have nothing to say."

Amar smiled. "Really. Darla says her baby is your son, Paul junior. She's very excited to bring him to see the Christmas surprise I told her you had arranged."

His face tightened. "She doesn't know anything about all this."

"That's too bad, Mr. Reicher. I think she may be very disappointed about what she finds here today."

He looked away a moment.

Kenny was out of patience. "That little girl your friends took better be safe," he warned, stepping closer. "If something happens to her…"

Reicher glared at Kenny. "She's fine. Nothing will happen to her if Dr. Case is delivered as requested."

Amar shrugged. "You see, Mr. Reicher, that is not going to happen. We have the doctor, and he is the important one. I'm sure you realize this. And as much as we want his daughter to be safe, she really is not our top concern."

Kenny bit his tongue to prevent calling him a liar. But he understood the tactic. He didn't like it, but he understood it.

"I don't think the doctor will see it that way," Reicher argued, the fear in his eyes impossible to conceal.

"I have a onetime offer for you, Mr. Reicher," Amar said. "You tell me where my friend Jamie and the girl are and—assuming they are unharmed—I will allow you to

leave with your girlfriend and your son when they arrive."
He laughed. "Hell, I'll even throw in a little bonus for that
Christmas surprise. But, if you waste this opportunity, there
is nothing I can do for you."

Kenny shook his head. "He doesn't deserve a deal. I say
we just beat it out of him."

"But I've already called Darla and she's on her way."
Amar checked his watch. "We have maybe ten minutes
before she arrives."

"Okay," Reicher said. "Just don't hurt her or tell her
about any of this."

That was easier than Kenny expected. Maybe too easy.
"Tell us where the girl and my friend are being held."

"They're in a house on Trinity Road. I can give you directions."

"How about you take my friend there," Amar suggested.
"That way there are no miscommunications."

"But what about Darla and the baby?"

"I'll let them know to go home and wait. You'll be there
soon."

Reicher looked from Amar to Kenny. "How do I know
I can trust either of you?"

Amar withdrew a knife, opened the blade and sliced it
through the bonds holding Reicher to the chair. "I suppose
you're just going to have to take a chance. If you're not willing to take a chance, then you're in the wrong line of work."

Kenny grabbed the guy by the collar. "Let's go." He
shoved him toward the door.

Amar leaned in closer to Kenny. "Once you have Jamie
and the girl, just leave him at the house and get back here.
We're running out of time."

Kenny nodded. "I just hope Jamie doesn't regret trusting you because I sure as hell do."

In the corridor before they reached the stairs, one of the men working on Amar's team approached Kenny and Reicher. "This way, gentlemen."

They were led to a door that opened into a six-car garage. Outside the garage, one of the black sedans Amar's people had used waited as if everyone had known this was the way things would work out.

"I'll be your driver," the man said as he opened the rear passenger-side door.

Kenny waited for Reicher to get in, then he dropped into the seat next to him. He removed his weapon and held it ready. "Don't waste my time," he warned Reicher.

Reicher gave the driver the street address.

The drive took longer than Kenny had hoped, but he didn't know a lot about the area. Trinity Road was closer to where they had been in the Excalibur house than where they'd ended up today. Staying in the same general vicinity as the home invasion for hostage containment made a sort of sense, he supposed.

Trinity Road led away from the more heavily populated areas and had older houses set back off the road. It was heavily wooded in some areas.

"Up ahead on the left," Reicher said.

When they turned onto the long drive, a man with a weapon emerged from the woods.

Kenny poked the muzzle of his weapon into Reicher's side. "Unless you want to die now, I would suggest you think carefully before you speak to this guy."

Reicher nodded, then, hand shaking, powered his window down. "I'm here to pick up the girl."

"Good luck with that," his comrade said. "That lady with her opened a window and they took off. I've been looking for them for the past hour."

Kenny's pulse thumped with the news. He barely resisted the urge to grin.

"We'll help you look for them," Reicher said. "Get in the car." He slid toward Kenny.

The other guy got in. As he closed the door, he looked at Kenny. "Who the hell are you?"

Kenny pressed the muzzle of his weapon to the man's forehead. "Toss your gun into the front seat."

He hesitated.

"Do it," Reicher said. "We're not going to win this one."

The new guy reluctantly did as ordered.

"Anyone else here?" Kenny asked.

The new guy shook his head. "Just me."

"Drive up to the house," Kenny said to the driver.

The car rolled forward, stopping at the small ranch house. Kenny and the driver emerged and ushered the two men into the house. Kenny walked through. Spotted the raised window in the bedroom and smiled.

"Go Jamie." He crossed to the window and surveyed the area into which the two had taken off.

Back in the living room, the driver had the two standing with their backs against the wall. Kenny looked to the driver. "You have anything we can use to secure these two so we don't have to shoot them?"

The driver nodded and hurried out of the house.

Kenny looked to the guy who had been guarding Jamie. "How long ago did they escape?"

"Maybe an hour."

Damn. They could be anywhere by now. Maybe even back at the Excalibur house. "If I don't find them, I'll be back."

When the two were secured, Kenny and the driver headed outside.

"Let's make sure they have to walk out of here if they somehow manage to get loose."

"Good idea," the driver agreed.

"What's your name?" Kenny asked while he slashed the tires.

"Landon."

"Well, Landon," Kenny said as he got back to his feet, "maybe we need the car's fob to ensure it's no use to anyone."

Landon nodded and went back into the house. Half a minute later, he returned with the car's fob. He popped the hood and did something under there. Kenny wasn't much of a mechanic so he had no clue what. He could change a tire and check the oil. That was about the extent of his vehicle maintenance skills.

When Landon closed the hood, he said, "They won't be going anywhere in this vehicle." Then he dropped the fob on the ground and used the heel of his boot to disable it as well.

"Take the car," Kenny decided, "drive slowly along the road. I'll walk and have a look around in the woods."

"You got it," Landon said.

Kenny scanned the overgrown grass and quickly spotted the signs of recent movement. He followed that path into the woods.

"Jamie!" If they were still in these woods, maybe they would hear him calling.

Once he was deeper in the woods, the path wasn't as easy to follow. He trudged through the underbrush and called Jamie's name over and over.

The sound of a car horn blowing had him stalling in his tracks. He listened. Coming from Trinity Road. Maybe Landon had found them.

Kenny started to run through the woods. When he

emerged, he was in the yard of another property. He kept close to the tree line along the yard's border since he had no desire to get shot. Then he saw Landon's car on the road. Kenny broke into a hard run.

As he reached the road and the car, the rear passenger window powered down. "Looking for me?"

Jamie. His knees almost gave out on him. "You and Lillian okay?"

She nodded. "We're good. Get in."

Kenny opened the front door and dropped into the seat. To Landon, he said, "Let Amar know we're headed back with what we came for." He turned to Jamie then. "Where were you?" He glanced at Landon. "How did he find you?"

"We were hiding in the church a mile or so up the road. The guy who'd been holding us had come through looking for us, but he didn't think to look under the altar."

Kenny laughed. "But you thought to hide there."

Landon ended his call. "Smart move," he said to Jamie. "I spotted the church as we drove in. When we were told you had escaped on foot, I figured you went to the church. That's where I would have gone."

Kenny had to admit he would probably have done the same. He looked to Lillian then. "Your parents are going to be very happy to see you."

She nodded. "Jamie saved me."

Jamie smiled. "We did it together."

Kenny was just thankful they were safe. He was pretty sure he'd never been so relieved in his life.

"I don't think that guy was very good at his job," Lillian suggested.

"We're just lucky he wasn't," Jamie pointed out. She looked to Kenny. "And we're very lucky that my friend is really, really good at his job."

Chapter Fifteen

Stonewall Drive,
Noon

Lillian wanted food so they had to stop. Thankfully, she recognized where they were pretty quickly once they were on the main road and directed the driver to her favorite drive-through. Jamie wasn't really hungry, but she understood the necessity of eating. She hadn't gotten any sleep, so forgoing food was not a good idea. She needed her head clear and her body energized.

"So this is the place." Jamie assessed the mansion where the doctor and his wife had been taken.

"This is it," Poe said, surveying the estate as the car parked in front of the house.

It wasn't as new as the doctor's mansion, but it was every bit as ostentatious in its own right. The whole situation was over the line. One rich guy kidnapping another to get what he wanted. How screwed up was that? Maybe growing up a Colby made her understand at a fairly young age how completely upside down the world could be, but there were still times, like this one, when she just couldn't get past the reality of how bad it really was. More than just upside down.

What was wrong with these people?

The part that bothered her the most in all this was that she actually got it. These people were desperate. Desperate people, no matter how wealthy, did desperate things, creating desperate situations.

Jamie got out of the car and held the door for Lillian. The girl was still shoving fries in her mouth when she got out. Poor thing, she really had been starving. Kids were like that. She remembered when she and Luke were that age. They were always clamoring for food—especially fast food.

The double front doors opened, and Abi stood in the doorway. "Welcome back."

Jamie's first thought was to punch him, but what kind of example would that set for Lillian? It was better if she behaved herself until the two of them had a minute alone to talk in privacy.

"Let's get this show on the road," Jamie shot back. "I'd like to see my brother."

Abi stepped aside and gestured for her to enter. "The doctor and Mrs. Case are waiting in the great room."

Lillian stuck close to Jamie as they walked through the entry hall and on to the great room. Like the Case home, the whole place was decked out for Christmas with a massive tree and tons of garlands. Under the tree, dozens of wrapped presents waited.

Mrs. Case gasped and rushed to her daughter. She paid no attention to Jamie, which was good. Dr. Case did the same.

Poe gave her a nod from the other side of the room. Jamie responded in kind. This was the best part of what they did—reuniting families or couples after a situation had pulled them apart. They didn't always get this moment.

After a good deal of hugging and weeping, Dr. Case

stepped back from his family and walked toward Abi. "Let's get this done."

"Very well." Abi gestured to the door. "You know the way."

Jamie glanced at Poe. "I'm going with them."

Poe nodded. "I'll hang around here."

Jamie hesitated. There were many things she wanted to say to him—things she probably should have said before now—but all of that would have to wait. Jamie needed to know what was happening with the doctor. This was the part that her brother's life depended upon. Poe would look after the daughter and the wife.

She wasn't allowing Abi or the doctor out of her sight until Luke was free. Whatever else happened, she intended to see that her brother was brought home safely.

Abi led the way down to the walkout basement area. There they walked through a massive game room and into a short corridor with no windows. At the end of that corridor was a door like one found on a bank vault. Jamie wasn't sure whether to be startled or impressed. Abi entered the code as if he'd been here many times before. Jamie decided she could safely assume the owner of this place was Abi's employer.

The door opened and they walked into a small curtained off area. The sort of space found in a mobile hospital setup. There was a sink, a temporary shower and a smaller curtained off dressing area. This, she surmised, was the prep area for the space beyond. No doubt a state-of-the-art surgical setup. Now she was totally impressed.

Case glanced back at Jamie and Abi and then started to strip off his clothes. He didn't need a block of instructions on what came next. Jamie turned her back and gave him some privacy. When the water in the small shower started running, she faced Abi once more.

"This guy has a surgical suite in his basement?" Was this for real?

"When he made the decision to go this route, he went all out."

Jamie shook her head. "This is way over-the-top, Abi."

The water in the shower stopped, preventing the need for Abi to respond. Jamie kept her back to Case as he dressed in what she presumed would be his surgical scrubs and gown. A sense of dread that would not be tamped down climbed into her throat. What if the patient died? Case was unquestionably a skilled and highly sought after surgeon who hadn't lost a single patient so far—according to his bio. But that didn't mean it couldn't happen. No matter that she and Abi had done what they were expected to do, would Luke still be released if the patient didn't make it?

Focus on the now, Jamie. Don't borrow trouble.

Case opened the curtained door and entered the surgery suite. The glimpse Jamie got of the room beyond this prep area was stunning. She couldn't imagine the money spent to prepare for this…but then, what was the value of a loved one's life? Most likely it was whatever a person possessed.

Abi gestured to the rack of scrubs. "If you're planning on going inside, you need to scrub down and dress for the occasion."

"We don't have to shower the way the doc did?" Jamie would be the first to admit that she could use a shower, but she didn't want to miss a moment of what was happening.

"Not unless you're planning to help with the surgery. But since he already has a nurse, another surgeon and an anesthetist, our assistance is not required."

Jamie gave a slow nod. "I'd like to see what's going on in there, considering I have a great deal to lose."

"Understandable." Abi peeled off his sweater, grabbed the bottle of Hibiclens soap and started the necessary process. Jamie did the same. They scrubbed down and pulled on surgical gowns.

When they stepped beyond the larger curtain, Jamie was almost startled. The lights. The equipment. It was incredible. The real thing—maybe even more state of the art than the average surgery suite found in hospitals. Right in the center of it all was a surgical table complete with the patient and surrounded by all the necessary equipment and, apparently, personnel. A clear enclosure separated that center area from the rest of the room. It was like a room with invisible walls inside a bigger room.

She watched as they prepared the patient—not an adult... a child. Her chest constricted.

As Abi had said, there were three people besides the surgeon, all suited in surgical gowns. Two working closely with the doctor, the other standing at the patient's head. The anesthetist.

The setup really was incredible. She shouldn't be surprised. If this was going to be done right, they needed not only the proper equipment, but also the proper personnel as well. No expense appeared to have been spared.

Another man, middle aged, stood well beyond the activity on the other side of the smaller surgical room. Was this the child's father?

Jamie leaned closer to Abi so she could whisper. "Is that him?" The doctor and those working around the patient were talking among themselves. She didn't want to distract or disturb them.

"Yes." Abi followed her lead, speaking in a whisper. "The father—my employer."

"Did you know the patient was a child?" Jamie understood that the patient's age didn't make what they had done right…but it somehow made it more palatable.

"I did. That's the only reason I agreed to the job."

Jamie's attention shifted to the ongoing procedure. The conversation between the doctor and those helping was so soft that she couldn't make out their words through those clear walls. It was the sounds of the machines that made her feel oddly discombobulated. Or maybe it was the whole situation that created such a sense of being overwhelmed.

"Should we go now?" She suddenly felt out of place even watching.

"I'm staying. You don't need to."

She nodded. "Okay. Going upstairs then."

Jamie exited the sterile environment, peeled off the surgical gown and pulled on her sweater. She tossed the gown into the provided hamper and opened the door. As she walked out, the door closed behind her, locking her out. She flinched at the sound or maybe it was the idea of what was happening in there.

Forcing her mind away from this thing they had done, she considered that she should call her grandmother and let her know she was okay and that the procedure was happening. Hopefully, Luke would be released soon. She shook herself. Good grief, it was Christmas Eve. She needed to see if anyone had heard from her parents.

One thing was certain—this was the most bizarre holiday of her life.

The trudge up the stairs was harder than she'd thought. She supposed she was more exhausted than she had realized or maybe all the emotions were just catching up with her. She had necessarily restrained her feelings related to Luke being held hostage. Now they were working overtime to bubble up.

Upstairs, Lillian and her mother were on the sofa in the great room, watching television. Mrs. Case looked as exhausted as Jamie. There was no shortage of guards. All dressed in black and stationed at every door and at the larger windows. Not just to keep the doctor in either. To keep new intruders out, she supposed.

Worry tugged at Jamie's brow. Where was Poe? She walked to the front door and had a look outside. No Poe out there. Then she walked back through the great room and on to the kitchen before she found him.

He stood at the island, a host of vegetables piled around him. He glanced up as she neared. "I decided to make a salad. Fast food never fills me up."

She went for a smile, but didn't quite feel it happen. "Sounds smart. Can I help?"

"You interested in cucumbers?"

"Sure. A salad isn't a salad without cucumbers."

She washed the long English cucumber and selected a knife. "Thick or thin slices?"

"Prepper's choice."

She thought about bringing up the morning's event and then the identity of the patient downstairs, but decided she needed to think on it for a while. There was a lot wrong with how those hours went down, but she couldn't be certain it had been what she now suspected.

Poe grabbed a couple of carrots and started to chop. He was very skilled.

"You've had lessons," she suggested.

"A class in Paris." He shrugged. "Another in Rome. I love to cook."

How had she not known that?

When they had prepped all the veggies and tossed them into a larger bowl, they cleaned up. The mundane work helped with the questions and emotions nudging at her. A little more *mundane* would be most welcome.

Poe tossed the hand towel on the counter by the sink. "I'll see if anyone is hungry."

"Do you have a cell phone? The guy who drove us to the other location took mine."

"Sure. Amar gave me another." Poe passed his cell to her. "I'm glad you're back, Jamie."

"Me too."

"I was worried. Really worried."

She nodded. "I've worried a lot during this thing."

He held her gaze for a moment longer as if he had more to say, then turned and headed for the great room.

Jamie had a feeling they both had things they needed to say.

She walked to the sink and stared out the window as she entered Victoria's number. As always, her grandmother answered on the first ring. "It's me," Jamie said since the number would not be familiar.

"I'm so grateful to hear your voice. Are you all right, Jamie?"

"I'm fine. Tired, but fine. The surgery is taking place now. Hopefully, Luke will be released soon."

How was it that saying the words almost made this thing feel like it was a normal mission? This was not normal. It was not even close to normal. They had broken a good number of laws, not to mention they had kidnapped a man and his family from the other thugs who had attempted to kidnap them. Add to that how someone on the opposing team had kidnapped her and the girl and they'd had to escape.

How crazy was that? Worse, she still couldn't even begin to fathom what the coming ramifications would be.

Mrs. Case and Lillian came into the kitchen with Poe. He served them both as if he'd trained at a five-star restaurant. Even when Lillian insisted there should be meat on a salad, he managed to rummage in the refrigerator and find deli slices of turkey, chopped it and added it to Lillian's salad.

The man was good. He was kind. Jamie smiled. And handsome.

"I can send the jet for you and Luke when you're ready," Victoria insisted, drawing Jamie's attention back to the call. "I'm anxious to have you both home."

That was the thing. No matter where Jamie lived and worked, Chicago would always be home.

"Sure." Whatever Victoria wanted to do would be fine by Jamie. At this point any sort of vacation from her everyday life would be great. "Have you spoken to Mom and Dad today?"

"I did and I'm so happy to say they'll be coming home tomorrow. They've decided that as much as they've enjoyed their little getaway, that Christmas is about being at home with family. I didn't tell them what was happening with Luke. I'm hoping the two of you will be here by the time they arrive and that this whole nightmare will be behind us."

Jamie hoped so as well. "I'll call you as soon as I lay eyes on Luke."

They exchanged goodbyes and Jamie took Poe's phone back to him. "Thank you."

"Everything all right with your grandparents?" He heaped salad onto a plate.

"Yes, and she just told me that my parents are coming

home tomorrow so it'll be a good day." As long as she got Luke back home safely.

He passed her the plate. "Eat."

Jamie thanked him and joined the Case family at the island.

Mrs. Case set her fork aside and turned to Jamie.

Jamie braced for her fury. Not that she could blame the woman. Look what they had done to her family...to their holiday plans. The thought sickened her. She couldn't tell the family that she'd only taken part in this because her brother's life was at stake. They certainly didn't need any added stress after all they'd been through. Besides, what kind of excuse was that? Who was to say whose family was the more important one?

No one...because that was not true any way you looked at it.

"Lillian told me about how you helped her escape that man. How you helped her run to safety and to hide."

Jamie managed a smile that felt like an imitation at best. "It was a team effort." She and Poe shared a look. She suspected he didn't feel heroic any more than she did.

Lillian blushed. "You're a superhero. Like in the movies."

"You were pretty heroic yourself, Lillian. You were strong and brave. You should be very proud of what you did too. Like I said—a team effort."

Mrs. Case smiled a weary expression as she turned back to her salad. Jamie felt sick at the idea of what she must be thinking. Though the woman was obviously grateful that Jamie had helped her daughter, she likely recognized as well that Jamie was part of the original kidnapping crew. That reality couldn't be ignored.

Lillian picked at her salad, eating mostly the turkey, before skipping back into the great room to resume the movie she'd been streaming.

Poe took his salad and followed her.

Jamie forked the greens and took another bite. She generally liked salad, but it all tasted bland today. She suddenly wished she had gone with Lillian and Poe. Sitting here with Mrs. Case and feeling what was no doubt the weight of her mounting accusations was not exactly sparking her appetite.

After an entire minute of silence, the older woman said, "My husband is very upset. He feels this entire event is a travesty."

It was actually, and Jamie wasn't going to try to excuse her actions. She had done what she had to do to keep her brother safe. She wouldn't do things any differently if she had to do it over and over again.

"He has," Mrs. Case went on, "tried very hard not to think of all the patients he can't save. He is only one man. But it has been very difficult. The burden of all those other lives has weighed heavily on him. Particularly in light of what his brother did for months before we realized what he was up to."

She didn't explain further, and Jamie didn't ask. She was already aware of the twin brother's deceit.

Mrs. Case went on, "The past few hours have driven that point home. It's one thing to know what's happening, but another altogether to be faced with the reality."

Jamie could only imagine how horrifying the ordeal had been and the number of emotional levels that horror had hit. As Mrs. Case had already said, the weight of having to turn patients away was awful enough, but to be forced to look at a child who desperately needed that help, and whose father was willing to do anything to make it happen, was immeasurably painful.

Working hard to keep her voice steady, Jamie confessed, "I will tell you I am not proud of the part I played in this. But—"

"If you hadn't," Mrs. Case argued, "my daughter might be dead. My husband might even be as well. Or me. You and your people kept us safe."

Jamie opted not to correct her. Yes, she, Poe and Abi may have provided a buffer between the Case family and the bad guys from the other team, but the truth was they weren't that different. They'd all been here for the same goal ultimately—to get Dr. Case to do what they wanted.

"They wanted twenty million dollars," Mrs. Case said. "For our daughter."

"There was a ransom demand?" Jamie wasn't aware that had happened, but she wasn't entirely surprised.

"Oh yes. Once you and Lillian were taken away, another man informed us of what they expected. We had twelve hours to pull the money together—which was absolutely ludicrous—before they were going to kill Lillian."

"Wow...that's terrible." Jamie replayed those minutes over in her head. The men had operated on a reasonably professional level. They had appeared prepared for what they had come to do...mostly. "They told me nothing. I had no idea."

"Your people saved us—*you* saved our daughter."

As much as Jamie appreciated being called a hero, there were some things that didn't add up for her. First, a twenty-million-dollar ransom demand should have come with a bigger team. What kidnapper who believed an asset was worth twenty million dollars only sent along one guard with that asset?

This was wrong somehow. Frankly, everything that had gone down felt wrong on some level.

There had been just three in the other crew in the first place. Three. With a twenty-mil ransom demand. Oh yeah, there was something very wrong with this situation.

Poe came to the door. "Jamie." He hitched his head toward the great room.

Jamie produced a smile, one slightly more real this time, for Mrs. Case. "Excuse me." She slid off her stool and went to the door. "What's up?"

"We need to talk."

She followed him beyond the great room to the entry hall. The guard there seemed to sense their need for privacy and stepped outside to monitor the door from there.

Poe glanced around. "Something is off with what happened this morning."

"I couldn't agree more." She hitched a thumb toward the kitchen. "The wife just told me there was a ransom demand for Lillian. Twenty million dollars."

Poe shook his head. "That's crazy. One of those guys—from the two left behind when the one took you and Lillian—basically split after you two were gone. Abi called in a backup crew to clean up the mess, but let's face facts, we already had more than three—besides us—here in the first place, which begs the question, how were we overtaken by three thugs?"

Jamie had an idea about that. "I think it was a setup to make the Cases believe we're the good guys."

"You mean we're not," Poe said with a shake of his head. "Don't answer that. I already know what we've been in this op." He blew out a big breath.

This was just another aspect of this whole business that weighed on Jamie. "I shouldn't have let you get involved with this."

He harrumphed. "Like you could have stopped me."

"We just have to make sure the rest of this goes off without a hitch. The family gets taken back home and no one dies."

Her chest tightened as she thought of Luke.

Keep him safe.

3:00 p.m.

BY THE TIME the doctor and Abi surfaced, Lillian had fallen asleep, and her mother was pacing the floor.

Jamie wasn't sure what would happen next, but if they were all lucky, it wouldn't involve the police. Or worse, the FBI, considering they had kidnapped the doctor and his family.

"How did it go?" Mrs. Case asked, looking tattered around the edges.

Dr. Case gave her a nod. "Very well. I'll be seeing him when we return from our vacation for a follow up. Until then, the doctor who assisted me will keep an eye on him. But I'm not anticipating any issues."

Jamie shared a look with Poe. That was certainly not the announcement she'd anticipated.

"A car will be here for you and your family in ten minutes," Abi explained.

Wait. Wait. Was this it? No accusations. No cops. No nothing?

Dr. Case turned to Abi. He looked from him to Poe, then to Jamie. "I realize what has happened today. Don't doubt that I am fully aware." His gaze lit the longest on Jamie.

This was the part she had been expecting…dreading.

"But in reality, all the three of you took from my family were a few hours of our time." He glanced at his daughter. "I wonder if you—" he looked from Jamie to Poe and then Abi again "—had not made the decision to help the child downstairs, what would have happened to our family? Those other men were clearly unconcerned for the safety of my family. Their only desire was money." He shook his head, regret clear on his face. "The idea that my work has come to this tears me apart. Anyone who needs the help I can provide should be able to have it without such theatrics. This has opened my eyes to what I know I must do next. It wasn't bad enough what happened before…" He heaved a heavy breath. "The only answer is that more surgeons must be trained in this procedure. It's the only way to see that we meet the need of all…not just that of certain patients." He exhaled a weary breath. "Thank you for helping me to see this more clearly."

Abi nodded, but said nothing. He turned to Jamie and motioned for her and Poe to follow him to the kitchen. They gathered around the island.

"A car will be arriving shortly." He set his gaze on Jamie's. "The driver will take you to your brother's condo. Luke will be delivered there at approximately the same time." He turned to Poe then. "If you need a different car, just say the word."

"I'm going with Jamie." Poe looked to Jamie. "We have a mission report to complete."

Abi nodded. "Very well." He smiled. "We make a good team."

Jamie laughed. "Except for the fact that you were keeping all sorts of details from us." She leaned in closer and spoke more quietly. "Like the three guys from this morning. Give me a break. After the doctor's monologue in there, you really expect me to believe that was a coincidence? And where did you find them? Thugs-R-Us?"

Abi didn't smile, but the twinkle of amusement in his

eyes was unmistakable. "No one is calling the police," he said. "In my humble opinion, that implies it was a brilliant strategy."

"You couldn't have warned us?" Poe argued, sounding more than a little ticked off.

Abi bumped him on the shoulder with the side of his fist. "The goal was authenticity. It's hard to fake, wouldn't you say?"

Poe held up a hand. "Whatever."

"In any case," Abi said, "thank you for your help. Your car will be here any moment." He smiled at Jamie. "You'll be pleased to find Ian Michaels behind the wheel."

Whoa. Now wait a minute. "How did you get in touch with Ian?" Poe had told her that Victoria had sent Ian to provide any necessary backup, but that was the last she'd heard about him being here. Too much had gone down for her to even think about Ian. She decided it might be best not to mention this to her grandmother's long time loyal investigator.

"I called your grandmother," Abi explained. "I told her you would be ready to depart within the hour and she said Michaels would pick you and Poe up for transport back to Chicago." He chuckled. "She also invited me to your Christmas party. Unfortunately, I'm unavailable. I'm sure you understand."

"Of course. You're a busy man." Jamie barely resisted the urge to roll her eyes.

"One more thing," Abi said. "For the record, the ransom demand for Luke…" He shrugged. "Just a little something for more of that authenticity."

Jamie did roll her eyes that time. "Good to know." She extended her hand. "Until we meet again, Abi."

He gave her hand a shake. "I am certain we will." He turned to Poe next and extended his hand.

"I, for one," Poe said, "hope to never see you again."

Abi laughed. "I'm confident that can be arranged."

When the first car arrived, Jamie, Poe and even Abi stood on the portico and waved goodbye to the Case family. As the car drove away, Lillian turned around in her seat and waved some more. Jamie kept waving until the car was out of sight.

"This must be the enigmatic Mr. Michaels," Abi said as a second car rolled up to the house.

Jamie turned to face her old friend. "Take care of yourself, Abi."

He hugged her. She didn't resist. Given their occupations, it could easily be the last time they saw each other.

Poe only allowed the other man a nod before walking away.

Ian emerged from behind the wheel and gave Jamie a hug. "I am so glad to see you," she admitted.

"Always." Ian drew back. "Let's go pick up your brother."

Jamie and Poe relaxed in the back seat as Ian drove away, though it was impossible to relax completely until she laid eyes on her brother.

The drive to his condo felt like a lifetime and when they arrived, Luke was sitting on the front steps. Jamie rushed out of the car and into his arms.

"I didn't have a key to get inside," Luke said.

Jamie laughed. "Oh my God, it is so good to see you. I've been worried to death."

He shrugged. "It wasn't so bad. I played video games the whole time."

Jamie resisted the urge to kick him. "Don't tell Poe," she warned. "I'm not sure he would take it as well as me."

Luke made a zipping gesture across his lips. "I won't say a word."

"Come on." Jamie ushered him toward the door. "There's a key under the mat."

"Who put a key under my welcome mat?" Luke frowned. "That's like the first place a burglar looks."

Jamie decided not to tell him that she'd put the key Abi had used under there in case she needed to come back. To her way of thinking, if Luke was missing, there was nothing else in the condo worth worrying about.

Inside, he looked around and groaned. "I need to water my plants."

"Pack your bag," Jamie told him. "I'll water your plants. We have a jet waiting for us."

They were going home. Together. For the first time in far too long.

Chicago
Tuesday, December 25

Christmas Day

Chapter Sixteen

Colby Residence,
7:00 p.m.

Victoria surveyed the buffet and the table in her dining room. Pride welled in her chest. She was so very grateful that her favorite caterer had been able to pull this off on such short notice.

Everything was perfect. The food, the desserts, the lovely drink venues. There was Wine Avenue in one corner, Champagne Falls—a fountain—in another and Everything Else Lane—with nonalcoholic choices—in yet another. The whole setup was so creative.

"It all looks lovely," Lucas said as he moved to her side.

She smiled up at him. "The decorations too." Lucas had been the one to oversee that part of the preparations. How he'd gotten holiday decorators on Christmas morning was a mystery. But then, Lucas was a man of many talents.

He'd never failed to accomplish a mission.

"I think we should share a private toast before the guests start to arrive," he suggested.

"Good idea."

They wandered to the champagne fountain and allowed the flowing bubbly to fill their glasses.

"To family," Lucas said as he tapped his glass against hers.

"Family," Victoria echoed. She closed her eyes and drank deeply. She was so very thankful that her family was home.

Jamie and Luke had arrived just before midnight last night. Victoria and Lucas had been up until two this morning just looking at those beautiful kids and pinching themselves. And listening to the story of all that happened in Nashville. The best part was that their grandchildren were safe, and they were home.

Jim and Tasha had arrived home this afternoon. The kids had gone to have some private time with them. Jim said they planned to tell them about the cancer and how fortunate they were that the treatment appeared to be doing its job. If all continued on this course, by spring Tasha would be cancer free.

It was all they could have hoped for.

"I think Poe is a very nice young man," Lucas said, drawing Victoria from her deep thoughts.

She smiled. "He is, and I'm quite certain he's madly in love with our Jamie."

"Well, of course he is," Lucas boasted. "She's brilliant, beautiful and...he doesn't deserve her."

Laughter bubbled from Victoria's throat. "You would say the same thing about anyone who showed an interest in her."

"I would. And I would be correct in my deduction."

Victoria nodded. "You would."

"She and I talked for a bit this morning," Lucas said before drinking more of his champagne.

"Really?" Victoria had seen the two of them having another cup of coffee after everyone else had left the kitchen this morning. "What did you talk about?"

"I asked her to come to work for the agency."

Victoria's heart skipped a beat. So many times she had wanted to ask Jamie that question, but she'd always satisfied her desperate hopes with simply letting Jamie know that she was welcome at the agency if she ever wanted to be there. Not once had Victoria come right out and asked.

"How did she react?"

Lucas inclined his head and considered the question for a moment. "She seemed surprised but not offended in any way. She asked me if the suggestion was only coming on the heels of the fright we had with Luke's kidnapping."

"What did you tell her?" Victoria couldn't wait to hear this.

"I told her that of course any and all things of that nature impacts our feelings, but this latest event wasn't the reason I asked."

Victoria's eyebrows went up. "I'm sure she was surprised by that claim."

Lucas shrugged one shoulder. "Perhaps, but it was true. I asked because I think we need her. The agency needs her. I've stayed on top of what she's doing for IOA. Like all these suitors, they don't deserve our granddaughter. She belongs at the Colby Agency."

Victoria struggled not to allow the sting in her eyes to become evident. "She is the one who should fill my shoes one day." Her voice wobbled a little, but it was the best she could do.

"Just a few weeks ago," Lucas went on, "Jim said the same thing."

Victoria felt taken aback by the news. "I wasn't suggesting Jim shouldn't run this agency. He has every right."

"He is aware of how you feel. You've asked him to do this before, but he always defers to your choices regarding agency matters."

This was true. She'd tried to retire, to turn the reins over to Jim, but he'd always come up with a reason that she should return.

"Do you think he feels as if I don't trust him or that anyone here doesn't trust his ability?" The notion twisted inside her like barbed wire. She loved her son. She wanted him to have what she and his father and Lucas had built. Jamie should be working with him and one day she absolutely should step into Victoria's shoes. But first, Jim would have his time.

"I think he doesn't trust himself to sit at the top. He loves this agency, and he loves being a part of it, but he does not want to be *the one*."

Victoria nodded. "I see. I'm sorry I didn't realize how he felt."

Lucas touched her cheek with a fingertip. "Jim doesn't make that easy."

This was true. She moistened her lips and asked, "What did Jamie say?"

"She wanted to think about it for a bit, but she promised to give us an answer soon."

At least it wasn't an immediate no. Victoria finished off her champagne. "That's all we can ask for."

"Indeed," Lucas agreed.

The doorbell rang and they put their glasses on a nearby tray and hurried to answer. Forget Paris. There was nothing like family and friends at Christmas.

Ian and Nicole were the first to arrive. In the next half hour, everyone from the agency who was available had arrived. It was a houseful for sure.

Victoria was so very thankful to see Tasha and Jim. Luke arrived with his parents, looking very handsome in a white suit, shirt and tie. Before she could grab Luke in a hug, he kissed her on the cheek.

"You look ravishing, Grandmother."

Victoria grinned. "Thank you, Luke. You look pretty amazing yourself." She hugged him and he kissed her temple and whispered, "I love you." She peered up at him. "Love you too." Then he hurried off to say hello to Lucas.

"Luke is right. You look great." Jim hugged her. "Merry Christmas, Mom."

Victoria hugged him fiercely. How she loved this man. "Merry Christmas to you and Tasha." She drew back, reached for her daughter-in-law and hugged her a bit more gently. "You two look incredible." How very strong this woman was. Victoria was so proud that she was the mother of her grandchildren.

"Thank you, Victoria." Tasha smiled. "And thank you for having this beautiful party."

Victoria barely restrained her tears, but she refused to cry considering all the blessings they had received in the past forty-eight hours. Lucas rescued her by coming for hugs of his own.

Lastly, Jamie and Kenny arrived. Victoria lost her breath when she saw the two of them. Jamie wore a pale blue sheath, and she looked stunning. She and her mother were nearly the same size and Victoria suspected the dress was Tasha's. Kenny looked quite dapper himself in a black formfitting suit, crisp white shirt and black tie. As a couple they were quite spectacular. The perfect power couple with their whole futures ahead of them. She hoped their relationship worked out.

The food tasted as wonderful as it looked. Lucas had set the Christmas music to a soft whisper and the smiles and laughter that filled their home was the perfect finishing touch. This Christmas was all that Victoria could ask for.

"Grandmother."

Victoria looked around to find Jamie standing beside her. To her gorgeous granddaughter she said, "I hope you're enjoying yourself."

Jamie smiled, the expression so big and beautiful it filled Victoria's heart with renewed pride. "I'm having a wonderful time." She hesitated a moment, then continued, "I spent some time this afternoon talking with Dad and then with Poe."

Victoria was afraid to breathe. Of all the things she had faced in her life, this might very well be one of the scariest.

"I've decided to put in my resignation at IOA and come to work with you and Grandpa."

As much as Victoria wanted to shout and jump for joy, she held it back and remained cool and calm. "That is wonderful to hear. And you're certain about this?"

Jamie laughed. "I am certain. I've been thinking about it for a long time. I'd like to be closer to my family. Running around all over the world has lost a bit of its mystique."

"If you change your mind..." Victoria offered.

"I will not," Jamie said resolutely. She looked across the room to Kenny. "You should know that Poe is coming as well, but I'll let him tell you."

Victoria beamed. "I am so pleased. I'm certain your father and mother are pleased as well."

Jamie's eyes turned a little watery then. "They're very happy about it."

Victoria hugged her granddaughter. "Merry Christmas, sweetheart."

Jamie drew back. "Merry Christmas to you, Grandmother."

"I hope I'm not too late."

The deep male voice with just a hint of a British accent drew everyone's attention to the man who'd entered the room.

"Abi," Jamie said. "I thought you couldn't come."

Looking very handsome in a black suit, shirt and tie, Abi crossed the room and pressed his cheek to Jamie's. "I rearranged a few things." He looked to Victoria then. "How often does one get invited to a Colby Agency party?" He gave Victoria the same treatment. "Thank you for inviting me."

Victoria gave him a nod. "Glad you could make it."

"Well, just look who the cat dragged in." Kenny appeared next to Jamie. He thrust out a hand. "Merry Christmas, Amar."

He shook the offered hand. "Merry Christmas, Poe."

Victoria decided that maybe this party had needed a little jolt of excitement and intrigue.

It was the perfect Colby Agency Christmas, as well as a celebration of the next generation.

* * * * *

Wyoming Undercover Escape
Juno Rushdan

MILLS & BOON

Juno Rushdan is a veteran US Air Force intelligence officer and award-winning author. Her books are action-packed and fast-paced. Critics from *Kirkus Reviews* and *Library Journal* have called her work "heart-pounding James Bond-ian adventure" that "will captivate lovers of romantic thrillers." For a free book, visit her website: www.junorushdan.com.

Books by Juno Rushdan

Harlequin Intrigue

Cowboy State Lawmen: Duty and Honor

Wyoming Mountain Investigation
Wyoming Ranch Justice
Wyoming Undercover Escape

Cowboy State Lawmen

Wyoming Winter Rescue
Wyoming Christmas Stalker
Wyoming Mountain Hostage
Wyoming Mountain Murder
Wyoming Cowboy Undercover
Wyoming Mountain Cold Case

Fugitive Heroes: Topaz Unit

Rogue Christmas Operation
Alaskan Christmas Escape
Disavowed in Wyoming
An Operative's Last Stand

Visit the Author Profile page at millsandboon.com.au.

For all who served in the Marine Corps. Once a marine, always a marine. Thank you for your service.

CAST OF CHARACTERS

Rip Lockwood—Tough as nails, this former marine and current president of the Iron Warriors motorcycle club will stop at nothing to keep a vow he made years ago—protect Ashley Russo and get justice for the murders of both their brothers.

Ashley Russo—This dedicated sheriff's deputy must decide how far she's willing to go for justice. Even if it means teaming up with the biker she's not quite sure she can trust.

Todd Burk—Nicknamed Teflon because the authorities can never get any charges to stick to him. As the leader of the new outlaw motorcycle gang, the Hellhounds, he has declared war on the Iron Warriors and Rip. He will mercilessly eliminate any threats to his drug operation.

Daniel Clark—The sheriff is a reasonable man, but he won't tolerate anyone messing with his deputies.

Mitch Cody—A deputy and good friend of Ashley's.

Holden Powell—Chief deputy of the sheriff's department and best friend of Angelo Russo, who was murdered.

Stryker—President of the Sons of Chaos outlaw motorcycle gang.

Chapter One

Rip Lockwood crossed the field of his elderly landlady's property, heading to his Airstream parked a few hundred feet away, to grab a screwdriver to repair her dishwasher. Wishing he'd worn his jacket in the chilly November night air, he noticed his front door ajar. Only cracked a couple of inches, but he hadn't left it open.

He drew his gun from its holster on his ankle and trained it on the door. Glancing around, he searched for anyone lurking outside as a lookout or any sign of a parked getaway vehicle. Nothing that didn't belong and no one around, from what he could tell.

A slam from inside the trailer, followed by dishes clattering.

Creeping closer, he caught the creaking tread of heavy footfalls across his floor. More than one person. He listened carefully. Two were skulking inside.

"Hurry up," one said from deeper within, trying to keep his voice low.

Rip eased onto the wood deck under the awning and up to the door. Pleased with himself for oiling the hinges last week, he swung the door open wide and rushed inside the Airstream.

Two men—one with a tall, burly frame and the other with an average build—wearing black hoodies and ski masks spun in his direction. The tall one grabbed the microwave from the counter and hurled it at Rip.

He blocked the blow of the sturdy appliance, but a third guy emerged from the bedroom behind him and charged. No way to sidestep the inbound assault in the tight confines, Rip took aim. But the heavyset guy tackled him around the waist. Rip's weapon discharged at the same time, three bullets hitting the ceiling. He and the guy fell out of the trailer, tumbling off the deck while wrestling, and hitting solid, cold ground.

Unfortunately, the stocky guy landed on top of Rip. Another squeeze of the trigger and a shot fired off low to the side, the slug spitting bark from a tree. The thickset man landed a blow across Rip's face before knocking the gun from his hand and sending it sailing across the grass.

Rip threw a hammer fist up into the man's chest, the meaty part of the swinging blow hitting the solar plexus. Gasping for air, the wind knocked from his lungs, the heavy guy fell backward.

The tall one rushed forward with the microwave hoisted overhead, ready to bring it down on Rip's skull. Rip rolled out of the way an instant before the appliance smashed onto the ground. Still on his back, Rip used the position to his advantage and kicked at the other man's knees. Felt a kneecap give way with the snap of broken ligaments. The man hollered in pain.

As Rip tried to climb to his feet, a punch caught him in the ribs. A second fist struck him in the kidney. The thickset guy hit hard, like a boxer. Rip could guess who it was, but rather than focus on identifying him, he needed to immobilize him first. He spun, vision blurring, swinging his elbow up and around, using the added momentum to drive the blow hard into the side of the guy's head. If he'd punched him with that much force, Rip would have broken his hand, whereas his elbow barely registered it.

The heavy guy staggered, clearly disorientated, but he was strong and could take a solid punch. Rip charged straight at him, a wounded bull, lifting the heavy man off his feet and slamming him backward against the ground.

Steel glinted in the moonlight. His gun.

They both went for the weapon.

Then Rip reconsidered. Instead, he launched a fist into his assailant's face, throttling him with jabs until his attacker was dazed.

Where was the third guy?

Adrenaline hot in his veins, Rip reached for his gun. In his peripheral vision he spotted a shadow moving. His fingertips grazed cold steel. The third assailant tried punting his head off with a front kick. Abandoning the gun, Rip jerked away from the incoming boot, but not fast enough. The tip caught him in the jaw.

The tang of blood filled his mouth. He scrambled up onto his hands and knees, reaching for the sheathed Marine Corps KA-BAR on his hip. Or rather, the one that should've been on his belt.

Swearing, he realized he'd left the knife in his trailer.

Mr. Average, who'd gotten in him the jaw, stood with gloved hands clenched and a knapsack on his back. The tall man, now limping, pulled a 9mm gun from his waistband that had been concealed by his sweatshirt.

Rip groped around for something, anything he could use as a weapon, and his fingers closed around a large rock.

"No!" the average one said to the tall guy, his tone sharp with alarm, his palm raised. "Remember, you can't shoot him."

The voice familiar, Rip thought he might be able to pinpoint it.

The man holding the gun hesitated. "No, I just can't kill him."

Rip threw the rock, hitting the guy holding the gun square in the forehead. The man swore, stumbling backward and holding his head with one hand while maintaining a shaky grip on the pistol with the other. Rip spun on to his knees, ready to lunge.

A shotgun cocked, not too far in the distance, pumping a shell into the chamber. The sound was loud and unmistakable. "You're trespassing!" Mrs. Ida Hindley called out. She was his landlady and friend and the closest thing to family that Rip had left. "You better leave because I shoot to kill."

That warning was meant for Rip. He dropped to the ground before Ida opened fire. She could only see a few feet clearly in front of her and that was in bright light. Eighty big steps away, at night, she was just as likely to shoot him as his attackers.

The shotgun cracked, sounding like a mini explosion, the shell getting dangerously close to the big guy.

The three assailants took off toward the woods, one hobbling impressively fast.

Ida pumped off one deafening shot after another, changing her aim each time, determined to hit something. Even if it only ended up being trees and his trailer.

The men disappeared into the darkness.

Motorcycle engines grumbled to life, the sound faint, the sight of the bikes concealed by the woods. They must've been parked on the auxiliary road near the property. Seconds later, the bikes sped off, and Ida was finally out of ammo.

Rip lumbered to his feet and started making his way to Ida. She had lowered the shotgun to her side, but better to be safe than sorry. "It's only me," he said, in case she had extra shells in the pockets of her robe. "They're gone."

Getting closer, he spotted her late husband's snub-nosed revolver in her other hand.

"Are you all right?" she asked.

"I'll live." He slipped the shotgun from her trembling hand, touched his jaw and winced. "You're going to kill someone one day."

"Only a trespasser who deserves it." Giving him a sly grin, she took the arm he offered, and they headed to her house. "I dare anyone to doubt that I would, son." Even with her frail body racked with rheumatoid arthritis, white hair in rollers, wearing winter boots and a flannel bathrobe over pajamas, she was a formidable woman who shouldn't be tested.

"Well, I'm not fool enough to doubt you, Auntie Ida." They might not be related by blood but were still kin.

Shoving the revolver in her pocket, she wheezed, and he slowed their pace.

Tragedy had claimed the lives of their closest relatives. When he was a young teen, Ida had taken him in along with his younger brother. Despite her love and lectures and desperation to keep them away from the motorcycle club their father had been a part of, they had joined the Iron Warriors MC anyway.

If only they had listened.

If only they hadn't chased after some illusory birthright.

If only Rip hadn't failed to protect his brother, he might still be alive.

If only...

"Now, what was all the ruckus about?" she asked.

"MC business," he said.

"Iron Warriors business or Hellhounds?"

The Iron Warriors were his, at least those who still wore the MC cut displaying their patches and insignia, and he had their unwavering loyalty. The Hellhounds, the newly formed OMG, outlaw motorcycle gang, were his cross to bear.

Somehow Todd Burk had dragged the club so deep into illicit and illegal activity, right under his nose, that Rip had to put a stop to it, drawing a line in the sand. In the end, Rip had made a mess of things and caused his club to split.

Those who agreed that they should not deal drugs stood with him as Iron Warriors. The vast majority who didn't, who loved the money, who craved power and refused to give any of it up, had broken away with Burk as their leader and become the Hellhounds.

The group's existence was yet another failure Rip had to atone for and deal with.

He helped Ida up the steps of her back porch and inside the house. "It's best if that's all you know." Gently, he set her down in a chair.

"There's been a lot of ugly, unfortunate *MC business* around here and in town lately." Ida was back up on her feet, plodding to the refrigerator. She grabbed milk and went to the stove.

"Precisely why I don't want you to pull another stunt like that," he said, setting the shotgun on the kitchen counter. "Understand? I don't want you to get hurt."

She waved a dismissive hand at him. "I've had eighty-nine good years on this earth. They weren't always easy, but I've gotten to see the world, make my mark on it, known the love of family and cherished friends." She put a delicate hand on his arm and squeezed. "What I will not do is hide in here while someone I care about is in danger out there." She pointed through the window at the land in the direction of his trailer.

"I don't want you to risk your life for mine." No one should die to save him.

Giving a dry chuckle, she poured milk in a pan and turned on the fire. "Remind me, how old are you?" She counted on her fingers. "Thirty-five?"

"You flatter me. Thirty-eight."

She opened a cabinet and grabbed hot chocolate. "My life has been full and rich, though not with money." Another dry laugh. "When my time comes, I'll be ready. And I want you to be at peace with it. But you've got more than half your life ahead of you, son."

Things had only escalated with Burk, going from bad to worse. Rip had been extorted, shot at, and had his tires slashed. No matter how hard he tried to avoid bloodshed that would only lead to a war, he wasn't so sure he'd outlive Ida. And after tonight's incident, with her getting involved, he'd reached a crossroads.

If he allowed this mayhem to continue, Ida would be burying him before the new year.

"I wouldn't be so sure about that." He dug out the cold compress from the freezer and put it on his face. "I haven't done much good with the first half of my life." Maybe there wasn't much point in the second half. "What do I have to show for it?"

"You left this small town and the club to join the military because I begged you to."

And he'd also left his brother behind, who refused to leave.

Rip had seen the dark side of the MC culture and when Auntie Ida pleaded, no, *dared* him to see what else there might be in the world for him, he didn't back down from the challenge.

Ida got out mini marshmallows and caramel syrup and

set them on the counter, but not the chocolate syrup when she knew he liked a drizzle of both on his cocoa.

He was lucky to have her in his life, someone willing to shoot his attackers and make him hot chocolate. Dropping into a chair, he propped an elbow on his leg, resting his head in his hand, and put the compress to his face.

"You saved lives in the Marines," Ida continued. "Looking around here, you can't see it. But dig out your Navy Cross and look at that. It's proof you made an impact. Not only on those you saved, but for their mothers and fathers and siblings and spouses and children. You also came back home to make an even bigger difference." He opened his mouth to protest, and she raised her palm, silencing him. "You haven't achieved what you set out to do. Not yet." She handed him a cup of hot cocoa. "Not yet," she repeated. "But there's still time. And where there's a will, there's a way. Even if we don't like the way forward or it happens to be unexpected, there comes a point where we have to make a choice. Do we keep at it, using the same methods that haven't worked. Or find a new way to fight."

There was time. As a Marine Raider, he was trained to deal with disaster and eliminate too many types of enemies to name. Stopping terrorists was his specialty. He was going to use his skill set and whatever time he had left to take down Todd Burk.

War wasn't a possibility that he could prevent. It was already on his doorstep, and he was in the thick of it. But the one thing he knew how to do was fight a war.

He needed to be ruthless to win. Even if doing so killed him.

Ida picked up two mugs and left the kitchen.

"Why did you make three cups of cocoa?" How did he not notice until now?

She shuffled down the hallway and he followed behind her.

Red-and-blue flashing lights pulled up in front of the house.

"You called the sheriff's department?" he asked. Irritation sparked through him. "I can't talk to the law about MC business."

No one snitched. Not even about this. That was the code. They lived by it. Died by it. Honored it. Even a legit biker and upstanding citizen like him did not get the authorities involved.

"But I got the pretty deputy to come," she said.

Gritting his teeth, Rip sighed. There were a couple of female deputies in the sheriff's department, but instantly he knew she was talking about the gorgeous one he had a complicated relationship with. "You asked for the one who hates me?"

And Ashley Russo had every reason to despise him, the club and everything the MC stood for. No matter how hard he'd tried to break down her wall of disdain—and he'd tried very, very hard—it was never enough to get her to change the way she looked at him.

There was a rap at the door. Light from the headlights and flashing strobes outlined a slender athletic shape wearing a cowboy hat through the glass pane of the door.

"I thought you two had some kind of thing going on. That you were at least friends," Ida said.

"Friends trust each other. That's not the case here. We've formed a tenuous…" He was at a loss for what to call it. Association? Acquaintance? Civility? No word was quite right. "I guess we do have some kind of a *thing*." But it was held together by gossamer threads. One wrong move on his part and it would snap.

"That does explain all the questions she asked me a few weeks ago about whether you were living on the property against my will and if you were paying a reasonable rent or if I wanted you to leave. But I cleared it up. Set her straight about you. She gave me her card, with her personal cell phone number on the back, and told me to call her anytime, especially if there was trouble. So I did, tonight."

"What? Why didn't you tell me? When was she here?" *How was any of that friendly?*

Another knock. This time louder.

Ida looked at him with a wry grin. "There's a thin line between love and hate. Now open the door and act like the man I raised you to be."

"She blames me for the death of her brother," he admitted, his voice low.

He remembered like it was yesterday, the conversation Ashley had overheard at her brother's funeral, the way she came up to him, a fearless seventeen-year-old girl, slapped his face, pounded on his chest and screamed her anger and grief.

Ida's smile fell. "Is she justified?"

Rip didn't pull the trigger but shared the blame for Angelo's death and for his own brother's. "In a way, yes."

"Then it's high time you took responsibility for it and started righting your wrongs."

Scratching his head, he wished Ida had warned him she had called the authorities. More specifically, one deputy in particular.

Ida switched on the porch light and the one in the foyer and gave him a *get-on-with-it* look.

Dropping the cold compress onto a side table, Rip stalked up to the door and opened it. His gaze met the deputy's, her whiskey-brown eyes narrowing a fraction. He gave her the once-over, surprised she wasn't in uniform. Her dark hair hung loose, falling past her shoulders rather than pulled into a ponytail or the tight braid she sported whenever he'd seen her working. Form-fitting jeans accentuated her long legs and rounded hips. A tucked-in flannel shirt and leather jacket didn't do much to flatter her figure. But her classic hourglass shape on her five-foot-seven frame made it impossible to ignore the fact she was no longer a girl.

He flicked a glance over her shoulder. She had driven her personal truck, using portable red-and-blue emergency lights that could easily be mounted to the dash or windshield with suction cups, rather than a patrol SUV. "Are you off duty?"

The deputy unhooked her badge from her belt and held it up, making it clear she was working even if she might be off duty.

"I'll ask the questions." She gestured past him into the house.

The star in her hand reminded him what he *didn't* like about her. Rip stepped aside, opening the door wide.

She came in, bringing with her the cold and the crisp, clean scent of frost.

Ida handed the deputy a mug. "I made it just the way you like it. With mini marshmallows and caramel syrup."

"Thank you," she said. "But you shouldn't have gone to the trouble."

Rip glanced down at his mug. He had neither the zhuzh of marshmallows nor syrup.

Sipping his plain cocoa, he shut the door and followed them down the hall. His gaze slipped below the deputy's waistline and belt with flashlight, pepper spray, handcuffs and holstered gun, and locked onto the gentle sway of her hips. He liked her curves, and she had plenty of them. Appreciated the strength of her body from a combat standpoint. But he had to fight against the primal physical interest, the spark of heat that flashed inside him whenever she was near.

Inside the kitchen, he hurried to the table and helped Ida ease down into a chair. In the evenings her arthritis got worse, making her stiff.

The deputy glanced around the room, her gaze lingering on the shotgun on the counter, and took out a notepad and pen. "I'm responding to a report of shots fired. The best way for me to do my job efficiently is if you're honest when answering my questions," she said, all business, staring right at him as she spoke. "You might not be a Marine anymore, but tonight I need you to abide by the same uncompromising integrity of the corps instead of your MC code of silence."

"Once a Marine, always a Marine," he said, not turning away from her face, which he liked even more than her figure.

Satin-smooth complexion. The golden brown hue of her skin showed her multiracial heritage. Italian on her father's side. Creole on her mother's. Not that it was one thing about her, like her high cheekbones, but rather the complete package, the sum of her parts, that he found captivating. He could look at her for hours and often struggled not to stare.

"A distinguished Marine," Ida chimed in, her voice full of pride. "Ripton lives by a set of core values that have formed the bedrock of his character."

"Really? Is that so?" The deputy didn't filter the sharp skepticism from her tone. "What kind of core values?"

He understood the law enforcement game she was playing. When a cop thought they might have trouble getting answers from a person, they warmed them up, getting them talking about something the reluctant party was comfortable with first.

Unfortunately for her, he'd been playing this game far longer and was better at it.

"I do my best never to lie unless there's good cause. But I never cheat. Never steal. Don't break the law." Honor, strength to do what was right, commitment—an unrelenting determination to achieve victory in every endeavor—made him who he was.

He'd tried to tell her this before but she either didn't listen or didn't believe him.

"I only hope that's true." She stepped closer, dangerously close, inches separating them, studying his face as if searching for the truth, and heat flared again, coaxing him to thaw. Enticing him to strive for something far deeper than friendship with her.

But he backed away from the deputy, going around to the other side of the table. Regardless of how attractive he found her or how drawn to her he was, or that he needed to, and intended to, make amends for her brother, he had to be the same with her right now as he would be with any other badge investigating. Stone-cold.

An iceberg that wouldn't crack.

Chapter Two

Staring up at Ripton Lockwood, with her being at least six inches shorter than him, Ashley fully expected him to answer every question with a half-truth or simply evade giving a real answer at all. He might still consider himself a Marine, but instead of wearing a military uniform, he usually wore a biker cut.

Though he didn't have on the leather vest covered in patches now.

He was not only a member of a notorious motorcycle club but also the president of the Iron Warriors.

The MC had been a blight in the towns of Laramie and Bison Ridge for as long as she could remember. Corrupting the youth, recruiting them into their ranks with sparkly promises, neglecting to disclose that not everything that glitters was gold.

A few things gave her a glimmer of hope that Rip might be honest about tonight's events and, if so, possibly help her with her one-woman crusade. Ida Hindley's high praise of him. The DEA's recent deep-dive background report on him that only showed two red flags: his motorcycle club affiliation and no verifiable source of legitimate income. There was also the fact most of his rotten-apple bikers had broken away, forming a new, dangerous faction—the

Hellhounds—under Todd Burk. The man who had brutally killed her brother.

Now the Hellhounds seemed hell-bent on putting Rip six feet under.

Maybe the enemy of her enemy could be a real ally?

The way he answered her questions would tell her. "Mrs. Hindley told me you were fixing her dishwater, left to get a tool from your trailer, and then she heard gunshots."

Rip stared down at her with that uneasy stillness to him. He possessed a coiled readiness, a wariness that made her nerves hum, giving him a more lethal vibe than any other MC gang member. Nothing on the job ever made her nervous.

But he did.

He wasn't quite like the other bikers. Guarded, sure, but he didn't taunt authority as though invincible, certainly didn't back down from it, and he didn't run in a pack.

For all the years she'd seen him around, she'd usually encountered him alone. More baffling was his living situation with Mrs. Hindley. Apparently, Rip had taken care of her debts, saving the land she was about to lose due to outstanding unpaid property taxes, and still paid her rent.

The question was where did he get the money?

He didn't have a nine-to-five job, and whenever she asked about employment, he'd given cagey responses.

The elderly woman had been eager to explain why Rip had done so much for her, but Ashley had been called away to respond to a 10-80, chase in progress.

She was bound and determined to figure out what Rip's deal was.

"That's right," Mrs. Hindley said, holding her cocoa between her hands. "And then I called you."

Instead of 911, which puzzled Ashley, but she wasn't going to squander this rare opportunity.

"Walk me through what happened," she said.

Rip pushed up the sleeves of his shirt, revealing corded forearms and tattoos, then pulled out a chair for her to sit. His gaze never left her, always watchful. Especially of her.

She decided to change course. "Why don't you show me where the altercation happened while you walk me through it?"

"Out at my Airstream." He turned to Ida. "Will you be all right until I get back?"

Sipping her cocoa, Ida waved a hand at him. "I don't need a babysitter. You're the one who needs looking after."

Grabbing his black sheepskin bomber jacket from a hook, Rip smiled and gave a low, husky chuckle far sexier than Ashley wanted it to be. He opened the back door and, standing against the jamb on the threshold, held it for her.

She hesitated.

Not that she feared him. Oddly, not once had he ever made her afraid. She simply didn't care for his politeness, how careful he was never to stand too close—*she was the one always stepping within arm's reach, maybe to test him*—the way he seemed aware of his height and strength and how intimidating it could be.

The dark jeans and gray Henley he wore did little to hide his sculpted chest and muscled arms. Another stark reminder of his physical capabilities.

If only he acted less chivalrous and more despicable, it would be easier to cling to her lingering doubts about him.

"You'll be safe in the dark alone with me, Deputy. Don't worry, I won't bite. Unless you want me to." His slow grin made her skin tingle.

It was devilish and inviting, and she had to fight very hard not to grin back at his effortless charm.

She'd been alone with him plenty of times and always

felt safe, but they'd never been together in the dark. This flirty banter of his was just a game, so she decided to play by putting her hand on the hilt of her gun. "I'm not worried because I'm armed."

Ashley brushed past him, their bodies grazing, and she couldn't ignore the hard, rugged wall of muscle beneath his clothes. The smell of him. Soap and leather and pine. Up close, his eyes were a startling blue-gray that commanded attention. His features were sharp and chiseled, his square jaw unshaven. The sheer size of him never had her strategizing how best to take him down if necessary, because she didn't consider him a personal threat.

In fact, whenever she drew near him, her stomach fluttered as it did now.

Instantly, she became aware of her mistake. Physical contact. She wished she'd had him lead the way and gone out behind him.

Rip might be ridiculously—*disarmingly*—good-looking, but she refused to be attracted to a selfish man who ran from responsibility when he could have prevented her brother's death.

He shut the back door and slipped on his jacket.

Ashley walked beside him. "How long have you lived here?"

"Depends on the perspective."

An answer that told her nothing. He was good at giving those. "I need to know for my investigation and the report. You agreed to cooperate."

"Did I?" He raised an eyebrow. "Don't think so."

She thought back to the brief conversation in the kitchen. He was right. "You said you wouldn't lie."

"I said I do my best not to." He flipped up the collar of his jacket against the wind. "And I haven't lied to you. *Ever.*"

Another flutter whipped through her on his last word, but she deliberately tamped it down. "Why did you call me if you're only going to stonewall?"

"Ida called you. Not me."

She stopped walking. Once he did too, she hiked her chin up at him. "Would you prefer a different deputy to handle this?"

Shoving his hands in his pockets, with a hint of a smile on his face, he stared at her. That incisive, intense gaze and the sharp intelligence behind it made her squirm a little on the inside.

"I'd prefer none at all," he said, running his fingers across his head. Gone was his slightly too long sable hair that fell past his collar in favor of a buzz cut that made him look harder, edgier. Sexier.

"I already called it in to the station. So, it's me or someone else."

"You're in civilian clothes and driving your personal vehicle. Why are you here off duty?"

Technically, she wasn't off duty. For the past couple of months, she'd worked around the clock on a special assignment. "Ida called. I told her that if she ever needed me, I would come."

"Because you're worried about me?"

Odd way to phrase it. "Because I'm worried about her with you."

His jaw twitched as he seemed to chew on that. "I prefer you. Over the others. Since I've got no choice." He turned and continued to his trailer.

At the Airstream, she pulled latex gloves from her pocket, slipped them on and looked around outside, noting the damaged microwave oven on the ground.

Rip picked up a gun and held it up by the hilt. "It's mine.

Discharged four times. Once out here, hitting a tree. The other three inside the trailer into the ceiling."

She opened an evidence bag, and he dropped the sub-compact gun—SIG P365, she guessed—inside. "I thought you'd be a good shot, as a Marine."

"I am. When I intend to shoot, I don't miss. All the shots were accidental. The discharge happened during a scuffle."

She glanced at his hips. No holster. "Where were you carrying?" she asked, shaking the bag.

Pulling up his pant leg, he revealed an ankle holster.

"Got a concealed carry permit?"

He took his wallet from his inner jacket pocket and fished it out.

She looked it over. The permit was in order. She handed it back to him. "Shouldn't have your gun too long. This is only a formality. Procedure. I'll call you when you can get it back." His number was one of the few she had pro-grammed in her phone, though she rarely had reason to use it. "Why do you live way out here, so far from town, on Mrs. Hindley's land?" she asked, trying again now that he was talking.

Since age nineteen, Ashley had lived in Bison Ridge, away from town, in the house her grandmother had be-queathed her. It was peaceful, surrounded by nature. Not unlike here.

"It's an arrangement that works for both of us."

Still being cagey.

"I noticed your motorcycle parked at Mrs. Hindley's house instead of in your driveway out here." The suspects would have heard his engine approaching and prob-ably would've hightailed it out of there before he got close enough for an altercation if they only wanted to rob him or trash his place. "Why?"

"Ida needed a refill on her blood pressure medication. She wanted me to wait until the morning to get it, but I insisted since the pharmacy in town was still open. I parked at the house when I got back. We chatted for a while. Then she wanted me to look at the dishwasher because it had started leaking."

"Walk me through what happened," she said, and Rip explained everything from finding his door open to Mrs. Hindley firing her shotgun. "Can you describe what they looked like?"

"They wore ski masks, black hoodies and gloves. One was average height and build. The other was an inch taller than me but with slightly less bulk. The third one was thick around the middle. Stocky."

"Any distinguishing marks? Visible tattoos?"

"No. But the tall one is limping after the altercation."

"Did you recognize their voices?"

He hesitated and then shook his head. "Can't put a definitive name to any of them."

His choice of words had been careful. Too careful. "But you have some idea who they might be?"

"I don't care to speculate. Sorry, Deputy."

But if he did, no doubt he'd name three Hellhounds.

Sighing, she stepped inside the trailer and looked around. It was in a shambles. Broken dishes on the floor. Cushions ripped open and stuffing pulled out. The mess would take a solid day to clean up and furniture would have to be replaced.

Three guys to trash one trailer was a lot. Overkill really, unless they'd wanted the backup in case they encountered Rip. Three against one and he'd done substantial damage. Impressive.

"Did they take anything?" she asked.

He stood near the door under the bullet holes. "I haven't had a chance to look, but I don't have anything of value. I don't keep cash in here."

She walked over to him. "What about drugs?"

"I don't do drugs. Never used. Never dealt it. Also, don't condone the trafficking of it."

She searched his face and, strangely, believed him. If he was into drugs, she supposed he'd give her one of his *non-answer answers* to avoid lying.

Passing him on her way back outside, she caught the masculine smell of him again. Her body tightened against it. Outside, she was grateful for the fresh air.

"You know this is a crime." She gestured at the trailer.

"What, assault with a microwave?" he asked, the corner of his mouth hitching up.

She bit back a smile. "I wasn't referring to that." She pointed higher, to the colorful pepper-shaped lights strung up along the awning on the outside of the Airstream. This was her first time at his home, and she realized how little she knew about him. "Putting up Christmas decorations before Thanksgiving."

The holiday feast at her parents' house would be next week. This was the hardest time of year for her, for the entire family, since her brother had been killed right after Halloween.

"You're one of those, huh? A believer that the holidays shall not overlap. Ida is the same. She calls the lights sacrilege. But I like having them up for longer than a month. The festive feel of it, though I've got nothing to celebrate."

She eyed him for a moment. "We can sweep for fingerprints, but since they wore gloves, I doubt we'll get any other than yours and those of visitors."

"No visitors. Not even Ida comes in here."

"No lady friends?"

He leaned against the side of the trailer, that laser focus of his full bore on her. "Are you asking as part of your investigation?"

Honestly, she wasn't sure why she'd asked. "Curious."

"No lady friends, Deputy."

"You mean that you bring here. I guess that's what your clubhouse is for." The MC had a clubhouse, if it should be called such, that Rip had built. Once again, raising the question of how it was paid for if not by illicit means? A massive single-story building that took up almost half a block. She'd heard the rumor that every member had his own bedroom at the club. After they partied hard, everyone had a private space to sleep or continue having fun with a woman. Not only that, but they also reportedly had a bar, game room, armory, conference room, gym, and a stage with stripper poles. *Classy.*

"If that's what you want to think, go ahead, but you'd be wrong about me."

"Why so cryptic?" She wasn't inquiring about MC secrets, only if there was a woman in his life, or occasionally in his bed. Not that she cared either way.

"Why so curious?" he countered.

"Can't help it." Particularly when it came to him. "It's what I do—ask questions, investigate, solve problems."

"I meant no lady friends. Period. Before you ask, no, I'm not gay. Only single. And when the clubhouse belonged to the Iron Warriors, I never used the room designated for me to sleep with women."

Something important in his comment registered.

"What do you mean *when* the clubhouse belonged to the Iron Warriors?" The answer dawned on her, but it didn't make any sense. "The clubhouse belongs to the Hell-hounds now?"

A shadow crossed his eyes. "I gave it to them."

"What?" That wasn't akin to giving a bully your lunch or the money in your wallet, but more extreme, like giving them your entire house or life savings. "Why?"

Rip wasn't the type to roll over and give in. Was he?

Her gut clenched at what this could mean. The Iron Warriors were losing the battle against the Hellhounds. Rip was losing.

Where would that leave the town? If Rip and his guys were a blight, then Burk and his posse were a plague.

"The answer to that question is none of your concern," he said, his tone matter-of-fact, his stance unyielding. "Has no relevance on your investigation."

"It's connected. Todd forming a new gang. You giving him your clubhouse. The clubhouse you built for them. The other day, Ida told me someone slashed your tires. And now this. I'm sure there's now one Hellhound with a limp. Be honest with me."

"You want the truth?"

"Yes."

"Move on," he said, and she caught the warning as well as the worry in his voice. "Ida only called you tonight because she thought I might be in trouble or hurt. I'm fine."

She squared her shoulders, irritated at his straightfor-ward manner of telling her zilch. Glancing back at the trailer, she tried to regroup. "Deputy Livingston will be out to sweep for prints. Maybe one of them got sloppy and we'll get lucky."

"Not necessary. I'd prefer not to have any further intru-sion in my home if we can avoid it."

Frustration welled inside her. "Can I give you some advice?"

"Certainly. Doesn't mean I'll take it."

"In this turf battle between the Iron Warriors and Hell-hounds, don't become a person of interest." She needed him free to help her, not investigated or locked up behind bars.

"Well, I *am* an interesting person."

She sighed, her breath crystallizing in the air. "Anything else you can tell me about what happened here tonight?"

"Nothing. And believe me, I wish I could."

"Thanks for the paperwork I'll have to do tonight since I have to file a report that will lead to nothing." She put away her notepad. "If you find anything missing, let me know."

Little point to her coming out here, let alone looking at his trailer, though it was nice to finally see where he lived. Maybe she could make this trip worth her while. She had to ask him sooner or later for help and couldn't wait for him to make another random visit to her house.

"Sorry about the paperwork and that I couldn't be more helpful," he said, almost sounding sincere. "I wish I hadn't taken up so much of your time while you're off duty, Deputy."

His politeness and formality were galling.

"You and I have history," she said. He owed her for her brother's death, and she was going to make him clear that debt. But over the years, he'd watched out for her and cease-lessly endeavored to build something beyond their complicated bond of obligation. In the back of her mind, she couldn't be sure he wasn't trying to use her. A powerful thing if a motorcycle club president had a cop in his pocket.

"That we do," he agreed.

"You show up at my house maybe twice a month to check in on me." Sometimes it was closer to every eight to ten days. Rip seemed to always be doing that. Looking out for her. Making sure she was okay. At first, they only talked outside on her porch. Then he started bringing food—tacos, empanadas, savory croissants from the café, delectable, irresistible items that got him inside the house, and once even a bottle of whiskey. She'd told him she preferred tequila. For her recent—twenty-fifth—birthday, instead of giving her the usual bath oils, luxury candles or silk kimono robes that she loved but would never buy for herself, he'd given her a bottle of Clase Azul twenty-fifth anniversary tequila. Someone at the office told her it cost three thousand dollars. Good thing she hadn't mentioned who'd given it to her, or they would've thought it was a bribe. That was what she'd suspected after learning the price. "It's weird, the way you only call me Deputy. Even when we bump into each other in town and I'm in plainclothes. Or when you're at my house."

He always parked around back, like his presence at her home was a dirty secret, and maybe for her it was, but she never let him past her kitchen.

She'd been grateful for the distance the use of her title provided, preventing them from ever getting too close, but now she needed that distance erased.

Rip folded his arms. "That's what you are."

"It's my job title. Not *who* I am." In a small town, it was hard to be someone else once you clocked out of your job, but she didn't always have to be Deputy Russo. "Use my first name. When you do, I'll know you haven't forgotten. About my brother. About the misery you could've prevented."

Something flashed across his face. Guilt? Pain? Whatever it was, it was real, honest.

"I haven't forgotten," he said. "I'll never forget. Burk will pay for Angelo. For everything. I swear it."

The words hit her, not as a blow, but more as a sudden, swift bear hug. Strong and reassuring.

He was a hardened Marine who had sworn to defend his country—once he'd even sworn to protect her, too, on the day her brother was buried. Back then, she couldn't hear it, wouldn't believe it. Now she suspected Rip didn't take oaths lightly.

Still, she didn't trust him completely either, which put her in a difficult position, because she was going to have to put her life in his hands.

"Why do you live here? Mrs. Hindley is itching to tell me." Ashley needed Rip to share, to open up further. DEA Agent Welliver had hammered home the importance of it when trying to cultivate an asset. Oddly, it made her wonder if that was what Rip had been up to all this time, with the visits to her house, asking her personal questions—trying to recruit her, but to what end? "I want to hear it from you. Will you give me that?"

He sighed. "My parents died when I was thirteen. Ida took us in, me and my brother, Thatcher. *Hatch*, that's what everyone called him. She cared for us when no one else would. She had lost her husband and her daughter and needed someone to love. Would've been less heartache for her if she'd rescued a couple of stray dogs instead and let us go to foster care." The regret in his voice was thick.

His candor touched something deep inside of her she hadn't expected.

"I'm out here to look after her," he continued. "To give her what company I can. Fix whatever breaks. Get her groceries. Make sure she takes her medication. She needs me now, though she'd spin a different tale, so I'm here."

Rip was an enigma. He'd told her things about himself, details that painted him as a good guy. A great one in fact.

All of which she doubted and questioned until talking to Ida. Ashley had seen many things that made her wonder why he was ever in the MC, much less a club president. Sponsoring blood drives, holding fundraisers for the elementary school to cover the cost of pre-kindergarten, the way he was helping Ida when he didn't have to. How he watched out for Ashley. Not once had she had any problems with the Iron Warriors since he took over the club. Rip was both laudable and lamentable.

She struggled to reconcile the dichotomy.

"What happened to your brother?" She knew that Hatch had tried to rob a strip club one night while drunk, with some other bikers. He'd been caught and, while in prison, someone had killed him. Stabbed him with a shiv. According to the report, one of the guards suspected it had been related to a drug deal.

If Burk had been involved, Rip might let something slip.

His lips firmed. "I failed him. The same way I failed yours."

Ashley approached him, cautiously, as one would a wild animal being cornered. Not that she expected him to attack her. But her situation meant risking her life all the same. She couldn't afford to make a mistake. Not with him.

She drew as close as possible without touching him and could see the stormy blue-gray of his eyes in the illumination from the string lights above his head.

He stiffened, pressing his back to the side of the trailer as though he wanted to get away from her. But he didn't walk off, only shoved his hands in his pockets.

"I need your help," she said, her voice a hair above a whisper, even though they were alone.

His brows pinched together. "With what?" His tone matched hers.

"Taking down Burk, once and for all."

Straightening to his full height, he leaned in a little. "I warned you to stay away from him. Told you I'd handle it."

"Yeah, seven years ago. How has that been going for nearly a decade?" she asked, and he lowered his gaze. "You don't get to do that. I want you to look at me."

He lifted his head, his eyes meeting hers, but everything about him frosted over, putting distance between them, even though they were only inches apart. Might as well have been miles.

"I'm going after him," she continued. "But I need you." She had to be careful about how much to tell him until he agreed to help her.

"*Need*, huh. Tempting words coming from you," he said with sudden, cool remoteness that still managed to warm her. "But I'm not sure what you're saying. Are you asking to get dirty with me?"

Ashley hated the power he had over her, to make her belly flutter or her thighs tingle with the slightest innuendo. She cursed him in her head. "I have sensitive information I'm going to act on. I could use your help."

"I can't work with a cop. Cooperation is one thing. Collaboration is quite another. The code—"

"Forget about the MC code. For once. Please."

He stared at her for a long moment, as if looking straight through her, down to her soul.

When he didn't respond, she asked, "Did you mean it when you said you'd protect me?"

He gave a curt nod. "Of course."

"Then help me," she implored with every fiber of her being. It might be the only way she could take down Burk's operation and get out alive. "Do you have any idea what this takes?" To her chagrin, she heard her voice threaten to break and he dropped his head back against the trailer. "For me to come to you and ask? Please, I need you on this."

"I can't." His jaw tightened. "Just leave this to me. I'll handle it," Rip said, anger or annoyance edging his voice.

"When? In the next seven years? Seven days? Do you even have a week? Because you can't handle anything if you're dead. Tonight was only a taste of what's to come. Burk is turning up the heat on you. The word around town is it won't stop until you're finished. As in cold in the ground." She studied him, hoping to see a crack in the ice wall he'd thrown up between them. Nothing. "Forget it. I knew asking you was a waste of time. I'll do it on my own."

She spun on her heel, but before she could take two steps, he caught her wrist and whirled her back around, stealing her breath.

It was the first time he'd ever laid a finger on her. At her brother's funeral, she'd wailed as she thrashed him, beating him with her fists, and he'd done nothing to stop her or defend himself. He'd simply taken it until her parents had hauled her off him.

But now he had her wrist locked in an iron grip and dragged her so close she could feel the heat of his body. His eyes flashed hot enough to singe, a muscle in his jaw ticking. His face was so near hers his chocolaty breath brushed across her lips. She couldn't tell if he wanted to kill her or kiss her, and for a heartbeat she wondered what his mouth would feel like on hers.

"I don't know what you're planning," he said in a harsh whisper as his thumb stroked along the inside of her wrist. "But whatever it is, I'm telling you it's a bad idea. Stand down and walk away from it, Ashley. Do you hear me?"

Her pulse pounded from his touch. From his fury. From

the bittersweet sound of her name on his lips. From the jolt of unwelcome desire.

From his blunt order that shook her to the core.

How dare he try to tell her what to do?

She was no longer a teenage girl. She had been with the sheriff's department since she was of legal age to join. For nearly seven years, she'd worn the badge and done as he asked, staying away from Todd Burk, his MC brother, while he *handled* it. Not anymore. She was done waiting. "Shame on you. For asking me to back down. For not helping me, when I have never asked you for anything. I've finally got a chance to stop Burk and I'm taking it. I'll handle it while you keep running from your responsibility."

Ashley yanked her arm free from his tight grasp and marched off toward her truck.

DEA Agent Welliver had given her the tip she'd been waiting for. The final piece had been Rip, but...

Shaking her head, she whisked away her disappointment. She didn't need him. It would be riskier without him, a lot riskier, but she could do it alone.

Come hell or high water, she wasn't going to be like Rip. She wasn't going to fail.

Her mission wouldn't end until she stopped Burk's drug-running operation and the man was behind bars or dead.

Chapter Three

Pushing through the front door of the first-ever Iron Warriors clubhouse, Rip hated the emotions running riot through him. Anger. Shame. Defeat.

No. Only a temporary setback.

Rip had lost a battle, but not the war.

Taking off his sunglasses, he sat in a rickety chair and looked around. In the early afternoon light, the ultra-rural cabin situated in the middle of nowhere looked even more dilapidated. Almost a twenty-minute drive outside of Laramie or Bison Ridge, it was a sufficient spot for privacy, to gather with his men and strategize without any of their plans getting leaked.

For far too long, Rip had been trying to take care of the problem named Todd Burk, without any of his other brothers in the MC being collateral damage.

The task had proved impossible.

Todd had layers and layers of separation from most of the illegal activity, insulation by the very men Rip had been trying to protect.

The sheriff's department had done half the work of cleaning up the club, without Rip's involvement, by shutting down Burk's prostitution ring with help from the FBI. Todd had a few civilian sleazeballs running the day-to-day of handling the women and clients. Two low-level Iron Warriors had been collecting the money, funneling it back to Todd. They were arrested but refused to incriminate Burk.

Nasty business that had opened Rip's eyes to what had been transpiring unbeknownst to him. A couple of months later, he learned about the drug trafficking when his own brother was killed. Hatch had been behind bars for armed robbery, serving nine years. A dangerous, foolish act that never would've happened if Rip had been around instead of serving in the military. Hatch kept getting into trouble in prison and his sentence extended with every infraction. Then his brother had gotten caught in the middle of a turf war between rival gangs selling narcotics behind bars. That was how Rip discovered Todd had been sneaking drugs into the prison somehow and turned Hatch into a dealer.

Rip had dug around with the type of professional scrutiny he'd used in the Marines.

Todd's operation was extensive. Not only was he dealing locally, but also to every university and college within a four-hour drive of town, poisoning communities and killing kids.

What Rip hadn't been able to ascertain was Todd's supplier, the schedule and location of major shipments, how the cash flowed and was being laundered. He also couldn't prove that Todd was behind any of it. Rip could only decree that the club would not mess with drugs. No transporting or dealing them.

But Todd had been prepared and called the decision to a vote.

One Rip lost.

Those same guys he'd been trying to protect had stabbed him in the back, figuratively, siding with Todd and trading in their Iron Warrior cuts to be Hellhounds.

Now Rip would get as ruthless as required to complete the job, even if it meant half of the new OMG ended up behind bars. A necessary sacrifice as long as he kept Ashley out of the fray.

He looked over at the few men seated that he had left, a whopping four, whom he'd called together this afternoon.

"Meeting here feels like a slap in the face," said Quill, his vice president. A senior Warrior twenty years older than Rip, Quill had seen the club go through many phases and lots of change, but even he was having difficulty with this one. "Being in this run-down shack while the *Hellhounds*—" he spit on the floor "—are in the house that you built."

To clean up the club and steer it toward the straight and narrow path, Rip had to give them a way to earn money. Legitimately. He fell back on what he knew. Combat and defense. He'd formed the Ironside Protection Service. Whether someone needed a single bodyguard or full squad detail, conspicuous or covert, Ironside answered the call. Once they developed a solid reputation, work had begun to pour in, the gigs had gotten better, more lucrative. They had raked in plenty, to pay for the tricked-out clubhouse, to keep them flush in cash and, he had thought, mistakenly, to appease their greed.

The whole time he was busy focused on building a law-abiding legacy, Todd was just as busy expanding the criminal enterprise. The worst part was that Todd had the brains and clever sense to keep it quiet and his methods concealed from Rip and those loyal to him.

JD grimaced. As the group's sergeant-at-arms, he was third in rank. "How could you give it to those ungrateful, traitorous fools?" JD asked.

For so many years, Rip had been careful, not keeping

anyone too close because he couldn't afford any additional vulnerabilities. But last month Todd had taken his one weakness and exploited it anyway.

"Give me the clubhouse or I'll spill blood," Todd had said. *"And not just the Iron Warriors'. I won't waste a bullet on Ida. But you won't be around forever to protect the pretty little deputy, and once you're out of the picture, she'll pay the price."* A wicked grin pulled at his mouth. *"It won't be quick, and it won't be painless. Maybe a couple of guys will show her a 'good time' first."* He licked his lips.

Disgust swam through his veins as he recalled it. After Rip *showed* Todd what he thought of that proposal, with his fists, going so far as to break his nose, he'd given Burk the keys and signed the deed over to him.

"A building isn't worth bloodshed," Rip said.

Quill rolled his eyes, leaned back in a creaky chair and put a boot up on a table, kicking up dust. "Let those boys build their own place. Danger comes with the territory for us. If we get to hold on to what's ours, we can take whatever they dish out and give it right back."

They could.

Ashley couldn't.

She was smart and strong and a sharp deputy, but the badge wouldn't keep her safe. The depravity Todd was capable of, combined with his utter lack of respect for women—the guy even beat and cheated on his own old lady—meant he'd order some lowlifes under his thumb to hurt Ashley, bad, and then kill her. Not only to get to Rip but just for fun. "I don't want a war spilling over into town. Innocent people will suffer the consequences," he said.

"Are you talking about Ashley Russo?" JD asked, and all the other curious gazes in the room swung to Rip.

It was common knowledge that he'd watched over her

and ensured no Iron Warrior messed with her, but he'd kept it secret from Ashley how he managed to do that. Todd's vile threat only made Rip more determined to shield her. From everything, including herself.

"I am," he admitted. "But also, Ida. And your families. Once bullets start flying, bystanders could be hit."

Quill nodded. "You make a good point. The sheriff's department will only make things difficult for us, and cops are likely to die if Todd becomes so unhinged as to go after *your* deputy."

My deputy?

A part of him enjoyed the sound of that far too much. Ever since he'd seen her swimming in the lake with some friends, almost nineteen years old, climbing out of the water in a modest one piece, laughing, sparkling, radiating light, he'd considered how it would be if she was his.

The more pragmatic side of him was aware she didn't even like him and deserved much better than he could offer. So, he kept his distance and put Quill in charge of watching her, ensuring her safety with the full power of Ironside services at his disposal.

But the way she'd asked for his help, the imploring look on her face, the plea in her voice had been a sucker punch straight to his heart. That was the last conversation he'd wanted to have with Ashley. Upsetting her. Angering her. Disappointing her.

Denying the one request she'd ever made of him.

He'd almost caved. *Almost.* But helping her would not only go against the code but also meant allowing her to get in the middle of this war, which was exactly where he didn't want her. He needed to figure out her reckless plan and stop her before it was too late.

Her defiance last night, when he was only trying to keep her out of the line of fire, still had him bristling.

"This is going to come to a head, sooner rather than later," JD said. "There's only room for one club in this town."

An unfortunate truth. It was the reason Todd had called a vote to split the club instead of replacing Rip as president. This left those not loyal to Todd isolated and vulnerable to attack.

Todd was eventually going to try to kill him unless Rip got to him first.

"Rather than a full-frontal confrontation, there's a better way to handle this," Rip said. "Ironside is mine. They can't bring in cash through it without me. The authorities already shut down their prostitution ring." He'd had no idea women were being trafficked and pimped out in portable tiny homes that routinely changed locations. But Todd had at least three or four degrees of separation preventing law enforcement from charging him. "The only thing left is drugs."

"I heard he's expanding that," JD said. "He's got big plans."

Rip nodded, having caught wind of the same rumors. "And we need to know what they are."

"It'll turn out like every other attempt to get Todd." Quill heaved a loud, long sigh laced with weariness. "Teflon won't go to jail."

Since the cops could never make a charge stick to Todd, the club had given him the apt nickname "Teflon."

Rip also doubted the man would ever see the inside of a prison cell and wasn't counting on Todd's arrest as part of his plan. "He's most likely getting his drugs from a cartel. We need to figure out the inner workings of his operation and bring the hammer down. Find a way to seize a shipment. A big one that he can't recover from financially. One that puts him in the crosshairs of the cartel."

"So they take him out for us," JD said.

Rip nodded. A lot of moving parts to piece together to make it happen. But possible.

"That might work," Quill said.

Based on the expressions of the others, they weren't opposed to the idea, but they weren't sold on it either.

"How are we supposed to do that?" asked Saul, one of the skeptics.

"We start with a weak link. A little guy in the food chain," Rip said. "One of his dealers. Someone who will talk to us, but also someone we can rattle to keep quiet about sharing information. Any ideas who we can squeeze?"

JD snapped his fingers. "Yates. He acts tough, but it's smoke-and-mirrors. I'm telling you that dude will rat to save himself when it comes down to it. I think he might even do it just because he doesn't like Todd and the way he gets treated."

Burk didn't respect many of his brothers. That was why it had come as such a shock to Rip that so many had sided with him. Was it out of coercion? Fear? Bribery?

It certainly wasn't out of loyalty or love.

"But what if Yates doesn't know enough?" Quill asked. "Todd is a slippery snake. I'm sure none of the dealers will know everything we need to make this happen."

A safe bet that Rip wouldn't wager against. Getting information from one of the dealers was only a maneuver that would lead to another. Rip had already made a preemptive move before he'd given Todd the clubhouse. He'd left behind a parting gift. A voice-activated audio transmitter with a SIM card hidden in the room or rather the *chapel*, where they held *church*, their official club meetings. When its built-in sensor detected a sound over sixty decibels, it automatically dialed a preset number, Rip's primary burner phone. Then he could listen in. Thus far, he hadn't learned anything noteworthy, but at the same time, it also meant Todd wasn't aware of the bug.

"Yates isn't going to be the endgame guy," Rip said. "One step at a time. First, we find out what he knows, then we take it from there." His men nodded. "Something else I need you to do. Talk to the boys who we thought were loyal, who we never assumed might side with a drug dealer. Find out why they're wearing different patches now." At the moment, Todd outmanned them. Anything Rip could do to whittle down the numbers and spare some good people jail time, he would. "And be discreet."

Chapter Four

Ashley zoomed the telephoto lens in on the front of the Hellhound clubhouse. Ten bikes were out front. Over the past several hours that she'd been seated in an unmarked patrol SUV across the street, she'd snapped pictures of six members. None of them had a limp. But instinct told her to be patient.

Apparently, the ones inside, whom she hadn't seen, weren't early risers. Nearly noon and they hadn't shown their faces yet. She didn't know if any women were inside. Besides the Harleys, no other vehicles were parked out front. Not that there couldn't be some concealed in the adjacent four-bay garage.

They'd accepted a food delivery about an hour ago.

Why were they all holed up in there on a Saturday instead of at home with girlfriends, wives, their families? Half of them had kids.

Mustering together, getting their stories straight.

She looked around. There wasn't much traffic out here on Rock Grinder Lane. No homes or businesses in the desolate area on the far outskirts of town, aside from a couple of warehouses farther down the dirt road, a trucking company and a defunct cement plant. Other than a few 18-wheelers and vans that had passed earlier, there was plenty of privacy for the OMG.

The front door of the clubhouse swung open. Todd Burk sauntered outside smoking a cigarette, followed by three members of his crew. One was average height and medium build. Another was a heavy guy with a barrel-shaped torso. The last guy, bringing up the rear, was tall and had a distinct limp. Every time he put weight on his bad leg, he winced.

"Gotcha," she muttered to herself, snapping pictures of them talking.

Not that she had fingerprints, a detailed description of them to go on, or any evidence to link them to the attack last night on Rip. But those were the perpetrators.

Ashley only had to prove it. She took a couple more photos.

Todd patted the tall one on the back, saying something to him and the others. The three guys nodded as Todd turned, glancing around. His gaze landed on her.

She zoomed in for a close-up of his face.

He smiled, though there was nothing pleasant about it. His grin was pure evil. He gestured for the others to go back inside, then he jogged across the lot through the opening in the gate, and over toward her.

Stay away from Burk. Rip's voice rang in her head.

But she had kept her distance. Nothing she could do about the man crossing the street. She certainly wasn't going to speed off like she feared him. Even though she'd been afraid of the man since she was seventeen.

Ashley set the camera in the passenger's seat, started the SUV and lowered her window. Heart thrumming, she unfastened the strap on the holster at her hip with the flick of her thumb and rested her hand on the butt of her duty weapon.

Todd took one last drag from his cigarette and flicked it to the ground.

"That's littering," she said as he approached.

"Good afternoon to you, too, Deputy Russo. Feel free to write me a citation. I'd be happy to pay. I must admit I'm surprised to see you here."

Anger always overrode her fear when she saw him, but this was the first time they'd come face-to-face and spoken. "Someone broke into Rip Lockwood's trailer last night and attacked him. I'm here investigating. You wouldn't happen to know anything about that, would you?"

"No, ma'am. A break-in and assault. How unfortunate. The thought of a former brother under siege." He gave a mock shiver. "Terrifying. It's good the sheriff's department is investigating. But it looks like you're just taking pictures. Which is fine. I welcome it. Nothing to hide. In fact, I was counting on someone from your department swinging by today." Another vicious grin tugged at his mouth. "Just surprised that it's you." He let that dangle between them for a moment. "Want to come on over, ask us some questions inside *my* clubhouse?"

No way that was happening. "Why are you surprised it's me out here?"

"Well, your boyfriend paid a steep price to keep the devil away from you, but in spite of that, here you are, taking pictures, in front of the devil's house. Tempting him." He licked his lips. "Not wise. I bet Rip doesn't know you're here. He would not be happy." Todd shook his head as though reprimanding a child.

"What price did Rip pay?"

He raised his eyebrows. "You don't know?" A dark chuckle rolled from him. "Then I can't say. I don't want to be the one to spoil the surprise. But the gesture was grand. Undeniably romantic. You should ask your boyfriend."

Hearing Rip referred to as her *boyfriend* irked and intrigued her. Why on earth would Todd or anyone else for that matter think such a thing?

"There's nothing personal between me and Rip," she said flatly, not wanting him to see he'd struck a nerve.

A look of surprise and she dared guess possibly even delight swept over his expression. "You're not his old lady?"

"Old lady?" That was a serious term of endearment reserved for a woman a biker was committed to. But there was nothing romantic or sexual between her and Rip. No *ship* of any kind. No relationship. No friendship. Nothing.

"Yeah. I get you wanting to keep it secret. You've both got to keep up appearances with you wearing a badge. But you can tell me. You two a thing?"

Something prickled through her, some kind of omen, at him pressing the question, at him asking at all. If people thought that, if the sheriff did, could it hurt her job, damage her reputation? "Not that it's any of your business, but no."

Wicked satisfaction spread wider over his face.

She realized with a sinking sensation in the pit of her stomach that she'd somehow made a mistake. But she'd only been honest.

Todd drew closer, resting his forearm on the frame of the open window.

She tightened her grip on her gun.

"You may not be intimate with your protector, but make no mistake, it's personal. Rip really should remedy that technicality." Todd sucked his teeth. "One never knows how much time they've got. Life can be short. With the slew of mishaps that he's endured recently, he probably hears a phantom clock counting down in his head. *Tick. Tock. Tick. Tock.*" He chuckled again, making her skin crawl. "Are you sure you don't want to come in?" He hiked a thumb over his shoulder at the clubhouse. "We make a mean cup of coffee. Could probably scrounge up a Danish or a doughnut for you, too."

"Yeah, I'm sure. The boys will all say they don't know anything, the same as you. Their alibi will be that they were here at the club."

"Sounds about right." He winked at her, and it was all she could do not to wrap her hands around his throat and squeeze. "Suit yourself, Deputy. You drive safely back to the station, you hear?" He tapped on her door, jogged back across the street and slowed to a hurried stride, disappearing into the clubhouse.

Doing a U-turn, she rolled up the window and cranked the heat. She headed toward town, churning over everything Todd had said. A lot to unpack.

No doubt in her mind, Rip was in grave danger.

As much as she wanted her concern for him to be strictly related to the operation she was planning and the part she had hoped he'd play, it was hard to deny that it was also deeply...personal.

Hating that Todd Burk had been the one to make her face that uncomfortable truth, to feel it, she groaned.

She glanced in the rearview mirror. Through the dust on the dirt road that her tires kicked up, she spotted a black van behind her.

Todd had expected the sheriff's department. Probably to question his crew about last night. Whenever they were interviewed, they always told the same lies, as if reading from a script that Todd wrote. But the way he'd been looking forward to the arrival of law enforcement was concerning.

It niggled at her even more how strangely pleased it made Todd to learn she wasn't Rip's woman.

Ashley watched the black van speed up a bit. She told herself that it couldn't be anyone after her. Not in broad daylight while she was in a patrol vehicle. But still she sensed something was off. Just nerves after speaking with Todd, her brother's murderer, inches away from her face, taunting her. Given that she'd yearned so long for justice, and she finally had a chance to hurt the man that had killed Angelo, who could blame her?

Pressing down on the gas, Ashley drove a little faster, anxious to get off the barren strip of road and to reach the well-populated town center.

The van stayed back behind her some distance. She couldn't make out the driver, front passenger or license plate in the cloud of dust. What had made her think the person behind the wheel had been chasing her?

Todd hadn't threatened her, and after all, she'd only been taking pictures.

Still, she couldn't shake the unease curling through her midsection. She got on the radio. "This is Russo, who else is on patrol?" With her splitting her time and focus between the sheriff's department and the DEA, she couldn't remember.

"It's your favorite deputy," Mitch Cody replied.

He was a good guy and they got along well. "Where are you right now?"

"Black Elk Trail. Why? What's up?"

Not far from her. Only a few minutes away. "It's nothing. I'm on Rock Grinder, passing Cloverleaf now," she said, referring to the cluster of dirt roads named after boot spurs. "I was over at the Hellhounds clubhouse. Had a chat with Burk."

"I'm sure it was pleasant." His voice was laced with sarcasm.

"He invited me in for coffee and doughnuts."

"Ooh la la. Aren't you special."

As a matter of fact, she got the impression that she was, somehow, because of Rip, but not in a good way. "Anyhow, there's a black van behind me. I can't make out the plate. I don't think it's following me. Probably from the trucking company." But she wasn't sure and that was what troubled her. "It's silly, but something in my gut told me to check in."

The van sped up, closing the distance between them.

"Never ignore your gut." His tone sobered. "I'll head your way."

Ahead, the road made a sharp turn to the right and then back to the left. Only a little farther and Rock Grinder would connect with the wider, better-paved main street into town, which Mitch would turn onto any second.

Ashley came around the corner as the sun peeked through the clouds, shining over the landscape. She caught the glint of something up on the horizon ahead of her. Checking the van's distance behind her in the rear-view mirror, she spotted a man lean out of the passenger's window, wearing a gaiter scarf pulled up over his nose, a second before she heard a loud distinctive crack—*a gunshot*—followed by another.

Both back tires on her patrol SUV blew.

Tightening her grip on the steering wheel, she fought to maintain control of the vehicle, but it was impossible. The rear end fishtailed, the tires skidding across the loose earth at the edge of the road. The SUV keeled hard to the right and rolled, sliding on its top before crashing into a tree in the ditch below the road, the passenger's-side window shattering on impact. The airbag deployed, making her cough from the dust particles released in the air.

Stunned, Ashley hung upside down, the seat belt cutting into her. The airbag was now hanging deflated in her face. For an instant, she couldn't move, couldn't breathe.

The sound of the other vehicle's engine roaring toward her fired her into action.

She hit the seat belt button, tumbling onto the headliner of the ceiling covered with pieces of the window. Glass shards cut into one palm. Aware the van had stopped, she drew her weapon and got back on the radio. "Shots fired. I repeat, shots fired. My tires were hit. My vehicle crashed in the dry ravine just before Nine-Point Star Trail. I'm in need of assistance. Suspects are still on the road."

Ashley fumbled for the door handle.

Jammed. The door wouldn't open.

If she crawled through the broken passenger's-side window that faced the road, it would leave her exposed to possible gunfire.

She aimed at the driver's window and pulled the trigger. Glass shattered.

The engine of the van revved and tires peeled off, screeching. She kicked away the remaining fragments of glass around the frame, scrambled out and got her bearings with her Glock at the ready.

Ashley ran up the incline, out of the ditch, and took aim. She fired two shots, one hitting the back door before the van turned onto the main road.

Sirens blared. Seconds later Mitch raced by in pursuit of Todd's thugs.

Drawing in a deep breath, she winced. Her ribs throbbed and her skull ached. She touched the wetness on her forehead and looked at her fingers. Blood.

Todd Burk had come after her.

Whatever protection Rip had provided over the years was gone and they were out of time.

Now, she needed to go after Burk. Tonight. There was no telling what might happen tomorrow.

PARKING AT THE crime scene at Fuller's Pharmacy, Ashley glanced around for the sheriff. She spotted Deputy Livingston suited up in protective clothing—white overalls with a hood, goggles, face mask, gloves and plastic overshoes—to prevent DNA cross contamination. Holding his kit, he headed inside. As she cut the engine, Sheriff Daniel Clark walked out of the pharmacy, tugging off his latex gloves.

Ashley climbed out of her truck. She was no longer woozy from the accident and the emergency room had cleared her for duty. No concussion and nothing broken. She ducked under the yellow police tape cordoning off the area in front of the drugstore.

"I heard about what happened," Sheriff Clark said. "Are you okay?" He gestured to the small bandage on her forehead.

"Only a scratch. It's fine."

"It's not fine," he said, his expression stern.

Of course, it wasn't. Deputy Mitch Cody had apprehended the driver and shooter. A couple of prospects, two young guys hoping to become full members of the Hellhounds.

"Did the perps talk?" he asked.

"They claim they didn't like the sheriff's department taking pictures and acted without any of the other Hellhounds' knowledge."

The sheriff pursed his lips. "And Burk? What did he have to say for himself?"

"According to Mitch, it was the same story. Burk even had the audacity to act horrified that potential members of his club would shoot at a cop."

"Do you think they went after you because of your association with Ripton Lockwood? Hurt him by hurting you?"

More likely to offend Rip than hurt him by going after

someone under his protection. It seemed like a leap, but then again Todd had a lot to say about Rip and the questions he'd asked her gave the impression he believed she was Rip's old lady. "Anything is possible."

"Regardless of the reason, I should've had you hand off this investigation to Cody first thing this morning. The MC has an issue with cops and an even bigger one with female cops."

Rip wasn't like that. He didn't have a problem with women in positions of power or authority, but when she'd joined the sheriff's department, he'd told her in no uncertain terms that he didn't care for her putting on the badge. Not because he disliked cops, but he didn't want her in harm's way, let alone pursuing the bad guys.

"Mitch has got it from here," she said.

"The Hellhounds and Todd Burk can't think they're going to get away with this. An attack on you is an attack on all of us. On the law itself. I'll pay them a visit later. Bring Cody and the fire department."

"Why the fire department?"

"Because I've got a sneaking suspicion that I'm going to smell smoke when I get there. Might have to bust through a few walls to make sure it's not electrical."

The sheriff was a good man and only wanted to look out for his people, but things were going to escalate. Todd's reign of terror was just getting started. The sooner he was dealt with the better for everyone. "What do you have inside?" she asked, wanting to change the subject.

"Homicide. Someone shot the pharmacist once in the head, twice in the chest and slit his throat."

"Unusual. Not what we typically see in a robbery." Perpetrators were normally in a rush to grab what they could and get away from the scene. "One in the head. Maybe in the chest. But not three bullets and a fatal knife wound."

"I think someone was sending a message," the sheriff said.

What kind of message and sent by whom? "Was it the father or the daughter?" Fuller's was the largest drugstore in town. Multigenerational, family owned and operated. Kind, decent people.

"Father. I need to track down the daughter to see what she knows. She was scheduled to work today. Looks like she logged in earlier on one of the computers, but there's been no sign of her."

Over his shoulder, Ashley watched the news station van along with the purple Jeep that belonged to journalist Erica Egan parking near the scene. "Media is here."

"I'm surprised it took them so long." The sheriff glanced behind him. "I better go speak with them. Did you need something? Shouldn't you be resting?"

No rest for the weary. Or the wicked. "The hospital cleared me. I just wanted you to know I'm going dark for the next couple of days."

"The DEA is sending you undercover?"

Debating again about whether to be forthright with the sheriff, she decided against it. "Something like that. The situation is urgent. A window is open. Now or never." She had jumped at the chance to be assigned as a liaison to the DEA's Rocky Mountain task force. Finally, she thought she'd be able to cut off Todd Burk's drug operation at the source. How naive she had been to assume the DEA cared about her small town or any of the others that Burk was poisoning. They had their own targets and objectives, and though she'd done plenty of good work with them, none of it had brought her any closer to her goal of stopping Burk.

So she was going undercover. Technically, she was still attached to the task force and working within the constructs of their mandate, but the DEA wasn't directly sending her. "I'm tracking down the drug supplier to the—" she caught herself from saying *the Iron Warriors*, the change was still surreal "—Hellhounds. I'll be out of pocket and unreachable until I'm done."

"Can you say where you're going?"

The less he knew the better for them both. In case things went awry, she didn't want any of this to blow back on him. Only her butt would be in a sling. "North."

"Tell Agent Welliver to keep you safe. I want my deputy back in one piece, preferably unharmed."

This went against her instincts, her training, her deep-seated desire to do things by the book, but drugs had now spread to the high school. Kids were getting addicted and dying younger and younger. Lives were at stake. Including Rip's and hers. This was bigger than the rules. It might be the only way to clean up the town and get rid of Todd Burk.

Just this once, she had to go rogue.

She gave the sheriff a measured smile. "I'll let you know as soon as I get back."

"You do that." He turned toward the media approaching the crime scene.

Her cell phone rang. Heading to her truck, she pulled it from her pocket and looked at the caller ID. The man must have a sixth sense. "Russo," she answered.

"Checking to see if you're squared away," Agent Welliver said. "Were you able to get Lockwood as an asset?"

"Not quite." She got into her truck out of the cold and started the engine.

"My recommendation is to keep working on him. I did a deep dive into Lockwood. No red flags other than his association with the motorcycle club. Honorable discharge from the military. Glowing performance reviews. His last commander said that Ripton was a man of focus, commitment and sheer will. He'll be your best way in and with his Special Forces background as a Marine Raider, you couldn't have a better person at your side."

She swallowed her bitter disappointment. It could take weeks to convince him to help her, and with Burk getting more hostile with each passing day, they were out of time. "If you could assign one of your agents to assist me for a couple of days—"

"We've been through this. The DEA is after big fish. Major dealers. Heavyweight gangs. Cartels. Not low-level dealers. The best I can do is pass along any intelligence to you that might be of interest."

According to one of Welliver's informants, a small motorcycle club in southern Wyoming, which had been narrowed down to her town, got their drugs from a pill mill—a place where bad doctors and clinics handed out prescription drugs like candy—and made their contact through someone known as LA, who was with another MC. The Sons of Chaos up in Bitterroot Gulch.

The town was outside of her jurisdiction as a deputy, but as a liaison of the task force, she had legal authority throughout the province of the Rocky Mountain Division of the DEA to investigate.

"Maybe the sheriff can get another deputy to help you," Welliver suggested.

They were short-staffed as it was, and Sheriff Clark was under the impression she was getting all the support she needed from the DEA. Her approach was thorny and not without great personal and professional risk, but necessary.

"That won't be possible," she said.

"Probably for the best anyway. You'll need a real biker with you to get anything out of the Sons. You need Lockwood."

Shaking her head, she slapped the steering wheel. "I've tried."

"Have I taught you nothing?" Welliver gave a dry chuckle. "Try harder."

The lessons she'd learned from him had been hard and ugly and most she wanted to forget. He operated in the gray, as she was doing now, all for the greater good. If she succeeded in this and needed DEA cover in explaining her actions, he'd provide it. If her op fell apart, then—

"You've mentioned that he feels protective of you. Something to do with the death of your brother. Exploit it. Better yet, sleep with him."

The suggestion was a complete blindside, leaving her stomach fluttering. First Burk, now Welliver. "What, sir?"

"If you do, I think you'll have him wrapped around your little finger."

"No, it wouldn't work." Not on Rip. He wouldn't take the bait. Even if she thought that he might, she'd never consider doing it.

"Might sound indecent but agents use a honey trap on occasion because it does work. If he's been protecting you from the Warriors all this time, then there's an emotional element that runs deeper than guilt or obligation. Trust me. If you get physical with him, the guy will do whatever you ask. I can practically guarantee he'll help."

"I can't."

Not that Rip was lacking in physical appeal. It was the exact opposite. Last night when he'd touched her, there had been something beneath the anger, a different kind of heat. No matter how hard she tried to convince herself the sparks had merely been a product of the argument mixed with adrenaline, she still wondered what his lips would feel like on hers.

Every time he'd visit, the rumble of his bike drawing closer, a thrill of anticipation went through her. After a while, she'd stopped feeling guilty about the way her pulse quickened when he came into sight. He had a way of pushing her buttons. Every single one of them. Gave her that strange, fluttery feeling with a look. Made her thighs tingle with simple innuendo. She'd always suspected he'd be an amazing lover. Once, after a couple of shots of tequila from the bottle he'd brought over, she'd been tempted to invite him to her bedroom for dirty, hot, pity sex, no strings attached, but then he'd addressed her as deputy, and the thought of Angelo and Burk—a man Rip viewed as his MC brother—had sobered her.

Why did Rip have to be a biker?

Then again, a dyed-in-the-wool biker was precisely what she needed right now.

Regardless of how much she wanted justice, she wouldn't trade her body, manipulate Rip using feminine wiles. Not that it would work anyway. Rip's charm could come across as flirtatious, but he wasn't attracted to her. Constantly reminding her she was nothing more to him than a deputy and an obligation.

"That's not a line I'm comfortable crossing," she added. "I won't operate that way. I'll find his pressure point and push."

But she already had, and it hadn't worked.

"Then Russo, you need to find an active *trigger* point. The difference being the latter is very painful. And make it hurt when you push. I'm talking excruciating. If your op turns up anything worth my while, let me know. Remember, you can't do this alone. To try would be suicide. Good luck." Welliver disconnected.

Ashley racked her brain over how to persuade Rip to do this without seducing him. Because that was not an option. He was against the dealing of drugs and had big reasons to take down Burk. Now more than ever. But working with a cop went against his MC code.

She had to give him a compelling justification to overlook that detail. Something he couldn't ignore. Something bigger than that code. Maybe she'd been too careful last night about not revealing her plan. He'd only help her if he understood the magnitude of the risk she was taking, the high degree of danger involved.

Being cagey like him got her nowhere.

The one thing she couldn't share quite yet was that Todd had sent his prospects after her. Telling Rip would only distract him from the bigger picture. Knocking Todd's lights out would be temporary and would only provoke the devil to act more violently. The only real solution was putting an end to Burk's drug business and locking him up behind bars.

To do that, she would have to trust Rip. She needed to put the rest of her cards on the table with him and let the chips fall where they may.

She took out her phone and sent Rip a text message.

Your gun is cleared. I'll give it back. Meet me at Angelo's grave. Thirty minutes.

Chapter Five

Rip had a bad feeling about meeting the deputy, much less at her brother's grave. Yet, there he was, riding his Harley, headed for Millstone Cemetery.

Deep in his gut he knew she was still determined to carry out whatever plan she had, no matter how dangerous.

He was equally determined to keep her from painting a bull's-eye on her back.

Pulling up to the cemetery, he spotted Ashley's parked truck and something inside his chest clenched.

Chance had put him on a collision course with her seven years ago. Rip had heard about his brother's arrest, taken leave from the Marines and gone home to find out what happened. While there, Quill had told him about Angelo Russo. A first-year college student who had been in the wrong place at the wrong time and witnessed Todd trying to take advantage of a teenage girl. Todd had killed Angelo. Threatened the girl and her family into staying quiet. And had gotten rid of the gun tying him to the crime.

All speculation and deduction. Todd had only ever alluded to being responsible, at least to Rip.

Quill had insisted Rip go with him to the funeral to pay their respects to the family. At the time, he didn't understand why the older biker wanted him to go, but once there, he realized it had been an emotional ambush.

"*Your father always wanted you to be an Iron Warrior,*" Quill said.

"*And I joined.*" He'd wanted to wear a cut and ride a Harley since he was five, but the club didn't fulfill him the way he had imagined it would. Fantasy had been better than reality.

"*Only to leave. When you were meant to lead.*"

The Marines had given him an unexpected sense of purpose and belonging and family the MC never had. Just like Ida told him it would. "*I'm on the career track.*" He'd gotten great assignments, tough, but career-builders that put him in the fast lane for promotion. "*I was thinking about being a lifer.*"

A four-year enlistment had turned into ten. Why not make it a full twenty or more?

"*A lifer?*" The dismay in Quill's voice was cutting. "*You made a vow to us first.*"

"*I'm still an Iron Warrior. Wear my colors whenever I ride, no matter where I am in the world. When I'm here, I attend church,*" he said, referring to their meetings.

"*Not good enough. Your leaving created a vacuum that Todd Burk has filled. The boy is a bad seed. Has sway like I've never seen before. If you had been here, in charge of the club instead of Larson, the way you were supposed to be, the way your father meant you to be, none of this would've happened. Your brother wouldn't be in jail along with those others. It was Todd who put them up to the robbery. And Angelo Russo wouldn't be dead,*" Quill said, the words stabbing Rip like a hot knife to the gut. "*The only reason Burk felt so confident and cocky to kill that kid is because he's got a gang on his side. You never would've allowed that snake to wear the patch and get a choke hold on the MC by getting more filth like him to join. Todd is running amok, getting worse every year, and will drag the club in a direction it was never intended to go by any of the founding members like me and your father. This is on you, Rip. You were selfish and ran away from your responsibility. There are many who'd still support you to take up the mantle. How many more brothers need to get locked up? How many more kids need to die before you take your place as president?"*

"Is it true? You could've prevented this?" a tiny female voice said as a teenage girl dressed in black, with dark brown hair in two long braids, stepped out from behind a tree. Her face was still damp, her cheeks flushed, her eyes swollen and red from crying during the service. Ashley Russo. "It's your fault my brother's dead?"

The men make the club. *He'd heard that a thousand times. The president guided the MC, but his real power resided in whom he did and didn't allow into the club. One devil could be like a cancer, spreading, eating away at what was healthy, slowly killing what was once good.*

The Iron Warriors always had a dark side, but didn't abide rape and didn't gun down teens. Quill and a few of the others had been grooming Rip to lead. Someone young, strong, principled, with fresh ideas, who would protect the moral constructs of the bylaws. But he'd never wanted the job, which they'd said made him perfect for it. And so, he'd run from the responsibility to lead.

Rip was an eerily excellent judge of character, the closest thing he had to a superpower, and never would've let someone like Todd Burk join if he had been president. The Iron Warriors were supposed to defend the town. Not decimate it.

As he stared at the girl, seeing the devastation in her eyes, the sorrow on her face, her pain called to him, and with his heart aching for her, he gave the only answer that he could. "Yes."

Her anguish flipped to anger. She stormed up to him and slapped him hard, her small palm making his cheek sting. "Then you should've been here!" She curled her hands into fists and beat his chest. "You should've stopped him!" Her screams were bloodcurdling, the sound resonating in his soul as she shouted and sobbed.

Quill moved to grab her, but Rip held out an arm, stopping him.

This innocent young woman was grieving and in anguish. She couldn't do this to Burk, but she could do it to Rip. And he let her.

Until her parents raced over, horrified. It took them both to haul the slip of a girl off him.

"I'm going to kill him!" she cried. "I'm going to kill Todd Burk!"

"Stay away from Burk," Rip said, his voice low and firm. "I'll take care of him."

"She didn't mean it," Mr. Russo said, his voice shaky with fear.

"I meant it!" the young woman spit out. "I'll kill!"

"Please don't let that animal hurt her." Mrs. Russo's face was awash in agony and alarm. "He's already taken our son. Don't let him take our daughter, too."

"I'll protect her." Rip took a tentative step toward them but stopped when the mother cringed and the father held up a hand in warning. "No Iron Warrior will hurt her. I swear it."

The girl's parents wrapped their arms around her and hurried away.

"How are you going to keep that promise?" Quill asked.

Rip turned to him. "I haven't signed my reenlistment

contract yet." Something kept telling him to wait. To hold off as long as possible. Most Marines had to sign twelve months before their service date ended. Raiders could wait up to six months, a special exception that no one talked about, because of the stressors of the job. "Rustle up support for me in a vote as president. I've got a ton of leave saved up. I'll be back as soon as I can. Until then, I want the girl to be watched and protected. Make sure she stays away from Todd and vice versa. Anyone who messes with her, even looks at her wrong, they'll have to deal with me."

RIP CAUGHT SIGHT of Ashley. She was kneeling at her brother's grave, brushing leaves off the headstone. As he approached her, he braced himself for yet another ambush.

He eased up alongside her. "I know why you asked me to come here. Effective, I'll give you that." Being back at Angelo's grave was a poignant kick to the gut. "But my answer will still be the same. I need you to trust that I have a plan to take care of Burk." He'd told her he would handle it and for too long he hadn't. But this time would be different.

Standing up, she gave him his gun.

His gaze flew to the bandage on her forehead. "What happened to you?" he asked, erasing the distance between them. "Are you all right?" He reached for her face, and she jerked away.

"Car accident. This is nothing," she said, gesturing to her head.

It took every drop of self-restraint not to reach for her again and double-check she was okay. She stood there, staring him down with those expressive eyes, and he suspected she'd only shoo him away once more if he tried.

To give himself something to do with his hands, he tucked the gun into his ankle holster. "How did you get into an accident?" She was proficient at everything. Always so serious and scrupulous. An excellent defensive driver.

"That's not what I want to discuss," she said. "You think you know why I asked you to come here, but you're wrong."

Silence fell between them. Not in a hurry to fill it, he waited for her spiel, steeling himself not to let whatever she had to say weaken his resolve.

Her face was stiff, her body tense, her obvious dislike of him palpable, which for some reason made him want to draw closer when he needed to stay as far away from her as possible.

"Once I leave the cemetery," she said, "I'm heading up to Bitterroot Gulch. Someone in the Sons of Chaos hooked Todd Burk up to his supplier. I'm going to find who and I'm going to cut off his drug operation at the source."

As she spoke it was like an invisible hand had reached into his chest and grabbed hold of his heart and squeezed. "You make it sound so simple."

"There's a difference between simple and easy. Regardless, it has to be done."

"The Sons are no joke." He knew those guys and was well acquainted with their president, Ben Stryker. Rip had a couple of things in common with the man. They were both prior military and tough as nails, but that was where the similarities ended. That gang wasn't to be trifled with. "You're playing with fire and you're going to get burned. If they find out you're a cop, they won't hesitate to do unspeakable things to you and then kill you."

She hiked her chin up at him, her expression so stubborn and her face so beautiful it hurt to look at her. "I guess I better not let them find out."

Scrappy as ever.

"You can't just walk in there and pretend with that group.

Have you even been trained for undercover work?" He seriously doubted it. She might be able to dress the part, but that was all. If by some miracle they didn't see beneath the facade she tried to put on, then they'd be entirely focused on her as a woman. Waves of dark brown hair and fiercely vibrant whiskey-colored eyes in a striking face that was a real gut check. Not to mention her body. Guaranteed to destroy a man. Heat prickled the back of his neck thinking about the way they'd look at her. They'd treat her like a biker groupie, though they had cruder terms, whose sole purpose was to slake the appetite of the guys. None of the above options was acceptable. "The Sons are a pack of animals. Those guys are a brutal, cutthroat bunch."

"That's why I need you. But since you refuse to help me, I'll have to do it alone."

Alone? "Sheriff Clark can't send you in there with no backup," he said, searching her face, and then saw the unthinkable.

She averted her gaze, a slight tilt of her head, as though hiding something, but also folded her arms, a defensive posture. He not only watched out for her, but he'd also studied her, knew her tells.

"He's not sending you, is he?"

"I'm on a task force with the DEA," she said, still not looking at him.

A chill slithered down his spine. "They most certainly wouldn't send you in alone."

"They go undercover alone all the time."

"It's what they're trained for. Not you."

"I can pull it off." But uncertainty flashed in her eyes.

"You're a lousy liar, Ash. You wouldn't even be able to bluff your way through a hand of poker with them. You can't seriously be thinking about trying to infiltrate the Sons of Chaos to get information. What are you playing at?"

"This isn't a game. And I'm done thinking about it. I'm doing it. Today."

"You're jumping into this too fast." She'd only first approached him about this yesterday.

"It has to be tonight," she said. "I can't afford to wait any longer."

"Why not?"

Averting her gaze again, she touched the bandage on her forehead. Then she caught herself and dropped her hand.

"How did you get into an accident?" he demanded.

"Work," she said, flatly, the one-word response not telling him a thing. "There's a window of opportunity with the Sons of Chaos. A Saturday night is my best chance. I'm going to do this."

Why was she rushing? "Hold off one week, and I'll give it serious consideration," he said, testing her. Considering and doing were not necessarily the same. A lot could happen in seven days to change her mind.

Her eyebrows drew together in contemplation that lasted a blink. "I can't wait that long. It has to be now."

"How about I call Sheriff Clark and see what he has to say about your plan?" he asked, not really thinking it through. He wouldn't jeopardize her job, but he also couldn't let her flirt with disaster.

Ashley whipped out her cell phone, pried off the back cover, and popped the battery out. "Go ahead." She shrugged. "The sheriff knows I've gone dark. And by the time you get him to believe you, president of the Iron Warriors, over me, his trusted deputy, which will take a while, it'll be too late."

Frustration burned at the back of his throat. What was she doing? "This is madness. I could call the Sons, tell them you're coming." Not that he had a number to simply dial, but if he dug, he might be able to get one.

"As you pointed out, they'll kill a cop. That's not the kind of call you'd make."

True. He'd never endanger her that way. "No matter how this shakes out, your job will be on the line if you try to go through with this."

Another shrug from her. "The only reason I ever put on the badge in the first place was to get Todd Burk. If I accomplish the goal, all will be forgiven. If I fail, the prospect of getting fired won't matter because my parents will have to bury me here—" she pointed to the empty plot beside her brother's "—next to Angelo."

She was willing to risk her badge and her life. "You would do that to your mother and father? They shouldn't have to bury another child."

Her eyes hardened. She was gearing up to be even more defiant, and in that moment, she reminded him of the innocent, reckless, daring-to-be-fearless girl who had slapped and punched him in this very cemetery. A different kind of man, a different kind of biker, would've made her pay for it. Might have even hit her back. But that wasn't him. All he had wanted back then was to take away her pain and keep her safe. The same as he did now.

"You would be the one doing it to them," she countered.

Too headstrong for her own good.

"You're asking me to break a vow," he said. "I'd give my life for you but that I won't do. Not even for you." If only she knew how much he'd already done and was willing to do on her behalf.

"I'm not asking you to break one. I'm asking you to keep two. You swore," she said, jabbing his chest with her finger, "justice for Angelo and to protect me. I'm asking you to keep both vows now. Or have you been stringing me along, simply placating me all this time?" Her words sucked the air right out of his lungs. "You can stay here and continue to do nothing besides offer platitudes and make empty promises. Or you can come with me. Help me. Not because I'm a deputy. Because I'm a sister seeking justice for her brother. A woman desperate to make her town safe again. Protect me, like you swore you'd do."

"I've been protecting you since you were seventeen." It hadn't been easy, especially once she became a law enforcement officer. The sacrifices he'd made, the scrutiny he'd been under. And now, no longer having the full might and force of his club behind him, with his chapter divided, could he still keep her safe while Todd remained unchecked? "Let me go instead of you. Stay here, out of unnecessary danger."

Her lips firmed. "Danger is everywhere. Closing in every day."

"For me, yeah. But you can stay away from it rather than throwing yourself headlong into it."

"For you *and* me," she said, and he wondered what she meant. "For the whole town. There's no hiding from it." She took a deep, shaky breath and let it out. "You think it's perfectly fine for you to go out and risk your life while there are different rules when it comes to me? I don't think so. This is my fight. I'm not sitting on the sidelines. Todd Burk has to pay for everything he's done. And I aim to be the person collecting."

The need for justice had driven her to become a cop, and he suspected it haunted her like a ghost, overshadowing every decision she made.

"Not just for my brother," she added, "but for everyone Burk has hurt or poisoned or killed. Get me through this with the Sons of Chaos and help me track down the supplier and, regardless of the outcome, any debt to me will be paid."

She was doing her best to box him in.

And he hated it.

She was a complication that he didn't need or want.

"Don't do this, Ash."

She eased forward, coming so close the tips of their boots touched, their bodies brushing. To a passerby, they probably looked like lovers, and that thought sent an ache through him.

Ashley tipped her head back, looking up at him. "Is there anything between us, besides your sense of responsibility?" She moistened her pink lips, and his gaze fell to her mouth and snagged there a moment. "Anything more?"

For him, plenty more.

Plenty that ran far deeper than he wanted her to know because she was off-limits. Every time his efforts at friendship with her had been met with skepticism or cool curiosity, a part of him was grateful he had failed to get closer. Because deep down when he paid her visits at her house, he no longer wanted to be confined to the kitchen and was ready to be invited into her bedroom. She stirred up his protective instincts as well as his desire. A powerful combination he was finding hard to resist.

But to tell her as much would give her ammunition to use against him and only a fool would do such a thing. "Anything more, like what?"

Stepping back, she lowered her head. "Never mind." She swallowed hard, her throat muscles jumping with the movement, and shoved her hair behind an ear. "I'm going with or without you. I'll follow this lead and put an end to Burk's drug trade, hitting him where it hurts, even if it's the last thing I ever do. The choice is yours, Rip. Whatever you decide, remember that you'll have to live with it." She marched off without giving him a chance to utter a response.

An icy breeze sliced through his jacket. He didn't mind the cold. In fact, he embraced the frosty wind. It helped cool off his temper so he could think straight. He had a lot to process.

Everything about this predicament grated. Ash going undercover. Rushing in. Unprepared. Unauthorized. With the Sons of Chaos. All alone.

His rule-abiding deputy was suddenly playing fast and loose with every rule in the book. And so help him, she was going to get herself killed.

Chapter Six

A tricky thing—not showing a hint of fear around those who could smell it, like sharks catching the scent of blood in the water. Even more challenging when it was the one emotion Ashley felt, second only to her resolve.

Being afraid did have the upside of keeping her mind sharp.

She sat sipping cola at the bar in Happy Jack's Roadhouse, doing her best to appear relaxed. In the mirror behind the shelves lined with alcohol, she looked over the twenty or so heavily muscled, tattooed bikers wearing leather vests with varying amounts of patches adorning them. Some wore hoodies or long-sleeved shirts under their cuts while a couple wore nothing at all despite the frigid temperature outside.

The Sons of Chaos owned the roadhouse—a seedy dive on the main floor with their private clubhouse upstairs—as well as the rinky-dink motel next door where she'd parked her truck in case she needed to make an inconspicuous getaway. The outlaw biker group used both businesses to launder money.

Two nights a week were open to the public. Thursdays were only for ladies looking to have the thrill of being with a biker. On Saturdays anyone, except for cops, was welcomed, making it the one night of the week she'd risk strolling in as long as she didn't have her badge. But she had gambled that she would also have Rip at her side and lost.

A flashing neon sign in front proclaiming Crime Happens Here had given her pause, but she'd still sauntered past the lined-up assortment of customized Harley Davidsons and hot rods into the roadhouse.

Inside, the place was crawling with bikers, their women, prospects. She'd spotted their president, a man they called Stryker, along with the vice president, but they were constantly surrounded by others. A couple dozen ordinary Joes and Janes were in the mix, playing pool, throwing darts, grabbing a bite to eat, dancing. Most of the women really should have been wearing more clothing than they had on. Attire ranged from sexy casual to downright skimpy. One even dared to prance around in cutoff shorts and cowboy boots. No way she was riding the back of a bike dressed like that in November.

To Ashley's surprise, more than a handful of women sported denim cuts that, on the back, read *Property Of* along with a man's name at the bottom.

The Iron Warriors had never considered any of the women they associated with or loved as property. And they had a policy of accepting any male prospect they deemed worthy regardless of skin color. A stark distinction from the Sons as she looked around, but they didn't seem to mind diversity among their groupies.

Feeling silly in her getup, Ashley kneaded the muscles in the back of her neck. Skinny jeans so tight she could barely breathe. Thigh-high boots. Backless, cropped, halter top. She was aiming to blend in and had overshot beyond her comfort level, going a tad too revealing. The problem was she had never had the wild, party phase. Her life since her brother's murder had all been about being prim and proper and then being a deputy. No parties. Hardly dating since guys seemed to lose interest after one dinner. She didn't really do makeup. And never did *this*—go to a bar and flirt with men to get information.

She wished she'd kept on her leather jacket after a big, brawny, hairy brute claimed the stool beside her and wouldn't stop trying to chat her up.

"Hotties don't pay for drinks." He leaned closer, his breath smelling of liquor and garlic. "Her next one is on us," he said to the bartender, who nodded.

"Thanks." She caught herself cringing ever so slightly in the mirror and forced herself to straighten and smile. "But I'm good."

He rested his massive hands flat on the bar top. Tattoos were inked on his blunt knuckles. From her vantage point, it took her several seconds to decipher what the upside-down letters spelled.

Lost. Soul.

Instead of *O*'s there were skulls.

She imagined how much damage those hands could do. Fists through walls and windows. Pounding flesh and cracking bone. The answer was a *lot* of damage. Not feasible taking him one-on-one, in the event things went awry. In spite of his relentless interest, this Neanderthal wasn't the right one to probe for information.

"Not much of a talker, are you?" he asked.

"Only when I have something to say."

He grinned, making the corded muscle of his inked neck flex. "I like the quiet ones." He put a meaty hand on her thigh. "Less talk. More action," he said, making her stomach twist.

The biker stroked her leg. His touch was worse than cobwebs across her face in a dark basement. She resisted the overwhelming urge to jerk away.

Picking up her drink, she spun 180 degrees on the stool, removing his hand discreetly. She looked around, trying to give him the message to move on. Her gaze kept darting to the door. Part of her clung to the unlikely possibility that Rip would walk into the roadhouse any second. She'd been in Bitterroot Gulch for over an hour. It took time to surveil the place, change into this ridiculous outfit and muster the courage to go inside.

Rip would've been there by now if he was coming.

She'd wanted to trust that his vow to protect her had been real. Not some hollow line. That when faced with the choice between keeping the MC's code and keeping his vow to her, he'd pick her in the end. To meet his responsibility to get rid of Burk head-on, so she no longer had a reason to hold any grudge against him.

A motorcycle growled up outside. A sliver of hope percolated in her chest. Seconds later, the door swung open.

Another biker waltzed in with his arm slung over the shoulder of a redhead.

Her heart dropped. It wasn't Rip.

I'd give my life for you.

That was what he'd told her, but Rip was a liar.

He always seemed to be there when she needed him. Flat tire on a dark road. He'd happened to ride by and changed it. As she was dropping off groceries at the soup kitchen, hands full, he'd appeared out of nowhere before a downpour started. Held an umbrella over her head and helped her carry the bags inside. The night she'd had too much to drink in a bar that never should've served her since she was underage, he'd snatched the car keys from her hand and taken her home. She'd come to expect Rip to be there, especially at a time like now.

If she was being honest with herself, it went much

deeper. She wanted to know he truly cared about her for some silly reason. Maybe because he'd spent so many years striking up casual chats that felt intensely intimate and got her to admit personal things, swinging by her house at night to make sure she was doing okay, giving her piercing looks that reached into her soul and heated her belly, trying to convince her he did care until she almost believed him.

She didn't want to simply be an obligation. She wanted to be a choice. For him to choose her. Not that any of it made sense.

Worse, she was such a fool for thinking the twisted bond they had ever meant anything.

"I'm Jimmy." The big scary biker turned around on his stool and rubbed the side of his leg against hers. "What's your name, sweetness?"

Why couldn't he take a hint? She crossed her legs, eradicating the contact. "Would you believe me if I said Sugar?"

"No, but I'm happy to call you whatever you want."

If this situation had the potential to turn into a brush-fire, then this guy was gasoline.

Her plan had been to chat up one of the ladies affiliated with the club, get a feel for which Son to approach. But her stalker had been all over her the second she walked in.

Maybe if she didn't make any more eye contact with him, he would buzz off.

"Yo, Jimmy." A Son wearing a red bandanna tied around his head strutted up along the other side of her. "Can't you see she's not interested? Time to give someone else a crack at her."

Jimmy swore as he made a vulgar hand gesture.

The other guy laughed, not intimidated. "Leave her alone, man. I heard your old lady is on the way over. If she sees you talking to her, she'll cut this chick. And I kind of like her face the way it is."

"Me, too," Ashley said, shifting in her seat toward Red Bandanna. "Would love to keep it unblemished."

Swearing again, Jimmy got up and skulked off.

"Thanks for saving me from his old lady's switchblade," she said.

"She's not really coming. When he finds out, he'll be back. So you've got until then to sit on my lap and show me some gratitude," he said, and a sour taste coated her tongue. He called over to the bartender. "Give me a Coke like the lady."

Red Bandanna had been watching and listening. She wasn't sure if she should be flattered or concerned.

"No shots or a beer for you?" she asked, putting on a pleasant smile.

"Been clean for two years."

She swallowed a groan at having first drawn a scary creep and now the only sober guy in the place. Would he even have the information she needed?

"Congratulations." She set her glass down on the bar. "Excuse me, I need to use the bathroom."

What she really needed was to regroup.

She hopped off the stool, grabbing her purse and leaving her jacket. The restrooms were situated partway down a short, narrow hall. At the end of the dimly lit corridor, she spotted the neon red Exit sign. For a moment, she considered using it. Just pushing through the door and getting out of that place. But she'd come here to achieve an objective. Running from the Sons of Chaos and Bitterroot Gulch would only lead her home, where Todd was waiting. She had to stay and finish what she had set out to do.

Besides, on taking a closer look at the door, she saw a sign that read Emergencies Only, Alarm Will Ring.

Ashley shoved into the bathroom. Going to the sink, she opened her purse. Inside it, she flicked off the safety on her personal firearm. A Beretta, and beside it was another gift from Rip. A stun gun. She had the unsettling sense she might have to use one or both before the night was over.

Staring at her reflection in the mirror, she washed her hands. The rough bangs she'd cut herself to hide the gash on her forehead didn't look too bad. She pulled red lipstick from her purse and reapplied. That and some mascara was the extent of her makeup, and fortunately it had been enough to attract two bikers.

Only the wrong two.

She had to make the most of Red Bandanna. He might not know about the drug supplier, but he could find out for her. She just had to be more persuasive with him than she had been with Rip.

Ashley finished drying her hands and tossed the paper towels in the trash bin. She opened the door, leaving the bathroom, and ran into a wall of muscle and the stench of alcohol. "Jimmy."

Before he muttered anything, she rushed past him into the hall, making a beeline for the main area. The last thing she needed was for him to force her back into the restroom, where he'd have her cornered and she'd have to use her gun. The equivalent of pouring gasoline on the brushfire. All the Sons of Chaos would come running.

Her new objective was to get out of that hallway unscathed.

"Hey." In a few strides, Jimmy was in front of her with a hand planted on the wall, blocking her from taking another step. "My old lady isn't coming. We're free to have some fun."

She suspected they had very different definitions of *fun*. "I don't want any trouble. Just another drink at the bar."

Ducking under his arm, she scrambled to escape out of the narrow, dim corridor but didn't get far.

He wrapped his arms, thick as tree trunks, around her waist, hauled her to him and swung her around, pushing her back against the wall. "Let's go take a ride on my bike. What do you say?"

Her heart thundered in her ears and her body turned to lead. "Not interested."

"First time I ever met a *mama* who wasn't."

She always found the word odd used in such context, but uglier terms existed. "Maybe that's because I'm not a groupie."

He grabbed her bare arms, pinning her to the wall, and leaned closer. "Then why are you here, Sugar?"

The hairs on Ashley's neck pricked as fear washed over her. She'd have to roll the dice with Jimmy instead of Red Bandanna. "Drugs."

"Selling?" He cocked his head to the side. "Or buying?"

She raised her chin. "Buying."

"Why didn't you say so? I can hook you up." He pulled out a little baggie with a variety of pills, keeping a strong grip on her arm. "Name your pleasure."

"I'm looking for more than you can supply. A lot more. I heard LA is the one to talk to. Can you introduce me to him?"

"Him, huh?" Jimmy's eyebrows knitted together as he narrowed his eyes. "How about you pop a pill first to prove you're not a cop?"

She didn't let any fear show even though the emotion nearly suffocated her.

"How about you take your hand off her and back away!" a deep, familiar voice said, making her pulse spike.

A voice that haunted her dreams. Rough and husky. Dangerous as a blade.

Rip.

Ferocious energy pumped off him as he stormed down the hall toward them. His eyes blazed with fury.

He came.

Her heart did a somersault in her chest, relief surging in her veins. She'd never been happier to set eyes on him.

"Saw her first," Jimmy said. "You'll have to wait until I'm finished."

Four bikers hurried down the hall behind Rip. More Sons of Chaos.

Can't be good.

"I say you're done. Right now. You've got two choices." Rip stepped up to him until they were toe to toe. He was dressed all in black, only his patches adding pops of color. "Remove your hand or I break it."

Jimmy's gaze raked over Rip's cut under his sheepskin jacket. "I don't care if you're a Prez or not. This is the Sons' house."

"And this is my old lady," Rip ground out with a fierce intensity that sent a shiver through her.

Jimmy hesitated, eyes flaring wide, like the words had stunned him as much as they had her.

She understood enough about biker culture to know that it meant she was off-limits to everyone else, regardless of club association.

Jimmy dropped his hand as if it had been burned and then raised both palms. "She didn't say anything about having an old man."

Rip advanced on him, vibrating with rage, fists at his sides. Jimmy staggered backward.

One of the Sons clasped Rip on the shoulder. "Ease up, Rip, he didn't know," Stryker said. "Misplaced anger. Your old lady should've told us."

"Yeah, you're right." Rip whirled and shot her a look that could cut through steel. Those intense blue-gray eyes of his stayed locked onto her as he closed the distance between them in two quick, threatening strides, causing her stomach to go into freefall.

Her pulse beat wildly as she stood rooted to the spot, strangely transfixed.

He pointed a finger in her face, something he'd never done before. "Next time you make it clear you're mine." The rough and rumbly words made her skin tingle. "Better yet, listen to me and when I tell you *not* to do something…" He let his voice trail off, his gaze boring into her, and the longer the silence stretched on, the more her nerves tightened until she trembled. "Don't do it," he said, in a deep, throaty growl.

She opened her mouth to give him some argument, but her mind blanked. "Sorry, baby." The words slipped out in a whisper.

He brought his hands up, cupping her cheeks, tilted her face toward his, and claimed her lips with his own.

Rip was kissing her. And it was hot and unyielding and possessive. Not controlled and characteristic of his rigid discipline. Or anything like she imagined, and she had thought about it whenever she drew too close to him.

But this was different. He was kissing her like he was starving. Consuming her. Needed her more than his next breath.

His tongue plunged deeper, sliding against hers. All Ashley could do was surrender to the spark of heat that flashed into a blaze inside her. She threw her arms around his neck, coming up on the balls of her feet to better meet him, giving in to the passion and promise in the kiss that had her forgetting about their audience.

His hands moved to her hips, and he lifted her up from the floor into his arms. She wrapped her legs around him, confused how all the fury that had been blasting off him a second ago had erupted into this.

Him pressed against her, his fingers fisting in her hair, his strong arm looped around her, his hot mouth on hers, and desire she'd never known surged through her.

Then he ended the kiss as abruptly as he had started it. They were left gasping for air, chests heaving. She opened her eyes, meeting the most intense, heated stare in her life, and her breath caught.

"Why was she here without you?" Stryker asked.

A muscle flexed along Rip's jaw. "Give us a minute." He didn't take his gaze from her. "I need a word with my woman in private."

The sexual current running between her and Rip had her body humming with electricity.

"Yeah, all right." Stryker waved the Sons out of the hall, and they left.

Rip set her feet down on the floor and pressed his hands to the wall on either side of her face and brought his mouth to her ear. "Sorry about the little show we had to put on. We needed them to believe it."

The declaration quickly sobered her. Of course, he was just acting.

The man was good. A little too good. But they both did what they had to. No big deal. Meant nothing.

So, why did her heart sink?

"You all right?" he whispered, his breath warm on her skin. "Did that guy hurt you?"

"No. I'm fine. But I didn't think you'd come."

"I'll always come if you need me, Ash." His voice was

a sexy, rough rasp. He made her name sound sensual. As if it were a caress.

Rip stroked her cheek, a gentle brush of his knuckles across her skin, a reverence that erased her doubts about what he valued more—his commitment to the code or to her.

He meant his vow to protect her. Ida and Welliver had told her Rip had saved lives in the Marines, earning one of the highest military decorations. The hero. Rip had that complex in his soul. She only wished she'd realized sooner.

"I can't bear the thought of you getting hurt in this," he said. "So, my options were either kidnap you to keep you from going. Or help you so you didn't get yourself killed."

"You understand my job is dangerous." She kept her voice low.

"This is different. You're in my world." He sighed. "Listen, I know how much you hate me, but for us to get through this, we've got to pretend to be a hot and heavy couple." He pulled back and looked down into her face. "Can you do that?"

Rip thought she hated him?

Ashley met his gaze. "I'm pretty good at bluffing," she said with bravado she didn't feel. "I'll give them an Oscar-worthy performance."

"I'm going to have to touch you. If you recoil, can't sell it—"

"Answer one question. Did it feel real, the way I kissed you back?"

Chapter Seven

As real as the air he breathed.

She'd kissed him back with a wild hunger that set his blood on fire.

"Yeah, it did," Rip said, realizing it was all illusion. He could only imagine what a struggle that must have been for her while he'd been in pure heaven. Not taking into account the Sons of Chaos that had been standing around watching.

He'd been interested in women and thought he had a crush on Ashley. But holding her and kissing her, he'd come to the revelation that he *wanted* her.

Wanted her in a way that he shouldn't, in a way that he could never have.

His desire was supposed to stay buried, a burning ball of yearning and guilt and anger, deep in his core. Never allowed to surface, to be dealt with, but it stared him in the face now.

The low-cut, practically backless powder blue top she wore hugged her ample cleavage. The midriff exposed an enticing flat stomach but had given him the pleasure of feeling her silky soft skin. High-heeled boots accentuated the length and curves of her legs. He'd always had the impression of her being tall, though it was merely the way she carried herself. Not that she was short, but in the skimpy top and heels, with no gun on her hip, she seemed much less formidable than usual.

Vulnerable. That was the word.

She looked vulnerable. And the most beautiful thing he'd ever seen.

It had been an uncomfortable realization when he saw that Son towering over her, with his hands on her. Made his blood boil. Granted, Rip had been relieved that she wasn't tied up somewhere, bound and gagged, but still.

Every instinct that flared had been primal. Visceral. The need to protect her a fist in his throat.

But he had to find a balance between his concern for her, his genuine affection, his frightening hunger for her and the need to keep his emotions in check.

Rip didn't normally have an issue maintaining a handle on his temper. But he had come close to punching that Son in the face and knocking out his teeth. He couldn't afford to make a mistake like that. Not when it could cost either of their lives.

"But I caught you by surprise," he added. "Now you're going to be anticipating it. I don't want to creep you out."

"Jimmy creeps me out. Not you."

Now he knew the jerk's name. "That's small comfort."

"To set the record straight, I don't hate you, Rip. Tried to, but never succeeded. I've just been angry. Partly at you. Mostly at Burk. At the Iron Warriors. At the lack of justice. I hated myself more for not being able to put Burk behind bars myself than I ever hated you."

He caressed her face. "I can understand that, and I know pretending to be with me isn't helping. I wish there was another way, but there isn't now."

"Kissing you wasn't so bad." She bit her bottom lip and he wanted to claim her mouth again. "You're really rather good at it."

Pride swelled in his chest. It had been a while since he

had locked lips with anyone, but he'd never kissed a woman the way he'd just kissed her. Full of relief and hunger and an urgent need that overwhelmed him.

Ash put her palms on his arms and ran them up to his shoulders, bringing her body closer until her breasts pressed against his chest. "I won't have a problem acting like you're mine or selling it to them." Rising on her toes, she feathered a kiss on his lips, and he didn't want to notice how right or good she felt in his arms, nestled against his body. "Think they're buying it?" She gestured with a tilt of her head.

He glimpsed down the hall. Sure enough, they had a captive audience.

"So far, so good. Did you give them your name?" he asked, not sure what alias she might've used.

"Sugar."

He glared at her, and she shrugged. "What if they had demanded a name? Taken your wallet to check your ID?"

"Someone in the DEA got me an ID. Ashley Roberts."

Sighing, he gave a nod of approval that she'd planned for that. He knew she'd worked on a DEA task force, which required her to bounce between Cheyenne and Fort Collins, but had been unaware about the need for a fake ID.

"We need to get out there," he said. "Once again, sorry for how we'll have to play it. For the way I'll have to touch you. And for the things I might have to say." The Sons treated their women like property and would only respect him if he did the same. He'd have to swallow his disgust and get into the role.

"It has to be done." She cleared her throat. "This is important. When we get out there, should I apologize?"

"To them? Hell, no. But saying it to me in front of them was the right thing. Good call." He took her hand, and they started down the hall. "Follow my lead."

"Whatever you say, *baby.*"

The endearment warmed his chest, despite being a part of the act.

Holding Ash's hand, Rip strode over to Stryker, who waited, seated at a table with his vice president and two other Sons. There was only one empty chair.

"She can wait over there with the other women." Stryker gestured across the room to the pool table where the scantily clad biker chicks had gathered.

Rip dropped into the chair and tugged Ash down onto his lap. "She stays where I can touch her." Just because the Sons wouldn't touch his *old lady* didn't mean the scowling women across the room wouldn't. Ashley could hold her own, but if they could avoid a brawl of any sort that would be best. "No worries. She knows when to be seen and not heard."

Leaning against him, she draped her legs across his lap and slid an arm over his shoulder.

Stryker cracked his knuckles. "If she were mine, I would've punished her in the hall instead of kissing her."

One of the dark things about the MC culture he always had difficulty with was how women were regarded as second-class citizens. The club was a means to an end for Rip, to safeguard Ash and deal with Burk, but with the Iron Warriors he didn't tolerate abuse in his presence. The one time Todd had tried to lay a hand on his girlfriend in the clubhouse, he'd put a stop to it and threatened to break his hand next time. *Property Of* cuts had never been acceptable in his club and he'd added to the bylaws that they never would. Some MCs encouraged cheating. He believed in loyalty. Not only among the men but also for the women who supported them.

"Well, she's not yours." Rip put a hand on her thigh and

curled an arm around her waist, tucking her closer. "And I don't like to damage what's mine." If he ever had the honor of being anything more to Ash than her protector, he'd cherish her every single day. "Can I talk to you without your boys?"

"Afraid not." Stryker shook his head. "Jimmy told us she's here looking for drugs. Didn't know you had a junkie on your hands. But it makes this club business."

Interesting. Rip hadn't anticipated that, and he'd considered a great many things before waltzing inside Happy Jack's.

It must have caught Ashley by surprise, too, based on the way she shifted in his lap, rubbing her soft curves against him, distracting him with her heat and sultry feminine scent.

A real relationship with her was out of the question, so he did his best to suppress his body's reaction. And failed.

He hoped she couldn't feel the way she aroused him, but there was no hiding it from her. What was wrong with him? How could the possibility of imminent bodily harm coupled with the friction from Ash against him cause such an intense physical reaction?

Must be the punch of adrenaline and the flare of hormones.

Rip reeled his thoughts in line despite the intimate way she stroked the back of his head with her fingers and pressed her lips to the side of his neck. "How is it club business?"

"Todd always griped about how you wouldn't let him deal." Stryker tipped his beer bottle up to this mouth. "You could go to him for what you need if it was just to get her high, but instead you allowed the matter to tear the Iron Warriors in two. Jimmy said she wants a supplier."

"*I* want a supplier," Rip clarified through clenched teeth. "Todd's. She was being overly eager, trying to find out for me." He rubbed his hand up and down her leg, stroking her thigh. "How does that make it a concern for the Sons?"

"We're getting to that." Stryker took another swig of beer. "Why the sudden interest in drugs? It's not your thing."

"But competition is. Todd wants to come for me and what's mine, so I'm coming for what's his."

With a sigh, Stryker set the bottle down. "Therein lies the problem. To connect you with his supplier is asking the Sons to take a side in your little civil war. Requires a vote, man."

His vice president leaned forward, resting his forearms on the table. "We could call a meeting upstairs, bring the matter to the table, but it'd be a waste of time. You won't have the numbers."

The Hellhounds had more support than the Iron Warriors. So much more in fact they were confident Rip didn't stand a chance of winning a vote.

He wanted to put a fist through the wall. "I need this," Rip said, considering a last-ditch play. Focusing on business and lining the pockets of the Sons might be enough to sway things. "I'll kick back five percent of my profits as thanks for making the connect."

"It still won't pass a vote," the VP said.

Since there never would be any profits, he could go up a bit, but if he ventured too high it would raise a red flag. "Okay, let's say ten percent."

Stryker stood, scraping his chair back across the wood floor. "We can't help you."

Ashley glanced at Rip, her eyes going wide in concern. But this discussion was finished.

Rip set her feet on the floor, shuffling her up as he stood.

He took her hand in his and squeezed, silently telling her to act cool about the setback.

Stryker walked around the table. "Sorry, man." He put a palm on Rip's shoulder and steered him toward the door. "If you'd come sooner, right after your club fell to pieces, I could've done more."

Sooner? How could a month have made a difference? Stryker was trying to tell him something, but what?

On the way out, Ashley grabbed her leather jacket from the back of a stool. If Rip hadn't been in the middle of Happy Jack's filled with Sons of Chaos, he would've helped her put it on. But chivalry was dead in that place.

Opening the front door, the Sons' president glanced over his shoulder and Rip did likewise. No one else was close by. As Rip passed him, crossing the threshold, Stryker said in a voice so low it was barely audible, "HT for ten."

Doubting Ashley had even heard the man, Rip gave one curt nod. Holding her hand, he went down the steps, practically pulling her along.

"We have to go back," she said in a harsh whisper.

The woman was going to be the death of him.

"Nope. Not happening." He hurried down past the bank of bikes to his. The Harley was in Ida's garage. Instead, he'd taken his Triumph Rocket. The motorcycle was sleek and powerful with ridiculous torque that hit the road like a berserker.

"We gave up too easily. We have to go back and try again."

Sometimes you need to know when to quit. "I know how badly you want this."

"Need this. It's the only way."

"We have to hold tight for ten like Stryker asked."

"When did he ask and what for?"

"Do you trust me?"

Ash didn't hesitate, she simply nodded.

He lifted her, seating her on his bike. "We need a reason to sit out here for a few minutes. Since neither of us smoke, we've got to keep up the ruse a little longer." Cupping her cheeks, he leaned in and kissed her.

The rush hit him again like water from a fire hose quenching the thirst of a man who'd been walking in the desert. Just as potent and intoxicating as before. Maybe even more so because when she wrapped her legs around his waist, holding him tighter, her fingers diving in his hair, rocking her pelvis against him, he groaned in her mouth.

Sure, they needed a plausible justification to hang around in the cold, but he would use any excuse for another make-out session, to hold her and treat her like she was really his. A taboo fantasy came to life. He'd always considered her off-limits, even after she grew into a woman and he'd seen her swimming that day, water glistening on her skin, shining bright as the sun, making everything inside him clench tight with need.

The world around him faded away, except for her and the possibilities he shouldn't be thinking about popping into his head. Of what he wanted with her if only he was someone else. Not some biker in an MC, fighting for his life. Not someone she was angry with and blamed for the delay in justice for her brother. Not someone a cop would be ashamed to be with. Not someone thirteen years older with his best years behind him.

If only.

He used those precious minutes. To imagine. To indulge in the feel of her lips and the warmth of her body pressed to his and the taste of her. To memorize the new carnal knowledge that would torture him later.

At the sound of approaching footsteps, a set of two, he pulled himself back, but stayed planted between her thighs. She blinked up at him, trembling, mouth slightly agape, dark eyes wide, uncertain.

Rip glanced over his shoulder. Stryker and his old lady were coming.

He looked back at Ash and ached to kiss her once more. Realizing this was probably his last chance, he took it. He dipped his head, catching her bottom lip between his teeth in a playful nibble, and kissed her again. Quick and hard. Then he eased away, helping her off the bike, and tugged her beside him. With his heart throbbing painfully from every twisted emotion those kisses had roused, he forced himself to focus on the business at hand.

"I'd tell you to grab a room at the motel, but it's wiser if you didn't stay the night," Stryker said. "You need to get your old lady a *Property Of* vest. Would've saved everyone some grief. Here's some patches."

The other woman offered Ash an envelope.

A fresh wave of anger rolled over Rip as he shook his head. "Not my style."

"Yeah, man, I'm aware," Stryker said. "You're too nice when you've got to be merciless. It's the reason you're losing the war at home. Trust me, you want it."

There was something more to the envelope. Rip nodded and Ash took it.

"Go grab us a room." Stryker smacked his woman's butt, and she hurried off toward the hotel, tottering on her high heels.

"What happened last month?" Rip asked, cutting to it.

"As soon as Todd formed the Hellhounds, he reached out to us. Asked to get patched over."

The news was a hard blow Rip didn't need. His heart

couldn't countenance the prospect. "He wants to turn the Hellhounds into a Sons of Chaos charter of Laramie and Bison Ridge?" That would give Todd powerful allies aligned with his interests, committed to supporting him in a war.

Stryker nodded. "He wants to roll you out, man. Only one club is going to survive in your neck of the woods. Todd has made a lot of friends here. After Thanksgiving, we're holding a vote with all the other charters on whether or not to let him join. I think it'll pass. That's why we can't officially assist you in your request."

Yeah, but he was sharing this information for a reason and not from the kindness of his dark heart. "And unofficially?"

"Unofficially, you're looking for LA. My sister, Lou-Ann," Stryker said, and Rip recalled one or two brief interactions with her. "She works for a dealer who operates a drug camp that runs a bunch of addicts. She used to pick up the junkies at a predesignated site, every two weeks, then drive them around for the day to various pharmacies filling scrips written by dirty docs. Big cities from Casper to Colorado Springs. Afterward, LA and the addicts would get flown to the camp, or the ranch as they like to call it, where they drop off all the pills, spend the night, and do it all over again the next day."

"Are you sure this is a major supplier? How much could they possibly get in a day?"

"LA told me that she brought in anywhere from 4,000 to 6,000 pills. A day. All controlled substances. Mostly opioids."

"That's major, but Todd is dealing more than that."

"Anything the dealer can't get with a scrip they get through a cartel."

Finally, a break. The lead they needed. "Can you give me her number?"

"I would, but she got promoted. Now she's at the ranch, managing distro. Out there, no cell phones and no guns for the workers, only for security."

Ashley put her hand on Rip's back, no doubt annoyed she had to stay silent, itching to voice the questions running through her mind.

Rip slid his arm around her waist. "Where's the ranch? Who runs it?"

"Don't know." Stryker shrugged. "Despite calling it a ranch, they're mobile and change locations every so often, but LA never discussed whereabouts or the owner. LA doesn't have loose lips. It's how she survives in that business."

"Then how do I find her?"

"Inside the envelope is the address of a pickup point. My guys would sometimes provide protection for her on the road, for the first day's run, making sure no one jacked her payload. She started by loading up a van with junkies at the pickup. Her runs always began on the weekend. Usually lasted two to three days. At night, they go to the drug camp. Give the workers food and their payment in pills. They like to do a big run before holidays, and Thanksgiving is in a few days. LA took off yesterday. Which means they're gearing up for processing. They either picked up some addicts earlier today or will tomorrow. You might get lucky if the pickup point is still active. Your best bet is to hang around there. Go as early as possible. Act like junkies looking to work for pills. If you make it to the ranch, tell my sister that Benji sent you." Rip raised an eyebrow, and Stryker added, "It's what she used to call me when we were kids. That'll let her know I really sent you. Maybe she can grease the wheels and help you cut a deal."

"You're sure that's Todd main supplier?" Rip asked.

"His only supplier. Everything he gets comes from those guys."

"I appreciate this, but what do you want for it?" Everything had a price.

"The ten percent you offered," Stryker said. "Only it comes straight to me. Not the Sons."

Greed wasn't enough for him to risk cutting out his club and going against their wishes. Presidents of an MC guided the club, they weren't dictators who ruled. Getting caught would result in severe consequences. "Why are you helping me?"

"I'm not helping you so much as I'm trying to hurt Todd. Earlier this year, at Sturgis, he got rough with some of LA's friends. One girl went missing. LA made the mistake of confronting him about it instead of coming to me first. He put his hands on her. Probably killed that friend of hers, too, who went MIA. If you mess with my little sister, you mess with me. Also, that dude can't be trusted. The way he stabbed you in the back and tore your club asunder." Stryker gave a low whistle. "I don't need that dirty fool wreaking havoc for me or the constant headache of worrying about when I'll get a knife in my back. If you can manage to crush him before the Sons vote on whether or not to patch his crew over, don't worry about the ten percent. We'll call it square."

"Thanks."

"Don't thank me yet. There are some Sons inside who don't much care for the way you operate. Letting her—" Stryker gestured with his chin to Ashley "—get away with that stunt she pulled, not making it known she was with you. That's something we would punish."

"Let me guess." Rip sighed, filled with frustration and exhaustion. "They also happen to be buddies of Todd."

"You got it. Look man, I have no beef with you. But some in the club already consider Todd to be an unofficial brother ahead of the vote. You're coming for his business. A righteous move in my opinion. But everyone knows the Iron Warriors are at their weakest. If you were full strength, it would be different, giving many a reason to pause. I suggest getting out of Bitterroot Gulch. Now. And expect some unfriendly company along the way."

Rip shook his hand.

"I'll do what I can to give you a head start," Stryker said. "Try talking them down. They think I'm out here schooling you about your lady. The fact that you 'accepted'—" he used air quotes, "—the *Property Of* patches might cool some heads."

Rip gave Ash a full-face helmet to put on while he grabbed the extra one that he had secured on top of an overnight bag with a pair of bungee cords to the back of his motorcycle. "Any time you can buy us would be good." Seconds, minutes, he'd take it.

Nodding, Stryker turned back toward the entrance of the roadhouse just as three bikers strode outside.

Rip shoved on his helmet and activated the two-way Bluetooth communication system. Grabbing his small overnight bag, he slipped the strap over his head, slinging it across his torso.

Ashley did likewise with her purse. "What about my truck?" she asked.

"Where is it?"

"Parked at the motel."

One red-faced hothead stormed around Stryker, but the president grabbed him by the arm as he continued to speak.

Rip got on his bike and cranked the engine, bringing it to life with a fierce growl. "Is your service weapon or badge inside your truck?"

"No. Left both at home." She climbed on behind him, resting her slim denim-clad thighs snug against the outside of his legs and fastened her arms tight around his waist.

"Then forget it. I'll send a tow truck to pick it up. I know a guy. We need to get out of here." He preferred together anyway, one ride. "Are you armed?"

"Always."

That was *his* deputy.

A pang of regret cut through him. What he wanted more than anything was for Ash to be his. But that was something that could never be.

He squashed the inconvenient desire and every distracting thought.

Because the one thing that mattered most was keeping her safe.

Chapter Eight

A cold knot settled at the base of Ashley's spine as they sped away from Happy Jack's Roadhouse.

She glanced over her shoulder and thought she saw people following them, but she couldn't tell if her tired brain mixed with the surge of adrenaline was playing tricks on her.

Rip raced down the long sleepy street as they headed for the highway and the relative safety of the open road.

"We'll get an hour or two away," he said in the helmet mic, over the comms system. "Get our bearings at a hotel and strategize how to handle the info Stryker gave us."

"Sounds good." The moment of calm gave her a chance to try and piece together what had just happened. "What does it mean if the Hellhounds become Sons of Chaos?" she asked. "Big picture."

"It would mean I'm out of time. It would mean added protection for Todd. That stopping him would be even harder. I can't believe how far out he's planned this."

"At least now we have a chance to hurt Todd by cutting off his supplier. Maybe even to goad him into doing something that the sheriff's department could nail him on."

"Yeah, but it's messy. Now I'm exposed no matter how this plays out."

"With Todd?"

"With everyone. Todd will know soon enough that I'm

going to come for him and how. They're going to mention you. If Todd tells the Sons that you're a cop, I don't know what the future will look like for me," he said.

The thought of this hurting Rip, upending his world, had the knot inside her coiling tighter. She wanted to save her hometown by stopping Todd Burk, not ruin Rip Lockwood's life in the process.

"Why didn't you listen to me and let me handle it?" he asked.

"Why didn't you just come with me to begin with?" she asked, throwing it back at him. "If we could've spoken to Stryker privately, this would've played out differently. His entire club wouldn't know."

"I needed to think. You only wanted to rush."

"Think about what?"

"How to help you without breaking a bylaw, the code," he said, and of course, he hadn't chosen her over the MC but had found a loophole. "Then I had to figure out exactly where you went. Once I connected the dots with it being a Saturday, only one place made sense."

"And what was the brilliant solution that kept you from breaking the code?"

"I called a vote to change it. With only five of us, the bind we're in with the Hellhounds, and considering my relationship with you, it passed, no problem. But it took time to make it happen."

"And what if it hadn't passed the vote?" Would he have abandoned her?

I'll always come for you if you need me, Ash.

Was that true?

She heard the growl of motorcycle engines roaring up behind them and turned to see flashes of yellow and black, three bikes coming up on their rear.

Gunfire erupted. One bullet pinged his bike.

"Should I shoot back?" She wasn't sure how the logistics of that would work. Firing behind her while holding on to him with only one arm.

"I'd prefer to outrun them," he said. "I'm going to need you to hold on tight. Wish you were wearing chaps."

Was he worried they might wipe out?

She stiffened against him, snapping her thighs securely around his as she tightened her arms on his waist. He cranked open the throttle and the bike exploded down the asphalt like a bullet.

The freezing wind whipped over them. The dashed lines in the middle of the road whizzed by so fast they almost appeared unbroken.

Her muscles twitched, aching to be released, needing to do something other than rely on Rip and his expertise in handling a motorcycle.

The length of black pavement separating them and the Sons in pursuit, who were shooting at them, continued to stretch.

"Fast bike," she said. "We're going to make it."

"Don't jinx us."

Too late.

A siren whined. Red-and-blue flashing lights appeared from the darkness and zoomed up behind them.

"They might be able to assist."

Rip didn't slow as they continued to fly down the road. "The Sons have got the police in their pockets around here. We're just as likely to catch a bullet from them as we are from a biker. Or worse, the cop stalls until they catch up to us."

The patrol cruiser wasn't far behind.

A train whistle blew.

Up ahead, the white crossing gate was already lowered

in front of his lane ahead of the train tracks. Yellow warning lights blinked. A train was coming, headlights ablaze.

He was going to try to outrun it and make the crossing.

She was all for taking chances, but one wrong maneuver, one miscalculation in the slightest, and ten thousand tons of steel would turn them into roadkill. "Rip, don't."

"We have to." His voice was steady, firm. "Don't let go."

What choice did she have? But could they clear the crossing in time?

The whistle blew again, reverberating in her bones. The long, high-speed freight train hurtled down the tracks, drawing closer to the crossing.

Twisting the throttle, he accelerated, and the bike surged even faster, the engine straining. Her stomach launched up into her throat as she clutched on to him for dear life, pressing the side of her head to his back.

The darkness, the rush of wind, pushed in on her, squeezing the air from her lungs. She dug her fingers into the thick leather of his jacket, hoping, trusting, praying.

He whipped across the dotted yellow line over into the lane for oncoming traffic and they rocketed around the crossing gate, barely zipping over the tracks—the glare from the freighter's headlights blinding—before the train roared by within inches of the rear tire.

The gust of the compression wave rocked them on the bike, the tail end swinging out. Rip slowed and rebalanced them and kept going.

Releasing the breath she'd been holding, she looked behind them. In between the train cars, she saw the police cruiser jerk to a halt, dust whipping into the air. The lights of three motorcycles pulled up alongside the vehicle.

A close call.

Deep down, she suspected there would be more to come.

IN THE MOTEL room off the interstate, Rip and Ashley had gone over the information Stryker had passed to them and strategized a flimsy plan to get to the drug camp. Start at the main initial point where the addicts waited to be picked up to make their rounds at pharmacies. With any luck, the location was still being used and tomorrow would be a pickup day.

"All the information I had to go on to get this far was intelligence from Agent Welliver with the DEA," Ashley said, seated next to him on the king-size bed. "He was in charge of the task force I'm technically still attached to. We should call him. See if he's willing to assist now that we know it's not just pills on the ranch."

"Worth a try."

The heat in the room had finally kicked in. He stripped off his jacket and MC cut. His cell phone rang. He dug it out of his pocket. "It's Quill," he said to Ash. "I'll put him on speaker. Just keep quiet. No more secrets or withholding information between us, okay?"

She nodded. "Agreed."

"Yeah," Rip answered.

"I spoke with the boys who we didn't expect to cross over to the dark side," Quill said.

"What reason did they give?" It could've been anything. Calling in political favors, backstabbing, bribery.

"It varied. Larger cut of the profits from Burk's new drug venture for two of them. But three guys weren't pleased with how you handled the situation."

Rip scratched at the stubble on his jaw. "What do you mean?"

"You tried to issue a decree of no drugs without taking a vote. They're upset that you didn't trust the system. Trust in them to have your back. Being a potentate who crushes the will of his people is being someone who destroys the backbone of an organization which you pledged to lead. A Prez must convince his members. Not coerce. Not decree."

Regret pooled in him. He'd been afraid to take a vote. And in acting out of fear, he'd created the very situation he hoped to avoid.

Ash put a hand on his leg. The concern in her eyes was a small comfort.

"They're right. I should've trusted them." Rip clenched his teeth and swallowed past the bitter lump in his throat. "Did anyone get info from Yates on what Todd's big new venture is?"

Quill sighed. "About that. Shane Yates is dead."

"How? When?"

"Sometime tonight. He replied to a text around seven thirty, agreeing to meet at the old clubhouse at nine, ready to spill details about Burk's operation. Never showed. JD swung by his place to check on him. The sheriff's department was there. Along with a detective from the Laramie PD. The Delaney chick. Crime scene tape was up. Wheeled a body bag out."

The sheriff's department and LPD? Seemed like overkill. "What's happening?" Rip asked, not really expecting an answer.

"No earthly idea, but the winds of change don't seem to be blowing in our favor. If I learn anything else, I'll call."

"I might be out of pocket and hard to reach the next day or two. If I am, don't worry about it. You'll eventually hear from me."

"Okay. Stay safe."

Disconnecting, Rip turned to Ash. "Can you find out what happened to Yates? He was one of Todd's dealers. We thought he'd be the weakest link to tap for information. He agrees to talk to us and then turns up dead. I don't like it."

"Sure. I'll pretend as though I'm checking in." She picked up the landline and called the sheriff's office. "Hey, Mitch. This is Ashley," she said over the speakerphone. "I'm out on assignment. Just checking in to say that I'm alive and well. What's going on in town? Anything new?"

"Everything is going to hell in a handbasket. Me and the sheriff went over to the Hellhounds hangout. Along with the fire department. Sheriff Clark tore through some walls with an axe. Burk seemed to get the point."

Rip slid Ash a curious glance and gestured for more information.

She shook her head and mouthed, *Nothing.*

Sounded the exact opposite of nothing to him. The sheriff was a levelheaded, cautious man. Rip thought he was well suited for the job and had even voted for him. Clark would never provoke anyone, least of all the Hellhounds, by busting holes in the wall of the clubhouse without good cause.

"Anything else?" she asked. "Any leads on the murder of the pharmacist?"

"No, but we've got another body. Two in one day. One of the Hellhounds. Shane Yates. Killed the same way as the pharmacist. One bullet in the head. Two in the chest. Throat cut. But it looks like the perp was in a hurry on the way out and dropped the knife used. Something to go on. LPD is bringing in Burk for questioning. Apparently, Yates was an informant for Detective Hannah Delaney. She's hot under the collar. I expect she'll hold Burk for as long as she can just to mess with him even if she can't dig up enough evidence for charges."

The police could hold him up to seventy-two hours before the prosecutor decided whether to charge him. The timing was a much-needed boon. The longer Burk was behind bars limited to making only one phone call the better.

The Sons of Chaos who had Todd's side in this war wouldn't be updating him on the events at Happy Jack's anytime soon. Rip only hoped it would be long enough for him and Ash to accomplish what they'd set out to do.

Once Todd learned about tonight's exploit, that he and Ashley were working together to bring him down, there was no getting around the fact that Rip would be left in a dangerous situation. Exposed. He'd have to make a tough choice.

One that was going to change his life forever.

Chapter Nine

Ashley paced near the landline on the bedside table. "You told me that if I found anything of interest to contact you," she said to Welliver, with Rip listening nearby. "Drugs from a cartel should catch your attention."

It was almost midnight, and the DEA agent was still in the office working. He had enviable stamina. A true workaholic. She knew getting assistance from him might take convincing, but she hadn't expected a flat-out *no*.

"Which cartel?" Agent Welliver asked.

"I don't know."

"How much product?"

"I don't know."

"Where's this supposed drug camp or ranch located?" She raked a hand through her hair. "I. Don't. Know."

"I appreciate your eagerness and commitment in getting this far. Really, I do." Welliver sighed. "Once you have more for me to work with, we can speak again. But tell me one thing, did you go into Happy Jack's alone?"

She flicked a glance at Rip. He sat on the bed, hands clasped, resting his forearms on his thighs.

"No," she said. "I had help."

"How did you convince him to do it? Did you sleep with Lockwood?"

Her stomach twisted into a pretzel.

Rip's gaze flashed up to her. His brows pinched together.

She reached for the receiver to take the call off speaker. Rip lunged, snatching her wrist, stopping her. He shook his head. *Leave it on.* He mouthed the words at her, indicating he intended to listen.

"No, sir," she said, her cheeks heating. "I told you I wouldn't do that."

"Really?" The surprise in Welliver's voice was like nails on a chalkboard. "I don't know what kind of hold you've got on this guy, but whatever it is, it's worth gold."

She squeezed her eyes shut, bracing against the embarrassment. The sheer humiliation.

"Get yourself and Lockwood into this drug camp. Find out what you can."

Jerking her wrist free from Rip, she grabbed a water and turned away from him, not able to look him in the eye. "I'll ask him. No guarantee he's willing to go that far." Not after learning she treated him like an asset. *Thanks, Welliver.* "Worst case, I go in alone." She twisted off the top and drank from the bottle.

"If you're telling me that he waltzed into the Sons of Chaos den with you and got you that information, then I'm telling you this guy will go off a cliff for you."

She choked on the water going down her throat. Chancing a glance at Rip, she hated what she saw. He was glaring at her, jaw tight, lethal energy starting to simmer beneath the surface.

Ashley was going to be sick.

"I'm impressed," Welliver said. "Once this all shakes out, he might face serious blowback."

Now he points this out. How this would leave Rip *exposed*. She should've considered any potential consequences to Rip sooner instead of operating with blinders on, solely fixating on nailing Todd Burk.

"If there is fallout for him, what can we do for him?" she asked. "What are his options?"

"Not if but when. And short of disappearing? Not much."

Her jaw went slack. "What?" She looked up at Rip.

He turned his back to her and crossed the room.

"Yeah," Welliver said, casually, "that happens in situations such as these."

Her heart pounded in her chest, a sharp pulsating roar that filled her ears. "If this could burn him, destroy his life, why didn't you warn me of the repercussions? Give me a heads-up?"

"Look, kid, you've got a tough exterior, but inside you're soft. You've got a heart. I didn't think you'd have the stomach to go through with it if you knew. But don't beat yourself up over this. Lockwood was a Marine Raider for ten years. Trust me, that dude considered every conceivable risk before helping you," Welliver said, only making her gut twist harder. "Focus on finishing this. Complete the op. Find the drug camp. If you can confirm ties to a cartel or anything big enough for me to take more interest, then I can help you. Best I can do. Hey, Jasper is in the next office. We've got something in the works tonight, but he wanted to speak to you if you've got a minute. Says you haven't been returning his calls."

Just when she thought this conversation couldn't get any worse, it did. "No, um, I, um," she caught herself stuttering, "I'm too busy to talk to him."

"Yeah, I bet. You've got your hands full with Lockwood."

Rip plopped down onto the bed and dropped his head into his hands.

Her chest tightened. "I've got to go."

"You know how to reach me," Welliver said.

Ashley hung up. Slowly, she turned to Rip and stared at his back. "I didn't know," she said.

"Know what? That you'd blow my life apart with this?"

She went over to him and sat beside him. "If you realized that this could happen, why did you come?"

He jumped to his feet. "You dropped a bomb on me that you were going to the Sons and ran off! You left me no choice!" he ground out, and her head spun, her heart aching. "What am I to you? Just some asset?"

Hesitation tensed her shoulders. She opened her mouth but was at a loss for the right words. "I don't know what you are to me."

For a long time, she'd thought of him as the one to blame for Angelo's death, right along with Todd. Later, his actions had separated the two men. Rip had been kind and sort of flirty in his aloof way, always offering to be there for anything she needed. Their conversations redefined him into a would-be protector. But she never knew what was real and what he simply wanted her to believe.

She'd convinced him to help her with this, like an asset. Because she needed him.

But he was never something to be used and discarded.

Rip leaned against the wall, muscled arms crossed over his chest, jaw set hard.

He'd risked everything for her, going to lengths no one else had ever done. Kissed her and touched her and made her feel things she didn't think possible.

The primal attraction heating her blood now as she looked at him left her breathless. But she didn't know what box to put it in, what label to give him.

"Who's Jasper?" he asked.

The question knocked her farther off-kilter. "What?"

"Jasper."

"He's, um, a DEA agent I worked with on the task force." Answering shouldn't fluster her the way that it did, as though she had something to hide, but she didn't want to talk about the other guy. Think about the things she'd done with him that she wished she could do with Rip.

"That's what he is. Who is he to you?"

She lowered her head. "No one."

It shamed and confused her that more heat existed when she was in the same room with Rip, a guy she'd convinced herself for years she had to despise, than with any of her past dates, including Jasper Pearse.

"I've never lied to you," he said. "Have enough respect for me to be honest."

This shouldn't be so difficult to spit out but it felt like admitting to an affair when there was nothing between her and Rip. "Jasper and I slept together while working on the task force in Fort Collins."

No other man had ever followed up after a date, showing any eagerness to get to know her better. Other than Jasper. Her interest in him had been lackluster at best, but it was an opportunity to finally explore something romantic. Something sexual. It had been her first and only time being intimate with a man, but she'd felt more desire, more raw, hot need for Rip when he had his hands on her than she'd ever had for Jasper. No one but Rip had kissed her so thoroughly, so passionately that he had possibly ruined her for every other man out there.

Something about her attraction to Rip unnerved her. An attraction he couldn't possibly reciprocate.

"Are you two still together?" Rip asked.

She was startled by the odd undertone she could have sworn she heard in his voice.

Was he jealous?

What if all this time it was desire lurking beneath their arguments, the flirty banter, the endless tension and prying conversations that always got too personal?

That sudden thought seared into her brain like a brand, glowing red-hot and strangely urgent.

"No, we're not together. It was a brief, casual fling."

"How brief?"

"Why are you grilling me about an encounter with an agent, who I have no feelings for by the way, like some overprotective big brother?"

The color drained from his face as he grew still. Too still. Too quiet.

"We need to focus on Todd Burk," she said, redirecting the conversation. "We have to finish this. As soon as possible."

Staring at her, he said nothing. An emptiness fell over his eyes, the cool distance between them growing, spreading.

"There's something I haven't told you. About the car accident I had." She realized she was fidgeting with her hands and stopped. "Burk was behind it."

"What are you talking about?" His voice sounded hollow. Whatever numb mode he'd flipped into, he was still there, unsettling her. "He wouldn't hurt you, not until I'm out of the way."

Rip sounded so certain, but… "You're wrong."

"What am I missing, Ash?" His gaze sharpened, and he watched her far too closely. "What else haven't you told me?"

The harsh question came across like an accusation. One she deserved.

She'd deliberately hidden the circumstances surrounding her accident. Now there was no avoiding it. She had to tell him.

Ashley took a breath, steeling herself for how he might react. "I was taking pictures in front of the clubhouse. I think I found which three bikers attacked you. Anyway, Burk spotted me. He came over for a chat. Taunted me about some high price you paid. For me. To protect me. By the way, what was he referring to?"

"The reason I gave him the clubhouse," he said flatly, and she ached for how much he'd sacrificed. "Get on with what you were saying." His tone was ice-cold.

"Todd called the gesture romantic. I told him in no uncertain terms that there was nothing between us. Then he asked me point-blank if I was your old lady, which sounded preposterous."

Rip narrowed his eyes. "And you said?"

She stared at him like the answer was obvious. "The truth. That I wasn't. I left and then two prospects followed me, shot at me and ran me off the road."

Clenching his fists in front of his face, he shoved off the wall with panther-like grace. "I told you to stay away from him."

"And I did. Sort of. He approached me, not the other way around."

He stormed over to her, exuding masculine power, and she was strangely more comfortable with his anger than his silence. "The one safeguard, the biggest thing keeping you safe, you just stripped away. Like that." He snapped his fingers.

Seated on the bed, she tipped her head up at him. "How is that possible? What did I do?"

"After your brother's funeral, I had to go back to the Marines for a little while until my paperwork was processed. Do you remember an incident behind Delgado's?"

She thought back, combing through her memories, and came up short.

"You worked at the bar and grill part-time in high school," he said. "Went to throw out the trash. Spotted some Iron Warriors on their bikes. Decided to go over and make a scene. Threatened Todd."

Her shoulders sagged as she recalled. "Yes." It wasn't her proudest moment. She'd been in so much pain, the grief suffocating her, and then she'd seen Todd Burk and couldn't stop herself from venting her anguish.

"When you walked away and went back inside," Rip said, "Todd let it slip what he was going to do to you. Quill interceded, told Todd the only thing, the one thing that would stop him. The story he spun was that after the funeral, before I left, I was comforting you and fell for you. I staked my claim to you while I was home on leave…and that you were my old lady as far as the club was concerned."

She rocked back as though what he'd said had been a physical blow. "I don't understand." The words *my old lady* got caught in her mind and spun there. "Wouldn't I've had to know that I was your girlfriend, to pretend with you, like we did tonight, to pull that off?"

Letting out a heavy breath, he lowered his head. "Quill told everyone that it needed to stay quiet since you were only seventeen. When I came back to town, that explained why no one ever saw us together in public, except for us talking. As soon as you were of legal age, you joined the sheriff's department. Gave a different reason for us not to go public. They all think that you and I are together and that we want to keep it under wraps. Besides Quill."

Stunned, she sat there. "All this time, you've been lying about being with me?"

"I never asked Quill to lie or actually repeated it, but I perpetuated the story with my silence," he said, as though that made a difference. "Because it worked. Old ladies are off-limits. Period. The one rule Todd would respect until he eliminates me, but you've taken that away."

She reeled from the admission. "Wait. Help me wrap my head around this. For seven years, if I'm supposed to be your old lady, then you haven't had a real girlfriend or gotten serious about anyone?"

He shook his head. "No."

Narrowing her eyes at him, she found that hard to believe. "For seven years, *seven*, you haven't slept with anyone?"

"On occasion." He shrugged. "I'd go to Cheyenne. No one regular. Kept it discreet."

Oh my God. That was why he didn't have any female visitors at his trailer or sleep with women at the clubhouse. To add credence to the lie that they were together. In love. Committed.

"You can't collaborate with a cop, but you can sleep with one?"

"Yeah," he said with a reluctant nod. "There are clubs that have patches for a thing like that."

Gross. "Do you?"

"Of course not. I'd never brag or exploit you."

She believed him. He'd have too much honor to wear that kind of patch. But this story boggled her mind.

"What about me?" she asked, perplexed, trying to piece it all together. "I mean, how would you have explained it if I'd had a boyfriend." In high school, she'd been focused on getting good grades, graduating, taking it one day at a time without her brother, not dating. But once she'd started working as a deputy, she'd tried to build a full life. She wanted marriage, a family, thinking it might fill the hole inside.

"I figured I'd cross that bridge when I eventually came to it. But you haven't had a boyfriend, have you? Quill would've told me. Or you would've. Other than this *Jasper.*"

And she thought she would have shared it like she had countless other things, such as her awkward date with Dave, personal things about her family, things she'd never whispered to another soul.

But she hadn't. And Jasper had happened out of town. All the way down in Fort Collins. Where Rip and other Iron Warriors hadn't been watching.

The ugly truth of everything gelled and smacked her in the face. She leaped off the bed and strode over to him. "Are you the reason I haven't been able to date? That I haven't had a boyfriend? That after one dinner, every single guy, except for Jasper Pearse, seemingly lost interest in me?"

"How would I be the reason?"

"It's the only thing that makes sense. Has Quill been scaring them off? Have you?"

"What?" The denial on his face slowly shifted, realization dawning in his eyes. He shook his head like he didn't want to believe it and then took out his phone. Punched in a number. Put the call on speaker.

After the seventh ring, Quill answered, "What's up, Rip?" He sounded like he'd been roused from sleep. "Thought I wouldn't hear from you for a while."

"I'm going to ask you straight and you better answer straight. Have you been sabotaging Ashley's dates? Keeping men away from her?"

"Huh?" Quill asked with a yawn.

"Give it to me straight," Rip demanded.

"Well, yeah. Me and JD let it be known subtly. We

planted a rumor around town that you two were together. Word spread faster than pink eye among toddlers. That did half the work."

Ashley thought back to a couple of years ago when Mitch had joked that the reason he couldn't ask her out was because she had a biker for a boyfriend. She hadn't taken it seriously, thinking it was his way of letting her down easily. It wasn't the first time someone had made that kind of teasing remark, but she'd chalked it up to how Rip would stop and talk to her whenever and wherever in town while he didn't give anyone else from the sheriff's department or most civilians for that matter the time of day.

"When any guys went sniffing around her," Quill continued, "JD and I rode up on them. Told them to lose her number. If they pushed back, well, then JD got off his bike. Looked them in the eye and told them to stay away from her. Every time they caved."

She should have chosen stronger men.

But that would explain why Dave, a nice guy who shared her fondness for Mexican food, had literally run from her when she bumped into him at the post office and asked if he wanted to grab some tacos and margaritas a second time. Because he'd been scared off. By Rip's henchmen.

"You brought JD into this?" Rip asked.

"Had to. I'm not as intimidating as I used to be. He understands and can be trusted."

Rip's free hand clenched into a fist at his side. "I never told either of you to do something like that!"

"You asked me to watch out for her after you caught *feelings* and didn't want to be the one keeping tabs. It had to be done. Let's say she started dating, got into something serious, then the story that you two were together would've unraveled faster than a yo-yo and painted a target on her back. If Todd ever found out the truth, she wouldn't be safe. And you know it. I won't apologize for doing my job."

"Unbelievable," Rip snapped. "You should have told me."

"Don't ask, don't tell, right? You didn't ask about my methods, so I didn't feel obliged to tell. Figured it was best that way for both of us. Straight enough for you, brother?"

Rip stabbed the disconnect icon on his phone and huffed a breath. "I'm sorry, Ash. This is my fault. I set out to protect you and roped Quill into helping me. This wasn't how it was supposed to be done. I never should've let this happen, let them interfere in your life."

Shock didn't simply surge through her. That was too simple. A mix of everything did. Surprise. Fury. Betrayal. Confusion. It rose up, twisted together and turned into rage with one target. Him. "But you did." She could spit nails. "Todd sent his goons after me because I told him the truth. Because you didn't bother to let me in on the big lie. Instead of keeping this a secret from me, you could've talked to me about it and explained. Given me a choice, a say in the matter."

"Talk to you about it? It's not as though you've made it easy to look out for you. You never listen to me. Or do what I tell you. Taking pictures at the clubhouse. Chatting with Todd. Running off to the Sons of Chaos. And where am I? Here, with you, ready to jump off a cliff, apparently, while my life is about to be blown apart, because I'm too foolish to help myself."

"I didn't ask you to vow anything to me any more than you asked Ida to take you and your brother in." Maybe he would've been better off if he had never made any promises and stayed away from her. "Don't get me wrong, everything you said is valid. The bind you're in with the clubs because of what the Sons know is on me and I'm sorry for it. But do you have any idea how your actions, Quill's, have made me feel? How it's damaged me?"

Rip's brow furrowed. "Damaged you? I don't understand."

"I could never figure out why no one was interested in me. At first, I thought the hot guys were simply out of my league. I came to terms with reality, accepted that I wasn't beautiful, lowered my standards. Told myself that the only thing that mattered was if a guy treated me well. Not what he looked like. Not if he excited me. Or made me feel anything at all inside besides boredom. Because the problem had to be me. I needed to try harder. I went so far as to force myself to go out with someone I didn't even like, only to have him reject me, too." The gnawing emptiness inside her opened up, spreading through her. "For years, I've gone through that. Do you know what it does to a person?"

A sense of defeat eventually crowded out the desperation. Hope and the chance for love slowly withered.

Being with Jasper hadn't been better. Their time together had left her emptier than being alone, so why bother.

Holding her gaze, Rip stood frozen, but she didn't want to see the pain echoed in his expression as though he were the one wounded.

Chapter Ten

"Ash…" He shook his head. "You're beautiful." So beautiful it hurts. "You deserved the attention of every guy out there even though you were better than all of them. I didn't think about how that story might grow and get out of hand. The way it might affect you." Maybe a part of him hadn't wanted to think about it, to question why a woman as stunning and smart and spirited as Ash was single. Deep down, he'd been too relieved not to have to cross that bridge. Not yet anyway. How blind he'd been. "I never meant to hurt you. I didn't realize."

"Why would you? How would you know the consequences of that lie or the repercussions of maintaining it? How lonely I've been." Her voice broke right along with his heart. "How badly I've wanted to be touched. To be wanted." Tears welled in her eyes. "To have what everybody else does. Affection from someone who has my back in this world."

Rip had no idea of the depth of her pain, and she would never know how truly sorry he was that she'd suffered.

But he had her back, no matter the circumstance. If only he was capable of being a vigilante, he would have taken out Burk long ago. Instead, he'd tried to do things the right way, to see her brother's murderer serving time behind bars. But in waiting, in being patient, he'd unintentionally robbed her of something she'd needed. For her to think she lacked in any way tore him up.

Easing closer, he curled his hands around her shoulders. Her cinnamon-anise scent filled the space between them and worked its way into his senses, overriding his anger at the mess of things. He pulled her to him and lowered his mouth to hers.

Letting out a shocked gasp, Ash shoved him away. "Stop it. You don't have to do that. Keep putting on an act. Pretend to be attracted to me. Give me a pity kiss to make yourself feel better about destroying any chance I had at a love life for the past seven years."

An act?

Sure, he'd hidden how deep his feelings for her ran because she never seemed interested. Any attempts he made to flirt were met with a cool, almost confused reception, like they were speaking two different languages. Every positive thing about him he'd tried to share she'd dismissed, choosing instead to look for the negative. Perhaps she'd simply never believed any of the good things, including his attraction to her.

If so, he'd done them both a disservice. No more being subtle. Time to be blunt.

"I wasn't pretending." Rip sighed. "My feelings for you have never been fake. I know you've never liked me. I didn't mean to overstep just now, but it was killing me, listening to you think you weren't desirable. You have no idea how men look at you. Even in your uniform I see it." He scrubbed a hand over his face, tamping down the jealousy that flashed through him as he recalled it. "I've wanted you for a long time. Thought about what it would be like, us, together. As a real couple. You're all I think about. All I hope for."

Rocking back on her heels, Ashley swallowed like something was stuck in her throat. "The kiss wasn't just an act for you?"

"The kiss was necessary. We had to get through it at Happy Jack's with the Sons believing we were a couple, but I didn't have to get *that* into it. Multiple times. I used it as an excuse to do what I've longed to for a while because I'm attracted to you. Want you in the worst way." There, he'd said it. Put his cards on the table.

A ragged breath punched from her lips as if squeezed from her lungs. Silence descended. Her gaze wandered as she rested against the dresser. Loose strands of hair hid her face, but he didn't need to see her expression.

He was probably the last man she'd want and if by some chance that spark had been mutual, he had to consider his entire world was about to change. But he didn't want her to think he'd bail or that she owed him anything. "Our history, our current set of circumstances, complicates things. I want you to know that I'm going to help you see this op through to the end. No strings attached."

"Thank you." Ashley let out a low breath. "It's not that I've never liked you," she said, her voice soft. "I thought I couldn't trust the things you've told me, couldn't believe in the goodness I've seen in you." She looked up at him. "Until tonight. Everything you've done…wiped away the doubt that's been keeping me from accepting how I feel about you."

He eased toward her, hoping she felt as deeply for him as he did for her.

"You're a good guy, Rip. I wish I could've seen it sooner. Believed everything you showed me. I'm sorry I dragged you into this. I wish there could've been another way. I didn't mean to ruin your life where you might have to go into hiding."

"Sometimes stuff has to happen, I guess. Without the way things played out at Happy Jack's neither of us would've been as honest as we have. Found out the truth." He'd never regret getting the chance to hold her, kiss her, and imagine.

She studied his face. "What if the vote to change the by-laws of the Iron Warriors to work with a cop hadn't gone in your favor?"

"The odds were pretty good, but I'd be here anyway. I would've waited until after we finished doing whatever is necessary to end this thing with Burk before I stripped off my patches and walked away from the club." He was prepared to give it all up.

"Really? For me?"

"This thing between us started out as an obligation I took upon myself. I'm not sure what it's become. All I know is that I'd do anything for you. The affection I have for you is real, and I want you in a way I've never wanted another woman."

Ashley pressed her palms to his chest. "I want you, too. Kind of scares me how much." She curled one warm hand around his arm and slid the other over the back of his neck. Her fingers stroked his hair, enticing him to soften.

But he couldn't ignore the uncertainty in her eyes. He no longer doubted that she wanted to sleep with him, but how did she feel about him?

"What am I to you?" he asked.

She was quiet, that beautiful gaze of hers stark. Perhaps she was surprised that he persisted in raising the question but also once more considering an answer. Then she looked away.

Again, she didn't know.

Not that he blamed her. First, she was angry at him and now she wasn't. Had questioned his character and now trusted in him without hesitation. Denied her attraction to him and now wanted to explore it.

But bikers and cops didn't mix.

Not to mention they were in different places in their lives. There would be fallout from his actions tonight. Once he rid his town of Todd Burk, one way or another, he'd have to leave before the Sons of Chaos came after him for payback.

"This isn't a game for me," he said.

"For me either." Lifting onto the balls of her feet, she leaned in, her mouth reaching toward his.

Rip locked down every muscle in his body and pulled his head back. "I won't be satisfied with one night." He stepped to the side, crossing the room. "With a brief, casual fling like you had with Jasper." The thought of that guy, any guy, touching her burned a hole in him. "I'd want more." A lot more. More than he had a right to have. Not simply rough, hot pleasure in a dark hotel room. The elusive more of a connection that was physical and emotional and serious.

"You don't understand. Jasper was convenient and he was interested," she said, as though that made things better.

"I'm convenient and clearly interested." A convenient asset, who could no longer hide his attraction to her.

Pressing a palm to her forehead, she lowered her gaze. "I slept with him because I didn't want to be a virgin anymore, okay?" Her voice was low, embarrassed. "But I didn't feel anything for him. That's why it was a meaningless fling." She looked up at him. "But this, us, it feels different."

Jasper was her first lover. Jealousy tangled with guilt and coiled within Rip. She'd simply given her virginity to the first yahoo who made it to a second date. Had a meaningless experience because she'd been denied the ability to have anything else.

He wanted to punch Quill and then himself for boxing her into that position.

"It wouldn't be fair to ask you for what I want." Even if she could give it. "The way I allowed Quill to handle things prevented you from dating and playing the field." Though Rip hadn't realized such horrible interference was happening, ultimately, the responsibility fell on his shoulders. "I won't take that away from you anymore. I'm thirty-eight. Doesn't feel old to me, but I'm already graying, and I've sown my wild oats. I know what I want. Who I want." Even if he didn't deserve her. "I can't undo my mistakes, but I can give you time. Without me or the club hovering, sabotaging your efforts to find what you've been looking for. Once we get Todd, put an end to him and I fix what I broke in the club, my obligation will be done. I'll move on from Laramie. And you can be free."

She blinked, her eyes filling with hurt, surprise slackening her features.

He didn't have time to choose his words carefully because if she kissed him again, he'd break apart and cave.

Rip snatched his jacket and helmet. "I'm going to run to that big twenty-four convenience store at the rest area we passed on the interstate. Get you some things for tomorrow. Sweatshirt. Sneakers. I've got an extra toothbrush in my overnight bag and you can sleep in one of my T-shirts. Don't wait up for me."

He left the room, shutting the door behind him.

Getting on his bike, he wrestled with his feelings. He wanted to make love to her more than anything, but she was special and deserved a man who would be serious about her. Who would be able to stick around and give her everything. To be everything for her.

Once some lines were crossed, there was no going back.

No doubt in his mind what she meant to him. He'd sacrifice everything, including his own desires, to make sure she got the chance to have the life she deserved.

ASHLEY CONSIDERED GOING after him but had no idea what to say.

What am I to you?

Because she didn't have an answer, he was prepared to push her away for good.

Something banded around her lungs, tight and squeezing. A depth and breadth of emotions she'd need time to sort through.

The secrets, the feelings they'd each unloaded were big and powerful and overwhelming.

She unzipped his bag, got toiletries and a T-shirt. A long shower gave her a chance to process, think, unwind. The water poured down on her, too hot, pricking her skin, but Ashley didn't care. When she toweled off, anxiety hadn't subsided, and putting on Rip's T-shirt didn't make it better. She climbed into the bed under the covers.

Sleep was impossible. She lay in bed, adrift and uncertain. Her life was caught in a whirlwind. This was the eye of the storm. The quiet, the calm, before more pieces of their lives got ripped away, changed forever.

Unease ticked through her over how Rip had left things. He'd been in her life, protecting her for seven years, letting his feelings for her grow, slow and steady and sure. But for her a cork had popped on the mix of emotions she'd kept bottled inside. Gushing and fizzing, overflowing into a mess.

Now he wanted her to simply contain it because circumstances made it inconvenient.

That part was unfair.

She stared at the red digital numbers on the clock. It wasn't until after two in the morning when she heard the purr of Rip's bike pull up outside.

He tiptoed into the room, not making a sound with the shopping bags, closing the door with a soft click.

"You don't have to be quiet. I'm not asleep." She sat up, bringing her knees to her chest under the covers and wrapping her arms around her legs.

He set the bags down on the floor. "You need to get some rest."

"We both do. But I need to talk to you first."

"You don't have to say anything."

"I do." She sighed, wanting to take her fizzy feelings and pour them into a neat glass he'd understand. "There are three phone numbers that I have memorized and know by heart. The landline to my parents' house, the sheriff's office and your cell phone."

"What does that have to do with anything?"

That was everything. He was one of the most important people in her life and she was only now realizing it.

"I don't know what you are to me because I never gave myself a chance to unpack it. During all the time we've spent together, throughout every conversation, every quick meal at my house, I've doubted you. While you were getting to know me, sharing who you really were, I refused to believe anything you told me was honest. Real. Until Ida and Welliver convinced me I should be looking at you differently." She released a heavy breath. "Whenever you're within arm's reach, I've been drawn to you, always tempted to get closer, daring to do so, curious to see what might happen, despite the fact you seemed determined to keep your distance. I tried to deny how attracted I am to you, constantly fighting against it. Told myself that it was just oxytocin, dopamine, norepinephrine. A chemical reaction in my brain that I couldn't trust."

Crossing his arms, he leaned against the wall. "The whole universe is a chemical reaction. But it's still real."

"You're right, and tonight changed everything."

"How so?"

"For one thing, you proved to me you're committed to stopping Burk. But there's more." She went to get up.

But he raised a palm, warding her off. "Stay there. Under the covers. Please."

"Then you come closer. Sit by me."

Rip hesitated a moment and then eased across the room and sat on the edge of the bed near her feet.

"Jasper gave me attention. Pursued me. I liked it and thought that meant I wanted him. But I was wrong. On my dates with him, I found my mind veering to you. Wasn't sure why. Sex with him—"

"I don't want to know." He hung his head and clasped his hands.

"It'd been fine. Nothing thrilling. Or sweet. Or special. But tonight, with you, was all that and so much more when you touched me and kissed me." Fireworks went off inside her body. "It was like my heart was beating so hard it was going to come straight out my chest. You made me ache, Rip, with real desire." She'd never experienced a hollow sensation between her thighs akin to pain. Never felt like she might die if she didn't get a man's hands all over her body. Not until him. "I don't want to fight what I feel for you anymore."

She crawled out from under the covers and climbed onto

his lap, settling her knees on either side of his thighs. Staring into his eyes, she slid her palms up his chest and then to his shoulders.

Rip stiffened while everything inside her eased. "Ash, please don't. You need to be free of me. Free of Todd. Free to see what your life could be without the pressure of this weighing on you."

Sometimes high pressure and intense heat were necessary to forge something new.

"I don't know what you are to me, but I need to figure it out." Despite the undercurrent of confusion, the suddenness of the tide washing away false beliefs, she couldn't ignore the truth that being close to him, like this, felt right. Absolutely right. Him. Here. The two of them. "What I do know is that you make me want to take off my clothes and throw caution to the wind and forget about every rule, Rip." She pulled the T-shirt over her head and let it hit the floor, exposing her body to him.

A harsh, shuddering breath rushed from his mouth as his gaze fell over her. "You need time. A chance to find someone, anyone else. Not me taking advantage of you. I promised myself that I wouldn't do this. That I wouldn't make love to you. Told myself that I wouldn't even take off my pants when I got back to the room."

Smiling, she cupped his handsome face and caressed his cheeks. He was an honorable man. Strong, fierce Rip, with his rugged good looks, cropped hair, stormy blue-gray eyes and that golden skin. Such a good guy, but right now, she wanted him to be bad in the best way. "Touch me. Hold me. Talk to me about all the things you've been trying to share but I've been too stubborn to hear. And if it makes you feel any better, I'm not asking you to break a promise to yourself. You can keep your pants on. But at least let me take your shirt off."

She pushed his leather jacket back from his shoulders. Tugged his arms from the sleeves. Stripped off his Henley. All hard-packed, well-honed muscle, without an ounce of fat. She slid her arms around his neck, pressing her body to his, skin to skin, melting into his warmth. His pulse raced beneath her touch as he stiffened.

"You and I are an impossibility." His somber tone tugged at her heart. "Where do you think this could go from here?"

"I don't know, but don't draw a hard line. Not when the sand around us keeps shifting. This thing between us runs deeper than anything I've ever known. Give me a chance to understand it. To fully feel it."

His piercing gaze was unwavering on hers. The awareness between them, the raw attraction, finally acknowledged, vibrated like sparks in the air, crackling with a new kind of electricity.

She brushed her lips over his and she trembled, or he did. Maybe both of them.

His jaw tightened, and still, he didn't put a finger on her.

Her heart couldn't take another rejection. Not from him. Not when she'd never wanted anyone more.

"Please, Rip," she said, filling her voice with every drop of desire running through her.

He looped an arm around her waist, cradled her cheek in one of his hands and stared at her like he was deliberating.

So, she slid her mouth against his and kissed him, insistent, determined, rocking her hips over the bulge in his jeans. Need twisted deep inside her. She yearned to explore his body until every contour was etched in her bones. No matter what happened tomorrow, or next week, she'd at least have that and this feeling.

Alive.

Electric.

Connected.

She clung to him. Pushing against him as if she could push herself all the way *into* him. Her pulse was a hammer, hard and resilient, thundering out a message—*don't let go, don't let go, don't let go.*

And finally, he kissed her back, his tongue sweeping over hers, delving deeper, drinking her in, erasing any questions or concerns, leaving only the powerful feelings she had for him. And in his arms, it was all that mattered. It was everything.

Chapter Eleven

The truth had a way of surfacing, regardless if it was convenient. The honesty Rip and Ash had disclosed changed things between them, for better or worse.

But redrawing physical boundaries complicated everything.

Rip sat behind the steering wheel of Ash's vehicle. The tow truck had dropped it off before sunrise and the driver had collected his bike, agreeing to take it on to Laramie for a steep fee. Then they drove to the address in Casper listed on the paper Stryker had given them. To a transport hub where they'd been waiting three hours.

Looking through binoculars, he stared out the windshield, staying vigilant, forcing himself not to look at Ash asleep in the passenger's seat, trying not to replay last night in his head. She'd taken off the T-shirt and had nothing underneath. All those soft, supple curves more beautiful than he'd imagined. Her killer body perfect to him. Sexy Ash.

Gutsy Ash.

Off-limits Ash.

Or at least she had been in some ways, but in one very important way to him she still was.

She had no idea how badly he wanted her. He'd tried to do the right thing, the noble thing, and he'd given her what he could. Kisses. Comfort. Tenderness. Pleasure again and again, with his fingers and his mouth, touching and tasting, and he'd reveled in her sweet cries of satisfaction. Then she'd asked for more, for him to be inside her. Need roared up like a wild beast, clawing through him, and he ached to have her. If he'd had protection in his wallet or had bought some at the store, he might've been a weaker man, but instead he kept his pants on as promised.

Ashley had been robbed of so much, he just wanted to give, not take.

Making love to her when he only had to leave later would've torn something from him. Something deep he didn't think he'd ever get back.

A part of his soul.

After the Marines and the club, he didn't have all that many pieces left.

Across the street, a small group of desperados had formed at the far end of the hub at the last bus shelter. Only seven. Every one of them had the anxious, fidgety vibe of an addict. Two looked as though they hadn't changed their clothes or showered in a few days and held a trash bag, partially full of items. The others had knapsacks, and one woman carried a huge tote capable of holding almost anything. They all appeared to be in rough shape.

With no one else around, they also stood out.

"Hey." Rip caressed her face with the back of his hand, brushing his knuckles across her cheek. "Time to get up." He hated to disturb her and wished he could've risked her sleeping longer.

Ashley stirred. Yawning, she stretched.

He took a small vial of peppermint oil he purchased from the store out of his pocket and applied a drop near the corner of each eye.

"What's that for?" she asked.

"The oil is an irritant. It'll give me those telltale red eyes that junkies tend to have." He slipped on a cheap pair of sunglasses. "Takes a few minutes to work."

"We got movement?"

"I think we're in luck." He handed her the binoculars.

She stared in the direction he indicated. "Either that or they're waiting for a ride to a Narcotics Anonymous meeting." She turned to him. "How do I look?"

They'd messed up the new clothes he'd bought, a sweatshirt and sneakers for her, and a flannel shirt for him by rubbing a jagged rock across the material, to tatter the fabric and scruff the shoes, giving their attire a worn-in appearance. If he'd had time, he would've gotten things from a thrift store to save them the trouble.

But her hair was pulled up in a smooth ponytail and her face too fresh and pretty to fit in.

"You need to be a bit rougher around the edges."

She removed the elastic band, fluffed her hair and redid the ponytail, making it sloppy with loose, chaotic strands framing her face. Pulling mascara from her purse, she flipped down the visor and lifted the cover of the vanity mirror. She applied mascara, but not to her lashes, and strategically smudged it underneath her eyes on the lids. She now looked like a party girl who'd had a hard night but was still beautiful.

"Much better."

They'd debated earlier and agreed it was best to play a couple. No way he'd be able to suppress his protective instincts if she was put in a compromising position.

"How much longer do you think until they get picked up?" she asked.

He shrugged. "No way to know for certain. Most of the

pharmacies around here open at nine, but Stryker said to be here early." He glanced at his watch. Seventy thirty. He popped open her glove box and shoved his primary burner phone linked to the voice-activated listening device at the clubhouse as well as his personal cell inside. "We should get out there. Try to blend in."

They exited her truck.

He braced against the frigid breeze with only an inexpensive fleece-lined windbreaker and the flannel shirt over his Henley to keep him warm. In a similar position, Ash shivered beside him as they crossed the street and turned the corner, heading toward the group.

They each had a backpack with protein bars, water, toothbrush, cheap burner phones that would be handed over in the event they were picked up and a rolled-up sleeping bag strapped to the bottom. Since he had no idea exactly what they were walking into, he erred on the side of caution.

With so many moving pieces, they didn't know where they would ultimately end up. So, he'd arranged for the same tow truck driver, Ganow, to collect her vehicle again and run it down to Laramie if necessary. Considering the exorbitant amount he was being paid, the guy didn't complain. Worst-case scenario, the drug dealers didn't show to pick up the group of addicts, there would be no need for the tow truck, but the guy still got paid. Win-win if you were Ganow.

As they neared the shelter, a scruffy guy with blotchy skin and an overgrown beard wearing a blue ballcap stared at them. The others noticed them but didn't take too much interest.

Once they were close enough, Rip gave a head nod to Mr. Bearded Blue Ballcap, BBB.

The guy didn't do likewise, only narrowing his eyes in

response. BBB was going to be a problem. The only question was how big of a problem.

Joining the seven individuals, they stood inside the shelter, shielded from the wind.

Rip put his back to a corner in the shelter, where he could see any approaching vehicles. Ash leaned her side against him, resting her head on his chest, and he curled a loose arm around her.

Six more strolled in while they waited.

An hour or so later, an unmarked white passenger van pulled up. The driver hopped out. A guy in his late twenties. Mirrored sunglasses. A well-worn leather jacket. Turtleneck. Torn jeans. Steel-toe boots. He finished smoking a cigarette and put it out under his bootheel.

He opened the passenger door and waved the group over. Everyone filed out of the shelter and up to the van.

The man opened a drawstring bag and set it on the floor of the van. "You know the drill. Cell phones inside."

A guy stopped in front of the driver and extended his arms. The driver patted him down, probably checking for weapons and wires, and searched his knapsack. Then the guy dropped his phone in the bag and climbed into the van.

So on it went until it was their turn.

Rip stepped forward, with Ash behind him. He caught the flash of a gun in the shoulder holster beneath the man's jacket.

"Hold on, you weren't here last time."

"We couldn't make it," Rip said, gesturing to Ash.

The driver eyed him and then looked Ashley up and down, taking her in too closely. Rip chalked it up to male interest and not suspicion. Not that either was good. The latter meant trouble now. The former meant trouble later. No telling what those guys at the ranch expected from female junkies, who were normally willing to do anything to get their next fix.

Everything inside told him to persuade Ash to stay behind, but he was certain she wouldn't agree.

"I don't know either of you," the driver said.

With a sigh, Rip shook his head. "Well, LA does. I'm used to riding with her. This is my girl's first time. But LA will vouch for us."

The driver cocked his head to the side. "Oh yeah? You sure about that?"

Rip took off his sunglasses, squinting at the light. His eyes should be nice and red by now. "Positive."

The driver scrutinized him for a moment as if trying to decide what to do. "You willing to bet *both* your lives on it? Because if LA says she doesn't know you, I guarantee you'll each get a bullet in the head."

Hesitation would only convey doubt. Rip opened his bag and extended his arms for the pat-down as his answer.

The driver nodded. "Okay. I'm up for a game of Russian roulette. Let's see whether you live or die."

Rip was used to taking high-stakes chances as a Marine Raider, accomplishing the mission as his sole focus. What he wasn't willing to do was gamble with Ash's life. She was a competent and capable cop, but asking her to stay behind—when she'd refuse because she mistakenly thought being a cop meant she was cut out for this—would only raise a red flag.

They were in this now. He just had to make sure he kept her safe.

After a less than thorough pat-down, where the guy had missed the gun in Rip's ankle holster, he waited for his bag to be searched. In the few seconds it took, Rip noticed the tight weave of the fabric on the drawstring bag for the cell phones. Inside, it was lined with a shiny silver material. A Faraday bag—blocked GPS signals to prevent location tracking and stopped remote spying. Whoever this crew was they were serious players, but if they had weaknesses at the pickup point, there would be more later that he could exploit.

Rip dropped his burner phone in the bag, waited for Ash to be searched and to dump her burner as well. Then they climbed in.

The driver started the vehicle.

They rode for about ten minutes before pulling up in front of a shady-looking pain clinic on Elk Street. There were no other buildings on the block beside the shoddy one-story. The sign on the door read Closed.

"Come on." The driver cut the engine and ushered them out. At the exterior metal screen door, he rang the bell three times and waved at the camera positioned above it.

They were buzzed in, the lock disengaging. The driver held the door open. They funneled in, forming a line. One by one they were directed into an office that only had space for a small desk and chair. A man wearing a white lab coat, presumably the doctor, sat collecting IDs. Not bothering to raise his head and look at anyone or even speak, he entered information into a computer and then handed back the identification card along with twelve signed prescriptions per person.

The driver took a thick envelope from the inner pocket of his jacket, dropped it on the desk, and they left. In the van, he collected the prescriptions.

Next stop was a small pharmacy three minutes away. They parked right as the place opened for business. The driver handed each person a scrip, enough cash to pay for it, and herded them inside.

STANDING IN LINE at a higher-end drugstore in Fort Collins, Ashley shuffled forward. The pace had been grueling. A merry-go-round of stopping at pharmacies, everyone filing out with their belongings rather than leaving them in the van, turning in the prescriptions, little to no wait getting them filled—courtesy of working for drug dealers, they were paid in cash, and then off to the next location.

No big chain store pharmacies. Only smaller, independent ones, lots of mom-and-pop places. They spent around fifteen minutes inside, thirty at most, with the driver, whose name she'd learned was Drexel, always waiting outside out of view of the cameras. Most likely didn't want to be captured on the surveillance video.

Whatever agreement had been reached with the owners of the pharmacies had been done in advance.

Getting back in line behind her after using the restroom, Rip curled his left arm around the front of her, tugging her backpack against his chest, his fingers stroking her throat.

A wicked heat curled through her belly, pooling deep inside her, and the memory of last night flooded her mind. The way he'd held her. Caressed her. Tasted her. Gave her such intense pleasure. The only problem was it had all been one-sided. He told her how much he'd enjoyed it, making her writhe with want, hearing the sounds of her satisfaction, but it wasn't the same as them coming together as one.

He pressed his mouth to her ear. "You good?" Concern was heavy in his tone.

"Yeah," she said low. Her nerves had settled now that she understood this part of the process and knew what to expect. The next part, where they were off to the camp, would kick up fresh jitters.

Nothing she couldn't handle.

She was well trained. Not DEA agent or Special Forces

trained but ready, prepared for anything. She could get through this. Still, she was aware that Rip's protective instincts tended to kick into overdrive where she was concerned.

In front of her, the weird guy with the beard and ball-cap stepped up to the pharmacist and handed over his prescription and ID.

"Not too late to back out," Rip whispered.

"As if." He needed to realize that her life wasn't more valuable than his. They could do this together, as a team.

"I figured as much. Just checking."

Her turn came. She followed the same procedure as the last eight times and then stepped to the side. Rip was the second to last to go up to the counter.

Those who had already turned in their prescriptions were already in the pickup line, paying with the cash Drexel had given them outside the store, and grabbing their white bag of pills.

"I'm going to go ahead of you," Rip said. "Use whatever time we've got to see if I can get Drexel to lower his guard a bit around me. If I can make inroads here, it'll be easier at the farm."

"Sure. I can buy you a minute or two by going to the bathroom. But I don't think it's going to be easy with Drexel."

He slid his arms around her shoulders, tugging her closer. "Speaking of not easy, things might get rough at the farm."

"I get it. I can do this." Security probably liked to have a good time with the women, trading sexual favors for pills, but she had Rip as an excuse. If she got cornered, a knee to the crotch would solve that problem. As for the countless other what-ifs, she'd take them one at a time.

He gave her a probing glance for a moment. "I know.

You wouldn't have gotten this far if you couldn't." His tone was warm, and from the look in his eyes, she could tell he meant more than this, here and now, but also the academy and every tough thing she'd been through as a deputy. "I believe in you." He gave her a quick kiss on the lips. "Do you trust me?"

She would trust him with her secrets, with her life. With her heart. "Of course."

"No matter what I might have to do, no matter what twists or turns come...*trust me*."

"Always." But his words sent a jolt of nervousness rushing through her.

"Next!" the pharmacist called out, not bothering to use their names, seemingly anxious to give them their pills and get them—the dregs of society—out of their place of business.

Rip went up to the pickup counter, grabbed his white bag and headed for the exit.

Ashley turned to the woman with the humongous tote. "Go on ahead of me. I've got to use the bathroom." She started toward the restroom and glanced over her shoulder.

Rip was speaking to the security guard at the front door before he headed outside. He dropped his bag with the oxycodone into the larger bag that Drexel held open as he waited for them on the sidewalk.

Hurrying inside the bathroom, she took the opportunity to use the facilities and wash her hands. No telling how long until the next pharmacy or where. She left the restroom.

Only a couple of regular customers were in the store.

A tense-looking pharmacist waited for her. Ashley gave her the cash and took her bag with the oxy from the woman and headed down the aisle.

She was just about to reach the door and caught Rip's

eye. His attention flickered between her and Drexel. The two were engrossed in a lively conversation, with the driver appearing more at ease with Rip.

Perhaps it had worked.

"Excuse me, miss." The security guard stepped forward, blocking the door. "I need to search your backpack."

Her heart fluttered. "What? Why?"

"I have reason to believe you stole something."

"There must be some mistake."

"Please take off your backpack and unzip the front compartment."

Stunned, she slipped off the straps and turned the backpack around to face the security guard. "I didn't take anything."

"I hear that all the time from you people."

She didn't take the comment as racist since the guard was Black and attributed it to her being in a group of addicts.

Across the street, a police cruiser pulled into the gas station and parked. Two officers got out and went into the convenience store.

The security guard unzipped the front compartment of her bag and peered inside.

"Satisfied?" she asked.

Frowning, he pulled out two bottles of perfume. "This is three hundred bucks."

Ashley stiffened, her legs turning watery, not understanding how it got in her bag. "I didn't put that in there." Her mind spun trying to make sense of it.

"Sure, you didn't." The guard grabbed her wrist. "I've got to call the cops."

"What?" She tried to jerk her arm away without getting physical. The two officers stepped out of the gas station, holding cups of coffee, and lingered as they spoke. "No. We can talk about this."

"You can talk all you want to the police," the guard said.

Drexel shouted something at Rip and pointed for him to go over to the drugstore.

Rip yanked the front door open.

But it was Drexel who asked from farther back, "What's the problem?"

"She stole something. I've got to call the cops. It's a class two misdemeanor."

Ashley glanced at Rip to see how to play this.

His expression was inscrutable, his blue-gray eyes going stormy, and her chest constricted.

Rip looked over his shoulder at Drexel. "My girl's a hardcore junkie, sorry," he said to him. "She does stuff like this sometimes. She isn't worth this kind of trouble."

A cold chill splashed down her spine, numbing her heart. Ashley shook her head, not believing this was happening.

"We've got to go." Drexel turned, facing the gas station, where the officers still hadn't gotten back into their vehicle. "I don't need any headaches on this run. We cut her loose. Get her pills and we're out of here." The driver made a beeline for the van.

She was ready…prepared for anything. Except for Rip betraying her.

Her stomach felt as though it had dropped into the spin cycle of a washing machine, churning and flipping.

Why hadn't he pulled this stunt at the first pharmacy? Why now? Why wait all day until they got here?

All the way to Fort Collins.

They were in Fort Collins, where she had people that she knew, who could straighten things out and give her a ride. He'd been planning this the whole time.

Rip marched inside the store and snatched the white pharmacy bag from her fingers. She narrowed her eyes at him and gritted her teeth, too blindsided to speak, anger drumming in her veins.

"This isn't betrayal," he bit out, as if reading her mind. "It's protection. I won't play Russian roulette with your life. Call a friend and go home."

Then he turned his back and left her behind.

Chapter Twelve

The wounded look on Ash's face once she realized what he'd done had taken a slice out of his heart. Still haunted him. Those sultry brown eyes—that warmed him like a shot of whiskey when her heated gaze fell on him—had flared with shock and then narrowed to cold slits. But pain had washed over her expression.

Another pang wrenched through his chest. He didn't want her to think this reflected what he thought of her capabilities or was some sexist judgment on his part.

It was purely selfish.

If something happened to her, when he could've prevented it, he'd never forgive himself. Headed to the farm, he needed all his attention on only one thing. The mission. With no distractions.

Worrying about her rather than the task at hand would've split his focus and gotten them both killed.

Once they'd finished at the last pharmacy in Colorado Springs, they'd driven to a municipal airport east of the city and loaded onto a Cessna—based on the size he guessed a Caravan outfitted mainly for hauling cargo—where a grungy pilot had been waiting. They sat on benches rather than seats, and the aircraft took off.

The plane passed Devils Tower—a distinct, iconic butte

that loomed 867 feet above the trees—and began a descent to land. They were back in Wyoming. The far northeastern part of the state.

Rip stared at the roll-up door for loading cargo. It was the same kind used for skydiving.

The Cessna touched down on grassland with a bumpy landing and rolled to a stop.

Drexel got up and yanked on the wide door, getting it halfway before using both hands to finish rolling it up. "Come on. Everyone out." He hopped onto the ground and led the way to a parked van nearby.

Another man, who wore a skullcap beanie and glasses, was behind the wheel.

As they got off the plane, BBB elbowed Rip, shoving past him. He'd let it slide this one time. Causing a scene wasn't his goal, but he let that guy push him around and it would only end up being a bigger deal later.

Everyone climbed into the van and settled in for the ride. Ten minutes later they drove into a camp. Tents, makeshift shelters, a couple of decrepit school buses, and a fifth wheel camper and a large trailer both connected to trucks formed a horseshoe. This was the drug camp.

The van came to a stop, and they exited. Everyone began forming a line in front of a third guy, and he followed suit.

"Lumley, I'm going to see the boss," Drexel said to the current driver, holding up the bag from the day's haul.

Lumley nodded. Drexel headed for the fifth wheel camper.

The third guy was lean, rangy and not too tall, with scruff on his face. He stood handing out payment in pills. The line inched along steadily, everyone waiting their turn.

Rip scanned the area, searching for Lou-Ann. He wasn't

sure if she'd remember him. Plenty of bikers had crossed her path over the years.

Near a picnic table, he spotted her stirring a large pot of something situated over the fire. Her blond hair was in a choppy, angular bob. She'd put on some weight. No longer rail-thin, she had a little meat on her bones. He was tempted to head straight for her, but all the addicts were only interested in pills. So, he stayed in line to blend in.

BBB came up from behind him, elbowing him to the side, trying to cut the line in front of him. Rip was fed up with this guy and hooked BBB's leg with his foot, tripping him. BBB couldn't regain his balance. Momentum carried him forward and he face-planted into the dirt.

Not knowing when to back down, BBB jumped to his feet. "Who do you think you are?" he said, lunging for him.

Rip had his fist ready to punch the junkie in the face and ring his bell nicely.

But the one in charge of the line got between them. "No fighting. Or you're out of here." He turned to BBB and dumped one pill into his palm from a large container.

"Hey, where's the rest? I'm supposed to get three, Perry!"

"You fight, you get less. Next time keep the peace." Perry looked at Rip. "Same for you." He doled out one pill for him. "Go get something to eat." He gestured to the picnic table.

The others were in line in front of LA, getting bowls of soup and then grabbing things from the two cardboard boxes on the table. Rolls were in one and snacks in the other. People were walking away with protein bars and chips.

Rip increased his pace without trying to look overly eager. He couldn't have a real conversation with her while everyone else was hanging around nearby, but he at least wanted to give her a heads-up.

The door to the fifth wheel camper swung open.

Drexel hurried outside and ran to the firepit, where LA continued to serve soup. "Lumley," he called over the other one.

Another man appeared in the doorway of the camper. Curly hair. With his height and wide shoulders and the light creating a shadow behind him, he was a menacing figure. He lowered a respirator mask from his face and leaned against the jamb, watching.

That was no ordinary camper. They were doing something with drugs in there.

Rip approached the fire. His gaze met LA's and he held it, steady, confident.

Drexel pulled his gun and the addicts scattered like roaches, disappearing into the darkness.

Rip kept walking until the muzzle of the gun touched his chest.

"LA, do you know this dude?" Drexel asked. "He claims he was with you on some of your runs?"

Squinting, she stared at him and cocked her head to the side like she wasn't sure.

"We first met at Sturgis," Rip said quickly. "Benji—"

"Shut up!" Drexel moved the gun from his chest to his head. "She shouldn't need any reminders if she knows you."

Lumley drew a gun from his waistband at his back but kept it down at his side.

"Yeah, I know him." LA nodded. "Rip Lockwood. He's cool. My brother made the connect for him to do a couple of my runs."

With his name put out there, his exposure only grew. He couldn't catch a break. At this rate, he'd have to go deep underground for the rest of his life. Provided he survived the ranch.

Drexel lowered his weapon, put the safety on and returned it to his holster. "Your lucky day. You get to keep breathing. No hard feelings."

"None taken," Rip said.

Drexel and Lumley walked away.

The others kept a safe distance, giving Rip the opportunity he needed, but he didn't know how much time he'd have.

"What are you doing here?" LA asked in a whisper. "You're no druggie."

"So, you remember me."

She arched an eyebrow and looked him over from head to toe. "You're a hard man to forget, Rip. Explain. Why are you here?"

He grabbed a disposable bowl and went to the pot.

"I'd skip the soup if I were you." She glanced around. "They lace it with rat poison. They don't want the same druggies sticking around forever, giving the DEA a chance to turn one of them into a snitch. The steady regulars only last three to four months. Always plenty of addicts out there to take their place."

His stomach clenched. He set the bowl down. "Todd Burk is making a big play at home. Believe me, I want to see him hurt more than you do. I need to sever this pipeline of his, making him hemorrhage until he bleeds out." Rip grabbed a couple of protein bars from one of the boxes.

LA smirked, appearing downright devilish in the firelight. "Music to my ears. That SOB has it coming."

"I heard about your friend at Sturgis and what he did. I'm sorry. But she's just one in a long line of his victims." He thought about Angelo Russo. Todd's comeuppance was long overdue.

"Not sure how you're going to accomplish that goal."

"Maybe I'm a buyer, offer to pay for Todd's product at a higher price because of the war going on at home." Even if the DEA wasn't interested in the bust, some law official in the county would be. Setting up a sting was high risk, but also high reward.

"Won't work." LA shook her head. "Not unless you've got more than seven hundred fifty thousand dollars on you right now."

"What?" he said in a harsh whisper.

"Buyers pay up front in advance of receiving their product. Todd has already forked over seven fifty."

Where did he get that kind of cash? His operation must be much bigger than anyone thought.

"I've already put a bug in the boss's ear." LA zipped her fleece jacket and pulled on the hood. "Todd claims this is his last shipment from us. I've heard he intends to set up his own drug camp close to home. That he's already intimidating doctors and pharmacists. His plan will hurt our business. The boss isn't too happy about it. So, he's taking steps to make him pay. Pay big." She pivoted and nodded to the camper. "They've cut his entire shipment of product with fentanyl."

It wasn't uncommon for dealers to grind down pills, add fentanyl and use a pill press to reshape the drugs, making them resemble real prescription drugs such as oxy, Xanax, Adderall and much more. The process was time-consuming and tedious. The worst part was that dealers weren't chemists. It only took two salt-sized grains of fentanyl to be lethal. Dealers did it to increase profits, stretch their supply and expand the number of addicts by juicing the potency of the other drugs.

"The boss is being generous with the fentanyl in this shipment." She warmed her hands by the fire. "It'll probably kill a quarter of Todd's customers. The rest won't get the same high as his regular product and will go looking elsewhere. Namely us. Those who die will bring him a ton of heat from the authorities. This is going to be a lose-lose for Todd."

Not to mention the unsuspecting people, many of them college students, who'd be getting far more than they bargained for. So many kids were going to die to make Todd suffer.

Rip kept the horror from surfacing on his face. "You must be talking about a lot of fentanyl."

"We sell quite a bit. Get it from the cartel."

"Mendez?"

LA shook her head. "Sandoval."

"There has to be another way for me to get my hands on that shipment." He had brainstormed about other ways to accomplish the goal in the wee hours this morning and all day in the van. "When is it supposed to go out?"

She shrugged. "Not sure. Maybe Tuesday or Wednesday."

"Tell me about your boss?"

"Farley." LA glanced at the fifth wheel camper, and his gaze followed her line of sight. No one was outside besides Perry, who was smoking a cigarette near the travel trailer. "He's Canadian. Ex-military. The guys who fly the planes used to work with him."

That was his way in. "Can you introduce me? Tell him I'm interested in working as security for him. Making deliveries, runs, anything that pays well."

"Tricky," she said, raising her eyebrows. "The boss doesn't take a shine to everyone. Especially not strangers. I had to prove myself doing runs for a year before he moved me over to distro."

"How does the distribution work?"

"Varies. Local drops made from wherever the ranch is located at the time, we do by van. Farther out, we use one of the planes. Drop the load with a beacon. Buyer tracks it via GPS."

"I need to meet him."

"I don't know." Glancing around, she stuffed her hands in her pockets. "Get yourself situated in one of the buses. Claim a cot. I'll see what I can do."

"Hey, all I need is an intro. No need to vouch for me any further. I'll do the rest."

Chapter Thirteen

Ashley sat in the passenger's seat of the sedan. They'd passed the sign that read Welcome to Laramie, Home of Southeastern Wyoming University.

The college was the biggest draw to the town. She'd gotten her bachelor's degree in criminal justice while working as a deputy, considering it one more tool in her arsenal in the fight against Burk. When all along, her greatest tool was also her greatest weakness.

Rip Lockwood.

Her chest was tight, achy. Her heart swollen and bruised over Rip's deception. He wanted to sugarcoat his betrayal as protection, but it stung, nonetheless. Because it meant he didn't trust her enough to be honest.

She couldn't be mad at him. Not while he was out there risking his life to take down Todd Burk. If only he'd let her help, be his partner in this. She was the one who'd brought him in on the plan after all. Besides, this burden was both theirs to bear.

They passed the smaller, unassuming sign marking the border of Bison Ridge.

Ten minutes later, Jasper pulled up to her house and parked beside her truck.

Ashley donned her emotional armor and girded her feelings. "Thanks again. For the ride back to Wyoming. For coming down to the police station to clear everything up when Welliver wasn't available."

"It's really no problem." He flashed a kind smile. "If this is what it takes to get to see you again, then I don't mind. I wish you'd called sooner. But I still can't believe this Lockwood fellow. What was he thinking ditching you like that?"

One thing for her to question Rip, but Jasper wasn't allowed. "He was doing what he thought was right. To keep me safe."

"Doesn't he realize he isn't authorized to act on his own?"

Technically, neither was Ashley, but she didn't know how much Welliver had shared. "He's a Marine. Special Forces."

"Used to be a Marine. That was what, seven or eight years ago?"

Irritation flared inside her. "Once a Marine, always a Marine. Whatever the situation, he'll be able to handle it and when the time comes, he'll contact the proper authorities."

"Are you sure he's not going to go vigilante and ruin any chance of you building a case?"

If Rip were going to turn into a vigilante and take matters into his own hands, regardless of the law, Todd would already be dead and buried in an unmarked grave where no one would ever find his rotting corpse. "I'm sure. Thanks again." She clutched the handle and opened the door.

"Mind if I come in to use the bathroom?"

She tensed, but how could she refuse. He'd spent too much time at the police station straightening things out and then an hour on the road to bring her home. "Of course."

Hurrying up to the front door, she racked her brain on how to get rid of Jasper without being rude. This wasn't her forte. In fact, she'd never been the one doing the rejecting before.

She unlocked the door and let him inside. "The bathroom is right through there," she said, pointing down the hall.

Setting the backpack on the floor, she couldn't wait to wash her face, shower, and try to get some sleep. Though she doubted she'd be able to rest, not knowing what was happening to Rip.

The toilet flushed and the faucet ran in the two-piece bathroom. She had her spiel ready. It would be short and sweet and would hopefully work without ruffling any feathers.

A moment later, Jasper came toward her with a sweet smile.

Yawning like she was exhausted, she stretched. "Wow, it's so late."

"After that long drive, I'm parched. Can I have something to drink?"

Who would say no to water? Besides a rude ingrate. "Certainly." She led the way.

In her kitchen, she grabbed a glass from the cupboard and went to the sink, wishing she had bottled water that he could take to go.

"Now, this is the kind of drink I'm talking about," Jasper said, excitement in his voice.

She glanced over her shoulder as she filled the glass with water.

Jasper was holding her extravagant, decorative three-thousand-dollar bottle of tequila. "Clase Azul. Ashley, I had no idea you had such fine taste. The sheriff's department must be paying better than I thought."

"It was a gift. Birthday present from someone special." From someone who thought she was special.

"I've got to try a shot of this. It might be my only chance.

Do you mind?" Jasper beamed, his green eyes bright, his face warm, his blond hair perfectly coiffed.

He reminded her of the frat boys at SWU she'd hoped would ask her out and call her back for a second date, eons ago. It would've only resulted in what she'd found with Jasper.

Nothing of consequence.

She was done with boys who didn't excite her, who didn't know how to pleasure a woman in bed, whose loyalty ran surface-deep, who wouldn't put her above everything else.

Who were so consumed with taking that they didn't understand the true meaning of sacrifice.

"I do mind, actually." It wasn't about sharing. If the tequila hadn't been a gift from Rip, she would've gladly given the entire bottle to Jasper, regardless of the cost, simply to get rid of him. "If you drink, you'll use it as an excuse not to drive. I'd feel bad about asking you to leave and get behind the wheel with alcohol in your system. Then things would get awkward between us because I don't want you to stay."

His perfect smile fell. "But why? I don't understand. Did I do something wrong? I thought we were starting a good thing. Didn't you have fun last time?"

Sex was supposed to be fun and passionate and meaningful. With Jasper, she'd only checked the no-longer-a-virgin box. That was all.

What she'd shared with Rip had been in a different universe. Undoubtedly one-sided in her favor, he'd done things to her that she'd only read about, stopping short of letting him go to home base or letting her give him any of the sweet pleasure he'd spoon-fed her body, but she'd been as affectionate as he'd allow.

Connection—that was what she had with Rip.

Ashley dug out one of the plastic cups she used for her

protein shakes and transferred the water. "You're a nice guy, Jasper, truly you are. It's just… I'm seeing someone else."

Surprise flashed across his face. "So soon? Already? I didn't realize we were even over."

"We never really started." Two dinners, one night of humdrum sex, and no further communication. "Did we?"

"Welliver told me not to get my hopes up, but I was certain I had a shot at something more with you."

"Why would you think that when I haven't returned any of your calls?"

"I guess ghosting a person should send a clear message, but I kept coming up with explanations for it because it's never happened to me before."

Welcome to my world. "I'm sorry if I hurt your feelings. I should've had the decency to explain. I know better than most how it feels. You didn't deserve to be treated that way."

"No, it's okay," he said, giving her a crestfallen look. "Who's the lucky guy? Please don't tell me it's that old, washed-up Marine turned biker?"

"He's far from old or washed-up." *More like mature, high-skilled, could-probably-kill-you-with-a-pencil Marine.* "And yes, it is." No hesitation. No doubt. No shame. "I'm with Rip Lockwood."

What exactly that would mean in the days to come, she wasn't quite sure, but for now her heart wasn't interested in anyone else.

LYING ON TOP of his sleeping bag that he'd placed on a cot in the bus, Rip stared at the ceiling. His mind churned; his body was restless.

He hoped LA could work out the introduction that he needed. With close to a million dollars on the line, not to mention countless lives, if he could sabotage that shipment laced with fentanyl, it would be a deadly blow to Todd. A move like that would be knocking down the perfectly positioned domino and the rest would fall, an unstoppable chain reaction until Todd Burk was dead or in jail.

The floor of the bus creaked. Feet shuffling slowly toward him.

Rip spotted BBB trying to creep up on him. Sighing inwardly, he lowered his eyelids to appear asleep while watching this dude, who thought he was being stealthy.

BBB had something sharp in his hand, a knife or homemade shank. Whatever it was, it could kill him. Hunched low, BBB slunk closer, easing past his feet, up beyond his legs, and raised the weapon in his hand, poised to thrust it in his chest.

Rip swung his legs around, knocking the man to the side, and jumped up as he grabbed BBB. He wrenched BBB's wrist hard, enough to sprain but stopping short of breaking it, snatched the shiv from him and pressed the sharp tip of the weapon to his jugular.

"I'm the last guy in the world that you want to mess with," Rip ground out. "Come near me again and I'm going to flip your off switch. Got it?"

Eyes wide with terror, BBB nodded. "Y-y-yeah. Got it." He scurried away and scrambled off the bus.

LA passed the scaredy-cat on her way in.

Rip hid the improvised weapon in his pants.

"You're up," she said. "Farley will meet you, but you have one chance to make an impression. Don't blow it."

He took off his windbreaker and the flannel shirt he wore over the Henley. "I won't."

As he left the bus following LA, the cold air nipped him. A temporary discomfort he ignored. He spotted Perry carrying a batch of drugs from the camper to a shipping container that was eight feet by eight feet. He held parcels of pills in various colors, roughly the size of bricks, maybe sixty or seventy of them, bundled together in plastic wrap. It looked like a small bale of pharmaceuticals. Perry set it on the ground and unlocked the storage container.

The man with wild, curly hair waited in front of the travel trailer. To his left beside him, Lumley and Drexel were chatting and smoking cigarettes. In the golden lights under the awning of the trailer, Rip saw that Farley's hair was red, his eyes a watery blue, his face weathered with a long, jagged scar running across his left cheek.

Farley stood, peeling an apple with a switchblade, but Rip didn't miss the tactical knife holstered on his hip. It was a Karambit. The small knife had a razor-sharp double-edged blade that curved inwardly, nearly semicircular, ending in a vicious point. In action, with the large round steel finger holes on the handle, a Karambit reminded Rip of a tiger's claw. A nasty piece of business if the one wielding it knew how to use it properly.

The only other person Rip had encountered carrying one had been Special Operations like him.

"So, tell me, why should I give a junkie, who'll do anything for his next fix, two minutes of my time?" Farley asked.

Two was better than one. "For starters, I'm not a junkie."

Farley cast a furtive glance at LA, who started fidgeting.

Drexel pulled his weapon again and pointed it at Rip. The kid was too eager to draw. The skullcap-wearing Lumley wasn't sure what to do and grabbed his handgun as an afterthought.

Farley raised a palm, giving them the sign to hold, but Lumley was the only one to lower his weapon. "Let the man explain what he's doing here if not working for pills."

"My girl is a junkie," Rip said. "I'm here because I need serious work with serious pay."

"Oh, really." Farley slid a slice of apple into his mouth. "How do you feel about serious risk?"

"Wouldn't be here if I couldn't handle it?"

"Are you a cop?"

Tipping his head to the side, Rip pulled up his shirtsleeves, revealing the tats that told his story from motorcycle club to Marine Corps. "Do I look like a cop?"

Farley narrowed his eyes. "I don't like smart mouths."

With his 9mm still raised, Drexel took a step toward Rip.

"He's the Prez of the Iron Warriors," Lou-Ann said. "He ain't no cop."

Gritting his teeth, Rip wished she'd let him handle it from here.

"If you're the president of the Iron Warriors, why aren't you working with Todd Burk?" Farley asked. "Doesn't he have to kick back a part of his cut to the club?"

"We didn't see eye to eye on the percentage points. Long story short, Todd formed a new MC. The Hellhounds. Now, we're at war. I'm looking to stick it to him any way I can. Requires the right sort of friends and resources."

Farley stroked his jaw as he scrutinized Rip, especially his tattoos. "It's rare, but not unheard of for things to go wrong during deliveries. I happen to know that Burk is indebted to the cartel. If he's not able to make a profit from his impending shipment, it would create trouble for him. The lethal kind. But I don't like blowback on my business."

"You mean, you don't like to get your hands dirty," Rip said.

The corner of Farley's mouth hitched up in a grin. "That's what middlemen are for. Let's say I hired you to handle Burk's next shipment. Free of charge to me, as a test. If his product happens to go missing, you take all the heat and deal with Todd Burk, so I never have to again. Dead men can't cause waves."

"What happens to the product?" Rip asked, though he already intended to turn it over to the DEA.

"Who's to say?" Farley shrugged. "If it got lost, finders keepers. But I'd want a taste of the profits."

"Ten percent."

"Forty. It's not as if you paid for it, and I remain your dealer in perpetuity."

Rip gave it a minute, pretending to weigh his options.

Clearly, Farley was a gambler. He was betting and betting big that Rip would eliminate Todd Burk for him, sell the tainted drugs, kicking back a whopping forty percent of the profits while taking the heat from the authorities once people started dying from the spiked drugs.

"You've got a deal." Rip offered his hand to shake on it.

Farley's half grin spread into a smile. "Not so fast. How do I know you're capable of *dealing* with Burk?"

Rip moved fast. He snapped his hand up, grabbing the body of Drexel's gun, and shoved the muzzle sideways to stay out of the line of any accidental discharge. Then he twisted the gun a half turn counterclockwise, nearly breaking Drexel's wrist. The gun fell to the ground. As Drexel howled in pain and clutched his wrist, Rip kicked the gun to the side into the darkness.

Keeping a lightning pace, he turned on Lumley. Skullcap was fumbling to draw his pistol. Once he pulled it free from his waistband, Rip snatched it. Stepping back, rather than aim it at anyone, he disassembled it. Removed the magazine. Ejected the bullet in the chamber. Pressed the two buttons on the side and slipped off the slide. Popped the spring free. Pushed out the barrel.

Eighteen seconds.

He held out the pieces for Lumley to take.

"A bit of a showoff, but I like you." Farley chuckled. "Were you MARSOC?" he asked, gesturing to Rip's tattoo of the Marine Special Operator insignia.

"Yeah. From the Karambit, I'd take it you were Canadian JTF," he said, using the acronym for the Joint Task Force.

"You'd guess correct." Farley's gaze dropped to his ankle. "You're also packing."

Rip tugged up the leg of his jeans, exposing the gun in his ankle holster. "What can I say? You've got shoddy security."

Drexel glared at him.

"Well, good help is expensive." Farley held out his palm and waited.

Reluctantly, Rip pulled out his gun and handed it over to him.

"SIG P365." Farley pulled back the slide, checking to see if a bullet was in the chamber. There was. "Nice weapon." He aimed it right between Rip's eyes. "I only do this kind of dirty business of backstabbing and double-dealing with people I can trust. Can I trust you, Rip Lockwood?"

No honor among thieves. Farley couldn't trust Rip any more than Rip could trust this drug dealer who had neglected to mention the entire shipment was laced with fentanyl.

"No. If I said yes, you'd know I was lying. What you can trust is that I'll take care of Todd Burk. He won't be your problem anymore."

Farley narrowed his eyes again. Then he cracked a smile. "As I said, I like you." He emptied Rip's magazine of bullets and handed it back empty. "Take a picture of Burk for me when you tell him his shipment got lost. I want to see the look on that weasel's face."

"I'll see what I can do."

This time they shook on it.

Chapter Fourteen

Dressed in civilian clothes, with her badge and her service weapon clipped on her belt, Ashley walked into the sheriff's department to let Clark know she was still breathing and to get an update on everything.

She kept her Stetson on, not intending to stay too long. Nodding hello to the deputy stationed at the front desk, she walked to the half door at the end of the counter and waited to be buzzed in.

The door clicked open. As she walked in, she glanced at the sheriff's office. He was inside talking to a striking, petite blonde.

Detective Hannah Delaney.

Her picture had been splashed all over the *Laramie Gazette* in recent months. She'd been put through the wringer. No law enforcement officer had gone through more hell than her, and Ashley did not envy the woman. However, Hannah had managed to catch the University Killer after nearly being his last victim, and gotten engaged to her partner on the case.

All is well that ends well. Ashley's grandmother used to say that.

Mitch flew out of his chair from behind his desk in the bullpen and hurried over to her.

"Where's the fire, Cody?" she asked, brightly.

Staring at her, he searched her face. "You haven't heard," he said in a whisper.

"Heard what?"

He took her by the arm, hauled her to the break room the size of a closet, stopped in front of the coffee maker and shut the door.

Drama was the last thing she needed this morning. "This is very cloak-and-dagger. What's up?" Then she caught the worry in Mitch's eyes.

"LPD released Todd Burk."

An icy wave of fear flooded every cell in her body. Fear for Rip. "No, no, they can't let him go." What if the Sons of Chaos reached out to him about everything that had happened in Happy Jack's? Not if. But when. Had they already called him? If so, would he think of contacting his supplier? Would he be able to? "I thought they were going to hold him for at least seventy-two hours."

"Detective Delaney had no choice but to cut him loose."

"But why? I don't understand."

With a sigh, Mitch put his hands on his hips. "The knife used to kill Shane Yates was the same murder weapon used to slit the throat of the pharmacist."

"Okay? What does that have to do with why they let him go?"

"We got prints off the knife. They didn't belong to Todd Burk."

"When have a set of prints at a crime scene ever matched his? It's probably some Hellhound who we need to interrogate because the odds are extremely high that Todd ordered the murder."

"You're not listening to me." Mitch clutched her shoulders as if to steady her, and dread crawled up her spine.

"We got a match on the prints. They belong to your biker boyfriend. Rip Lockwood."

Shock rocketed through her. What the hell?

She jerked free of his grip. "It's not Rip. He didn't kill anyone." Her mind whirled a second before focusing. "His place was burglarized Friday night. The knife must've been stolen."

Mitch looked anxiously uncomfortable. "You didn't list anything as missing."

"I meant to," she said quickly, without thinking. "It took him time to go through his things. He mentioned the knife was missing. But I didn't have a chance to report it because I had to go dark on something for the DEA." She grew lightheaded from the lie and the room started spinning. She hoped she didn't sound as suspicious as she thought she did.

Mitch frowned and crossed his arms. "What kind of knife was it?"

Swearing inside her head, she spun on her heel away from him. She pictured Rip. Sometimes he wore his Glock in a shoulder holster. Sometimes on his hip. She didn't know about the ankle holster. But he usually had a fixed blade. "KA-BAR." She opened the door.

Mitch slammed it closed. "Did he report it missing?"

"Let me open the door."

"If you march into the sheriff's office looking and sounding like you do right now, if you go in there and lie or try to protect Lockwood, you will lose your badge. Maybe not today, but when this all shakes out and the truth comes to light—"

"The facts, the evidence will prove without a shadow of doubt that Rip is innocent."

"Is he worth what you're about to do?"

"Yes." She tried to open the door again.

He leaned on it with his full weight, shutting it. "I'm your friend. Just walk back out the front door instead. Get in your car. Drive off. Calm down. Think it through. If what you're saying is true, then he doesn't need you to put up a defense for him in front of your boss. Let his lawyer do it for him."

"Move."

"Think it through, Russo."

"He didn't do this! If Rip was a cold-blooded killer, he would've taken care of Burk years ago."

"Right now, you need to be a deputy. Not his girlfriend."

Stepping away from the door, she took a deep breath. "You're right."

"I am?" Mitch cleared his throat. "I mean, of course I am. I just can't believe you're actually listening to me."

She needed to think clearly. Above all, she needed to be honest. Lying wouldn't help him.

"Did he really mention the knife was missing?"

She shook her head. "He hasn't had a chance to clean up his place, much less go through everything. But he wasn't wearing it when I was called over about gunshots reported. And I didn't see the knife on him the next day either. The three Hellhounds who broke in must have taken it from his trailer."

"Okay." Mitch nodded. "Just tell him to get a lawyer and turn himself in."

"I would…if I could."

"What is that supposed to mean?"

Her chest tightened with worry for Rip. "I need to update the sheriff on what I've been doing."

"And it concerns Lockwood?"

"It does." She'd dragged him into her one-woman operation to cut off Todd's drug supply and now he was alone, exposed. Vulnerable.

Because of her.

Lowering his head, Mitch sighed even louder this time. "Russo, what kind of hole have you dug for yourself?" Her friend looked at her with disappointment in his eyes.

"A big one." She held his gaze. "Please, get out of the way."

Mitch stepped aside.

She shuffled past him in the small space, opened the door and marched to the sheriff's office. Glancing across the hall, she looked at the empty chief deputy's office. She wished Holden Powell had been on duty today. Her brother, Angelo, had been Holden's best friend in high school. He'd have her back in this and would understand the lengths she had to go to in order to get Todd Burk. Knocking, she met her boss's gaze.

Sheriff Clark waved her in. "Deputy Russo. I'm happy to see you alive and well. This is Detective Hannah Delaney."

Ashley shook Delaney's hand while the detective remained seated. "Pleasure to meet you, ma'am. I admire your work and sympathize with everything you've been through this past year."

"Sometimes the job throws you into the meat grinder. If you're lucky, you come out in one piece, but never quite the same."

"I'm sure you've got some dark stories to tell."

The detective flashed a grim smile. "You have no idea."

"Detective Delaney, if that was all," Sheriff Clark said, standing, "I need to get an update from my deputy about a case she's working on."

"It would be best if she stayed." Ashley glanced between them as the sheriff's eyebrows pinched in curiosity. "What I have to tell you might have some bearing on her case."

"The Shane Yates murder?" Delaney asked.

"Yes."

"Well, go ahead." The sheriff gestured for her to speak.

For a split second, she debated how honest to be, but deep down she knew she had to tell him everything. "On Saturday, I left on a mission that was DEA-related."

"Yes." Clark nodded. "I'm aware."

Get on with it. Spit it out. "I misled you to believe that the DEA was sending me in with one of their agents. But they didn't feel the case warranted taking up their resources. They only want to go after big fish. Agent Welliver provided me with actionable intelligence, helped me strategize and then encouraged me to recruit Rip Lockwood as an asset and to have him assist me as my partner undercover, which is what I did."

Clark reared back, a stony expression washing over his features. His gaze flicked over her shoulder, behind her, to the hall. "Deputy Cody, unless you have a good reason to lurk outside my office, I suggest you return to your desk and get to work."

Ashley didn't bother to turn around; she could hear the shuffle of Mitch's footsteps hurrying off.

"Continue," Clark said, folding his arms across his chest.

Ashley clasped her wrist behind her back, standing formally at ease. "We went to Bitterroot Gulch on Saturday. Got information from the Sons of Chaos regarding Todd Burk's drug operation and then stayed the night in Misty Creek. I know that Shane Yates was killed that night between seven thirty and ten."

"How do you know that if you were out of town?" Detective Delaney asked.

"Because Bobby Quill from the Iron Warriors called Rip. I listened to the call on speakerphone. They all wanted to get information from Yates about the Hellhounds' drug operation. Yates responded to a text at seven thirty agreeing to meet them at their old clubhouse at nine. When he didn't show up, JD drove by his house. He saw the crime scene, you—" she nodded to the detective "—and a body bag. I also know that Rip's prints were found on the murder weapon."

The sheriff and Delaney exchanged a furtive glance.

"Explain," he said.

"I can't tell you how I know that, but I know for a fact that Rip didn't kill Shane Yates because he was with me that night. I can't speak to his whereabouts for the Fuller murder, but if the same weapon was used then it was the same person who committed both murders."

Clark glanced across at the bullpen through the window and shook his head, his gaze no doubt locked on Mitch. "What time did you leave town together on Saturday to go up to Bitterroot Gulch?" He opened his pad and grabbed a pen.

"We left separately, sir. But it's a three-and-a-half-hour drive to Bitterroot from here. He met me at Happy Jack's Roadhouse a few minutes after nine. We didn't stay long together inside. Maybe twenty minutes. We hung around the parking lot for another ten, waiting for Stryker, the president of the Sons. He gave us critical information that Rip is acting on now. Then we left and we were followed and shot at by three Sons."

"Can you prove Lockwood was with you in Bitterroot around nine last night?" Delaney asked.

"There were cameras outside of the roadhouse, which would have captured our arrival and departure." As well as their make-out session in the parking lot. "Also, I noticed a traffic camera at the main intersection less than a quarter mile on the only road that leads to Happy Jack's. We passed it separately on the way in and together on the way out. The motel we got a room at in Misty Creek also had surveillance cameras in the office. He was captured on it. I'm certain of it."

"Deputy Russo, did you and Lockwood share a room?" the detective asked.

Ashley stiffened. "The surveillance footage should be sufficient evidence to clear Lockwood of Shane Yates's murder. I don't see what bearing our accommodations would have on the case."

"You don't see, or you don't want to see?" Detective Delaney asked.

Ashley looked at the sheriff.

"Under normal circumstances," he said with a heavy breath, "I do my best to turn a blind eye to your association with Rip Lockwood because quite frankly I'd rather not acknowledge it. But since the nature of your relationship has significant bearing not only on a murder case but also a DEA-related operation, loosely related might I add and in a dangerous manner that I am not comfortable with, we need you to answer the question."

"We shared a room," Ashley admitted.

Detective Delaney crossed her legs. "Are the two of you involved?"

"It's complicated."

"I'll make it simple," the detective said. "Yes or no?"

"Yes. But as I've stated, there's proof that he was in Bitterroot at nine p.m. and could not be the person who murdered Yates. It is my belief that three Hellhounds broke into Rip's trailer on Friday to find something with his prints that they could use as a murder weapon. He injured one of them. A big, tall guy with a limp. Deputy Cody has the pictures I took of the three who I think are responsible for the break-in. Todd Burk is setting up Rip. I thought he wanted to kill him, but apparently framing him for murder is just as good to get him out of the way."

"To what end?" the sheriff asked.

"To have it all, with no opposition. Rip Lockwood is the one person that Todd Burk fears." Rightfully so because Rip had him in the crosshairs now. "The DEA-related operation was leading us to Burk's supplier at the ranch, a drug camp somewhere. But with Burk no longer being held in custody, Rip's life is in grave danger."

Detective Delaney straightened. "Wait a minute. Did you say a drug camp?"

"Yes."

"Before Yates was killed, he called me. Scared. Left a message that he had information about what Burk was planning next. Something about a *camp*, but it didn't make any sense at the time and I never got a chance to clarify."

"The drug camp that Stryker described was where they collected all the pills they received after a run. I rode undercover with Rip on part of one yesterday. They took us to a pain clinic. A doctor was paid to write various prescriptions for a bunch of addicts. For oxycodone, Percocet, Adderall. But mainly oxy. There was a man, Drexel, he was the driver and security, took us around to different pharmacies from Casper to Colorado Springs, though I only made it to Fort Collins, where we filled the prescriptions. Some kind of deal had been worked out in advance with the pharmacists. All smaller drugstores. Family-owned. Like Fuller's. Most just hurriedly went through the motions of filling the scrips to get us out of there, but a few looked as though they had been intimidated and coerced into compliance. What if Burk is trying to set up a similar operation here? And what if Mr. Fuller didn't want to cooperate and Burk found out that Yates was an informant, so he had them killed?"

Delaney was probably a fantastic poker player. Her expression didn't give away anything she was thinking.

"Ashley, it's not like you to color outside the lines," the sheriff said. "I want to know how long you've been misleading me about your work with the DEA, how deep it goes, and the specifics of everything you've done off-book. Anything you tell me will be fact-checked with Agent Welliver." Clark gave her a stern look of warning, but Ashley guessed that Welliver wouldn't return his calls until after he learned the results of the mission that Rip was still on. "Then I have to begin a formal investigation into your association, *relationship*, with Ripton Lockwood to see if it may have tainted any prior cases. Close the door and take a seat."

WEARING HER STETSON, Ashley walked out of the sheriff's office without her badge or service weapon. Suspended pending the results of the department's investigation.

White noise that had started in her ears as the sheriff began asking probing, invasive questions continued along with her out-of-body experience. It seemed she was floating to her truck rather than walking.

Sheriff Clark had doubted every word she said, she saw it in his eyes, but at least Detective Delaney had wasted no time starting the process to track down the surveillance footage in Bitterroot and Misty Creek. The Laramie Police Department would probably have it by lunch, certainly no later than the end of day, and Rip would be cleared of Shane Yates's murder and hopefully that of the pharmacist as well.

The only other good thing to come out of the interrogation was the three of them agreed Todd Burk was mostly likely behind this.

She climbed into her truck and simply sat there with no idea what to do next.

The loss of her badge didn't bother her. She only became a deputy for one reason and one reason only. To see Todd Burk behind bars. As long as justice was served, the results of the investigation didn't matter.

But she had no way to contact Rip and warn him that Todd was no longer being held in custody.

A buzzing sounded in her truck. She checked her cell phone to see if she had it on silent. But it wasn't coming from her cell.

The sound was coming from the glove box. She opened the compartment and tracked the buzzing to Rip's burner phone.

Ashley grabbed it. Instead of a phone number on the screen there was a six-digit code. She opened the flip phone and put it to her ear.

On the other end a bunch of men were cheering, whooping and hollering.

"All right, all right! Settle down. I told you I would be back lickety-split!" Todd Burk's voice.

Her pulse spiked. She stared at the phone, piecing together what she was hearing, how she was hearing it. Rip must have planted a listening device in the clubhouse.

She put the burner on speaker, took out her own phone and started recording.

"The cops can't hold me," Todd said. "No matter how hard they try."

"Teflon! Teflon! Teflon!" the Hellhounds cheered.

"Okay, let's get to business, boys," Todd said.

"Shane Yates is dead," a less than enthusiastic Hellhound said. "Murdered. You've got to call a vote for a member to meet Mr. Mayhem."

A vote to murder a brother in the club.

"Yates was a rat. He's been snitching." Todd went on to say foul things about Detective Delaney, calling her disgusting names. "He's not dead because of me. This is on her."

"We sided with you because you promised you'd be different." The same dissenter. "Rip didn't call a vote on you selling drugs, so we walked. On principle. But you're the same."

"I'm nothing like Lockwood!"

"You don't want to lead. You want to rule. That's not what we signed up for." Chairs scraped wood. She couldn't make out how many. Maybe three. Possibly four. "No member meets Mr. Mayhem without a vote. Snitch or not. We're out."

A door slammed.

"It's all right, boys. Let those weak punks walk. We don't need them anymore anyway. They served their purpose, sided with us in the vote that allowed us to form our own club. Now we can finish this with Rip. No vote necessary."

"He left town on Saturday," a different guy said. "Before Yates met Mr. Mayhem. He might have an alibi. Rip is one lucky dude. Maybe he can be persuaded to stay out of our way. He used to be our brother."

"Past tense," Todd said. "He's not a Hellhound. If he's not stopped, he'll bring down the empire we're building."

An empire of drugs and dirty money and death. Todd and his Hellhounds weren't building anything. Only destroying.

"Are you sure this is the best way to handle things?" a new voice questioned. "Letting Rip take the fall for the pharmacist and Shane? I mean, what if it doesn't work? Like Lyle said, he wasn't even in town when you had a brother killed. This might not stick to him and then he'll come for all of us. I don't know about you, but I don't want to be on his 'to-do things' list. Rip can be a scary, deadly dude when provoked. First you go after his deputy and now you frame him for murder. I'd call that provocation."

"Not me, *we*, brother. We're in this together," Todd said.

"I didn't vote for any of this!" a new dissenter called out. "I was in favor of expanding and starting our own drug camp. Not starting a war with Rip Lockwood."

"Quiet! Yeah, I wanted the cops to deal with Rip," Todd said. "So, I could see that self-righteous do-gooder rotting behind bars while I took everything that was his. Including his pretty deputy. But fortune shines on us, brothers. I heard from the Sons of Chaos. Guess who was in Happy Jack's with a cop the other night trying to get info on our drug supplier?"

"Rip wouldn't go in there with a cop, regardless of whether she's his old lady," someone called out.

"But he did! He called her his old lady, and they described her to me. Hot little number with light brown skin and long brown hair. Apparently, they were all over each other. We haven't seen Rip with a woman besides her. Definitely Deputy Russo. She must've lied to me the other day when I asked her about the two of them. Makes no difference now. I reached out to our supplier this morning. Just so happens Rip is with him. I told Farley that Rip is working with a cop. We don't have to worry about Lockwood anymore because his luck runs out today and I'm going to be there to watch. I've got the coordinates. Less than hour's drive north of town. All we have to do is go there and wait. He'll be delivered along with our drugs. Dead on arrival."

Chapter Fifteen

"Change of plans," LA said. "They upped the timeline for some reason. They're delivering Burk's shipment today. Be ready."

Change wasn't always good.

Rip finished eating the protein bar he'd purchased himself before arriving and washed it down with water. No need to take unnecessary chances consuming anything from the camp when all the food might be poisoned.

Putting on his windbreaker, he jammed the homemade shank into his pocket. He grabbed his backpack and got off the bus.

Perry went to the shipping container, unlocked it and opened the doors wide.

In the light of day, Rip had a full view of the contents. The quantity of drugs inside was staggering. A mother lode the DEA would salivate to get their hands on and be eager to take credit for the seizure of. This would make up for any wrongdoing on Ash's part or at least be taken into consideration if she were censured for breaking the rules.

Perry took a bundle of drugs out of the shipping container and locked it. The shipment had lashing straps criss-crossed and cinched tight around it. Hooked at the top was a small red device—the beacon.

"Load up!" Drexel called out.

The addicts crowded around the picnic table stopped eating and smoking. They gathered their belongings and began piling into the van.

Farley stepped out of the travel trailer, wearing sunglasses. His wild red hair was a hot mess in the wind. Taking a minute, he stretched his neck, arms, back, rolled his shoulders. Rip had done likewise before the sun was up. Farley slipped on a utility field jacket over his holstered gun and Karambit blade and started toward a second vehicle. "Rip!" He waved him over.

"Hey, what's up?" Rip asked, unease trickling through his veins.

"We're taking a separate plane to make the delivery," Farley said as Perry loaded the shipment into the van.

Rip stared at Farley. "You're coming?"

"I want to see to it that things go smoothly." Farley clasped his shoulder. "I need the warm fuzzy that you get to Laramie with the drugs. From there, it's up to you to deal with Burk."

Rip nodded, but his senses went on high alert. Farley preferred the middlemen to handle this sort of thing, so what was the real reason he was tagging along?

He suspected the answer meant trouble, but he played it cool. Got in the back of the van without protest or hesitation. Farley sat beside him.

Lumley drove with Perry riding in the passenger's seat.

A plane waited, engine running, on a landing strip that stretched off into vast, barren terrain punctuated by small piles of rocks. In the distance, trees, a range of mountains and Devils Tower were visible.

They parked and climbed out.

Lumley opened the back van door so Perry could grab

the shipment of drugs, but when he closed the door, he was holding a tire iron.

A blade or blunt instrument made the best weapon on an aircraft if you wanted to land in one piece. They boarded the plane without uttering a word. The aircraft was slightly smaller than the Cessna. A twin otter that had the same type of roll-up door.

Farley took a seat in the cockpit next to the pilot. With Lumley to his left, holding the tire iron, Perry to his right, Rip, on guard, buckled in.

The plane took off.

The two henchmen were antsy, gazes bouncing from the windows to the pilot, to Rip, to Farley.

None of this boded well for Rip. The lackeys didn't concern him. Farley was the unknown variable with his Special Operations background that made him wary.

They'd been in the air maybe forty-five minutes, definitely less than an hour, when Farley got up from his seat and shoved out of the cockpit. "We're here."

A shot of adrenaline that always came before a fight sparked through Rip's synapses. Muscles coiled. Ready for the inevitable moment to arrive.

Perry undid his lap belt. He went to the roll-up door, yanked it open, letting in a surge of cold air, activated the beacon on the shipment and tossed it out of the plane.

Hovering near the cockpit, Farley removed his sunglasses and slipped them into his top jacket pocket. "I got a call from Todd Burk this morning. He was released from police custody and couldn't wait to tell me that your supposed junkie of a girlfriend is a deputy with the sheriff's department. He also had a lot of colorful things to say about you. Like the only thing you'd do with a shipment of drugs is turn it over to the authorities."

"This is a war," Rip said, "and Todd's a liar. You can't trust anything he says."

"That may be true. In fact, it is true. Todd's a stinking liar for sure." Farley grinned, the facial expression tugging the skin around the gnarly scar on his cheek, making him look even more menacing. "But I'm going to take that weasel's word over yours on this because I know that he's a no-good criminal. Can't say the same about you." He pounded a fist on the wall of the cockpit. "Circle back around," he said to the pilot. Then he looked at Rip. "Time to jump."

"No parachute?" Rip asked with a wry smile.

Farley chuckled. "Why couldn't you be on my side of the law? I wasn't lying when I said I liked you."

"Get up." Lumley nudged Rip's arm. "And get moving. Burk is down there waiting to see you hit the ground. We promised him a show."

"Well, we don't want to disappoint him," Rip said, but it wasn't going to be him hitting the ground like a pancake if he had anything to say about it.

Lumley shoved him this time. "Let's go."

Near the open door, Perry stood hunched from the low ceiling, waiting for him.

Rip shook his head. "No way."

Staying back near the cockpit, Farley simply watched.

Lumley moved the tire iron to his left hand and grabbed the hilt of the 9mm stuffed in the front of his waistband with his right. "Unbuckle your belt. Now!"

Rip was seated at such a close range. The odds were high that Lumley could get off a shot and hit him somewhere that would do plenty of damage without puncturing a hole in the aircraft.

So, Rip did the only thing he could. He unbuckled his lap belt and got up.

Then Perry made the mistake of moving forward to grab him.

Training kicked in. Rip was a machine, programmed by the Marines for one purpose: to put down the enemy.

He fired a left-handed jab to the man's solar plexus, a tight network of nerves below the sternum, knocking the wind from him as he doubled over. Not giving Perry a chance to regain his breath, Rip grabbed him and whirled 180 degrees in anticipation of Lumley's next move.

Sure enough, in a panic the jerk had already pulled his gun. Lumley squeezed off two rounds. One bullet struck Perry in the back and the second in the head.

"Don't fire, you fool," Farley shouted. "You'll get us all killed."

Dropping the dead guy, Rip backed up closer to the door and prepared to take down the next one.

With a deer-in-the-headlights look, Lumley lunged at him. The guy swung wildly with the tire iron, but Rip pivoted out of the way, and Lumley hit nothing but air.

Rip launched a punch to his windpipe. When Lumley dropped the tire iron and gun and clutched his throat with both hands, his mouth open, struggling to breathe, not even a wheeze getting out, Rip knew he'd crushed his windpipe. He thrust Lumley toward the open door and kicked him out.

Something hard came down across Rip's skull, and piercing pain tore through the side of his head. The world blurred. He dropped, his head slamming against the steel bench, and hit the floor.

Farley. Farley had hit him with the tire iron. The former JTF operator had moved quick as lightning because he was also trained to kill.

Rip tried to regain his bearings, tried to swim through the dizzying haze of pain.

Move. You have to move.

Every second counted. He needed to end this fight quickly or the other guy would.

Farley yanked his leg, hauling him to the opening.

Frigid air rushed over Rip, energizing him. Adrenaline fired hot in his system, clearing his mind, but his head throbbed like someone was beating on his skull with a chisel.

Grabbing him by the windbreaker, Farley managed to shove Rip's head and shoulders out the door.

But with his right hand, Rip snatched onto a strap dangling near the rear wall, used for tying down cargo, and held strong.

Rather than trying to wrestle him out of the plane as one of his lackeys might've attempted, Farley drew his Karambit knife, hoisted the blade up and drove it down.

Rip reacted without hesitation, without emotion, without thought, and blocked with his left hand.

The blade plunged into his palm. Ignoring the excruciating pain, disregarding the fear of falling out the aircraft and plummeting to the ground, Rip let go of the strap keeping him onboard and grabbed the shiv from his pocket. Then he thrust the pointed end of the improvised blade up under Farley's chin.

The redheaded man stilled, a shocked expression on his pale face. Rip pulled the weapon free and stabbed again. This time in the jugular. It was done. Blood ran down Farley's throat, dripping onto Rip. He shoved Farley off him, knocking him deeper into the plane, and the former JTF operator keeled over.

Scrambling away from the door, Rip yanked the knife from his hand, letting it clatter to the floor. Not taking any chances, he checked Farley. The man was dead, his eyes open and vacant.

Rip peered out the door. Below on the ground, he spotted a black van and a couple of motorcycles—Hellhounds—in a wide-open space. The Snowy Mountain Range wasn't far to the southwest. They were somewhere north of Laramie, with no town around for miles.

Just then he caught sight of patrol cruisers from two different counties racing up, red-and-blue lights flashing. They surrounded the Hellhounds from the west and south, cutting off any escape.

Rip caught his breath, grabbed a gun and shuffled to the cockpit. Keeping the safety on, he aimed the weapon at the pilot.

"Don't kill me," the middle-aged man said, his eyes growing wide.

"I'm not going to kill you. But you are going to land. Right down there."

The pilot looked around at the ground. "I don't think there's enough room to taxi before I can stop."

"You had less space where you picked us up. Do it."

"Uh-uh." The pilot took another glance. "Pretty rocky down there. We could crash."

"I said I wouldn't kill you, but it's about to get a whole lot rockier for you if I shoot you," he said, aiming at the man's knee. Not that Rip needed to go that far. The pilot was scared of the cops. Rip needed to override that fear with the prospect of something worse. "Take us down and land."

After a moment longer of hesitation, the pilot nodded. "All right."

Rip's head pounded and ached. "You got a med kit?"

The pilot gestured to the wall behind the seat.

Rip popped open the kit, dug out some gauze and medical tape.

As the pilot circled twice, gauging where to make his approach, Rip quickly bandaged his hand, though it wouldn't do much to stop the bleeding. Once the pilot finally decided, he brought the twin otter down, taxied and braked to a stop.

"You're getting out first." Rip waved him along with the gun, and the pilot moved to the back of the plane.

The blood from the wound in his palm had already soaked through the gauze. Getting up, Rip winced from another gut-wrenching stab that went through his head, his vision blurring again. Pure adrenaline still pumping through him was muting the pain and keeping him moving. But it wouldn't last. He dreaded to think what state he'd be in once it wore off.

The pilot hopped out onto the ground and raised his palms.

Rip dropped the gun before he eased off the plane and held up his hands.

Several Hellhounds were in handcuffs. Freddy, Arlo and Clive—the same ones he suspected had attacked him at his trailer. They were loaded into the backs of cruisers.

And Todd Burk. He was down on the ground, facefirst, arms behind him, a knee in his back, as he was being cuffed. As they hauled him up, his gaze found Rip's.

Seething, Todd glared at him, and Rip smiled even though it cost him a jolt of pain.

Deputies from the neighboring county approached him and the pilot, guns at the ready, issuing instructions.

Doing as told, Rip and the pilot got down on their knees and put their hands behind their heads.

A door from one of the Laramie cruisers flew open. Ash

jumped out and ran, headed straight for him. She shoved past Sheriff Clark, who tried to hold her back, and kept sprinting for him.

Rip's heart lit up brighter than a stadium on Super Bowl Sunday.

Sheriff Clark hurried behind her. "It's all right!" He shouted to the other deputies. "Let her through. Rip Lockwood is with us."

For a split second, Rip wondered why she'd been inside the vehicle in the first place and why the other deputies didn't already know she was with the sheriff's department.

But every thought evaporated once she was in front of him, helping him up from the ground, her face slack with shock, her eyes wide with worry.

"Oh my God!" Ash's gaze fell over him. "You're covered in blood."

"Most of it is not mine." Grateful to be alive, he wanted to hold her, kiss her, but he was a bloody mess and there wasn't much time. His vision blurred again. Pain ballooned in his head like his skull wanted to explode.

Sheriff Clark came up beside them. "Good grief. What happened to you?" He glanced inside the plane and gasped. "Or rather, I guess you're what happened to them."

Ash touched the side of his head, and he winced. "You're bleeding. We need to get you to the hospital."

A deputy slapped handcuffs on the pilot.

"You're going to need him," Rip said, gesturing to the middle-aged man, "to fly you back near Devils Tower, where he picked us up. From there, it's a ten-minute ride..." He pushed through the fog encroaching on his brain to think. "Due east. You'll find the drug camp. Agent Welliver will want to know. There's fentanyl from the Sandoval cartel and enough drugs to make it more than worth his time."

He kept spewing every little thing he could remember. "Farley was in charge, but he's dead in the plane. Lou-Ann, LA, she knows about the dealings with the cartel and Burk. If someone cuts her a deal, she'll talk." He thought about her serving rat poison to the addicts they used as workers. "But the deal shouldn't be too good."

"Okay." Sheriff Clark nodded. "We'll take care of it."

"Come on." Ash curled an arm around his waist, slinging his left arm over her shoulder, like he needed her help walking.

And maybe he did, because a blinding bolt of pain lanced his head.

He took four steps forward, the world spun, and everything faded to black as his legs buckled.

Chapter Sixteen

Numb. Ashley was numb as she continued to wait for Rip to open his eyes and talk to her. In his hospital room, she lay in the bed alongside Rip, her head on his shoulder, her hand on his chest, listening, feeling him breathe on his own. The blinds were drawn, dampening the afternoon light without making the room too dim.

The hardest part had been the thirty-six hours he was in the ICU on a ventilator. The nerve-racking sounds of the machine, the overwhelming smell of disinfectant, constant reminders of how close he'd come to death. She didn't know if she could bear any of this, how to face the prospect of him not making a full recovery. So, she'd pushed such thoughts from her mind. As she'd sat in the chair, holding his hand and watching over him, one thing repeated over and over in her head.

I can't lose you.

I can't lose you.

Once he was moved to a regular room, relief had set in, but she still couldn't bear to leave his side for more than a few minutes. Not until he woke up. He was only here in the hospital because she'd dragged him into all this.

Ashley was considering going to the cafeteria for a cup of coffee when Rip stirred and finally opened his eyes.

Leaning up on her forearm, she peered down at him.

His gaze wandered before landing on her. "Hey, you." He sounded foggy.

She caressed his cheek, so happy to see him awake tears pricked her eyes. "Hey, you."

"My throat…"

"You were intubated," she said, and his eyes narrowed in confusion. "Want some water?"

He nodded. Groaned. Struggled to sit up.

"Take it easy." She helped him adjust and then grabbed the cup that she had ready for him. Once he was propped up and seemed more comfortable, she put the straw to his lips.

Rip sipped generously, draining the cup of water. "How long was I out?"

"Two days."

"Two?" He was quiet for a long moment. "Have you been here the whole time?"

"I have. I didn't want to leave you." She got an extra pillow from a table near the chair, put it behind his head and climbed back into the bed. "They put you into a medically induced coma to alleviate the swelling in your head and allow your brain to rest. You opened your eyes after they took you off the ventilator, but you fell back asleep. The doctor said it was from the medication, but that you're a remarkable healer." She rubbed his arm. "You're going to be fine."

He raised his left hand that was bandaged and clenched his fingers until he winced.

"Nineteen stitches," she said. "You're very lucky according to the surgeon who operated on your hand. Well, that's what everyone around here is saying. All the doctors and nurses." She caressed his cheek. "Which makes me lucky."

He lowered his eyes. "Are you still angry that I left you behind?"

"No." Her worry and fear for his life overrode any anger. "I understand why you left me in Fort Collins." If he was in better shape, she would've told him who had given her a ride home, but in his current condition she didn't want to risk upsetting him.

"What happened with the camp?" he asked.

"A major drug seizure for the sheriff's department and DEA. LA was arrested. She was willing to spill her guts about everything for a lighter sentence. All thanks to you."

Reaching for her, he brushed strands of hair from her face. "Thanks to us. That bust never would've happened if not for you. Your stubborn persistence. You're the one who got the lead from the DEA and made sure I didn't waste time getting up to Happy Jack's. If I had waited a day or two, planning, trying to handle it on my own, we would've missed the window of opportunity and Todd would've gotten his last shipment. Did Agent Welliver cover for you with Sheriff Clark?"

"He did. Spoke very highly of me and commended my efforts in recruiting you." But she had already been honest with her boss and nothing Welliver had to say was going to undo her suspension or could help with the internal investigation.

"Is everything okay with your job?" he asked, as if reading her mind.

The man had nearly died, and he was worried about her. "It's complicated. We can talk about it later. I'm just happy you're going to be okay and that Todd Burk is finally going to prison for a long time."

"They did catch him red-handed picking up a shipment of drugs."

"And we have a recording of him admitting to framing you for murder."

"Murder? What did I miss?"

"A lot. Is your KA-BAR knife missing?"

He thought for a moment and then nodded. "Yeah. I left it in my trailer. Those guys broke in and I couldn't find it afterward."

"They stole it. Used it in the murders of Dr. Fuller, the pharmacist, and Shane Yates. But I was your alibi for Yates. There's surveillance video of you in Bitterroot, proving you couldn't have been here in town at the time of his murder."

"How did you get the recording?"

"The burner phone you put in my glove box rang."

"The bug I planted in the chapel, the meeting room, must have been voice-activated. I forgot to tell you about it."

"When I answered the phone, I heard Burk bragging about everything. Including how his supplier, Farley, was going to kill you that day. I recorded it on my phone, but I was out of my mind with worry for you." With fear like she'd never known. She held his face in her hands and kissed him lightly.

But he moved his mouth from hers, and unease wormed through her. "The Sons of Chaos will be coming for me sooner or later. Word will get out about LA to the Sandoval cartel and then I'll be on their radar, too. I'm leaving town, Ash. Today."

She swallowed around the sudden lump in her throat. "You're not going anywhere today. They're running some more tests on you later this afternoon and the doctor needs to determine if you need rehab."

"I can do rehab anywhere. *If* I need it."

"The doctor isn't going to discharge you today."

"This isn't prison. They can't keep me against my will. I'll leave when I'm ready regardless of paperwork."

Putting her hand on his chest, she held his gaze and softened her voice. "You had a severe head injury. Let them finish running their tests today, to make sure that you're fine. It takes hours to get results." Everything in the hospital took forever. One long waiting game. "Tomorrow, if you're still determined to get out of here, you can do it then. Please. For me. For my peace of mind."

He sighed. "I'll wait until tomorrow," he said, and she smiled. "Only if you agree not to stay."

Her smile fell. "What?" Drawing closer, she rested on her elbow, lowered her face close to his and cupped his cheek. "Don't do this. Don't push me away. Not after everything we've been through together."

"You've been in this hospital for two days. Get some air. Go rest. Do something else besides fret over me. I'm fine."

"You're *going to be* fine. Provided you take the time to heal and listen to the doctor. You're not invincible."

"Never thought I'd see the day where you were begging to keep me in bed."

His flirty banter was back, which meant he was truly on the road to recovery.

"You could have plenty more of those days." She brushed her lips over his and held his gaze. "You just have to want them. Want me."

Someone near the door cleared their throat, drawing their attention.

Quill and JD entered the room.

"Sorry to interrupt," Quill said. "We can come back later."

"No." Rip waved them in. "Ash was just leaving."

"To get a cup of coffee," she quickly added and glared at him. "I'll be back." Then she leaned in, bringing her mouth to his ear. "Whether you like it or not. If you think you're going to slip out of the hospital and sneak out of town, think again." Putting her hand on his chest, she snuggled up close and kissed him on the lips in front of his MC brothers. The long, slow kiss left no doubt about her feelings for him, and maybe because they had an audience or he was too tired to fight her, whatever the reason, he kissed her back, soothing her heart.

She climbed out of the bed, grabbed her purse and, ignoring the confused stares of the Iron Warriors, left the room. In the hall out of sight, she stood still a moment and listened.

"You're welcome, brother," Quill said with an attitude.

"What are you talking about?" Rip asked. "Welcome for what?"

"For her. Looks like she's your old lady after all. And that would not have happened if we hadn't been scaring off every dude that came near her."

"I'm still not happy about your interference, but I don't know what she is," Rip said. "What I do know is that I have to leave town as soon as possible and she's not coming with me."

We'll see about that, Ripton Lockwood.

RIP WAS A man of his word. The measures he'd taken over the years had derailed Ash's love life. Now that Todd Burk was in jail on charges that were going to stick, she could be free. To live her life as she wanted. To date. To have fun. To find love. To settle down in town, where she had a career and her family and roots.

Not running away and going into hiding with him.

"Have you heard anything from the Sons?" Rip asked.

JD nodded. "Oh, yeah. Stryker found out his sister is in jail because of you. The Sons want your head on a pike."

"Your old lady's, too." Quill raised his eyebrows.

"They asked the Hellhounds to take care of you two,"

JD said, "but they're a mess after Todd and the others got busted. At least that's what Will tells me."

Will was one of the surprise voters that had been against Rip because he hadn't trusted in the process and in the members to make the right decision.

Rip believed that deep down, Will was still loyal to the Iron Warriors and under new leadership, he'd return.

"Get the word out that Ash is with the sheriff's department. It'll be a deterrent. Once the Sons know I'm gone and I've left her behind, they'll think I don't care about her. But before I leave, I'll talk to Sheriff Clark about getting her protection and give him enough information to take to the FBI about the Sons and their prostitution ring. That'll put many of them in jail and leave the rest in real chaos." LA didn't know about Ash, which meant she'd stay under the radar of the cartel.

JD crossed his arms. "You can't go starting a war with the Sons by giving the FBI information without a vote, Rip."

"You heard Will. They want me dead. I'm already at war with them. That's why you need to strip me of my patches and excommunicate me. To protect the Warriors from any blowback."

Quill blanched. "No. No way. We won't do it. There has to be another alternative."

"There isn't." Rip had given it serious consideration. Strategized all the options. "Quill, I want you to support JD for president."

JD shook his head. "I don't want the mantle."

Smiling, Rip understood what the others had tried to teach him years ago. "That's one of the reasons why you're perfect for the job. You'll do great."

Ashley walked back into the room, holding a cup of coffee. She stopped at the foot of his bed and met Rip's gaze, and his chest tightened. She was so beautiful. So full of light. Special.

He didn't want to leave her, but he also didn't want to endanger her.

The best thing to do was to set her free.

"I appreciate everything you guys have done for me," Rip said to them. "Everything I've asked. For trusting me. For having my back. For watching out for Ash." He took a breath, finding it difficult to continue. He wasn't the sentimental type but was getting a bit choked up. "Even though I won't be an Iron Warrior anymore, you'll always be my brothers."

Ash stiffened, her eyes going wide in surprise.

"One drink before you leave town?" Quill asked.

Rip gave a noncommittal gesture. "I can't make any promises."

"I don't want this to be the last time I see you. In a hospital bed. Not wearing any underwear." Quill grinned.

Rip chuckled. "I'll see what I can do."

"You were a great Prez, Rip. I learned a lot from you," JD said.

"Make me proud. Lead them in the right direction."

Quill and JD took turns tapping a fist on Rip's shoulder. On their way out, they did the same to Ash.

There was a knock on the door. Chief Deputy Holden Powell came in and tipped his cowboy hat in greeting. He was the one man Rip thought might've ended up with Ashley. He had been her brother's best friend. Holden and Ashley had chosen to be deputies at the sheriff's office, and worked long hours together. But according to Ash, Holden always treated her like a little sister and now was happily married to a nurse.

"Holden," Ash said, "what are you doing here?"

"I wish it was better news," the chief deputy said gravely. JD eased toward the door. "We'll get going."

"You two might want to hold on." Powell stepped deeper inside the room. "Since it's Thanksgiving tomorrow, the district attorney wanted Burk and the other three Hellhounds to be moved to county lockup today. Earlier, as they were being transported, they managed to break out."

Rip swore under his breath. *Teflon.*

"In the process, they killed Deputy Livingston and injured Deputy Cody," Powell continued.

"Oh no!" Ash moved closer to Powell. "Is Mitch going to be okay?"

"He's out of surgery. Lost a lot of blood. Needed a transfusion. But he's going to make it."

Ash's face hardened. "You should've told me sooner."

"I'm sorry. I know you two are good friends, but you were waiting for Rip to wake up. I didn't want to add more to your plate of worries until I had to. The US Marshals have started a countywide manhunt for Burk and the others. In the meantime, we're working with the Laramie Police Department to have an officer assigned to each of you around the clock," he said to Ash and Rip.

Todd and the others would be looking for a place to hide. Someone vulnerable, someone alone whom they could exploit. "Ida. She'll need protection while I'm in here."

Holden tipped the brim of his hat up. "The LPD can only spare enough personnel to watch each of you."

"Ida is fine." Ash came around to the side of the bed and put a hand on his arm. "She's been with my parents the last few days."

"She went willingly?"

Smiling, Ash nodded. "Not a single complaint."

Didn't sound like his Aunt Ida.

"My mom had been checking on her several times a day to make sure she was all right and was taking her medication. Eventually, she just invited her to stay over. Ida seemed more than happy to have the company," she said, and that was a great relief to Rip. Ash turned to Powell. "You can have one officer watch our family. The other one can cover both of us. We'll stay together."

She was good at boxing him in and getting what she wanted. He'd give her that.

But *our family* struck him in an unexpected way. It almost gave him hope he and Ash could be together, their families joined as one.

Powell looked at Quill and JD. "We're hoping the Iron Warriors could keep an ear out and let us know if you hear anything."

JD nodded. "Of course. The sooner you catch them, the better for all of us."

"Everyone needs to stay vigilant," Chief Deputy Powell said. "Todd Burk and his cohorts are armed and desperate. With the marshals searching for them, we think it won't take long for them to be apprehended."

Ash's gaze found Rip's. The look in her eyes made his heart constrict. Too many emotions surfacing, battling for dominance. He didn't like it clouding his judgment, thawing him when he needed to be ice-cold—the only way to make tough decisions.

"I'm still getting out of the hospital tomorrow," he said to her. "But I won't leave town. Not until Burk has been captured."

Chapter Seventeen

In her parents' kitchen, Ashley finished putting away the last of the food. "I really appreciate you going to so much trouble to make Thanksgiving special."

"It was nice to have more people at the table this year," Mom said. "Instead of it being the three of us. And I'm pleased you finally brought a man to dinner. I didn't expect it to be that one, a biker, but you seem happy around him. Light up whenever you two are in the same room. Your father and I have noticed how he looks at you, too."

"How is that?" She still wasn't sure what was going through Rip's head.

He acted determined to push her away, but she was known for her stubborn persistence.

Mom gave a knowing smile and a soft chuckle. "The man is in love with you."

Air caught in her throat. *In love*. Their relationship had been a complicated, slow burn and then a sudden rolling boil. He'd give his life for her, and she wanted to spend her life with him. Love…was the perfect word.

"Are you sure?"

"I'm certain of it. The real question is how do you feel?"

She went to her mother and took her warm hands in hers. "I didn't realize how deeply I felt for him until I saw him covered in blood and watched him collapse. Sitting with him in the hospital, I would've given anything for him to open his eyes. Anything."

"I never knew what to make of Rip, but after everything he went through to get Todd Burk arrested, he's got our approval. We just want you to be happy."

"I will be. Once Burk is back behind bars." And Rip accepted they were meant for each other. "Tomorrow, I need to sit down with you and Dad and share my plans for the future."

"Not tonight?"

Ashley needed to get Rip on board with the plan first. "Tomorrow." She hugged her mom. "I love you."

"I love you, too, sweetheart."

She went into the living room.

Rip and her dad were coming down the hallway from the bedroom.

"We just tucked Ida in for the night," Dad said.

"She really loves it here. Thank you for taking care of her while I was gone." Rip shook her dad's hand. "There's something I'd like to ask, though it might be a huge imposition."

Ashley sensed what it would be. "Rip, I think you should wait until tomorrow. We'll come back. Okay?" One clear discussion about leaving would be best. "It's late and I'd like to get going."

Eyeing her, Rip hesitated.

She looked away from him and hugged her dad. "See you tomorrow. Love you."

"Love you more, jelly bean."

Hating when her dad called her that, she groaned.

Rip followed her through the living room.

She opened the front door and stepped out onto the porch. "An officer will stay parked out front until the US Marshals find Burk and his crew."

"Don't worry about us. You two go enjoy the rest of your evening." Dad lingered in the doorway, watching them get into her truck, and waved as they drove off.

"Drop me at my trailer. The other officer will stay with you."

"Rip—"

"Ash, we're not going to argue about this. I said I won't leave town. I'm not going to run off."

"Fine, no arguing." She turned on the radio and drove. Ten minutes into the ride, rather than take the road that led to the Hindley property, she took a left, heading for Bison Ridge.

"This isn't the way to my place."

"No, it isn't, because we're going to mine."

"Ashley."

"Is that going to be a thing?"

"Is what?"

"You using my whole name when you're cross with me?"

"I want to go to my trailer."

"The one you haven't cleaned up? Sure thing. But first, I want to show you something."

"Okay. I'll play this game. What?"

"Something you've never seen before."

He growled, the low rumble in his chest sounding sexy instead of scary. "Tell me what it is."

She pulled up in front of her house and threw the truck in Park. "That would spoil the surprise. But trust me, it's important. Afterward, I can take you straight home, if you still want to go," she said, and he narrowed his eyes at her. "I'd take that deal if I were you. It's the best one you're going to get." She pocketed her car keys.

"Fine." He got out, slamming the truck door, and stomped up to the porch.

The police officer parked behind her vehicle.

She went to the driver's side of the patrol car and he rolled down the window. "We're going to be here for the rest of the night. Can I get you some coffee or something?"

He held up a thermos and a plate of dessert covered in plastic wrap. "Your mother was kind enough to take care of me and the other officer who is watching your family's house. Have a good night."

"Thank you." It was a shame those officers had to be out in the cold, keeping guard on Thanksgiving, but hopefully the marshals would end this ordeal with Todd Burk once and for all.

Ashley hurried up the porch steps, past a brooding Rip, and opened the door. She stepped inside, but he stayed on the porch.

"What's wrong?" she asked. "I promise it's a good surprise. It won't upset you and we won't argue."

"It's just that you've lived in this house for five and a half years, I've been here countless times, but this is the first time I've come in through the front door."

She reached for him, taking him by the arm, and pulled him across the threshold. "Why did you always come around back?" She closed the door, locked it and put on the chain.

"You didn't seem thrilled about my visits. In case your family or a friend stopped by, I figured it would be best if they didn't see my bike."

She took his hand. "I felt like you were just as bad as my parents, checking up on me, giving me a hard time for living out here by myself."

"A young, pretty woman living alone with no neighbor in shouting distance tended to worry me. A lot."

She led him down the hall. "It made me feel like you underestimated me. My ability to handle myself if something were to happen."

"I never underestimated you, Ash. I just prefer to over-estimate other people's capacity for evil."

"Guess I didn't think of it that way." She stopped in front of her bedroom. Holding his gaze, she backed up into the room, tugging him along with her.

He halted in the doorway. "What are you doing?"

"At first, I was annoyed when you'd stop by, but after a while, I looked forward to your visits. Every time I heard the rumble of your bike coming, pulling around back, I'd get these electric tingles and a part of me couldn't wait to see you."

"You hid it well."

"I'm sorry. I just wanted to be sure this thing between us was real, and not you trying to manipulate me, or use me because I was a cop. That you really wanted to see Burk in jail. It was taking you so long to handle him."

"Revenge would've been easy, but you wanted justice. He was slipperier than I anticipated."

She set her purse on the dresser and held out her hand for him.

Rip sighed like the weight of the world rested on his shoulders. "Why are you doing this? I have to leave. Soon. Your family, your job, your life, are here."

"You're asking the wrong question. Ask me the right one. The one from the motel."

His gaze bore into hers. "What am I to you?"

She took a deep breath, but she wasn't confused or un-sure. This time she was certain of her answer. "You're my anchor. The one I confide in." She shared so many things with him first, some she'd never even told her parents. Wanting to be a deputy. Enrolling in college. The problem she had with a sexist professor. Her worst nightmare—that the authorities would never get Burk. How she wanted to get married and have a couple of kids. That she avoided monthly karaoke night with the sheriff's office and Laramie Fire Department because she had an irrational fear of singing in public and only did it at home. "The one person who has *been* there for me. Protecting me. Helping me. Sacrificing for me." She didn't realize she was moving toward him until she was touching him. "This thing between us hasn't been conventional, but it's real and I'd be lost without it. Without you." She took another deep breath. "Because I love you."

Nothing had ever felt so right or sounded so true. She eased further back into her bedroom.

And this time, he followed. "You shouldn't say those words lightly."

"I haven't."

He took her in his arms. "I want more than a night."

"I know." She slipped his jacket off, letting it hit the floor, and then hers.

"I want everything with you."

She unbuckled his belt, transfixed by his piercing gaze. "Then we're on the same page."

"But how? What about your job? Your family?"

Putting her hands on his cheeks, the scratchy stubble forming a beard tickling her palms, she brought his face to hers. "We're going to be together. We'll discuss the details later." After they made love.

His mouth took hers and he kissed her, a deep, sensual kiss that had her moaning and losing her balance. Digging her hands into the material of his shirt, she wanted him inside her, no long foreplay, only the fast, frantic rush of passion. She pulled the Henley over his head and started unbuttoning her shirt.

"Wait," he said, and she hoped he wasn't going to come

up with another reason why they couldn't be together. "We're going to do this slow and easy. I want you to remember the first time I make love to you. For it to burn in your memory for all the days and nights to come."

The first time I make love to you. There would be other times, other ways they'd do this.

"You hide it well."

"What?"

"Being such a romantic."

He caressed her cheek and gave her a soft grin. "Do you still have any of those bath oils and candles I bought you?"

She nodded. He bought her the most luxurious gifts. She only used them on special occasions, savoring them. "The oils are in the bathroom. I'll light the candles."

Not only was he a generous lover but a romantic, too. Jasper hadn't taken it slowly or thought of her pleasure. Within minutes, it had been done, and she hadn't felt any different, even though she was no longer a virgin.

But this…making love to Rip would change everything.

He went into the bathroom and started the water. She dug out the large, scented soy candles that smelled like a lush tropical paradise and lit them. She set one on each nightstand and carried the other two to the bathroom, where she found Rip standing in all his glory, without a stitch of clothing on.

Her mouth dropped. He was beautiful. Rugged. A work of art she couldn't wait to get her hands on. "No fair, I wanted to undress you."

"Next time." He took the candles from her and set them down. They reflected a soft white light in the mirror, providing the only illumination in the room. "There is one thing," he said.

No, no, no. "This is happening, Rip."

He smiled and it was a rainbow after a storm, glorious

and filled with promise. The hot look in his eyes sparked heat low in her abdomen. "I don't have protection. I didn't plan on this."

Oh, not what she was expecting him to say. "I used a condom with Jasper."

"Please refrain from mentioning other men when I'm naked and about to make love to you."

"Sorry," she said with a shake of her head. "Anyway, I had a checkup after." She pressed her hand to the heavy stubble lining his jaw, enjoying the way it scratched her palm. "I'm clean and I take the pill."

His eyes changed. The desire from before turned even darker. "It's been a while for me, but I'm clean, too."

"Then I don't want there to be anything between us."

No barriers. No past. No secrets. Just the two of them. She wanted to open her soul to him.

He stripped off her shirt and unfastened her bra. Crouching, he pressed kisses to her stomach before slipping off her shoes. He unbuttoned her jeans and pulled them down. She touched the top of his head, balancing herself as he tugged them off.

Her knees trembled. Who was she kidding? She trembled all over.

Rip planted a kiss at the apex between her thighs, his warm breath coursing through the silky material of her panties, unraveling her in thirteen different ways. Then he gripped the waistband and slid them down, allowing her to step out of them. Leaving them on the floor, he stood and looked at her.

Fixing her attention on his mouth, the shape of his full lips, the sexy crook of his smile, she shivered. Grabbing a clip from the counter, she pinned her hair on top of her head while he shut off the faucet and checked the temperature.

Rip held out a hand, helping her into the claw-footed porcelain tub filled with bubbles that smelled divine. He climbed in on the other side, the water sloshing, and eased down, careful not to get his bandaged hand wet. His legs stretched out, and she clamped her knees together, making room for him to surround her.

In the candlelight suffusing the room, he bathed her gently, tenderly, caressing every inch of skin. No one had ever taken such care of her. Been so patient with his affection. And when he finished, she bathed him. She was familiar with the top half of his body but enjoyed the new spots she hadn't yet explored. Stroking him in places that made him groan, and she understood what he meant about liking to hear her pleasure because hearing his lit her up inside.

Every kiss, every touch, every stroke heated them until their desire for each other reached a torturous simmer. She was ready to climb on top of him and have him right there in the tub. His restraint was phenomenal.

"I can't wait any longer," she admitted.

Another heartrending smile. "Me neither."

They got out and hurried, towel-drying each other off.

Rip bent over and scooped her up off the floor, lifting her in his arms.

"You'll hurt your hand," she said, worried about him. "And what about your head?"

He was already moving out of the bathroom and set her down on the bed. "I've got this."

She scooted higher on the bed and lay back. He climbed up, prowling closer.

Excitement pulsed through her and goose bumps pebbled her skin.

Island scents drifted in the air—Tahitian vanilla, white musk, night-blooming jasmine. He settled between her spread legs, caressed her cheek with the knuckle of his index finger, moved to her mouth and stroked her bottom lip with his thumb. She caught the tip between her teeth, bit down lightly, and sucked.

"God, you are amazing," he said, his voice filled with the same awe she felt looking at him. "So sexy."

He kissed her, a searing brand of possession and passion, his hand diving between them, his fingers stroking that place she ached most. He knew precisely how to caress her to make the rush of desire flood her body, to make her tremble with longing, and she became lost. So sweetly lost in him. And this time the pleasure was both theirs to share.

His thigh settled between her legs, and she opened herself, pressing the warmth of her most intimate spot against him. Desire roared through her, so intense, so urgent, she swore the world quaked.

Need took over as he entered her slowly. She cried out, not in pain but in a kind of triumph. Gripping his hips, she urged him to move faster, deeper. Sensation swamped her with a force she'd never felt before and she wanted more. Lots more.

They rocked together as one, clinging to each other, breathing hard, climbing higher. Not just having sex or hooking up or having a fling but making love. Committing to each other.

This new dimension of their relationship was sensual and nurturing and hot and better than she'd imagined. All these years she'd been searching for something she couldn't fully define, and here she'd found it in the one man who had been there for her all along.

Rip.

Chapter Eighteen

Holding Ash in his arms, in her bed, Rip felt like he'd won the lottery. If this was a dream, he never wanted to wake from it. "How do you feel?"

"Different. Revered and ravaged," she said, and he laughed. "I wish I had waited for you. Waited for this. Instead of blowing my first time on Jasper."

He patted her butt softly, playfully. "Please, do me the favor of not mentioning him again. Ever."

"Okay, okay. But I will say one more thing."

Rip groaned.

"You'll appreciate this. You gave me my first orgasm, in the motel," she said, and he did appreciate it.

"Well, I've given you plenty of those. Five so far, not that I'm counting, and more to come. Pun intended."

She elbowed him lightly in his side. "Humble. But I am looking forward to lots of other firsts with you, like our bath." She rolled on top of him and peered down into his face. "Have you ever been married?"

"Yes." Suddenly, he wished he had been the one who'd waited for her. "It was right after I became a Raider. Spec Ops. The marriage lasted less than two years. She couldn't handle me being gone all the time. Didn't like being lonely. I came back from a deployment to find her living with another guy." The memory no longer stung. It had happened a lifetime ago.

"What was she like? I mean, what's your type?"

"You're my type." He slid his arms around her waist. "Beautiful, bold, brave. Loyal." Mandy had only been pretty. He'd been in lust with her, mistaking it for love. His ego had been more hurt than his heart when the marriage ended.

"So, I won't be your first wife," she said, and the sadness in her tone and her eyes stopped him from making a joke about how he'd never promised marriage.

"No. Not the first. But the last. The only one to matter. My dad used to talk about how my mom was the great love of his life. You're mine." He kissed her. "I love you. I have for a few years."

"Did you fall in love with me before or after you started bringing me tacos?"

"I *wanted* you before the tacos, but I think I realized I'd fallen in deep when I started bringing you candles and bath oils and—"

"And the booze."

He chuckled. "Yeah."

"There was one night," she said, slipping her leg between his and snuggling against him, "where I wanted you so bad, I came close to inviting you to my bedroom."

"Why didn't you?"

"You called me deputy and it…shifted my thoughts back into alignment."

"That's why I did it. Called you deputy all the time. To keep me focused on not crossing the line between us." He put a knuckle under her chin and tipped her face up, so he could look into her eyes. "Speaking of which, what about your job?"

Sighing, she rolled off him onto her back and stared

up at the ceiling. At the lack of eye contact, he braced for what she might say.

"Don't get upset, but the sheriff suspended me because I misled him about the DEA mission, and the current status of our relationship prompted an investigation."

"What?" He leaned up on his forearm and peered down at her face. "I can talk to him. Try to clear it up."

She pressed her index finger to his lips. "I'm not worried about the internal investigation. I'll be cleared, but I still quit."

He moved her finger from his mouth. "Ash, you can't."

"I already did. The sheriff asked me to reconsider, said he didn't want to lose a good deputy and that the investigation was only procedural. I told him that a law enforcement officer has to do things by the book. But to get Todd, it required me to bend the rules. I had to work in the gray. I don't regret it and I also don't think I should wear the badge anymore. Todd was arrested and when he's found, he won't slip out of those charges. He was the only reason I became a deputy in the first place. I achieved what I set out to do. You were in the hospital, and suddenly, you were all that mattered to me. So, I quit. It's done. Tomorrow, we'll tell my parents and Ida that we have to leave. Together. Besides, I can find a new job wherever we decide to make our new home. Not law enforcement of course, but something to help people that also pays the bills."

He wrapped an arm around her waist. "You don't have to worry about paying bills. I bring in plenty of money."

Turning onto her side, facing him, she raised an eyebrow. "Clean, legit money?"

He chuckled. "Yeah, of course. I started a company. Ironside Protection Services."

"I've heard of it. That's you? How were you able to hide

being the owner from the DEA? It didn't come up in their deep dive on you."

"I was Special Forces. I know how to hide things I don't want others to know. Over the years, I've expanded a great deal into Montana, Idaho and Colorado. I employee a lot of veterans."

"Guess I could do protection work."

He trailed his fingers over her spine, loving the feel of her nestled against him. "I bring in close to a million a year. You can do what you want. Handle management. Source intel. Lead a team. Stay home with me and we can practice making babies."

She sat up and stared down at him. "A million *dollars* a year?"

"Yep."

"And you pay your taxes?"

He laughed. "On time. Every year. I swear it's all aboveboard. You can trust me, honey."

"I know I can. It's just I had no idea."

"That's the point. For no one to know."

"You're full of surprises. The good kind." She gave him a peck on the lips and hopped out of the bed. "I'm going to go to the bathroom and clean up."

"I'm starving."

"There's a strawberry rhubarb pie on the counter and shepherd's pie in the fridge."

"Both are my favorite."

"I'm aware. I've been paying attention, too, over the years and I had planned for you to stay here. The strawberry rhubarb is from the Divine Treats café and the shepherd's pie is from my mother's kitchen."

He pulled on his boxer briefs. "Want anything?"

"Glass of water." She paused, thinking. "Ooh, this is

a night to celebrate. Calls for Clase Azul. I'll meet you in the kitchen. Give me a couple of minutes." She disappeared in the bathroom, shutting the door, and he heard the faucet turn on.

His head buzzed. Not from pain. Not from swelling. From this high of being in love, of knowing that Ash loved him back, wanted to build a life together.

He padded down the hall, passing her living room, and entered the kitchen.

A draft sent a chill over him. The back door creaked. Slightly ajar. The bottom windowpane had been busted in, broken glass on the floor.

Then he sensed movement behind him before he heard it.

He grabbed the first thing within reach—a cast-iron skillet from the dish rack on the counter—and swung around.

The iron pan collided with the barrel of a twelve-gauge shotgun that Freddy was holding. A blast exploded, shattering the window over the sink.

Rip swung again, smashing the pan against Freddy's fingers and then across his head, sending him to the floor in a whirling sprawl.

Heavyset Clive had a baseball bat. Tall, burly Arlo limped forward, raising a 9mm.

Over their shoulders, Rip glimpsed Todd Burk stalking down the hallway toward the bedroom.

"Ashley!" Rip ducked, taking cover behind the kitchen island as Arlo opened fire. He grabbed the shotgun from an unconscious Freddy.

When those men, former brothers, had attacked him at his home, he'd gone easy, only dislocating a kneecap.

Now they were here, going after Ash, and he'd show no mercy.

SINGING TO HERSELF in the mirror, she wondered where they'd go, if he already had a city or town picked out. Would they even stay in Wyoming?

Boom.

"What the hell?" She shut off the water and listened.

"Ashley!"

Her heart stuttered. *Rip.*

She snatched the long purple kimono robe from the hook on the back of the door, put it on and tied the belt.

Gunfire erupted deeper in the house, from the kitchen, sending her pulse skyrocketing. She opened the bathroom door and froze. Todd Burk stood on the other side. In her bedroom. His black hair was wild, his eyes crazed. He had her in height, he had her in weight, and he was holding a hammer.

In milliseconds, she located her gun and pepper spray. Both in her purse. On top of the dresser that Todd had pushed in front of the closed bedroom door.

Panic wanted to ice her brain. It snaked through her belly, slithered up her throat, made her hands shake until she balled them into fists. Fear threatened to swallow her, but her anger, her seven years of grief, her bottled-up pain were stronger.

A vicious smirk tugged at his mouth, and he raised the hammer.

She kicked him in the crotch as hard as she could. As he doubled over, she rammed the fleshy part of her palm up into his nose. Once. Twice. Bone crunched. Then she kicked him again, this time thrusting the heel of her foot into his gut, shoving him back, putting space between them.

More gunfire came from the kitchen.

Todd stumbled and fell near the dresser, blocking her

escape, but the hammer slipped from his grip and clattered to the hardwood floor.

She bolted for her nightstand on the other side of the room.

Cursing and grunting, Todd was up. He leaped onto the bed with the hammer in his hand.

She grabbed the handle of her top drawer and pulled it open, but Todd lunged, taking her down to the floor. The breath was knocked from her. Lights starred behind her eyes when her head rapped hard against the floor. She still held the handle, but the drawer had been yanked free from the nightstand, the contents spilling around her.

She felt around for what she was looking for. She'd seen it fall to her left.

Crouched on top of her, Todd raised the hammer. She swung her forearm into his head, across his face. A move Rip had taught her after she graduated from the academy to keep her from breaking her hand. Then she went for his eyes, raked furrows down his cheek.

He howled like a wounded animal. Ashley grabbed his arm holding the hammer with her hands and bit him, as hard as she could, drawing blood.

The hammer fell, but with his free hand, he punched her. The blow stunned her, but she kept moving.

His bloody hand was shaking. She only wished she'd been able to take off a finger.

Head clearing, she scrambled with him for the hammer. His hand closed over it first, but she didn't stop fighting for it.

"The boys are taking care of Rip. So you and I can play."

Todd's face was close to hers, his body pinning her in an obscene way. His wrist was slippery with his own blood.

She cursed as she lost her grip.

Smiling, in control of the hammer, he ripped open the top of her robe, exposing her breasts. "I want a taste of what Rip's been protecting all this time before I kill you."

She sagged, but reached out, searching the floor with her fingers, hoping, praying, the weapon might be nearby.

There! She found it. Her hand closed around cool aluminum. "You're not man enough to take what's his."

A lecherous smile curled his lips and something in his eyes made her stomach clench like a fist. "We'll see when I'm done with you."

With her finger, she flipped the on switch. Blue sparks snapped and sizzled, drawing his gaze down to her hand.

She shoved the stun gun into his side.

Todd let out a piercing wail, falling off her to the side, shuddering and convulsing. The hammer dropped to the floor.

One to two seconds of contact caused unbearable pain, muscle cramps and dizziness. She shocked him again. Todd and his flunkies had broken into her house, assuming she was alone and weak. They had been thinking four against one. Had planned to do unspeakable things to her and then kill her.

A geyser of pain and rage welled up in her and exploded. She hit him with her fists. In the face. In the gut. In the stomach. Screaming, she kept punching. The red haze clouding her vision darkened every time she landed a blow.

She never heard Rip calling her name. Or the battering of the door. Or him busting it down and shoving the dresser aside.

His arms were around her waist, her back pressed to his chest, and he was hauling her off Todd. She was still swinging and kicking when he carried her to the corner of the room.

"Ashley!"

She wasn't sure how many times he'd yelled her name before it registered.

"Look at me. Not him."

Chest heaving, she tore her gaze from the sight of Todd, crumpled and bleeding on her floor, to Rip. Met his eyes. Those riveting blue-gray eyes anchored her. The immediate connection calmed her. The red haze of fury dissipated, and tears fell from her eyes.

"I need to know. Right now," Rip said.

"What? Know what?" Then she realized he'd been talking to her, but she hadn't heard him.

"Todd Burk. Do you want him dead…or in prison? I need to know, right now before I call 911."

She glanced back at the man who had killed her brother, who had caused her family unfathomable suffering.

"Look at me when you decide." Rip's voice was sharp, sobering.

Finding his gaze and holding it, she took a long, ragged breath. "I want him to burn in hell for what he's done." Staying focused on this man, whom she loved, whom she was safe with, who would do anything for her, she then thought about her brother, remembered the promises she'd made her parents when she joined the sheriff's office. "But I want him to rot in jail first."

She wanted justice.

Not vengeance.

"Good choice, honey." He sat her down in a chair. Yanked a cord from the lamp on the bedside table. Tied Todd's hands behind his back. Ran from the room for a minute. Hurried back with duct tape and a phone pressed to his ear. "The four escapees the marshals are searching for broke in and attacked us. I believe the officer outside is dead."

Rip finished the call on speakerphone, giving the 911 operator Ashley's address, as he doubled the restraints on Todd's wrists with the tape and bound his ankles.

He grabbed their clothes and ushered her to the hall. Quickly, he dressed her and himself. Looking her over, he wiped blood from her face, and she winced from the tenderness in her cheek where Todd had hit her.

"Sorry I didn't get to you sooner," he said, regret heavy in his voice.

She leaned against him, needing his strength, his support, and he wrapped her in a bear hug. "He had a hammer. He was going to rape me." She shivered at the prospect of what might have happened if Rip hadn't been in the house. But he had been there dealing with the others. "I don't know what choice I would have made if you hadn't stopped me."

"I do. You would've made the right one." He tightened the embrace. "I believe that. I believe in you."

"But how can you? After the way I hit him. I didn't think I'd be able to stop."

"Todd had that coming and deserved everything you dished out. Deserves far worse. But I know because in all the years when you weren't sure what side of the law I was on, you never asked me to put him down like a dog, shoot him unaware in the back and bury him in a deep hole somewhere no one would find him. You never would have."

It had crossed her mind, but she could never bring herself to utter the words. To ask someone to commit murder. Not that Rip would have ever gone through with it. He was a good man, the best kind of man, who believed in justice. Not revenge. "What about the others?"

"Two are still breathing, but they're broken. They're going to have a tough time in prison wearing casts."

She pressed her head to his chest. "I'm glad it's over. I'm glad you're here."

"I'm the one who's glad. That you're safe and okay."

"What if you hadn't stayed? What if you had gone back to your trailer?" A shudder racked her body.

"But I'm here. Because you're stubborn and persistent. Because you had the guts to tell me how you felt about me and then had your way with me in bed to get me to stay."

Pulling back and looking up at him, she gave him a grim smile.

"That's my Ash, head held high, a warrior to the bone." He took her chin between his thumb and index finger. "I'm never leaving you again. It's you and me together from now on."

She nodded. "Together."

He lowered his mouth to hers and kissed her, long and slow and deep, and her heart melted as everything else faded away.

Ten months later

RIP STOOD BESIDE ASH, with his arm around her shoulder, in front of Ida Hindley's grave in Millstone Cemetery. Though he couldn't be with Ida during her last months, he was comforted knowing that she had lived to see her ninetieth birthday, and in the end, had been surrounded by love and hadn't been alone, thanks to Ashley's parents.

"It was a lovely service," Ashley's mother said to the small group.

Only her parents, Quill and JD had been invited. An announcement about her passing would be put in the paper along with her obituary once Rip and Ash left town again. They'd only flown in for the funeral.

"Of course, it was." Rip smiled, looking at her simple headstone that read *Ida Hindley, Beloved Wife, Mother, Auntie and Friend*, along with the years of her birth and death. "Auntie Ida planned it herself. She claimed it was so I wouldn't have to do it and that's partly true, but she was also a perfectionist and wanted it done right."

Ashley's father laughed. "Even when it came to making the bed. If I didn't do hospital corners, it was done wrong."

Fond memories sprang to mind and his chest filled with gratitude and love. "Thanks to her, making a bed and shooting were the two things I didn't have to worry about learning how to do when I joined the Marines."

"She was a good woman," Quill said.

"With Rip and Ashley gone, Ida appreciated you two paying her visits," Mrs. Russo said to Quill and JD.

JD nodded. "She played a mean hand of pinochle and enjoyed taking our money."

"I didn't know pinochle was a gambling game," Ash said, resting her head on Rip.

Quill laughed. "It was the way Ida played it."

"Tired?" Rip asked Ash, tightening his arm around her.

"Starving." She put her hands on her belly, nearly the size of a basketball, and rubbed. Her wedding ring, a diamond eternity band, sparkled, catching the light. "I'm always hungry."

"I was the same when I was pregnant." Her mother put a hand on Ash's rounded tummy. "You said you'd tell us the sex in person. We've been waiting."

"What are you having, man?" Quill stepped closer. "Boy or girl?"

Rip looked at her. "Do you want to tell them or should I?"

Ash shrugged, a mischievous gleam in her eye. "Let's do it at the same time. One, two, three. Boy."

"Girl."

Everyone looked at them, confused.

Her father's face lit up. "Oh, my! Twins? Is my jelly bean having two beans?"

Ash nodded. "A boy and a girl."

Everyone took turns giving them hugs and offering congratulations.

Then her mom broke down in tears.

"Don't cry." Ash kissed her cheek and comforted her. "This is good news."

"The best news possible." Her mom sniffled. "It's just that your dad and I retired early. With Ida gone, we have no reason to stay here. We miss you. We want to see the baby, the babies when they're born, watch them grow up, but…"

Rip took out a handkerchief and gave it to her. "Ash and I have been talking about that. We were wondering if you wanted to come live with us. Well, not in the same house. But walking distance close."

Her mother went slack-jawed with surprise and looked at Ash as if to check whether the proposal was real.

"Yes, Mom. We want you guys with us if that's what you want."

Ash had broached the subject and he had been open to it. They had even made plans to bring Ida. He'd always wanted a big family. If he could give his kids grandparents, who wanted to be hands-on and in their lives every day, then he would. It was also a huge plus that he'd make his wife ecstatic in the process.

An easy win-win.

Her father grabbed him in a bear hug. "Thank you, Rip."

"Sir, you're more than welcome. We're happy to have you."

"We told you at the wedding. No more sir or ma'am or

Mr. and Mrs. Russo. It's Dante and Emily. Or if you'd prefer, Mom and Dad. You're not our son-in-law, but our son."

They'd gotten legally married at the Justice of the Peace in the United States, only the two of them. Then had a small ceremony in Paris with Ash's parents and Auntie Ida. At the Place du Trocadéro, overlooking the Eiffel Tower. Ash had wanted to do it in Europe, since she'd never been, and he thought she'd love it. Her parents and Ida had been impressed and her mother couldn't stop crying happy tears. For their honeymoon, they'd traveled for a month, going wherever Ash wanted.

"All right. No more formalities." Rip nodded, sticky emotions surfacing. He'd have to work his way up to calling them Mom and Dad. "Don't sell your house. Don't change your routine. Just have two bags packed and ready. One day, we'll call with instructions. Follow them to the letter. Don't say goodbye to anyone. Okay?" It was similar to how he'd handled things for the wedding. The obstetrician thought the babies might come early. He was planning for a December birth and to have her parents relocated by Thanksgiving.

"Yes, yes," Dante and Emily both said.

"Will we ever see you guys again?" JD asked.

The district attorney had plenty of evidence to put Todd, Freddy and Arlo away, including for the murder of the police officer who had been assigned to protect them. Clive hadn't left Ash's house alive. Fortunately, the case was so solid against the others it didn't require either of their testimonies in court. Their sworn affidavits would suffice. Many of the Sons of Chaos had been arrested, including Stryker, when the prostitution ring was busted. But the Sandoval cartel was still a potential problem waiting to happen.

"No, you won't." Rip shook his head. "I'm sorry."

"We understand." Quill patted him on the back. "Thanks for still kicking Ironside work to the Warriors."

"It'll help keep the club legit," JD said, proudly wearing his president patch.

"Now that's all settled, can we eat?" Ash asked.

"Let's go to the house," Emily said. "I have plenty of food prepared."

"Good. I'm hungry." Quill patted his own round belly, heading for his bike.

Once they finished lunch, they would go to the Laramie Regional Airport, where Rip had a chartered plane waiting. Staying any longer than the day wasn't wise. Not a chance he was willing to take with his family, now that the cartel knew his name and involvement in the seizure of the drug camp.

They started for the car when Ash stopped suddenly.

"The babies are kicking." She put his hand on her belly.

After a second or two he felt it. Like a powerful one-two jab from inside her. Took his breath away every time. "They're so strong."

She smiled. "Fighters like their dad."

"And their mom."

"I was thinking about names. How about Hatch Angelo and Elizabeth Ida?"

The suggestions warmed his heart, choking him up in a way he didn't expect. This beautiful woman never stopped surprising him in the best ways. He nodded. "Great choices, but only if you really love those names."

She pressed a palm to his clean-shaven cheek. "I love you. And I think those names would make us both happy."

"Thank you. For loving me. For marrying me. For giving me this family I've always wanted." Far too long he'd been looking to the motorcycle club and the Marine Corps to give him that intangible piece missing to make him feel whole. But this was it. Ashley, the babies, her parents, even Quill and JD. This was what he'd been missing.

"I wish I'd seen it sooner," she said. "How remarkable you are. Seen that I could trust you. That we were meant to be."

No, he rejected that. Immediately. He looped his arms around her and pulled her close. "Everything happened as it was supposed to. Without all that came before, we would never have been here. Sometimes things have to happen, to push us, to show us, to get us where we never thought we'd be."

Not in a million years had he thought it possible for Ash to be his wife and the mother of his children, that he would even ever be a father.

"Then I'd go through it again." She stared at him with light and love. "All seven years. Walking through fire. To get to the other side, to be here with you now."

He really had won the lottery, because Ash was the remarkable one.

The great love of his life.

* * * * *

INTRIGUE

Seek thrills. Solve crimes. Justice served.

Available Next Month

Tracking Down The Lawman's Son Delores Fossen
Twin Jeopardy Cindi Myers

....

Cold Case Protection Nicole Helm
Wyoming Christmas Conspiracy Juno Rushdan

....

Danger In Dade Caridad Piñeiro
Holiday Under Wraps Katie Mettner

Larger Print

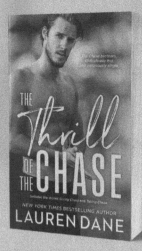 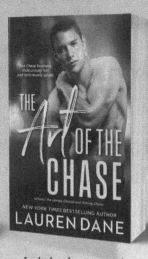

Subscribe and fall in love with a Mills & Boon series today!

You'll be among the first to read stories delivered to your door monthly and enjoy great savings.

WE SIMPLY LOVE ROMANCE